BECAUSE SHE LOVES ME

OTHER TITLES BY THE AUTHOR

The Magpies

Kissing Games

What You Wish For

WITH LOUISE VOSS:

Forward Slash

Killing Cupid

Catch Your Death

All Fall Down

MARK EDWARDS

BECAUSE SHE LOVES ME

THOMAS & MERCER

Published by Thomas & Mercer, Seattle

www.apub.com

Amazon, the Amazon logo, and Thomas & Mercer are trademarks of Amazon.com, Inc., or its affiliates.

ISBN-13: 9781477824863
ISBN-10: 1477824863

Cover design by bürosüd° München, www.buerosued.de

Library of Congress Control Number: 2014935332

Printed in the United States of America

For Archie and Harry

One

'Look up.'

Over the past three months my eyes had been poked, stretched and lasered. They had endured brilliant light and foreign bodies, had air and liquid puffed and squeezed into them. They'd been stared at and discussed and invaded, clamped open and taped shut. They'd endured pretty much everything an eye can endure. So when the nurse asked me to look upwards so she could apply the drops, told me this might sting a little, I – well, I didn't bat an eyelid. This was nothing.

One summer night, I almost went blind. It was only the skill of a surgeon at Moorfields Eye Hospital, where I sat now, waiting to be seen, that saved my sight. Even then, after the 2 a.m. emergency surgery, they told me it was unlikely the sight in my left eye would return fully. When it did, I saw it as the first sign that my luck was changing.

The second sign – or so I thought, in those breathless, heady first days of our relationship – was meeting Charlie.

I was the youngest person in the waiting room by thirty years and the only person on my own. The white-haired man in the corner was accompanied by his wife, who kept reading out excerpts from her magazine, one of those real-life mags, full of stories about unfaithful spouses, child abuse and kids with cancer. There was a gang of three elderly ladies opposite me, hunched beneath the glaucoma poster, and an Indian man with a young woman who I assumed to be his daughter. Two old men in dark glasses walked past, one of them cracking a joke about the blind leading the blind.

There was no one I could have asked to come with me. I worked as a freelancer so didn't have any colleagues. My sister Tilly was my only surviving relative, apart from an aunt and uncle in Sussex whom I hadn't seen for years, and I didn't have a girlfriend. I suppose I could have asked my best friend, Sasha, to accompany me, but she was busy and would have had to take a day off work. I didn't like to ask.

I had barely admitted it to myself but I was, if not lonely, at least tired of being alone. In the days and weeks that followed the operation, I had sat around on my sofa trying not to feel sorry for myself and imagining how good it would be to have someone to look after me. If I hadn't split up with Harriet, if I had a flatmate, if my parents weren't dead. I despised self-pity but sometimes, during those days when I had to sleep sitting upright and my spatial awareness was so screwed that I couldn't negotiate my way around my flat, let alone the outside world, I wished I had someone to laugh with when I bumped into the coffee table for the hundredth time.

Now I was better, but it was getting harder to kid myself that I enjoyed being on my own most of the time. I wanted a girlfriend – I wanted companionship and sex and love – and was on the verge of trying internet dating. It was going to be my New Year's resolution: to find someone.

I picked up a newspaper from the table and leafed through it. Pages 4 and 5, along with the front page, were dedicated to a story I and most of the country had been following with grim interest: the trial of Lucy Newton, a care assistant in a nursing home who had been accused of murdering eighteen residents. The Dark Angel – that's what the tabloids called her, the second most-prolific British serial killer of modern times, the new Harold Shipman. Attractive, statuesque, icy, probably psychotic: she was a newspaper editor's dream, and there were dozens of websites on which her supporters and detractors argued viciously about her innocence. But as I was reading about her testimony – she claimed she was being set up by her former neighbour – the drops started to work, my pupils dilating so I couldn't focus on text or anything within arm's length.

I wished I'd remembered to bring my headphones. Since my operation I'd spent a lot of time listening to audiobooks, each one consuming days. Instead, I was left to daydream and watch people as they walked past the waiting area.

After half an hour, I was twitching with boredom. There was a coffee machine across the corridor. I rummaged in my pocket, pulling out my phone, keys, several pieces of paper and my eye drops, before finding a pound coin. Standing up, trying to juggle the various objects in my hands – the three old ladies watching me with interest – I dropped the coin.

Stopping and swearing under my breath, I chased it as it rolled across the corridor – and collided with a young woman walking past the waiting area.

'I'm so sorry. I—'

I stopped dead, the words – whatever nonsense I was going to come out with – stuck in my throat. Even though my eyes were dilated, I could see her clearly; more clearly, in fact, than I had seen anyone in a long time. She was beautiful. Red hair that hung just past her shoulders, cut with a fringe. Huge green eyes. Full, cupid's-bow lips. A smattering of faint freckles. She was wearing a white blouse and a pencil skirt, and her NHS ID hung around her neck. Maddeningly, I couldn't focus on the words so couldn't read her name or job title.

She crouched and produced the pound coin from beneath her shoe and I could make out the outline of a tattoo on her ankle, a vibrant hint of colour hiding beneath her conservative black tights. I guessed she was a few years younger than me, about twenty-six, but she looked more grown up than I did in my scruffy jeans and cardigan.

Her eyes shone with amusement as she handed me the money. 'I recommend the hot chocolate.' Her voice had a soft northern lilt.

I stared at her. I can honestly say that if anyone had asked me before this encounter to describe my ideal woman, she would be it. A composite of all the girls and women who had moulded my taste: the girl who sat in front of me at primary school; the divorcee two doors down who used to come out to collect the post in a silky black robe; the lead actress in my favourite TV show; the first girl I kissed. Here she was, the perfect woman, standing before me.

'The coffee is like cow's piss,' she said, her eyes shining with mischief.

I wracked my brain for a clever response while she continued to smile at me. Before I could think of one – to be honest, seasons would have come and gone before I'd come up with a good line – I heard a man say my name.

'Andrew Sumner?'

Mr Yassir Makkawi, the baby-faced consultant ophthalmologist who had seen me on my visits to Moorfields since my operation, stood outside his room.

The red-haired woman gave me a final smile and walked away down the corridor.

'Nothing wrong with your eyesight now.'

'Huh?'

Mr Makkawi raised an eyebrow and I realised I'd been staring at the woman's receding form. She turned a corner and vanished. I wanted to run after her.

Instead, I went into the consultation room and did as I was asked. I looked at Mr Makkawi's right ear, then his left. I looked up and down, and at the coral reef of veins that lit up inside my eye.

The consultant examined his notes and nodded with satisfaction.

'Very good. Everything looks excellent. I'm going to be able to discharge you.'

'Oh, thank God for that.'

He put his hand on his chest. 'I'm deeply offended, Andrew.'

'Well, you know.'

He gave me a lopsided grin. 'You've done very well. I know you may not feel it, but you're very lucky. Extremely lucky.'

As I left his office, I pumped his hand vigorously. He looked taken aback, as if no one had ever done this before. But I felt so grateful and relieved. I wanted to rush to the gift shop and buy him a present.

I left the hospital with newfound strength. One of the darkest periods of my life was over. I forgot all about the red-haired girl in the corridor. All that mattered was that I was well again.

It's hard now, after everything that's happened, not to wonder about what, statistically speaking, should have been. If I hadn't dropped that coin, if my consultation had ended five minutes later, if I'd popped into Starbucks when I left the hospital instead of going directly to the station.

In this parallel version of my life, everything would be different. I would have gone on a series of internet dates. I would have met a nice girl. It would have all been very pleasant and I wouldn't be lonely anymore.

In this alternative future, I wouldn't be sitting here among the smoking wreckage of my life, wondering about what might have been.

Nobody would have got hurt.

Nobody would have died.

Two

I walked down City Road to Old Street Tube station. Silicon Roundabout – many of my clients were based here, a mixture of web start-ups and small publishers. The design agency that I did most of my work for is based a short distance away on Clerkenwell Green. I'm a web designer and although it sometimes feels like there are more of us in London than there are rats, I'm able to make a living from it. I even had a little money saved, although three months without being able to work had drained my bank account. *I must call Victor*, I thought, as I descended the steps of the Tube station.

It was late-December, just after five in the afternoon, and the station was packed with Christmas shoppers and office workers on their way home. I would send Victor a Christmas message when I got home, remind him of my existence. Fortunately, he'd been very understanding of my situation and had told me there should always be work for me. 'At least until the next fucking recession comes along,' he'd said on the phone, unable to resist the urge to say something gloomy.

I was so deep in thought about work, money and the Eeyore-like tendencies of my main employer that I didn't notice her at first. The platform was crowded and devoid of festive spirit and I was tempted to turn back, go and sit in the pub until rush hour was over.

The train came and sucked hundreds of passengers inside, leaving those of us who weren't desperate to get home standing on the platform. I looked towards the departures board to see how long I had to wait – and there she was.

The woman from the hospital.

I froze. This was it: my second chance. But I hesitated. A woman that gorgeous would definitely have a boyfriend. Several, probably. She was out of my league. I was hopeless at this sort of thing. Half a dozen excuses why I should leave it ran through my head.

If I hadn't been in such an ebullient mood, I probably would have done nothing, regretted it for a day then forgotten all about her. Instead, I shouldered my way through the crowd until I reached her, trying to persuade myself that I was confident and that rejection would be better than not trying at all.

'You were right, you know,' I said.

She looked up with surprise.

'About the coffee in the hospital. It did taste like piss. Though I think it was more like horse's piss than cow's.'

Perhaps it wasn't the best way to start a relationship, with a little white lie. I hadn't tried the coffee. But it was the best opening line I could come up with. For a horrible moment I thought she didn't recognise me, that she thought I was a random nutcase.

But she hitched her bag onto her shoulder and said, 'No. Definitely cow.'

She was still wearing her ID round her neck and with my pupils returned to normal I could read it. Charlotte Summers. Her surname made me smile. Charlotte Summers and Andrew Sumner. It was a sign.

'Charlotte,' I said, sticking out my hand. This was so out of character for me but, like I said, I was on a high after getting the news from Mr Makkawi. 'I'm Andrew.'

She returned my handshake with a firm grip, her hand dry and warm. I couldn't believe she hadn't run off yet. She actually seemed pleased to be talking to me. 'I'm Charlie when I'm not at work. Are you an Andy?'

'You can call me Andy if you like.'

She wrinkled her nose. 'Nah, I prefer Andrew. Sounds more grown up.'

The train clattered into the station and Charlie and I were propelled onto it by the surge of the crowd. We found ourselves pressed together beside the door, other bodies clustered around us.

'Where are you going?' I asked.

'London Bridge.'

'Me too. Then an overground train to Tulse Hill.'

'Is that where you live?'

I nodded. 'How about you? Are you one of those north-of-the-river types?'

'Oh no. I live in Camberwell. Proper London.'

'You don't have the accent,' I said. 'I'd guess you're from some-where up north.'

She laughed. 'Yes. That great wilderness beyond the M25.' She stage whispered. 'I come from a tribe in a primitive little village called Leeds.'

'Oh yes, I've heard tale of it. You escaped though.'

'Yes. Though my seventeen brothers are hunting me even as we speak. With specially trained hunter pigeons.'

We talked. Were we flirting? It definitely felt like flirting, though maybe she thought I was an idiot and was awaiting her first opportunity to get away. I couldn't take my eyes off her face. She was even more stunning than I'd originally thought. She had a little chip out of one of her front teeth, and the heat of the Tube train had made the skin around her collarbone flush pink. I badly wanted to kiss her.

I told her I was from Eastbourne and she told me she'd been to Brighton, which is what people always say, and then we passed Bank and I became aware that we were about to get off the train and would probably get separated. Forever.

'I just had some excellent news,' I said. I told her about being discharged.

'That's fantastic.'

We pulled into London Bridge. I was going to have to get off. I would never see her again. She appeared to be deep in thought.

'So how are you going to celebrate being released from Moorfields?' she asked.

'I don't know.'

'Going to go out with your girlfriend?'

'I don't have one.'

The doors slid open and commuters began to push past me. I stayed rooted to the spot, trying to prolong the moment.

I didn't need to. Before I could gather the courage to ask her out, Charlie took me by the arm and pulled me off the train. We stood on the platform, jostled from all sides. Charlie stood firm, the other passengers flowing around her like water past a rock.

'Come on,' she said. 'I'll buy you a celebratory drink. You do drink, don't you?'

We went to a pub off Borough High Street, an ancient place with twinkling Christmas lights hanging from the timber beams and dozens of workers sinking one last pint before going home to the kids.

As we entered the pub, a middle-aged couple stood up to leave and Charlie grabbed their table, attracting evil stares from a man and woman who'd been waiting at the bar. She ignored them.

'Red wine,' she mouthed at me.

I could feel the couple whose table we'd 'stolen' glowering at me but I was in such a good mood their daggers bounced off me. There was a mirror behind the bar and I caught my reflection. My hair, dark brown, stuck up at the back no matter how often I tried to flatten it down. I was still slim, despite my sedentary lifestyle, and I'd been told I had good cheekbones. I looked scruffy, though, and had bags under my eyes, though these were mostly obscured by my glasses. Spending so much time on my own, I didn't worry too much about my appearance, but what would Charlie think? I assumed, from the way she'd asked me here for a drink, that she wasn't horrified by what she saw.

I bought Charlie's wine and a pint for myself, then sat down opposite her.

'So, what happened to you?' she asked. 'Why were you at the hospital?'

I took a long sip of lager. 'I had a detached retina.'

'Nasty.'

'I know. But it's all better now.'

She downed half her wine in two gulps. 'I feel all better now too.' She put on a funny Eliza Doolittle voice, a mangled blend of Cockney and Yorkshire. 'I'm only an 'umble project manager, so I don't know much about eyes. What caused it?'

'They don't really know. Apparently, it's something that can happen to people who are badly short-sighted.'

'Really? Let's see how short-sighted you are.' She took my glasses from me and tried them on, instantly adopting the sexy geek look. 'Whew! You really *are* blind.'

She handed my glasses back and asked me to tell her more about what had happened.

'It was weird. First thing, I noticed a couple of floaters – you know, those little dots that sometimes appear in your vision and, er, float around. Then I saw this shadow that started here—' I pointed to the corner of my left eye '—and slowly spread across my vision. I was trying to ignore it, thinking it was just something that would pass.'

'Typical bloke.'

'Yeah. I would rather die a slow, painful death than go to see a doctor. Eventually, I Googled it, learned about detached retinas, about how the retina peels away from where it should be, and how I could go blind if I didn't get to the hospital straight away. That was when I called a taxi.'

We finished our drinks and Charlie went to the bar. The aggrieved couple were still there. They looked like they worked in the City, in their forties, wearing expensive suits and with expressions that said they weren't used to being fucked with. They were talking loudly about how they were going to spend Christmas skiing in a five-star resort 'away from the plebs and all our fucking relatives and their brats.'

When Charlie sat down I told her the rest of the story. About how I'd been rushed into surgery in the small hours of the morning, how all I could remember was being wheeled down the corridor, then waking up with my eye taped shut and a complicated prescription for eye pressure tablets and four different kinds of drops. I had a gas bubble in my eye which would keep my retina in place while it healed. All I could see out of my left eye was a big, wobbling bubble that obscured everything I looked at. I had to sleep sitting upright so gravity would keep the bubble in place.

I spent those first ten days listening to books or watching box sets with my good eye. The tablets bent my senses and made everything taste peculiar, especially alcohol, meaning I didn't drink for two weeks, though when I went out my depth perception was so awry that everyone thought I was drunk.

'It was a pretty shit few weeks,' I said to Charlie, able to laugh about it now.

'You're lucky not to have lost the sight in that eye, then? Though I reckon you'd look good with an eye patch.'

I resisted the urge to put on a pirate voice.

Charlie said, 'What's your problem?'

It took me a moment to realise she wasn't addressing me but the couple at the bar.

The woman was visibly taken aback and moved to turn away but the bloke she was with sneered at Charlie. He was drunk and I felt a prickle of concern that things might escalate into, if not physical violence, then at least the verbal kind.

'*You're* our problem,' the man said.

Charlie sat up straighter. 'Oh really? Why's that?'

'You nicked our table.'

She opened her mouth with mock horror. 'Oh my goodness. Did you hear that, Andrew? This is their table. I didn't realise that, did you?'

'Shut up, slag,' the woman said.

'Ginger minge,' added the man.

Charlie looked shocked for a split second, then laughed. '*Ginger minge*! Wow, I haven't heard that one for a long time. Since secondary school, in fact. Well, yes, it is ginger, as a matter of fact, not that I wear much hair down there. But colour-wise I like to go natural – unlike you.'

She looked pointedly at the woman's dyed-blonde hair.

'Perhaps rather than concentrating on us, you should keep an eye on your husband,' Charlie went on. 'If he looks at the barmaid's tits one more time he's going to go blind.'

The man's face went crimson.

'And mate,' Charlie said, 'you might be interested to learn that while you were in the loo, your bird here had a good look through your phone. Checking your texts, by the look of it. Doesn't trust you – and who can blame her?'

'You what?'

The man and woman glared at each other.

Charlie swallowed the dregs of her wine, grabbed my wrist and said, 'Let's go.'

As we left the pub, she turned back. 'You can stick your bloody table up your collective arse.'

We ran out into the street, Charlie laughing and wiping her eyes. '*Collective arse*? What the hell was that?'

'Oh my God,' I said, panting. 'Are you always like that?'

It was freezing outside and she exhaled mist as she spoke. 'No, I'm usually a pussy cat. I haven't scared you off, have I?'

The truth was, I'd found it mortifyingly embarrassing, but also exciting. 'No.'

'Good. What do you want to do now? Actually, I want to get out of these clothes.' She laughed. 'You should see your face. I mean, I want to get changed, Andrew. These are Charlotte clothes. I need to get into some Charlie stuff.'

She hailed a black cab and instructed the driver to take us to Oxford Street. She led me into the huge Top Shop and immediately started rummaging through the clothes racks.

With arms full of tops and trousers and skirts, she strode over to the changing rooms. For a moment, I thought she was going to ask me to follow her in, but she looked me up and down and said, 'Do you want to get some new stuff too? Have you got any money?'

'Yeah. OK.'

This was fun. I rode the escalator to the next floor and found a new pair of jeans and a party shirt. I paid for them then went into the changing room where I tore off the labels and put them on. With my scruffy old clothes in a carrier bag, I went back downstairs to find Charlie, who had done the same as me. Now, she was wearing a tight-fitting snakeskin dress that shimmered gold and green.

'Not bad,' she said, looking me up and down.

'You look . . . amazing,' I said.

'Thanks. Actually, you look better than not bad, but I didn't want to stroke your ego.'

'I don't have an ego.'

She raised an eyebrow. 'Everyone has an ego, Andrew.'

She was right. It thrilled me to hear her say I looked good.

She grabbed a bottle of perfume and gave herself, and me, a quick squirt as we left the shop. We headed up Oxford Street and into Soho. I wanted to take her hand but didn't dare. Actually, what I really wanted to do was grab her and push her into a shop doorway, pull her against me and feel her mouth on mine.

Instead, we went into a bar where we drank cocktails, then another bar, and then a walk through air so cold it almost sobered me up, to Leicester Square and a club, the name of which escapes me now but which was so loud it made my ears ring for a day afterwards, the drinks ludicrously expensive, the dance floor crowded and sticky underfoot, the toilets full of wankers snorting coke . . . But none of that mattered. I was drunk, I was high on Charlie's company and I felt as if I was floating through the crowds of revellers.

There was a moment on the dance floor that will stay with me forever. A Calvin Harris track was playing, and Charlie was dancing in front of me, holding my gaze and smiling as she swung her hips and shoulders, the lights pulsing and throbbing, and I was aware, even as I lived it, that this was going to be one of the highlights of my life. When I was old this song would come on the radio and I would be thrown back in time to this golden moment, when I was young and dancing with a beautiful woman in the greatest city in the world and all my troubles were behind me and my life stretching in front of me. Then I stopped analysing the moment and melted into it.

We tumbled out of the club at two a.m. into the bitterly cold night. I put my arm around her and she didn't protest. Her hip was bony and solid in my palm. I still hadn't kissed her.

'That was fun,' she said. She yawned. 'And now I'm pooped. I have work in the morning. The last day before the Christmas break.'

There were still a lot of people around. As we walked towards the taxi rank, Charlie flicked her thumb over her phone, texting someone.

A tall man was walking along the pavement towards us. He had a great mop of blonde curly hair. He had his head down, shuffling his feet. Then he looked up and the moment he saw us he crossed the road.

'That was weird,' I said.

'Huh?' Charlie looked up from her phone.

'Some guy just crossed the road like we were a couple of terrifying would-be muggers.'

'Ha – really? Well, you are scary looking, Andrew. I didn't want to say, but . . .'

The tall curly-haired man had vanished into a side street.

'Do you want to share a taxi back to south London?' I asked. 'I mean, it can drop you at yours first . . .'

'You're sweet. But I've just arranged to stay with a friend who lives around here. I'm sorry. I just can't face having to make the journey back in tomorrow morning.'

'No worries.' I felt gutted.

'Give me your number,' she said, handing me her phone. I tapped it in and she saved it to her address book, then looked up at me. 'I've had a great time helping you celebrate, Andrew Sumner.'

'Me too, Charlie Summers.' I didn't want to say goodbye to her.

'I'll call you in a couple of days and we can do it again. Or something more sedate. How does that sound?'

My good mood returned immediately. 'That sounds awesome.'

'Like, totally, dude.'

'Don't tease me,' I said, smiling.

Which was when she kissed me. Slipping her arms around my waist, she tilted her face upwards and we kissed. It seemed to go on for a long time. Someone wolf-whistled as they passed us in the street. It was the best kiss of my life.

She strode away, leaving me standing by the taxi rank, completely smitten. And the amazing thing was, she seemed to like me as much as I liked her.

Three

'What's the matter, bruv? You seem distracted.'

It was Christmas morning and, as always, I was spending the day with my sister, Tilly, in her purpose-built apartment in Eastbourne.

She manoeuvred her wheelchair closer to my armchair, the glass of Buck's Fizz on her tray sloshing dangerously. The room was full of presents and discarded wrapping paper; the fairy lights on the plastic tree flashed on and off and a boy band mimed to their biggest hit on *Top of the Pops*.

'I'm fine,' I said. 'Feeling a bit sick after that huge dinner.'

'You're so full of compliments.'

I laughed. 'I didn't mean it like that, sis. Come on, let's go out, get some air.'

It had been six days and Charlie hadn't called or texted, and no matter how many times a day I fiddled with my phone, making sure the volume was turned up, that I had reception, that I hadn't missed a call, it didn't ring or chime. Why hadn't I taken her number? I didn't even have an excuse to go to the hospital now I'd been discharged, though that would have been pretty sad anyway. I had to face it. She wasn't going to call. We'd had one great night out together, a single kiss and that was it.

Time to move on.

The day before Christmas Eve I was sure I'd seen her near my flat. I'd been out to buy some last-minute presents and wrapping paper, feeling glum, willing myself to forget about Charlie and embrace the Christmas spirit. As I turned into my street, a long road with a mixture of Victorian and Edwardian semis and converted houses not far from beautiful Brockwell Park, I saw a red-haired woman turn into the alleyway opposite my building. Weighed down by shopping bags, I broke into a slow run. The alleyway led through to a new development which bordered the park. There was no sign of her. I walked down the alley and over the fence into the park. Some kids were stomping in a pile of leaves and a man was talking enthusiastically to a cocker spaniel, but there was no red-headed women.

I shook my head. *Great, now I'm hallucinating her*, I thought.

'You're definitely not with it today, are you?' Tilly said as I pushed her along the promenade.

The sky was battleship grey and the wind whipped in from the English Channel. There were some crazy people swimming in the foamy sea, their skin tinted blue as they emerged from the water onto the pebbles. The seafront was busy with children trying out their new bikes, families taking a post-lunch stroll and couples walking arm-in-arm, unwittingly making me envious.

'I met someone,' I said. 'But I think she's got away already.'

'Ah,' Tilly said. 'She must have received my warning note.'

I told my sister about Charlie and about how she hadn't called.

'Her loss,' Tilly said.

I sat on a damp bench beside Tilly and we looked out to sea, silence settling over us.

'Do you miss them?' she asked.

My eyes filled with tears and I clenched my teeth hard, swallowing the bruise in my throat. 'I do on days like this. They'd be happy that we're spending the day together, though.'

'Undoubtedly. Pleased my big brother's here to look after me.'

'You do all right on your own, though, don't you?' I needed her to say yes.

'Oh, of course. I'm an independent woman.' She started humming the Destiny's Child song.

'You should audition for *X Factor*.'

'Go for the big sob story vote, you mean? There'd be a shot of me talking about the car accident. They could show photo-montages of us when Mum and Dad were alive while I sang "Tears in Heaven" in my wheelchair. There wouldn't be a dry eye in the country.'

'You'd win for sure.'

'Nah, I'd get voted out in disco week.'

A couple wearing matching purple fleeces walked by, giggling like they were heading straight back to bed for some mutually satisfying sex.

'So this girl . . . Want to talk about it?' she asked.

I sighed. 'No. There's no point.'

'I always thought you and Sasha would get together. She's lovely.'

'Sasha? She's my best friend. Neither of us would want to ruin that. Plus we don't fancy each other.'

'What?' She expressed mock outrage. 'How could anyone not fancy you? That's crazy talk.'

'Well, yes. How about you? Is everything all right?'

'I thought you were going to ask about my love life for a moment there.'

'Oh?'

She smiled. 'There's nothing to tell, unfortunately. Though there is a very cute guy in the apartment next to mine. Biceps like grapefruit. Plays basketball . . . I might have to go along and watch him. Also, there's this guy at work who I'm pretty sure has got the hots for me.'

'I'm sure he has.' Tilly was gorgeous. Light brown hair, almond eyes, cute like a children's TV presenter. She had a lot more success with the opposite sex than me. She worked as an editor for a children's publisher who was based here on the south coast.

'I just wish he'd do something about it. It's been months and I'm horny as hell.'

'Tilly!'

'Sorry.' She held her hands up. 'Big brother leaves his comfort zone. Well, if you know anyone who wants some hot sex with a girl who can't run away, send him my way. As long as he's hung like . . .'

'Oh God, please.' I covered my ears.

'I do miss them, though,' she said, lurching back to the original subject.

'Just you and me, kid,' I said, and I took hold of the back of her chair and walked on before I had to start pretending to have something in my eye.

The accident had happened when I was sixteen. The four of us were heading home after a weekend away at Center Parcs. I hadn't wanted to go, thinking it was for kids, but we'd had a great time swimming, playing badminton and riding around on bikes all week. Dad had even let me drink, though Tilly wasn't allowed, to her disgust.

'It's not like I'm an alcohol virgin,' she'd muttered to me when our parents were out of earshot. 'In fact . . .'

'Tilly, shut up.'

She had always embarrassed me and made me smile in equal measure.

Mum and Dad had been arguing a lot before the holiday; she seemed irritated with him all the time and I'd been worried they were heading for divorce. But, apart from a couple of episodes related to his forgetfulness, they seemed happy and relaxed together and had even, to my teenage horror, kissed and held hands. Yuk.

'I hope you're lucky like me, Andrew,' Dad said out of nowhere while he barbecued sausages behind our cabin.

'What do you mean?' I asked, fixated on the sizzle of the meat, my stomach gurgling.

'I hope you find a woman like your mum. Someone who really loves you and is good to you.'

I grunted.

'But make sure you sow some wild oats first, eh?' He winked at me and I shuffled away in search of the ketchup.

On the way home, a huge thunderstorm cracked the sky open as we hit the M25. Rain bounced hard off the windscreen and all the cars put their lights on as the world darkened around us. Dad was driving, leaning forward in his seat like being a couple of inches closer to the windshield would help him see through the torrents running down the glass.

Despite leaning forward, he didn't see the lorry that swerved in front of us out of the slow lane until it was too late. All I remember is Dad yelling, Mum trying to grab the wheel, Tilly screaming and a great jarring screech of metal and smash of glass as the car flipped over like a toy.

Dad was killed instantly.

Mum died in the ambulance on the way to hospital.

Tilly was crushed beneath the overturned lorry, her legs shattered beyond repair.

The lorry driver emerged with a single scratch, a bead of blood tracing a line from his forehead down to his lips.

And me: somehow, my corner of the car escaped the lorry. I suffered some bruising, mild whiplash, and I pissed myself with terror. But physically I was all right.

The lucky one.

On Boxing Day, which we spent eating leftovers and staring at the TV in the traditional manner. I went on a bit about my money worries and my need to find more work, but Tilly appeared preoccupied. She kept drifting off and though she smiled when she was talking to me, a couple of times I caught her reflection and saw she was frowning, anxiety creasing her brow. But she denied that anything was wrong so I left it.

Shortly before I was due to leave, Tilly's personal assistant, Rachel, arrived at her flat. Rachel was the woman who helped my sister do the things she couldn't manage by herself, a person who helped her live an independent life. There had been times when I had wondered if that person should be me and had even volunteered. Tilly had point-blank refused, saying that it would ruin our relationship, that she wanted me to be her brother, not her carer. I was relieved in a guilty way.

Rachel rode a huge black and silver Harley Davison and, according to Tilly, treated it like her baby, taking it to conventions, spending every spare minute polishing and tinkering with it. She was tall with sharp cheekbones and short black hair. She looked a little like she should be the guitarist in an early-eighties all-girl rock band and had well-developed arm muscles, from lifting Tilly, that I was envious of.

She came into the flat and dropped her crash helmet on the side, handing Tilly a wrapped bottle before noticing me.

'Hi Rachel,' I said. 'Good Christmas?'

She half-smiled, her hand moving towards her lips. She had a habit of concealing her mouth when she spoke, like she was ashamed of her teeth, not that I could see anything wrong with them. 'Pretty boring, actually. Mostly sitting around listening to my mum and dad bickering. Parents, they're such—'

She went pink as she realised what she'd said. 'Oh God, I'm so sorry.'

'Don't worry about it,' Tilly said and I smiled in agreement.

Rachel looked at my bag. I was going home by train. I wouldn't drive on motorways. I didn't really like driving at all and avoided it wherever necessary.

'Do you need a lift to the station?' she asked.

'What? On your bike?'

Behind me, Tilly made clucking noises. 'You're such a chicken.'

'I'll need a helmet,' I said and Rachel smiled behind her hand. 'There's one here. I got it when I took Tilly out for a ride.'

'It was awesome,' said Tilly, grinning at my surprised expression.

'I guess I've got no excuse then. Actually, I've always wanted to ride a Harley.'

I bent to kiss Tilly's cheek and said goodbye.

'Relax, Andrew,' she said. 'I think you'll enjoy it.' She waved me goodbye. 'Good luck finding work. You can always come and stay here if you can't pay your mortgage.'

'Thanks, sis.'

I straddled the monstrous Harley, all gleaming silver chrome and black rubber, and held on to the sides of the seat. The bike accelerated away without warning and for a moment I thought I was going to fly off the back, so was forced to cling on to Rachel as she roared through the traffic, heading into town, breaking every speed limit like the rules were designed for other, mere mortals. My heart was in my mouth, my mouth was dry, but it was exhilarating and strangely sexy, even if it was Rachel I was holding on to. I imagined what Charlie would look like wearing the leather outfit Rachel had on; pictured us racing along American highways with Charlie's arms wrapped tight around me, the wind whipping her hair . . .

'What did you think?' Rachel said, flipping up her visor as I disembarked outside the station.

I was still shaking off the images off Charlie in black leather. 'Yeah, it was fun. In a terrifying way.'

'You can't beat it,' Rachel said. 'When we all go out riding together, it's the best feeling in the world.'

'All?'

'Yeah, I mean me and the rest of the chapter.'

I recognised the terminology. 'You're a Hells Angel?'

'No, we're not Angels. Not proper ones, anyway. It's just a motorcycle club – we call it "the chapter" as a kind of joke.'

'I see.' I pictured the kind of men Rachel hung out with: long hair, beards, tattoos, attitude.

'Andrew . . .' She looked at the ground.

Uh-oh, I thought. When someone says your name like that it's rarely good news. 'Yes?'

'Have you got five minutes for a chat before your train?'

'Um.' I checked my watch. 'I've got fifteen, actually. What is it?'

She got off the bike. 'Let's go get a cup of tea and I'll tell you. It's about Tilly.'

She bought two cups of tea and we sat down at a greasy Formica table in the station cafe. Rachel's expression and tone of voice had me worried. Was there something wrong with Tilly that I didn't know about?

Rachel fidgeted with the zip on her leather jacket. When she spoke to me, she avoided eye contact, her focus slipping around the room. 'I've wanted to talk to you for a while. But I need your word that you won't tell Tilly I've spoken to you. She'd freak out and fire me.'

Now I was really concerned. 'It depends what it's about.'

She fidgeted some more, her hand straying repeatedly to her mouth as she spoke. 'I'm really worried about her. I'm sure you know that she's always been prone to black moods, days when she is snappy and down and, to be frank, feels sorry for herself. But recently it's been getting worse and worse. The good days are less common than the bad days now.'

I was shocked. I *didn't* know that Tilly suffered from black moods, beyond the occasional grump that everyone in the world suffers.

'I think the doctor has put her on a different antidepressant, but since Jonathan dumped her . . .'

I raised my palms. 'Whoa. Hold on. Antidepressants? And who's Jonathan?'

She appeared genuinely shocked, meeting my eye for the first time. 'I didn't realise you didn't know. I thought you and Tilly were close.'

'Obviously not as close as I thought.'

'I'm sorry. OK, the crux of it is this: about a month ago she started seeing this guy who she met at the pool. I take her swimming a couple of times a week.'

'That's Jonathan? Is he disabled too?'

'Yes – he's an ex-soldier, lost his leg beneath the knee when he stepped on a mine in Iraq. Anyway, Tilly was completely smitten with him. She talked about him all the time.'

Not with me, I thought.

'He dumped her a couple of weeks ago. Out of nowhere. She thought everything was going brilliantly. She's been distraught ever since.'

I drummed my fingers on the table. The pub was empty and silent apart from the burbling fruit machine in the corner and an old man talking to his dog.

'Are you sure this is nothing more than her being heartbroken?' She raised an eyebrow.

'I'm not saying heartbreak isn't serious. But everyone gets down after they split up with someone they really liked.'

'It's more than that,' Rachel insisted. 'She keeps talking about how she's got nobody, how shit her life is, saying she's got nothing to live for. I think you should talk to her.'

What she had told me turned the blood in my veins to ice.

'But without giving away that you talked to me?'

'That would be ideal, yes. Like I said, she'd be really angry. If you could do something to cheer her up . . . show her she has got something to live for. What with you being so far away—'

'I'm only up the road in London.' It was seventy miles away.

'I know. But you don't see each other very often, do you?'

If I hadn't been so concerned about Tilly, I might have felt affronted by this woman, whom I barely knew, hinting that I was neglecting my sister. Instead, along with the chill of concern, the main emotion I felt was guilt.

'I need to think about what to do,' I said, after contemplating Rachel's words for a while. Part of me wanted to go straight back to Tilly's and talk to her, but I agreed with Rachel's planned approach. It would be better to be subtle. Plus I was so surprised by what I'd heard that I needed time for it all to sink in.

'That sounds wise,' Rachel said, displaying a rare smile. 'Thanks, Andrew.'

'No. Thank *you*. Tilly's lucky she has someone who cares about her so much.'

Rachel picked up her crash helmet and ran a palm over its smooth dome. 'If only she realised that.'

Back in London, I stopped for a coffee then headed for my connecting train.

My phone rang. It was a number I didn't recognise. My hopes surged – was it her?

'Hello?'

The call disconnected.

Annoyed, I switched my phone off. I needed to forget her. Get over it. I hadn't been dumped, like my poor sister. It hadn't even begun.

My flat is on the fourth floor of a Victorian terrace. Once upon a time, I guess it would have been an attic. It was cramped and the climb up the stairs was exhausting, but the view was fantastic. I could see the shining great transmitter in Crystal Palace, plus, in the other direction, I had a clear view across the park towards the Gherkin. The neighbours were nice. And it had been all I could afford. Both Mum and Dad had been insured and the money was put into a trust for Tilly and me. On my insistence, most of the money went to Tilly, to buy her apartment, but I'd had enough to put a deposit on this flat and pay for my education.

I carried my luggage up the stairs, chucked it on the bed and ran myself a bath. I thought about calling Sasha, see if she wanted to meet up, but remembered she was in Cornwall visiting her family. So I had a typical boring evening: I surfed the net, watched some TV, nuked something out of the freezer, played a bit of online poker.

At around eleven, I got undressed, ready for bed. My phone fell out of my jeans pocket and thudded on the floor. It had been switched off all evening.

As soon as I turned it on, it vibrated twice. I had a missed call and a voicemail. Both were from an unknown mobile number, though not from the number that had hung up on me earlier.

I listened to the voicemail.

It was her.

'Hey, Andrew . . . just going to wait a sec in case you're screening. No? Or maybe you are and you don't want to talk to me because I've been such a flake. Or maybe it was the kiss. Maybe you didn't like it. Though I thought it was a good one. Very good, actually. Oh God, I'm rambling.'

A smile spread across my face.

'So, yes, this is what happened: I lost my phone. I know, I know. Sounds like the oldest excuse in the book. But it's true, I swear to God. I lost it and didn't have your number because it was saved to my phone and not the thingy. I don't know the technical word for it. The cloud, or whatever. So, anyway, I thought that was it, that you'd hate me forever, or maybe be hugely relieved that this annoying girl who picks fights in pubs was leaving you alone. And then I was back at work today – no rest for the wicked – and did something a bit naughty. I looked up your details on the NHS database. Um, hope you don't mind.'

Mind? I was ecstatic.

'Give me a call. If you want to. I had fun the other night. Lots of fun. I'll probably be up late so call me whenever. Wake me up, I don't care. Bye!'

I punched the air.

Four

Charlie had arranged to come round at six. 'Don't worry about cooking me dinner or anything like that,' she said when I called her back. I probably should have waited till the next day, or even the day after. Make her sweat a little. But I'm not very good at playing it cool.

I wished I was cooking for her, even though I am hopeless in the kitchen, because it would have given me something to do to distract me. Instead, I spent the day prowling like a polar bear at the zoo, watching the minutes tick by. I showered, agonised over whether to clean shave or trim my stubble, spent ages trying to decide what to wear, tidied the flat three times, tried to work out what music should be playing when she arrived.

I had never acted like this before. Halfway through the afternoon I sat down and gave myself a silent talking to. This was ridiculous. She was just a girl. I'd only met her once. Then I started worrying. What if we didn't get on? What if she saw me and realised she didn't like me after all? Or vice versa, though that seemed highly unlikely.

The doorbell rang at five minutes past six, after I had convinced myself she wasn't coming.

'Hello,' she said, beaming at me and stepping forward to give me a hug. She smelled of expensive perfume and looked delicious, wearing a soft black dress and knee-high boots. 'It's freezing out here. Are you going to invite me in?'

'Of course. Come in.'

'If I was a vampire, you'd be screwed.'

'I wouldn't mind if you were,' I said.

'Well, if you want me to bite you . . .' She laughed. 'I feel a bit hyper. Sorry, I'm not normally like this.'

'Me neither.'

A look passed between us and I knew that any fears I'd had about awkwardness or not liking each other had been foolish. People talk about chemistry, about sparks flying between people, and that was exactly what was going on here. I had been strongly attracted to other women before, even thought myself in love, but I'd never experienced something as intense and *fast* as this.

I led her up the four flights of stairs and into my flat.

She handed me two bottles of wine. 'One white, one red. I wasn't sure which you prefer.'

'I'm easy. But you're red, yes?'

'Hmm, yes please.' Her eyes had gone over my shoulder, taking in the room. I left her to look around while I went into the tiny kitchen to open the wine. I grasped the worktop for a moment, telling myself to get a grip. Be cool.

When I returned she was looking at the computer, scrolling through my playlists.

'You don't mind, do you?'

I handed her the glass of red and took a sip of mine. 'Of course not.'

'In the old days – or so I've heard – you could go round someone's place and rifle through their record collection, take a look at their bookcases. Now you have to scroll through their iTunes or click on their Kindle. It's not the same, is it? I'm pleased to see you have some real books though.'

She stepped over to the bookcase and ran a finger along the spines. A lot of my books are graphic design tomes and photography, with a small collection of novels.

She took out an Ian McEwan book, flicked through it and said, 'I love this. I can't bear people who don't read. I think they must have something wrong with them, don't you?'

'I guess so.'

'Books, music, art, films.' She held up her glass. 'Good wine. It's what life's all about.'

I held up my own glass. 'To books, music, art, films and wine.'

She had missed something off that list, but I decided not to mention it. It was in the room with us already.

We clinked and she crossed to the window. 'Amazing view.'

'I know. It's even better from the bedroom.'

I realised what that must sound like but before I could speak she laid her hand across her breastbone and said, '*Andrew*. I've only been here five minutes. Oh, are you blushing?'

'I think I might be.'

'Quick,' she said. 'Change the subject before it gets awkward.'

She sat down on the sofa and I had a moment of indecision. Sit next to her or in the adjacent armchair? I sat beside her and we turned towards each other, knees almost touching. I groped for something interesting to say.

'When are you going back to work?' I asked.

'That is a change of subject. I've got a whole week off. Bliss.'

'So you're a project manager?'

She pulled a face. 'Boring, huh? I just happen to be very good at organising things and people. It's not exactly what I want to spend my life doing.'

I waited for her to continue.

'I did an art degree. That's what I really want to be doing. Painting. But there are thousands of us out there and the world needs more painters like it needs more politicians. So at the moment I do it in my spare time.'

We talked for a little bit about her art, about how she was trying to get some of her paintings shown at a big exhibition that was coming up, and then we talked a little about graphic design, though I didn't have that much to say about it. I mainly wanted to listen to her talk, to hear her melodic voice as she skipped about from topic to topic. She knew a lot about literature and music as well as art, and when she spoke, her passion for these things, for culture, for life, was infectious. She was funny too, and unusual. I had never met anyone like her.

I refilled our glasses.

'You must be doing okay from being a designer,' she said, 'if you could afford to buy this place.'

'Did I tell you I'd bought this place?' I couldn't remember much of the conversation.

'Yeah, you said something about having a mortgage.'

'Wow, Mr Interesting. But I can afford this place because of money I got from my parents.'

Charlie gave me another of her ironic looks. 'Ooh, are you rich? Have I lucked out?'

I hesitated. I don't really like to tell people about my parents straight away because I don't want them to feel sorry for me, and it can be awkward. I certainly didn't want Charlie to feel sympathy for me but, at the same time, I didn't want to keep any secrets from her, so I told her, keeping my voice as light as possible.

'Oh Andrew,' she said, her eyes shining with compassion. 'That must have really . . . sucked.'

I couldn't help but laugh. 'You could put it like that.'

'I'd like to meet Tilly. She sounds very brave.'

'Yeah, she is. But if you said that to her she'd tell you to fuck off.'

'Ha. My kind of girl. And then you had your eye thing. Sounds like you've had a lot of bad luck.'

I took another sip of wine, surprised to find that I'd finished my second glass.

'I've had some good luck too,' I said.

She raised an eyebrow. 'You won the Lottery?'

'No, I mean meeting you.'

She grinned. 'Oh God, that is *so* corny.'

But she put her arms around me and kissed me.

It was even better than the kiss we'd shared at the end of our night out. She was so soft, and her lips so warm, and heat radiated off her body as she pressed it against me. It was like being a teenager again: kissing for its own sake, not only as a prelude to sex. Charlie made little noises in her throat, her eyes shut tight, one hand on my chest, the other snaking around my back, slipping up inside my T-shirt.

'You're a very good kisser,' she said, breaking off for a moment. 'Have you had lots of practice?'

I just laughed.

We kissed some more, music playing in the background, our empty wine glasses at our feet. She took my hand and put it on her thigh, her dress hitched up, and soon my T-shirt was lying beside the wine glasses.

'Do you want to go to bed?' she asked.

I nodded. When I stood up, the room swam. Drunk on wine and Charlie. I held her hand and helped her up, realising I needed a pee. Typical – my bladder was determined to ruin the atmosphere.

'I need to go to the bathroom,' I said. 'The bed's that way.'

My bedroom had a dimmer switch and when I got back from the bathroom I found that Charlie had turned the light low. Her clothes were on the floor and she was in the bed, the quilt tucked under her chin. I stripped, wondering for a moment if I should take everything off or leave my underwear on, deciding to go for it. I kicked my shorts across the room.

'Fuck, your hands are cold,' she protested.

'They'll be warm in a minute.'

We stopped talking.

I won't pretend that our first time was amazing. I was too anxious about my performance, not yet familiar with her body, what she liked, what she wanted me to do. Our limbs knocked together, we both whispered apologies a couple of times. I had to concentrate hard to stop myself from finishing too soon, determined to make her come before me.

Not only that, but I was too aware that I was making love to Charlie, this woman who, in the few days I'd known her, had filled my head, knocked me out of orbit. It was impossible to sink into the moment, to become fully absorbed, because I was watching myself, recording the moment like someone taking a video on their phone at a gig, instead of enjoying the there and then.

Afterwards, Charlie lay with her head on my chest, her hair tickling my face.

'Do you think I'm easy?' she said, hoisting herself up and looking into my eyes. Her face and collarbone were flushed from her orgasm. She really was the most beautiful woman I'd ever seen.

'If you are, I must be too.'

'That's true. But there are different rules for guys, aren't there?'

'Stupid rules.'

She kissed me. 'Can you see me without your glasses?'

'Not much. I have to get really close.'

'They suit you,' she said. 'You've got that hot professor thing going on. You look cute without them too. Like a little mole.'

'Oh, thanks!'

'I like moles.'

'I like freckles,' I said, touching hers.

'Oh God, you really are corny.'

'I know. I just made myself sick.'

She rolled onto her side, propping her head up with her elbow, her free hand tracing patterns on my torso. 'How come you haven't been snapped up already?'

'I was going to ask you the same thing.'

She grinned. 'Plenty have tried to snap me up, Andrew.'

I must have looked worried, because she said, 'Don't worry, I'm not about to give you a speech about how I'm not looking for anything. On the other hand, I'm not going to ask you to marry me either.'

'Phew.'

'I do like you though.'

'Yeah, I can tell.'

She mock-slapped me. 'Watch it. So, anyway, you didn't answer my question. About why you don't have a girlfriend.'

'Oh. Well, I did have one until about nine months ago. We were together for a couple of years.'

The hand that had been drawing spirals on my flesh stopped moving. 'What was her name?'

'Harriet.'

'Harriet! Posh.'

I stroked Charlie's shoulder. 'She was a little bit posh, yes.'

'Did she have a pony?'

'As a matter of fact . . . When she was a kid, anyway. I think she had a couple.'

Charlie was silent for a second. 'So what happened with posh pony-loving Harriet?'

I shrugged. 'Oh, there was no big drama. We were together a couple of years, we talked about moving in together, but then it kind of went flat. Fizzled out. We're still friends though.'

Charlie's hand had started wandering up and down my torso again. 'Is that her picture out there in the living room?'

'Huh? Oh – no, that's Sasha. My best friend.'

There was a photo of Sasha and me on holiday in Ibiza on the wall by the door. We were standing on top of a large rock, laughing. It had been a fun holiday, quite debauched, in fact.

'She looks like a laugh.'

'Yeah, she's lovely. I'll introduce you to her.'

'Can't wait.'

She kissed me again, wriggling closer, and the kiss grew more passionate and Charlie came closer still until she was on top of me. We made love again, and this time I was fully absorbed, not worried about anything at all, great warm rushes of happiness enveloping me as Charlie made me feel better than I'd ever felt before.

Five

At some point during the next couple of days, I told Charlie about Tilly and my conversation with Rachel.

'So I need to find something to try to cheer her up,' I said. We were lying in bed. We had been in my bed for almost forty-eight hours, only leaving it to go to the bathroom or to eat or grab drinks.

'You think that's a better plan than simply talking to her?'

'Well . . . I think what I'd like to do is take her out somewhere and then talk to her, rather than turn up and say I want to have a word with her.'

'You're lovely,' she said.

I liked hearing her say things like that.

'What kind of thing does she like doing?' Charlie asked.

'That's the tricky part. She's really into sport – she supports Arsenal, for her sins – and she loves swimming. Other than that, normal stuff.' I shrugged. 'Stuff that girls like.'

'Stroking kittens, knitting, cooing over babies. That kind of thing?'

'Exactly.'

'Having their nipples slowly licked while their boyfriend slides ever so slowly into them . . .'

'Actually, Tilly is the only woman I know who's even ruder than you.'

Charlie smiled. 'I'd love to meet her.'

'You will.'

'And I'll try to think of some ideas. You're clearly a bit useless at that kind of stuff.'

'True. Thank you.'

'So. What I was saying about nipples . . .'

Charlie went home in the afternoon to do laundry and 'some woman stuff,' as she put it.

'Not meeting your other boyfriend?'

She didn't think it was funny. 'I'm a one hundred per cent monogamous person. I hope you are too.'

'Yes, of course.' I pulled her against me. 'Like I'd have enough energy left anyway.'

She kissed me softly. 'That's what I like to hear.'

It was the first exchange we'd had that made me think that she saw us as boyfriend-girlfriend. Some men might have been frightened by this development but I was delighted.

When she came back later, she was carrying several carrier bags full of shopping. She produced a market stall's worth of fresh vegetables from one bag – broccoli, red and yellow peppers, plump tomatoes, button mushrooms, a cauliflower smeared with mud – and a variety of spices and pulses from another. The third bag contained two bottles of wine. She opened one, commanded me to relax and have a drink and set about cooking what turned out to be the best curry I've ever eaten.

She rolled a couple of spliffs too, one of which she smoked with me while she was waiting for dinner to cook. I wasn't normally into drugs of any kind – hadn't been since university – but the weed made me feel so chilled and giggly that I wondered why I didn't do it more often. After dinner I laid the quilt on the living room floor and we made slow, stoned love to a playlist of old soul classics Charlie found on Spotify: Marvin Gaye, Donny Hathaway. Writhing in slow motion on the floor, it felt like we were making love for hours, the rest of the world eradicated by the intense focus of our desire for each other. It was extraordinary, like nothing I'd ever experienced before. It was like being in a fugue state, my whole body alive and humming, wanting to consume Charlie, to devour her, my mouth all over her, and hers all over me.

The trance was only broken when, in a stoned voice, I told Charlie her skin was 'softer than kitten's fur' and she roared with laughter, and then I did too and within moments we were rolling about literally clutching our sides, barely able to breathe.

'Ha, ha, bonk,' I said, when I was able to get some air into my lungs.

'What?'

'It's the sound—' A convulsion of laughter stabbed at me. 'The sound of a man laughing his head off.'

That set us off again.

Eventually, when we'd come down and calmed down, Charlie lay on her front beside me, legs crossed at the ankle, showing off the small mermaid tattoo on her right ankle, and said, 'Can you get your sister to come up to London on Saturday?'

'I expect so? Why?'

She laid her head on one side and smiled. 'I have a surprise for you.'

Charlie asked me to meet her by the London Eye at noon. At Victoria station I steered Tilly through the vast crowds, many of them apparently heading to a football match. Tilly and I stopped en route to the taxi to grab a doughnut, my treat.

'What's all this in aid of?' she asked in the back of a black cab. 'The doughnut?'

'The excursion! You don't invite me up very often.'

Traffic was slow and I was concerned we'd be late to meet Charlie. No matter how much I'd begged, she wouldn't tell me what she had planned.

'Andrew?' Tilly said.

'I just thought it would be fun for us to spend a day together. Plus I want you to meet Charlie.'

'Wow. You've only known her for two minutes.'

'Yeah, but . . .'

'Oh. Em. Gee.' Tilly put on a silly voice. 'My big brother is in el you vee.'

'Stop it.' But I knew my face must have gone pink. I groped for something else to say. Although Tilly seemed amused, I was worried that flaunting my new relationship, when I was supposed to be helping to cheer up my recently dumped sister, was going to have the reverse effect.

We sat and watched the scenery roll by, a thin mist giving the London streets a soft-focus Saturday morning sheen. The cab dropped us by Borough Market. We were early and I wanted breakfast, so I bought us each a bacon roll, which made Tilly moan with pleasure, before heading down to the South Bank.

'Doughnuts. Bacon rolls. Is your plan for today to fatten me up and sell me to a hungry troll?'

'Damn. Rumbled.'

It was bitterly cold by the river and the Thames was the colour of a bruise, but the icy wind was invigorating, a wake-up slap that made my nose run and my eyes sting.

'Dad would have said this was brass monkeys,' Tilly commented.

'Are you too cold?' I asked.

'No, I like it. I always think I'm at my most attractive when my teeth are chattering and my nose is red.'

As we neared the London Eye, where Charlie had asked us to meet her, the morning crowds thickened. A street performer covered head-to-toe in silver robot make-up was setting up and the skater kids were already doing their stuff. Outside the National Film Theatre, early-morning shoppers browsed second-hand paperbacks. Then, in the distance, I saw Charlie and my heart did this little skipping thing.

'That's her.'

'Where?' Tilly asked.

'The beautiful one.'

Tilly pointed to a bag lady enjoying an early-morning can of cider on a nearby bench. 'What, her?'

'Yes. It was the scent of her crusty hair that first drew me to her.'

Tilly laughed. 'Hey, do you remember that homeless guy who used to live in Eastbourne – what was his name? Bobby Pole?'

Charlie had spotted us. She waved and walked towards us.

'Yes. Bobby Pole. Mum said she saw him once in the indoor market.'

'When he stopped and shook his trouser leg.'

'And a fossilised turd fell out.'

Charlie arrived. She was wearing a long black coat and was wrapped in a scarf with a green woollen hat completing the winter look. Spots of pink burned in her pale cheeks. She looked adorable. She grinned, showing the little gap between her two front teeth. 'What are you two laughing at?'

I told her the story of Bobby Pole and Charlie laughed like this was the funniest thing anyone she'd ever heard. Tilly and I joined in. I had never laughed as much as I had the last few days. I didn't know if my stomach could take much more.

'Tilly, this is Charlie,' I said when I'd got my breath back. 'Charlie, Tilly.'

They shook gloved hands.

'So you're the girl,' Tilly said.

'Oh no, don't embarrass me,' I said.

Tilly held up her hands, mock-innocent. 'Hey, I'm not going to say a word.'

'Please do,' said Charlie.

'So what are we doing?' I asked, redirecting the conversation.

Charlie gestured behind her. 'I've booked us tickets on the Eye to start with. Have you been on it before?'

Neither of us had. Tilly was delighted and wheeled herself along beside Charlie towards the big wheel, the two of them chatting like they'd known each other for years. Charlie gesticulated as she talked, her face animated. She looked like a movie star, the girl next door in an old American film, and I was struck by two emotions, one immediately following the other: joy, that she was with me; and fear, that at any moment she might disappear like she did after our first night out. I told myself to get a grip. Relax, enjoy it. She seemed to like me a lot. The way she looked at me reflected back the way I looked at her. And if she didn't care about me, didn't want to give this budding relationship the chance to bloom, she wouldn't be here now, taking my sister out, would she?

The London Eye was even better than I'd hoped, the city stretched out before us, proud and ancient and alive. Charlie pointed out her favourite buildings and Tilly recounted the time she and 'a load of other wheelchair kids' were taken to Buckingham Palace to meet the Queen. Charlie had a related story, about how the Queen had come to their school in Leeds and they'd all stood outside waving flags, hoping she'd brought her corgis with her.

'I'm not a big fan of the royals now, though,' she said.

'Oh, are you a republican?' Tilly asked.

Charlie waved a hand. 'Actually, let's not spoil the day with politics.'

I knew already, from watching the news with her, that anything Charlie saw as injustice made her angry. I had listened to her rage against some new policy the government had brought in, the so-called bedroom tax, and halfway through her diatribe I'd had to calm her down, pointing out that I wasn't the prime minister and couldn't do much about it. I liked the fact that she cared so much, though. It was another sign that she was a passionate person.

After the London Eye, we went on to Trafalgar Square and looked round the National Portrait Gallery.

'Charlie's an artist,' I pointed out to Tilly.

'An aspiring artist,' Charlie said.

'I really want to see some of your work,' I said.

'You will. Maybe you can pose for me.'

I was taken aback and Tilly laughed. 'If you get Andrew to pose for you naked, please don't ever show me the picture.'

That set them off again and led on to a conversation about penises that got ruder and ruder as we walked around the gallery, the two of them giggling like schoolgirls and pointing at portraits of historical figures and rock stars.

'Six inches, I reckon.'

'I'd say he's got a nine-incher.'

'A disappointment.'

Finally bored of this game, Charlie went into the gift shop and came out with a present for Tilly: a print of the Queen.

'Next time you meet her, you can ask her to sign it,' she said.

After that, Charlie surprised us by announcing that she had booked us a table at the excellent restaurant upstairs. 'I'm paying,' she said and when Tilly and I tried to protest she told us she'd won some cash on a scratchcard and was feeling flush.

We spent the afternoon walking around Covent Garden, looking in the shops, the two girls browsing the sales. Charlie bought herself a black silky top and bought me a new jumper, 50 per cent cashmere, which was exactly my kind of thing.

Towards the end of the afternoon, Charlie said she was going to run back to a shop we'd looked in earlier, and left Tilly and me alone.

'So?' I said.

Tilly raised an eyebrow. 'You mean, what do I think of her? She's lovely. Amazing. Sweet and gorgeous and a real laugh. Where on earth did you find her? Did you make her in a lab like those boys in *Weird Science?*'

I was thrilled to hear this. 'I'm worried she's too good for me.'

'Well . . .' Seeing my face she added, 'I'm only kidding, Andrew. The two of you look awesome together. It's great to see you so happy.'

'Thanks, sis.' I paused. 'What about you? How are you doing at the moment?'

'Me? I'm fine.'

'Are you sure?'

'Why are you asking?'

'Oh. I don't know. I just thought you seemed a bit down over Christmas.'

She looked at me suspiciously. 'Did Rachel say something to you? Only, she was acting very suspiciously when she came back from dropping you at the station. Plus she took ages. I thought the two of you had eloped. And then she was ultra-interested when I told her I was coming up to see you today.'

'No. She didn't say anything.'

'Hmm. Well, I'm honestly fine. I was seeing this guy and was upset when he gave me the heave-ho, but I'm not depressed or anything like that.'

'But . . .' I decided to come clean. 'Rachel told me you're on antidepressants.'

Tilly's face was stony. 'Did she? For fuck's sake. I wish she'd keep this,' she touched her nose, 'out of it.'

'She was worried about you, that's all.'

'So you decided you needed to do something to cheer me up? The poor crippled charity case.'

I was mortified. Her voice was loud and people around us, in the street, were gawping. 'Tilly. It's not like that. Rachel told me you were down and I felt bad that I hardly ever see you. It's not a charity thing. Come on, you know me better than that.'

She calmed down. 'OK. But, listen. Yes, I have been depressed. It happens. It's not something you can fix with a day out, but it's not a huge deal. I cope. I have medication which makes me feel better and I've actually been feeling pretty bright since Christmas. Looking forward to a new year.' She gazed into the crowd. 'And I really appreciate you trying to cheer me up. It's been a brilliant day and, despite being a bit useless when it comes to emotional stuff, you are a good brother, OK? Now give me a hug.'

I stooped to embrace her.

'I'm sorry,' I whispered.

'You've got nothing to be sorry about. But you can't fix me. You just have to be there for me.'

When I straightened up I saw Charlie standing a few metres away, watching us, a serious expression on her face. When she realised I'd seen her she came over.

'I'd better be getting back,' Tilly said.

We got a cab to Victoria and Charlie and I waited on the platform with my sister.

'Please don't sack Rachel,' I said. 'She cares about you.'

'Don't fret. I won't.' She looked up at Charlie, who was holding on to my arm. 'Be good to my brother. He can be an idiot but he deserves to be happy.'

I expected Charlie to crack a joke but her response was earnest.

'I'm going to make him happy,' she said. 'Don't you worry about that.'

Six

Hiya. Haven't heard from you since Xmas. You OK? Been trying to call. Can we meet up? I need to see you. Call me! S Xx

Charlie and I were in bed, again. Since our day out with Tilly we'd barely left the flat, only popping out to buy takeaways and wine, along with condoms and candles, which Charlie had insisted on for the bedroom. She'd bought scented bath oil too and some new pink-and-black underwear that had a Viagra-like effect on me. A couple of times, she'd popped back to hers to get clothes, check her post and so on, and I'd made a few solo trips to the off licence when it was raining outside, leaving Charlie snuggled on the sofa watching reruns of *Sex and the City*.

I felt drunk. When I closed my eyes, Charlie's face or body – her pierced belly button winking in the candlelight, the mermaid tattoo, the little chains of freckles that dotted her flesh – would swim into my vision. My jaw ached from grinning so much. My muscles and skin felt alive in a way they never had before.

It was as if a chemical explosion had gone off in my flat, Charlie and I the willing, happy victims. She didn't have to go back to work till January 4th, which was now only two days away. I was going to have to call Victor, start doing some work too. I was dreading it. I wanted to stay with Charlie in our little bubble forever.

My phone chirped and Charlie, who was closest to the bedside table, leant over and picked it up, passing it over. I read the text message.

'What's up?' she asked, reading my expression.

'It's Sasha. She wants to see me.'

'Oh – is she all right?'

'I'm not sure. Sounds like something's wrong. I'd better call her.' I kissed Charlie's cheek. She smelled of fresh sweat and lavender soap. 'I feel terrible. I haven't spoken to her all week. I didn't even send her a happy New Year message.'

Charlie and I had been planning to go out for New Year but had spent the night inside instead. Charlie said she wanted to be making love to me at the stroke of midnight, that it would be the best possible way to start 2014, and I had to agree.

Charlie sat up and pulled on a long T-shirt. 'I'm going to take a shower.'

I sat up too. 'Are you annoyed with me?'

'No, of course not.' She sounded irritated. 'Why do you ask that?'

'Oh, no reason.' I smiled at her and watched as she left the room, worrying a little about her sudden change in mood. But I set the worry aside – it was probably just me being paranoid. Harriet was always telling me that I was too quick to guess her moods and try to fix problems that didn't exist.

I called Sasha. She answered on the second ring. We arranged to meet that night.

'So?' Charlie said, when she came back into the room, damp from the bath, a towel wrapped round her. 'What's up with Sasha?'

'Boyfriend problems, by the sound of it,' I replied. 'She's been seeing this guy called Lance. He's married.'

Charlie pulled a face. 'Messy.'

'Yeah, it is. Anyway . . . I'm going to meet her at seven in Herne Hill.' I checked my phone. It was three now, just gone.

Charlie lifted the towel to dry her hair, giving me a full view of her naked body.

'That's cool,' she said, rubbing her hair. 'I have some stuff I need to do, anyway. Like ironing all my work clothes.' She groaned. 'I'll get dressed and go now.'

I reached out for her. 'Don't get dressed yet.'

She looked hesitant, just for a moment. Then she pulled the quilt aside and slipped underneath with me, her damp hair cold on my hot skin as she trailed kisses down my torso.

Before she left, she walked round the flat taking photos with her phone: the rumpled bed, the kitchen, which was full of empty wine bottles, the sink piled high with washing-up, even the bathroom.

'What are you doing?' I asked.

'You're going to think I'm a real sap, but I want to be able to picture you here when I'm not with you.'

'What, among all the mess?'

She put her arm around me and held the phone up to take a snap of us together.

'Say sausages.'

She took the snap then told me she needed the loo before she went. I sat and flicked through the newspaper, becoming absorbed in the latest news about the Dark Angel serial killer who had been found guilty of the murder of twenty-three elderly people. There was a photo of the guy who had discovered what she'd done, a former neighbour of hers. He said he hoped she would rot in jail and then burn in hell. Not for the first time, I was glad my neighbours were agreeable.

Charlie came back into the room, smelling of perfume. For a moment, she was caught in the sunlight coming through the window.

'Why are you looking at me like that?' she asked.

'Just . . . because.' I stood up and pulled her close to me, peering into her eyes, pretending to examine her. 'Are you real?'

She squirmed away. 'What do you mean, you idiot?'

'You seem too good to be true.'

I had expected her to treat what I was saying jokily but she was surprisingly serious. 'I'm really not that good.'

Apart from some of the more intense moments in bed, most of our exchanges over the past week had been light-hearted and playful. This new gravity took me aback.

'I was only messing around,' I said and, after staring at the carpet thoughtfully for a few long seconds, she finally smiled.

'I just want you to know that—' she began. 'Oh, this is crazy.'

I took her hands. 'What is?'

'Nothing. I'm being stupid, that's all. Ignore me. I'm about to start my period and it's making me feel a bit girly and emotional. Please stop me before I say something I regret.'

We hugged and I didn't want to let her go. But Sasha needed me, and it was time I stopped being such a bad friend.

⌣

As I was about to leave, my doorbell rang. It was Kristi, my cleaner.

'I completely forgot you were coming,' I said.

Kristi was from Albania, a slim woman in her early twenties with black hair cut in a bob, dark eyes and a prominent scar that ran down her left cheek. Of course, I'd never asked her about the scar, though I wondered about it in the same way I'd wondered what she would be like in bed when she had first started working for me. I'd hired her during a period when I was crazily busy with work, last spring, and had got used to her weekly visits, during which she mostly did my ironing, half-heartedly. She wasn't a very good cleaner, but I liked her and imagined a terrible background in which she sent home the pennies I gave her to a poverty-stricken mother, so I kept her on, always paying her slightly too much and telling her to keep the change.

'You want me to go?' she asked.

'No, no, come in.' I glanced around the flat. It was a mess and I noticed how Kristi wrinkled her nose. What did it smell of? Perfume? Sex?

'I will tidy up, yes?' she said, frowning.

'Yes please. Let yourself out, OK?'

I followed her gaze. There was a black, lacy bra on the sofa.

'Um . . . Maybe just do the dusting and hoovering? I'll tidy up later.'

I left her looking disapprovingly around the room. It was weird. Before meeting Charlie I thought Kristi was hot. Now she looked rather plain and uninteresting.

———

'Oh God, Andrew. Why am I such a cliché?'

'You're not. Well, you are, but these things don't feel like clichés when you're living them, do they?'

'That's almost wise.'

We were sitting in The Commercial, opposite Herne Hill station, pints half-full on the table before us.

I met Sasha at university. She was the girlfriend of a guy on my course whose name I could barely remember now. I got on with her much better than I did with him. We liked the same things – the same books, music, art, all the things Charlie had said made life worth living – and shared a sense of humour. We just clicked. But we didn't fancy each other, even though Sasha's boyfriend thought we did, and everyone said we should be together. It wasn't like that, though. I loved Sasha, but in a purely platonic way. This wasn't because she wasn't fanciable, either. She was very attractive, with straight dark hair, trendy dark-framed glasses and a curvy figure.

'If I was a bloke or a lesbian I'd be all over her like a rash,' Tilly said. 'Actually, she makes me come over all bi-curious.'

Yet another occasion when my sister made me cover my face with my hands.

Sasha was a web developer, a bit of a geek, who also loved science fiction and video games. She was recovering from a teenage obsession with *Buffy* and *Angel*.

The married-man thing was so unlike her. But this guy, Lance, was a programming genius, apparently, and had a touch of the Steve Jobs about him. Sasha told me she'd been unable to resist his advances, had tried not to think about his wife, whom he portrayed as a cold-hearted bitch who didn't understand him.

It was clichéd, all right.

'So what happened? Did his wife find out?'

She nodded glumly. 'How did you guess?'

'It had to be either that, or he decided he loved her and could never leave her.'

Sasha took a big swig of her pint. The lenses of her glasses were filthy, like they'd been splashed with tears. 'She phoned me. The wife. Her name's Mae. She said that if I went near her husband again, her brothers would track me down and, I quote, "cut off my tits and sew up my cunt".'

'Jesus.'

'It was really scary. I'm so glad I don't work with Lance anymore.' Her lower lip wobbled. 'I miss him, though.'

I trotted out all the stuff friends have to say in these circumstances: you deserve better, you need someone who really loves you. But I meant them, because as I said the words all I could think of was Charlie.

'He was kinky,' Sasha said, after she'd sunk another pint.

'Do I want to hear this?' I asked.

'He liked having USB sticks shoved up his bum. You know, dongles.'

I spat out my beer. 'Dongles up his bum?'

She creased up with laughter. 'Yes. But the plastic end, not the metal USB end.'

'Oh, that's all right then. Anything else?'

'Well . . . He liked wearing a nappy, and pretending to breast-feed off me.'

'What?'

She smiled. 'I'm joking.'

'Thank God.'

'About the nappy part, anyway.'

I went to the toilet, checking my phone while I took a leak. A couple of texts from Charlie, one saying that she hoped Sasha was all right, the next telling me she missed me and had been thinking about me. As I was leaving the gents, my phone flashed again. It was a photo – a selfie, of a topless Charlie.

'So what have you been up to?' Sasha asked when I got back to the table. 'Why have you been incommunicado?'

'Huh?' I was distracted, thinking about the picture I'd just received.

'What's going on with you?'

I stuck my phone in my pocket. 'I wasn't sure if I should tell you, what with your whole Lance thing. But . . . I've met someone.'

'Wow. Really? What's her name, what's she like and does she have any interesting fetishes?'

I told her all about Charlie. Twenty minutes later, after I'd paused for breath, Sasha said, 'She sounds . . . lovely.'

'She is.'

'She must be. I've never seen you like this before. You defi-nitely weren't like this with Harriet.'

'Yeah, well, I never felt like this about Harriet. Charlie has completely blown me away.'

'Your pupils dilate when you talk about her,' Sasha said, leaning forward. 'Uh-oh. You're in love.'

I was about to protest, but maybe I was. Did you have to be with someone for a certain amount of time before you were allowed to be in love with them? It did feel too soon to say the L word to Charlie, but I didn't deny it to Sasha.

'Wow, Andrew. I can't wait to meet her.' She paused. 'Oh, speaking of Harriet, did you see those photos she put on Facebook, the ones of her New Year party? It looked ay-may-zing.'

I shook my head. 'I've hardly been on Facebook recently.'

'You should take a look. And while you're on there you'll have to change your status to In a Relationship.' She gave me a big comedy wink.

My head was buzzing when I got back to my flat, which didn't look any tidier or cleaner, despite Kristi's visit. I needed coffee. While I waited for the kettle to boil I sat at my computer, the iMac that I used for work, and went on to Facebook to kill some time. Charlie had told me she wasn't on Facebook, believing it to be a poor substitute for real life, which I didn't agree with.

I remembered Sasha telling me about Harriet's party photos, and scrolled through my friend list to find her. I had 251 friends, most of them old acquaintances from uni or school, or people I had encountered through work. Harriet appeared to be missing from the list.

I double-checked by searching for her name and clicking through to her page. I could no longer see her photos. It appeared that she had unfriended me.

I was surprised. As far as I knew I hadn't done anything to offend or upset her. Then again, we hadn't been in touch for a while and maybe she was having a cull of her friends. I knew people who did that every so often.

I went to bed without thinking any more of it.

In the middle of the night, when I was tossing and turning, I slipped my hand under my pillow and felt something hard.

Groggily, I switched the lamp on and pulled the object out. It was a small parcel, fastened with a red ribbon which I pulled open.

Inside was a little heart-shaped box, about four inches across and made of cardboard. I lifted the lid of the box and found a tiny photo.

It was the photo Charlie had taken of me and her just before she'd left the previous afternoon. There we were, smiling at the camera, heads pressed together. Or was I confused? I squinted in the photo in the half-light. Yes, I'm sure it was that picture. We were wearing the clothes we'd had on in the afternoon. How had Charlie managed to print it and sneak it under the pillow? Too tired to think about it, I sank back into sleep.

Seven

I spent the next day catching up with life admin and looking forward to the night ahead. I hadn't seen Charlie for twenty-four hours which, in my newly loved-up state, felt like an eternity. This was her last night before she had to return to work and she was also spending the day catching up with laundry and paperwork.

I emailed Victor, my most regular employer, asking him if we could meet up this week, and he replied saying that I should come in the next day. I also, on a whim, emailed Harriet, wishing her a happy New Year and saying that I'd heard about her party. I didn't overtly mention the Facebook unfriending. I wasn't bothered about missing the party – it was in Buckinghamshire, where her parents lived, miles away.

She replied almost immediately.

Hey A!
Yeah party was wicked. I was going to invite you but thought you'd have more exciting plans. How are you? Any big news? We must catch up.
H xxx

I couldn't be bothered to reply, partly because I felt annoyed that she hadn't invited me and could only come up with a lame excuse.

My and Harriet's relationship had been one of those partnerships that came stamped with an expiry date, an uncomplicated and fun couple of years – we definitely went beyond our best-before date – that provided us both with someone to hang out and have sex with but was far from the love affair of the century. I did like her a lot and loved spending time with her. She was pretty and interesting and had loads of friends who became my friends while we were together. We used to say that we loved each other but, looking back, I think we said it more because we felt we should. It was an emotionally vanilla relationship. The only times I ever saw her cry were when she saw animals dying on TV or when she dropped a bottle of wine on her toe.

Now that she had unfriended me on Facebook, which I was a tiny bit offended by but not enough to make a fuss about it, I guessed this would be the very end of our relationship.

It was six now and Charlie was due any minute. I went into the bathroom to clean my teeth. Opening the bathroom cabinet to get out a new tube of toothpaste I noticed something I hadn't seen before: a bottle of Vidal Sassoon shampoo. Next to it, matching conditioner. Sliding the cabinet open further, I found a little roll-on antiperspirant, a small box of tampons and some Veet hair removal cream. There was a little brown jar containing some tablets too. The label told me they were codeine.

None of these items were mine. Charlie must have put them there.

I sat down on the closed toilet lid and thought about it. A friend of mine, Simeon, had once told me that his girlfriend, whom he was now married to, had moved into his flat by stealth: smuggling in her clothes, her toiletries, eventually so many of her possessions that there was no room in his wardrobe for his own clothes and they were living together. 'It was when I found her vibrator in the drawer where I used to keep my underwear that I knew she'd properly moved in,' he said.

Was that what Charlie was doing?

As crazy about her as I was, it had only been a week since we'd first slept together. A little soon to be shacking up, even if I was smitten with her. But part of me found it quite endearing and encouraging: she was expecting to be around here so much that she needed toiletries.

I made a mental note to ask her when she'd invite me to stay at her place.

I looked at my watch. She was late. Almost as soon as I thought this, she rang me.

'Hiya,' I said.

'Hey.'

'Are you all right?'

Her voice was thick with good humour. 'I'm excellent. Why don't you come down and see just how excellent?'

I opened the front door of my flat and peered down the staircase. 'Where are you?'

'I'm in the park, opposite your building. I'll meet you by the lake.'

She hung up.

Eight

To get to the park from my flat I had to walk through the new housing development on the other side of Tulse Hill. The gate was locked but there was a gap in the railings, partially concealed behind a shrub, which saved me having to climb over. I guessed Charlie had done something similar.

It must have been no more than a few degrees above freezing in the night air. The moon was almost full and the sky was mostly clear, but as soon as I moved away from the lights of the housing estate it grew harder to see where I was going. Bare, gnarly trees scratched at the star-pricked sky, whispered to me of a thousand childhood fairy tales and adult horror movies. Harmless objects such as benches and waste bins loomed out at me from the darkness. Something darted into a bush as I passed, making my stomach flip over. When a stray cloud took its sweet time crossing the moon, I found myself in absolute darkness and I was forced to pause on the path, pulling out my phone so I could use its weak light to illuminate my way.

She was waiting for me by the lake, actually a pond, towards the centre of the park. During the day, overfed ducks gazed disinterestedly at children chucking lumps of stale bread into the water while dogs sniffed at the railings and each other. A few years previously, on a bitter winter's afternoon when the lake was frozen over, a child had drowned in this pond after climbing the railings to attempt to rescue his Jack Russell which had leapt the fence and skittered across the ice. The outcome was predictable: the ice cracked, the boy got trapped, the dog survived.

At night, the lake was silent and motionless, the black water cold and uninviting. The ducks were elsewhere.

'Charlie?' I said, not sure why I was whispering.

She was standing beyond the fence, next to the water. She appeared to be wearing a long black coat – but when I got closer I saw that it was more like a cloak, thin and rippling whenever the wind caught it. The breeze licked at it now, lifting it, revealing a bare glimpse of white leg.

'Come over,' she said. Her voice was low but clear.

'What are you doing?' I asked, climbing over the waist-high railing. I could see her clearly now. Only her face and hair were visible, the black cloak wrapped tightly around her.

I stepped towards her and into her embrace. She smiled at me and kissed me softly. This was surreal but exciting.

I tried to speak, to ask more questions, but she pressed her mouth against mine to hush me, and I understood that it was my role to stay quiet. She took my wrist and pulled my hand inside the robe, where it met naked flesh. I ran my palm over her ribcage, stroked her shoulder blade, then brought it back round to cup her breast, sliding my thumb over her erect nipple. I was aroused now, and I tried to press more firmly against her, but she stepped away.

She let the robe slip from her shoulders and to the ground. She was naked and part of me wanted to grab the robe, wrap her up and keep her warm. But before I could do anything, she stepped into the water.

'Charlie!'

I couldn't believe what she was doing. I watched, stunned, as she walked slowly into the lake until it covered her legs and then her hips. She turned to me and smiled. She looked like a water nymph, straight from that pre-Raphaelite painting. What was it? I looked it up later: *Hylas and the Nymphs*, John Waterhouse. A handsome youth, drawn to his presumed death by strange, beautiful women. Staring at Charlie now, pale and half-submerged, her skin catching the moonlight, I was torn between two urges: one, to get her out of there, out of the bitterly cold water, and take her home to the warmth of my flat; and two, to slip with her into the dangerous, icy depths, to abandon sense and, instead, embrace my senses.

She beckoned me and I hurriedly undressed, leaving my clothes and glasses in a pile, until I stood naked and aroused before her. I hesitated – this really was insane – and then stepped into the water. It's hard to describe quite how cold it was. And even harder to describe why I kept going rather than leaping out.

It was Charlie. She magnetised me. But I also felt like she was daring me, testing me, that to stop would have made me less of a man. Plus I wanted her, was literally being led by my penis towards her. So I gritted my teeth and tried to ignore the burning cold as I stepped deeper into the water. The bed of the lake felt slippery against my soles and I feared what might be down there: broken bottles, old cans. For a second I had a flash of that boy who had drowned here, picturing his body lying beneath the water, small hands reaching out for me . . .

I reached Charlie and she wrapped her arms around me, pressed her body against mine, kissing me deeply, her tongue in my mouth. She folded her hand around my cock and moaned. She was shivering; we were both shivering. She stood on tiptoe and positioned the tip of my penis against her.

'Lift me,' she said into my ear, and I did. She was lighter than I expected, and she wrapped her strong legs and arms around me and we both gasped as my cock pushed into her.

I came within seconds. I don't think I could have held her much longer than that. As I gently put her down, Charlie started giggling.

'I'm cold,' she said. 'My teeth are actually chattering.'

I started laughing too. What the hell were we doing? We splashed our way out of the water and I wrapped Charlie in the robe before hurriedly pulling my own clothes over my wet skin. I pulled Charlie against me and felt her trembling.

'Let's get—' I began, then stopped.

'What is it?' she asked.

I stared into the trees that ringed the lake, peered into the shadowy spaces between them, and said, 'Hello?'

Charlie followed my gaze, her eyes wide.

'Did you see something too?' I asked. When she shook her head I said, 'I'm sure there was someone there, watching us.'

'Oh please, don't.'

Tentatively, I approached the trees. There was no one there.

'Let's get out of here,' I said. My whole body felt like it had been encased in ice for a thousand years, like that Stone Age man they found in the Italian Alps. And right now, I needed to get back to the warmth and safety of my cave.

I was still thawing out half an hour later as Charlie and I sat at opposite ends of my bath. A gentleman, I had taken the end with the taps and the plug. Soap bubbles covered Charlie up to her shoulders. She took a sip from her condensation-streaked wine glass.

'I still can't believe we did that,' I said.

She laughed. 'Me neither. It was fun though.'

I wasn't sure if that was the right word. It was intense, unforgettable – but fun?

'I wasn't wearing a condom,' I said.

She scooped up a handful of bubbles and blew them at me. 'You're such a worrier. It's OK. I'm on the pill. And I'm trusting that you're not wildly promiscuous, so your chances of having a disease are low.'

'I'm definitely not, nor have I ever been, wildly promiscuous,' I said.

She paused, took a sip of wine. 'So, what's your number?' she asked.

'You mean, how many women have I slept with?'

She smiled. 'Uh-huh.'

'Seven,' I said, after taking a few moments to count in my head. 'Including you.'

I had expected her to say something like 'is that all?' because, compared to most of my friends and from reading survey results in magazines, mine was a low number. But she said, 'I know Harriet already, and me of course. Who were the other five?'

I ran through the other girls.

The first had been Laura, my girlfriend when I was in the sixth form at school. We were both virgins and after many heated petting sessions, finally went all the way while babysitting a neighbour's toddler. We stayed together for another few months after that, splitting up when we both went to university.

There were Junko and Helena, two one-night stands when I was a student.

Then I went out with Sarah for two years, starting in our third year of uni, before she left me for a guy she met at the office where she worked.

After a long period of involuntary chastity, I had a brief thing with a woman called Karen, ten years older than me, whom I had met through Victor. Karen and I both had meetings at Victor's office at the same time and had got chatting while waiting in reception.

Victor had found our tryst highly amusing and, until we split up, made constant jokes about being guest of honour at our wedding.

Karen was by far the best in terms of passion and technique, until Charlie came along. Karen and I had been an unlikely match: she was experienced, worldly, at ease in her own skin, while I was gauche and awkward. I'm still not sure what she saw in me. Enthusiasm, perhaps. Energy. She had recently split from her long-term partner and, even when we were having sex, seemed sad. Beautiful and sad. One day she told me she thought we shouldn't see each other any more, and that was it. I ended our relationship feeling like a student who'd just graduated from a fun and rewarding course.

After that there was Harriet – who treated sex like a necessary bodily function – and then Charlie.

'That's it,' I said. 'My entire sexual history.'

She had been quiet as I had recounted my list. 'And who was best?' she asked.

'You, of course.'

She didn't smile. 'No, I mean apart from me.'

'Um . . .' I told her it had been Karen.

'The older woman. Are you still in touch with her?'

'God, no. I haven't seen her for years. It wasn't that kind of relationship, where you stay friends afterwards.'

She cocked her head to one side, studying me with those big eyes. 'What do you mean?'

'Well, it was just . . . We met, we had a sexual relationship, then we split up. That's all that relationship was about.'

'Just sex?'

'Yes.' I cleared my throat. 'I feel quite uncomfortable talking about it, actually.'

Charlie arched her eyebrows. 'I find it interesting. I want to know everything about you. Don't you feel like that about me?' Beneath the water, she stroked my thigh, squeezed it.

'I don't know. I don't really want to know your number.'

'Really? Why not?'

The truth was, I didn't want to know because I had this fear it would be too high. I knew that even if she'd had sex with one hundred men before me it shouldn't matter. But I also knew that it *would* make a difference. That was just the way it was. I would rather not know. Then I wouldn't have to care.

'Because the past is the past,' I said, resorting to cliché.

The bath water was growing cold and the candles that lit the bathroom flickered in the draft that crept in through the window.

Charlie was quiet for a minute or two, lost in thought. Eventually, she said, 'OK. I understand. But I would like to hear more about *your* past. I love hearing you talk, Andrew. And I want you to tell me everything.'

She wriggled forward, our legs pressed tighter together.

'But not now,' she said. 'Shall we go to bed?'

After we'd made love again, I remembered the things I had been meaning to ask her. Charlie had a way of sweeping the conversation along so that I'd forget everything I'd wanted to say. Like, she had never really told me about her background, her parents, where she went to school. Every day I resolved to get more information out of her – those were the parts of the past I was interested in – but some other topic always popped up.

I picked up the heart-shaped box that she'd left beneath my pillow.

'Do you like it?' she asked.

'It's lovely. But how did you do it? With the photo?'

She tapped her nose. 'Ah.'

'Come on, Charlie . . .'

'OK. I've got a tiny portable printer. It's in my bag now. I can plug my phone into it and print little photos. It's really cool. I did it in the bathroom while you were waiting for me, then slipped the box under your pillow.'

So that explained that.

I wanted to mention the toiletries in the bathroom cabinet, but she yawned and said, 'I really ought to sleep. I have to get up early for work.' She groaned.

'Do you dislike your job?'

She lay facing the ceiling, her eyes shut, bare shoulders just visible.

'I hate it,' she said. 'It's boring and stressful. Every minute I spend there is a minute of my life wasted. All I want is to be able to concentrate on my art.'

'One day.' I kissed her.

'You're sweet.' She opened an eye. 'Sorry, guys hate being called sweet, don't they? I meant to say you're butch and manly.'

'I don't mind being sweet.'

She closed the eye. 'Then you're even sweeter.' She yawned again. 'I really, really must sleep.'

'OK.'

She rolled away from me. 'Goodnight, Andrew.'

'Night.'

'I love you.'

I froze. Was I hearing things? We hadn't mentioned love at all up to that point. We'd only been together just over a week.

'Charlie?' I said.

But she was asleep.

I awoke at some point in the night from a dream in which I'd been drowning, small hands dragging me beneath the surface of an ice-encrusted lake, the green, rotting face of a young boy leering at me, flesh hanging in flaps from a grinning skull, an eyeball popping loose and bobbing towards me in the dark water.

I opened my eyes. I was shivering. I turned to embrace Charlie, seeking her warmth, and my heart skittered.

She was awake, propped up on an elbow. She was staring at me.

'I had a horrible dream . . .' I began, thinking I must have disturbed her. But as I started to speak she rolled over and appeared to drop off immediately.

My mind skipped about wildly: sex in the park with Charlie and how I'd been sure someone was watching us; Sasha's problems with her married lover; memories of Karen and Harriet; niggling anxiety about money. And above all this din, hearing Charlie say that she loved me.

It was a long time before I managed to get back to sleep.

Nine

Victor Codsall beckoned me into his office and shook my hand, gesturing for me to sit on one of the two sofas, flopping down on the other like he was unable to bend his knees. A stack of books, catalogues and magazines wobbled on the coffee table. Through the glass, I watched Victor's staff at the design agency wander to and fro: bright, trendy young things who brought their bikes to work and wore T-shirts with ironic slogans. According to Victor, they were all sleeping with each other.

'The whole fucking office is a festering Petri dish of disease,' he once told me, gloomily. Victor said almost everything gloomily, hence his nickname: Eeyore. A sketch of the depressive donkey hung on the wall beside a framed, signed Tottenham Hotspur shirt.

'How's your . . . ?' He pointed to his eye. Victor had found it hilarious that when I had my operation, the surgeon had drawn a black arrow above my eyebrow, indicating the eye to be operated on.

'Much better. Actually, I've been discharged.'

'Thank fuck for that,' he said. 'Not much call for blind designers round here. Although some of the shit this lot have been churning out recently, you'd think they'd all had detached fucking retinas.'

I didn't tell him that, actually, since waking up I'd been bothered by a floater in my left eye, a tiny circle that drifted across my vision whenever I blinked. I was trying not to worry about it. Mr Makkawi had told me floaters were normal, that I should only be concerned if I got a lot of them together.

We made small talk for a few minutes before I said, 'So I was wondering if you had any work for me? I'm available to work full time at the moment.'

'As a matter of fact . . .' He sighed, making it sound like he was about to tell me I had a terminal illness. 'We got a new contract come in this morning from this e-commerce site. They're planning some big new campaign – holidays, summer, beaches, young sexy people having fun and getting wasted . . . All that crap.'

'Sounds great. What site is it?'

'Wowcom. Big fashion site, based not far from here actually.'

'Oh.'

'Don't tell me – you ordered some fucking red trousers from them and they sent you pink.'

'No. It's just that I know someone who works there. My friend Sasha.'

Not just that, but Wowcom was the company owned by Lance. It would be strange to work for Wowcom, given what I knew about the owner and Sasha.

'That's great. You've got an in.'

We spent the next hour going over the details of the brief and Victor made a call to Wowcom to arrange a meeting later in the week.

'Sweet,' he groaned, at the end of the call. I wondered if, beneath the moaning, Victor was actually happy. He clearly adored his wife and children and was running a successful business. He was a self-made man. Rumour had it that he had grown up on one of the roughest estates in North London and that many of his friends were career criminals, drug dealers and gangsters with minders, huge houses and trophy wives.

All through the meeting, the floater in my eye danced and bothered me. But it was a relief to have some work, especially as Victor thought the project would take at least a couple of months.

I got up to leave.

'Oh,' he said. 'I forgot to mention. I saw Karen last week. She came to a dinner party round mine. She asked after you.'

'Really?'

'She's still single. Maybe she's getting the taste for young meat again. I reckon she'd be up for it if you gave her a call. Hey, what are you grinning at?'

'I've got a girlfriend now.'

'Oh really? What's she like? Obviously she's not going to be as hot as my missus – but hotter than Karen?'

I beamed. 'Much.'

'You're kidding me. Got a photo?'

I realised the only photo I had of Charlie on my phone was the topless selfie she'd sent me when I was out with Sasha, and I wasn't going to show him that.

'So I'll tell Karen you lied about having a girlfriend because you don't want to see her again?'

'Very funny.'

He saw me out. 'Actually, Karen was saying she needs someone to design a website for her. Just a personal site, a blog or something. Not a big enough job for me but maybe you should get in touch, earn yourself an extra couple of quid. Or who knows, she might offer payment in kind.'

'The only time you don't sound miserable is when you're teasing me,' I said.

He sighed. 'That's what I always say to my missus. Anyway, want me to ping her an email, ask her to get in touch?'

I hesitated. It might be awkward, seeing her. But the money would definitely come in handy.

'All right,' I said. 'That would be great.'

'So how does it feel being back at work?' I asked.

Charlie rolled her eyes. 'I don't want to talk about it. I'd rather talk about something interesting. Like sex.'

We were sitting in Starbucks near Old Street station, close to Victor's office. Charlie had suggested meeting for lunch. She looked great in her work clothes, with her hair neat and her crisply ironed clothes.

'I think the man behind you heard you,' I whispered.

She smiled naughtily. 'I can't help it. I want to drag you into an alleyway and have my wicked way with you.' She popped a grape into her mouth and sucked it. 'Why don't we go into the toilet now?'

Beneath the table she pressed her legs against mine and I felt my cock grow hard. It was frustrating, not being able to touch her flesh. At my flat, in those sex-drunk days between Christmas and her return to work, we couldn't keep our hands off each other, and didn't have to. But there was something deliciously tantalising about having to wait, knowing that when she finished work she would come round to mine and we could take our clothes off.

A thought struck me. 'How come we never go to your place?'

She pulled a face, like the grape she was eating was sour. 'It's horrible, that's why. There's no privacy. There, you wouldn't be able to push me over the kitchen worktop and enter me while we were cooking dinner . . .'

'Charlie!' I hissed, gesturing at the man behind her with my eyes as he looked round, shocked. She was so bad.

She smiled and sipped her fruit juice. 'I hate being Charlotte. I want to come home with you and be Charlie.'

I needed to change the subject before the urge to take her into the Starbucks toilet became too much. So I told her about the meeting with Victor and how it connected with Sasha.

She looked at her watch and grimaced. 'I've only got five minutes.'

'But you'll come round later?'

'Try and stop me. I'll make dinner.'

'You don't have to. I'm happy with a takeaway. Or I could make dinner.'

'Are you a good cook?'

'No, I'm terrible. Sometimes I have nightmares in which I'm forced to be a contestant on *Masterchef*. The whole nation could witness my humiliation. I once managed to set a pan of spaghetti on fire. Even my boiled eggs come out wrong. I'm probably the worst cook in the world.'

She reached under the table and squeezed my thigh. 'You can't be good at everything. I'd much rather you were good at cunnilingus than cooking.'

The man behind her almost fell off his chair.

'It feels wrong, though,' I said. 'Having a woman come round and cook me dinner. I don't want you to think I'm a typical sexist bloke.'

She stroked my cheek. 'I don't. Enjoy it, Andrew. I like cooking, I'm good at it, you're bad at it. Makes sense for me to do it, yes? You can learn one day and then you can cook for me.'

We moved on to talking about Tilly. 'How is she?' Charlie asked. 'Have you had any more clandestine cups of tea with her PA?'

'No. Rachel texted me to say Tilly seems a bit happier and to thank us for taking her out. I meant to tell you. She says she's keeping an eye on her.'

I went quiet for a minute and she asked what I was thinking about. I normally hate that question, but with Charlie I never minded.

'What about your family? Will I get to meet them?'

She frowned. 'That would be difficult. I don't have any family.'

Taken aback, I waited for her to continue.

'I told you that both my parents died when I was a teenager.'

I had no memory of her sharing this momentous fact. It certainly wasn't the kind of thing I'd forget. 'No you didn't.'

'I must have done. My mum died of cancer when I was fifteen and then my dad committed suicide a year later because he was so heartbroken and couldn't get over it.'

My insides had gone cold. 'You definitely didn't tell me any of that. Oh my God, Charlie. That's awful.'

She looked up at me through her lashes. 'But it's something we have in common, isn't it? We're both alone.' She stared at the table top then back at me. 'We *were* both alone.'

I tried to think of something appropriate to say but before inspiration struck she said, 'Right. I've got to get back to work. Back to being Charlotte again.' She stood up, kissed me on the lips and told me she'd be round about seven.

All the way back to the Tube, I racked my brain, searching for holes in my memory. Had she said anything about her parents? Had I asked? I couldn't think of a single time the subject of her parents had come up. She barely talked about her past at all. I knew she was from Leeds, and she had told me a few anecdotes about her childhood and stories from when she was at uni, like the time she'd fainted at a Green Day concert, how she and her friends went to karaoke every weekend, the day she crashed her car and wrote it off. There was a map of her body in my head: I knew her taste, her smell, how every part of her felt beneath my fingers. I could hear her speech patterns in my head as I drifted off to sleep. I knew what music she was into, who her favourite painters were, which varieties of wine she preferred. I knew all of that, but her past was a mystery.

I vowed to change that, to get her to tell me more about herself. After all, she knew most of my life story. I wanted to know everything about her. Because, and I knew this, felt this, even though I hadn't told her yet: I was in love with her.

When I got home I had a couple of emails waiting for me.

The first was from Sasha, updating me on the situation with Lance.

It's horrific. They've shunted me off to a different department, so I don't have to have any contact with him – which suits me! But it's like everyone in the office knows. The other girls are treating me like I've got some hideous contagious disease and the guys keep looking at me like I'm a nympho who will shag anyone. This creepy bastard called Jake who works in IT asked me if I wanted to go out for lunch, like if he buys me beans on toast at the greasy spoon at lunchtime I'll give him a BJ in the stationery cupboard in the afternoon.

I need to see you!! Can we go out this weekend and get REALLY drunk?

I replied saying yes, of course, let's meet up Friday after work – even though that would mean an evening apart from Charlie – though I didn't tell her about Victor and the contract with Wowcom. I wasn't sure how she'd feel about it so would tell her when I saw her.

The second email was from Karen.

Hi Andrew,

How are you? It's been quite a while. Hope you're well.
Victor told me you might be able to work on a website design for
me. It's nothing special – I need a site to show potential clients,
with a bio, a few articles, some testimonials, etc. Can you tell me
how much you would charge and then maybe we could meet to
discuss?

Thanks,
Karen

She was an HR consultant, a person who went into businesses and told them how to manage their staff more effectively. That's what she'd been doing when I met her at Victor's office, though it turned out that she and Victor were old friends. I was glad the email was so businesslike and impersonal. I fired back a quick response, telling her my day rate and that I would guess such a job would take two or three days (really, it depended how fussy she was). Then I spent a couple of hours pulling together some preliminary ideas for the Wowcom job.

Before I finished for the day, Karen replied to my email saying my day rate sounded fine and suggesting a couple of times for us to meet, both of which were later in the week. We agreed on Friday afternoon, so I could see her before going on to see Sasha.

———

Waiting for Charlie to turn up, I opened a bottle of wine and had a sort through some of my photography books. The email conversation with Karen had reminded me of an exhibition she'd taken me to see on one of the rare occasions we'd been out together.

She'd taken me to see some work by the photographer Rankin, who specialised in portraits of the rich and famous, along with more explicit pictures including nude shots of his model wife. Karen had bought me a Rankin book as a present and I wanted to look at it now – not to ogle the nudes but because there were some photos taken on beaches that I thought might provide useful inspiration for the Wowcom project.

I couldn't find the book. I searched the bookcase but it wasn't there. It was a large hardback and it couldn't have slipped behind the other books, and I was certain I hadn't lent it to anyone or taken it anywhere.

But before I could think about it any more, the doorbell rang, then rang again and kept on ringing, urgent, insistent. I went out into the stairwell and ran down the stairs as quickly as I could. Someone – Charlie, I assumed – was banging on the front door like she was desperate to get in.

I heaved the door open and she tumbled inside, panting.

She grabbed hold of me. She was cold but sweaty.

'Someone's following me,' she said.

Ten

I peered out of the door at the lamplit street, my heart beating fast. I couldn't see anyone.

'Are you sure?' I asked.

She nodded mutely. She looked terrified.

I stepped out onto the street, Charlie imploring me to be careful, and looked up and down the road. Apart from an elderly lady walking her dog, there was no one around. I went back inside and shut the door.

'Come on, let's get you upstairs,' I said. 'You're shaking.'

The first thing she said when we got into my flat was, 'I need a drink.'

She took a thirsty gulp of the wine I handed her and I steered her over to the sofa, sitting beside her, rubbing her cold arm.

'What happened?'

She hugged herself. Her face was very pale. 'I took a shortcut through the park again. I know, I know – it's a stupid thing to do. But I thought it would be fine.'

I waited for her to continue.

'I got about halfway through, just past the big house in the middle, and then realised there was someone behind me on the path. It was like they were hiding by the house and came out when they saw me. It was so dark I couldn't see him properly.'

I squeezed her hand.

'He followed me down the path.' The words gushed out. 'I didn't really want to look back but it was like he was gaining on me, going really fast, and all I could think of was that he was a rapist so I started running and he started running too and I just made it to the gap in the railings before him and I got through and he came through too and followed me down the street until I rang your doorbell . . .'

'Charlie, sweetheart.'

She was almost hyperventilating, and she clung to me on the sofa, shivering and crying silently. I held her like that until she calmed down, kissed the tear trails on her cheeks.

'We should call the police.'

'They'll just say I shouldn't walk through the park at night.'

'Maybe, but it's still worth it. What if he attacks someone else?'

I walked across the room to get my phone.

'Please, Andrew. I really don't want to call them. They'll tell me off for going into the park after dark.'

I weighed the phone in my hand. She was right: it was clearly signposted that you shouldn't enter the park at night. But I still thought it was worthwhile in case this man attacked someone else.

'Plus he didn't actually do anything, did he?' she said.

'All right,' I said. 'I'm going to phone them, say I saw someone go into the park, acting suspiciously. OK?'

She nodded.

While I waited for the police to answer I said, 'I bet it was the same guy who I thought was watching us last night.'

Charlie hugged her knees to her chest. 'Don't say that. I don't like the thought . . . that someone saw us having sex.'

I got through to the police and told them I'd seen a man in the park. They said they'd take a look but I could hardly see it being a priority.

She let out a long sigh. 'I'll be all right in a minute. I need more wine, that's all. And dinner. I popped into M and S and got us a moussaka and some salad. Is that OK? I know I said I'd cook, but I'm tired. Work was blah.'

'Perfect.'

She smiled at me.

'Promise me you won't do it again,' I said.

'What, buy moussaka?'

'Walk through the park at night. I couldn't bear the thought of anything happening to you.'

'Come on,' she said. 'Put the telly on. I need something mindless to cheer me up.'

———————

We ate dinner and drank more wine and pretty soon we were pulling our clothes off, doing it there and then on the sofa, Charlie on top. Afterwards I went to the bathroom and remembered the things Charlie had left in there.

'I saw you'd put some toiletries in my bathroom cabinet,' I said when I came out. She was wearing my towelling dressing gown, a fresh glass of wine in her hand.

She looked confused. 'Huh?'

'You left a bunch of stuff in the cabinet. Shampoo, conditioner . . .'

'I didn't put anything in there.'

'You must have.'

'I did leave some stuff in your bedroom – I left it in there by mistake when I was arranging my bag the other day. I was going to ask you about it. But I didn't put anything in the cabinet.'

'Oh. It must have been Kristi then.'

She sat up straight. 'Who's Kristi?'

'My cleaner.'

'You've got a cleaner?'

A programme I liked was starting on TV and I was half-distracted by it. Charlie picked up the remote and turned the television off.

'You've got a cleaner?' she repeated.

'Yeah. She comes once a week, does a couple of hours. I guess she must have found your things and put them in the bathroom.'

Charlie's whole demeanour had changed from tired but happy to tense and, seemingly, annoyed. I pulled on my clothes.

'What's she like? Some poor, middle-aged woman? A Mrs Mop?'

I thought about Kristi with her smoky eyes and killer cheekbones. 'No. She's pretty young. Albanian, I think.'

Charlie looked horrified. 'Oh God.'

'What?'

'It's so exploitative. Privileged middle-class white male gets poor immigrant to clean his toilet.'

I felt like pointing out that, as far as I could tell, Kristi had never been near my toilet. Apart from tidying up, I still wasn't sure exactly what she did. But I was dumbstruck by Charlie's reaction.

'I'm not exploiting her. She advertised for her services. I'm helping her out, actually. She needs the work.'

'Really? How much do you pay her?'

'I pay her eight pounds an hour.' That was after the agency's fee. 'Though I usually round it up to ten pounds an hour because she never has change.'

'What a hero.'

I couldn't believe this. I felt anger rising inside me. 'I'm not doing anything wrong, Charlie. I need a cleaner, she obviously needs work. I'm sure she's got far worse clients than me.'

'I don't understand why you need a cleaner anyway. This place is tiny, you're here all day. Can't you do it yourself?'

I explained that I'd taken Kristi on when I'd had my operation and found doing most things difficult.

'But you're all right now, so you can get rid of her.'

'I don't want to. I'd feel bad. She needs the money.'

Charlie stood up. 'Do you get off on it?'

'What?'

'Paying a young woman to degrade herself.'

I was aghast. 'Charlie! This is insane.'

'Or maybe she's too ugly for you to get a kick out of it.'

We were standing close now. This was crazy, but it was also exhilarating because, even as the blood heated in my veins and Charlie jabbed a finger at me, it didn't feel real. Were we really arguing about this? This was our first argument, and it was about a cleaner!

'As a matter of fact,' I said, 'she's really pretty. But you're being ridiculous. She's my cleaner, I don't want to get rid of her, and I am not exploiting her. I'm not degrading her and I certainly don't get a sexual thrill out of watching a woman vacuum my bedroom!'

She opened her mouth to speak again and promptly shut it. She closed her eyes too and inhaled deeply. I was pretty sure she was counting to ten beneath her breath.

'OK,' she said eventually. 'I'm sorry. I shouldn't have lost my temper. I've had too much wine and I'm still stressed after being followed. I just have a thing about people, women especially, being exploited.'

'I'm not—'

'I know, I know. I understand. It's not you – it's the injustice of the situation.'

'I don't think—' I began, but she cut me off.

'Can we talk about something else?' she said. 'Actually, can we go to bed? I'm tired, I'm a bit drunk and I don't want to talk any more.' She put her arms around me and kissed me. 'Do you forgive me?'

'Of course I do.'

She looked into my eyes. 'I love you, Andrew. I know we've only been together a couple of weeks, but I . . .' She trailed off, her expression shy. 'I feel embarrassed.'

I put my hands on her shoulders. 'Don't be embarrassed. I feel the same way.'

'But you won't say it?' she said with a little smile.

'I'm very happy to say it. I love you, Charlie.'

And with that, the argument was forgotten, and a minute later we were making love again, in bed, slowly, the intensity of it white-hot and all-consuming, the most intense it had ever been, and as she raked her fingernails down my back, and kissed me so hard I felt my lips would be bruised, I told her again that I loved her, and she whispered it into my mouth just before she came.

Afterwards, she lay with her front pressed against my back, her arms tight around me, her legs entwined with mine. She fell asleep quickly but I lay awake for a while. My vow to find out more about her past had gone by the wayside. Tomorrow, I told myself. Despite the weird argument about Kristi, and the scare with Charlie being followed, I felt content. In fact, the protectiveness I'd felt when she was scared, and the release after the argument – which was based on principles I admired even if I wasn't sure I agreed with them – made me feel even closer to her than before.

But I wasn't going to sack my cleaner.

Eleven

Karen was waiting for me in the little coffee shop in Islington, as we'd arranged. She stood up when she saw me and we kissed each other's cheeks, a habit she had picked up living in Paris in her twenties.

She looked great. Her dark hair was cut into a neat bob and she was wearing a cream cashmere sweater. I wasn't entirely sure how old Karen was, but my guess was somewhere between thirty-nine and forty-three. She'd never had children, told me that she'd never had the urge, although her eyes took on a sad, faraway look when she said this. She spent a lot of time doing yoga and Pilates. I still found it odd that we'd had an affair – and 'affair' was really the only word that suited it, even though it hadn't been illicit in any way.

'You look well,' she said, studying me, a smile at the edge of her lips.

'Thanks. You too.'

'You look like you're in love.'

I must have blushed because she clapped her hands together and said, 'How exciting. Who's the lucky girl?'

I spent the next ten minutes banging on about Charlie and how amazing she was, until Karen's eyes glazed over.

We turned to the subject of her website and discussed ideas while she showed me some sites she liked on her iPad.

Leaning towards her while she flicked between sites, I smelled her perfume and was thrust back in time to an afternoon we'd spent in bed together watching *The Graduate* and having sex that, not unusually, had been more like a lesson than anything else, Karen giving me gentle instructions as I went down on her: where to position my tongue, how firm, how fast, what to do with my fingers, and so on.

'Andrew? Have you zoned out?'

'Huh? Oh, sorry. I was just remembering something.'

She arched an eyebrow. 'Something good?'

I definitely must have blushed this time because she winked at me and said, 'Not the kind of thing you would want to tell your girlfriend about?'

I didn't reply. I felt guilty enough as it was. I definitely didn't fancy Karen anymore, and not just because the light that shone from Charlie cast all other women into shadow, but because that had been a period of my life that I wouldn't want to return to. I was a proper grown-up now.

'Does she know you're here?' Karen asked.

'Yeah, of course. Why wouldn't she?'

She shrugged. 'I don't know. Some women get funny about their boyfriends meeting up with their exes.'

'Charlie's not like that.' *Plus*, I almost added, *I wouldn't really class you as an ex.*

'That's good. There's nothing that kills a relationship faster than jealousy. It's why I split from Yuri.' That was her long-term partner. 'The last six months with him . . . well, I learned why they call it the green-eyed monster.'

I left a little while later, having agreed to show her a first draft the following week, and hopped on a bus to Farringdon, where I had arranged to meet Sasha.

The thing was, Charlie *had* been a bit weird when I told her I was meeting Karen to talk about designing a website for her.

She was getting ready for work, putting on her make-up. I loved watching her, a mug of coffee steaming in my lap, bright winter sunshine lighting up the flat.

'What?' she had said. 'You mean the Karen you were telling me about? Your former lover?'

I cringed. 'I hate that word.'

She turned from the mirror, eyeliner pencil between forefinger and thumb. 'She wasn't your girlfriend though, was she? You said it was purely a sex thing.'

I put my coffee down. When I had told Harriet about Karen, towards the start of our relationship, she had reacted in a way that had surprised me. She didn't care about any of the other girls in my past, but she took an instant dislike to the idea of this older woman whom I'd slept with but who had not been a proper girlfriend. She occasionally mentioned her during arguments, when she would shout, 'Why don't you go back to the Old Slapper?'

So I was immediately on guard when talking about her with Charlie, though the alternative would have been hiding that I was going to meet her. I didn't want to lie to Charlie about anything.

'It was all in the past,' I said. 'You don't have anything to worry about.'

Charlie glanced at me. 'When people say that, it usually means you *do* have something to worry about.'

'But you don't,' I said, somewhat lamely. I didn't know what else to say.

'Is she very beautiful?' she asked, turning back to her reflection and returning to the task of applying her make-up.

'No. Nothing like you.'

'Not even pretty, like your cleaner?'

I sighed. 'Don't start that again, please.'

'I'm only joking.' A moment later, she shouted, 'Fuck! Why can't I get this eyeliner to go on straight?'

She marched into the bathroom, leaving tension crackling in the air. I sipped my coffee and wished I'd never agreed to do this work for Karen. If Charlie and I ever split up – the thought of which filled my stomach with ice – I would never tell any future girlfriends about Karen.

'And after seeing Karen, you're meeting Sasha,' she said when she returned.

'Yes.'

'OK. Well, there's a drinks thing on after work today. I'll probably go to that.'

I got up to leave, kissing her goodbye.

'Have fun,' I said.

'Hmm,' she replied.

Sasha and I had a few drinks in an expensive bar in Farringdon before heading back on the train to Herne Hill, where Sasha had been invited to a housewarming party.

Sasha looked tired, with puffy eyes and the same greasy marks on her glasses that I'd noticed before. I wanted to take them off her and squirt them with washing-up liquid.

'How are you feeling?' I asked, as we walked up the road to the party. I had already told her about the work I was going to do for Wowcom and she had, to my relief, been delighted, especially if it meant I would be visiting her office occasionally.

'I'm all right,' she said brightly. A pause. 'Actually, I feel like shit. I know he's a come stain on the duvet of society—'

'Nicely put.'

'Thank you. But I was also kind of, you know, in love with him.'

'Poor Sash,' I said. 'Love. It fucks you up.'

'It sure does. Especially when the recipient of your love is married to a psychopath.'

I thought it was a little unfair of Sasha to direct her ire towards Lance's wife. Mae was, after all, the injured party in all this. But I was Sasha's best friend and it wasn't my place to take anyone's side but hers.

'But you're all loved up with Charlie, aren't you? You look like the cat who got the keys to the aviary. When I am going to meet this goddess?'

'Soon, I'm sure.'

'Good. Because if you wait too long I will begin to suspect that she is a figment of your imagination.'

We were almost at the party now and could hear the muffled thump of music up ahead. This was an expensive, quiet street and I could imagine the neighbours being pissed off by this noisy event.

'I've got a photo,' I said. I now had a number of fully clothed pictures of Charlie on my phone, lots of shots of her smiling or posing for me in my flat. I showed my favourite to Sasha. Charlie was sitting on the edge of my bed, wearing jeans and a white T-shirt, her hair all messed up, a shy smile on her face.

'Nice!'

'Gorgeous, isn't she? I can't quite believe she wants to go out with geeky old me.'

'You're a good-looking guy, Andrew. You don't realise that, which is one of the reasons you're not a prick. But I bet you and Charlie look great together.'

We arrived at the house, where a girl was being sick on the front steps.

Sasha said, 'I don't know if I'm the mood for this. Shall we go back to mine and watch a film? I think *Blair Witch* is on Channel 4 tonight.'

From inside the house, 'Blurred Lines' started to play and somebody whooped.

'*Blair Witch* sounds a lot less horrific than this party,' I said.

We walked back to Sasha's, which took us past the park. On the way, I told her about Charlie being followed.

'Bit daft, walking through the park at night,' Sasha said. 'Oh, did you hear about Harriet?'

'Her New Year party? You already told me.'

'No, not that. She was burgled. Someone broke into her flat – it was last weekend.'

'Oh shit.'

'I don't think they took much, but she said they completely trashed the place. They destroyed all her old photo albums, ripped them up and poured water all over them. They smashed up her computer and emptied out all the cupboards and drawers, just totally wrecked everything. Get this: they stole all her underwear. It's the only thing they took. Though just the nice lingerie, not the everyday stuff.'

'That's freaky,' I said. 'My God.'

'Yeah, she's devastated. Gone back to her parents. Said she feels violated, you know?'

I could imagine. I made a mental note to send her an email, saying I hoped she was OK. I wondered, briefly, if any of the underwear I'd bought her was among the stuff that had been burned; if she ever still wore it. I'd bought her some Elle MacPherson lingerie, which she'd worn all the time, and had got her a set from Agent Provocateur for Valentine's, which had cost a fortune.

Poor Harriet.

'It's made me take extra care when I go out,' Sasha said. 'I must have checked I'd locked the door about ten times before going out this morning.'

We went inside and watched the film. Halfway through I texted Charlie to say goodnight and to ask what she was doing.

She replied immediately. *In bed, thinking about you. See you in the morning :) xxxxx*

'Oh dear, you've got that look on your face,' Sasha said. 'Love-struck puppy.'

And then she started to cry. I sat and held her for a while until she felt better, at which point she announced she needed to go to bed.

'Thanks, Andrew,' she said, as I left.

'No worries.'

Her face was streaked with tears and there was a big damp patch on the front of my shirt.

'You deserve it, you know,' she said.

'What?'

'Happiness. I'm really glad you've met Charlie.'

'Me too.'

She blew me a kiss and I started to walk home, my coat wrapped tightly around me. My flat was a fifteen-minute walk from Sasha's.

I had just turned off the main road in order to take a shortcut through the quieter backstreets, when I heard footsteps behind me. I looked over my shoulder, a casual glance, and saw a figure in black, wearing a hood. The way they were walking – close to the walls, keeping in the shadows, their pace slowing as I turned to look – made me feel sick with nerves. I knew loads of people who had been mugged for their mobiles. It was an epidemic and I had just been walking blithely along the street staring at my iPhone in full view of any passing thief.

Or maybe it wasn't a mugger . . . I couldn't help but think of the person who had followed Charlie through the park, and the figure who I was convinced had been watching us that time by the lake.

I increased my pace, feeling in my pockets for weapons. I had my keys and I supposed my phone could do someone some damage if you hit them over the head with it in the right way. The person behind me – I pictured him as a muscular, wiry youth, the 'hoodie horror' who stalks middle-class urban nightmares – was gaining on me. I was only a few minutes from home now. I could be there in one minute if I ran. But what if the hoodie ran too and was much faster than me?

Heart thumping, I walked as fast as I could. I didn't dare look behind me, as if doing so would invite the hoodie to jump me. I had no idea how close he was now. Maybe I should call 999, tell them I was being followed. But I clung to the hope it was all in my imagination, that the guy behind me was an innocent heading home.

I could see my flat now. My keys were in my hand, ready. I broke into a jog, stealing a glance over my shoulder. The figure was nowhere in sight. Breathing hard, I reached the front steps of my building.

Someone jumped out on me.

I cried out with fear, my body flooding with adrenaline. I put my fists up, ready to fight, every muscle in my body tensed.

'Andrew?'

I blinked.

'Charlie? What . . . what are you doing here?'

Blessed relief washed through me. I looked around. No sign of the person who I had been sure was following me. He must have gone into one of the other flats on my road.

'I thought I'd surprise you,' Charlie said. 'You look like you're about to have a heart attack. What's the matter?'

I didn't answer her question. 'You told me you were in bed.'

She smiled impishly. 'I didn't want to spoil the surprise.' She took hold of the front of my coat, pulled me against her and kissed me. I was too freaked out to respond properly but she barely seemed to notice.

'You're freezing,' she said. 'Let's get you inside. I'll warm you up.'

Before we went in I took one last look down the street. Where had the person following me gone?

Twelve

Over the next couple of weeks, Charlie and I fell into a routine – though routine is not really the right word, as it suggests the mundane, tedium, life progressing without incident, each day another day closer to the grave. It wasn't like that at all. Every day with Charlie was a mini adventure, even the days when we didn't do much. She stayed at mine almost every night and the next day we would get up, have breakfast together, say goodbye as she went off to Moorfields and I settled at my computer to work, then meet up in the evening and go out to drink, watch a film or wander around London, exploring, following a book of walks Charlie had found in a charity shop that took us down river paths, across hidden marshes, through beautiful squares and into dark alleys.

Alternatively, we would spend the evening at my place, curled up on the sofa or in bed, or drinking wine in the bath. We drank a lot of wine, we watched silly TV shows and we continued to have a lot of sex. We were both insatiable, hardly able to make it from one room to another without pulling at each other's clothes. Most nights, I would fall asleep with Charlie holding me tightly, so spent and exhausted that I thought there was no way I'd be able to do it tomorrow, that my well had run dry. But the next day, we would be at it again.

Looking back, it was like we had been gripped by a mania that went beyond the normal lustful fun that fills the early days of a relationship. I knew we couldn't keep this up forever but, at the same time, believed that we would. We were having so much sex that I lost two or three pounds. My body looked more toned, my muscles pumped. I didn't care about the circles that were beginning to darken beneath my eyes. Who needed sleep?

One night, lying in bed, a thought struck me. 'You still haven't shown me any of your art,' I said.

'I know. I will. But I haven't had time to do anything lately.' She poked my chest. 'I've been distracted.'

The room was candlelit and cold outside the cocoon of the bed.

'That makes me feel guilty. I don't want you to stop doing what you love.'

'You're what I love,' she said, her voice thick and sleepy.

'Yes, but . . . You said you were going to do my portrait.'

There was no response. She was asleep.

⌣

The next day I had a meeting with Wowcom's marketing director, who appeared thoroughly bored and unimpressed with everything I showed him, though Victor would call me afterwards and say, 'You really wowed them at Wowcom.' I could never tell if he was being sarcastic. They wanted me to keep working on the project, though, and Victor told me he had some other clients he wanted me to meet.

'One thing,' he said. 'The client says your work is a little too sexy. I mean, sexy is good. Of course it's fucking good. But this isn't American Apparel or Playboy. You need to tone it down a bit.'

I was shocked. I'd used a few risqué images: young, beautiful people entwined, kissing on beaches. It was hardly explicit but there was, I had to admit, a lot of flesh on display.

Having coffee with Sasha after my meeting with the marketing guy, I told her what Victor had said.

She snorted. 'Sounds like your real life is seeping into your work.'

'What do you mean?'

'Come off it, Andrew. You told me you and your flame-haired sex-bomb are like a pair of rabbits on Viagra. It's interesting, because I would have thought that being sexually frustrated would make you more likely to produce sexy stuff. But with you it's the other way round.'

'I feel embarrassed.'

'And so you should.' She pouted, half serious. 'I feel very neglected recently. I haven't seen you properly for two weeks.'

'I know. I've been busy.'

She gave me a look.

'Why don't the three of us go out. Me, you and Charlie.'

She forked some of her carrot cake into her mouth. 'Hmm. As long as you promise to keep your hands off each other. I don't want to be made to feel like a gooseberry.' She laid her hand on her chest. 'My heart is still healing, remember.'

I stole some of her cake. She jested, but I knew she was still cut up about Lance, especially as she had to work in his office every day. I also knew that she'd received a couple of threatening texts which she was certain were from Lance's wife, Mae.

The first of these, sent in the middle of the night, read *I hope you die of cancer bitch.*

The second, again sent in the small hours, said *I've got my eye on you.*

I had suggested that she take them to the police. It had to be illegal to send threatening texts, but Sasha refused.

'Number one, I don't want to have to explain my love life to some smirking cop. Number two, I don't think Mae would be stupid enough to send me nasty texts from her own phone. She's probably using an unregistered pay-as-you-go.' She had sighed. 'All I can do is make sure I have no contact with him and wait for it to blow over.'

'Don't worry,' I said now. 'You won't be a gooseberry. When Charlie and I went out for the day with Tilly, we barely touched each other.'

'I admire your restraint.'

'I'm pretty sure you'll like her. She'll definitely like you.'

Sasha smiled at me, her mouth stuffed full of cake. She crossed her eyes and spoke with her mouth full, icing oozing from between her lips. 'How could she not?'

When I mentioned to Charlie that I wanted her to meet Sasha, her face fell.

'What's the matter?' I asked.

Charlie had come straight from work and was sitting at the little table in my living room, a glass of wine in front of her. She was leafing through an arty magazine.

'She won't like me.'

I sat down next to her. 'Of course she will.'

She didn't look up from the magazine. She turned the page to a photo-shoot in which models posed as murder victims, one stretched out in an alleyway with a slash across her throat, another tied to a chair with a plastic bag over her head. 'Girls don't like me.'

'Don't be silly.'

'It's true. Especially boyfriends' friends. They never like me.'

This sounded daft to me. Paranoid. 'Tilly liked you.'

Charlie glanced up from her magazine. She seemed tired, lacking her usual fizz and sparkle. 'Tilly's your sister. She's kind of duty bound to like me. Or at least pretend that she does.'

'But why do you think Sasha won't like you?'

Her mouth was a flat line. 'You're quite naive sometimes, Andrew. I'd like to meet Sasha. I want to get to know everyone who's special to you. But she won't like me.' She went back to her magazine. 'Just wait and see.'

———

After dinner, Charlie brightened. Once our food had gone down, she said she was going to freshen up and disappeared into the bathroom, then the bedroom. She was in there for a while and I could hear her singing to herself. She was actually a terrible singer but I found it endearing that she didn't care. She was singing a Katy Perry song, humming the lines she couldn't remember. After a while, she called for me to come into the bedroom.

I found her sitting on the bed wearing lingerie I hadn't seen before: expensive-looking, lacy and pure white.

'I've got a surprise for you.' She nodded towards the chest of drawers. 'We're going to make a movie.'

A video camera sat on the chest of drawers, pointing towards the bed.

'You mean . . . a sex tape?'

'Uh-huh.' She had a wicked smile on her face. 'Something special, just for me and you. Don't worry, I promise not to put it on YouTube. And you have to promise not to show it to anyone.'

'I promise.'

This was exciting. I stripped to my underwear and joined her on the bed. After a long kiss, she jumped up and adjusted the focus on the camera, pressed a couple of buttons.

'Action,' she giggled.

I felt self-conscious at first, aware of the camera pointing at us, feeling like I was being watched not by an inanimate piece of technology but by human eyes, staring, judging. But as Charlie and I kissed and touched each other and I grew more and more aroused, I relaxed and forgot about the camera.

I think it would be accurate to say that neither Charlie nor I were in charge in the bedroom. There wasn't one dominant party, one submissive. Sometimes, though, one of us would lead and on this occasion it was Charlie. She was the director here, and she prompted me with her lips, her tongue, her fingers. She moved her body so I would know what to do. She whispered for me to go slowly, faster, softer, harder. She ensured we were positioned so the camera could capture everything.

When we'd finished, when the tape was no longer running and we were both sated, exhausted, Charlie said, 'I can't wait to watch it.'

'Hmm. Me too.'

She wriggled closer to me, warm and affectionate, her hair tickling my nose. 'I've never done that before.'

I didn't respond.

We were silent for a minute and then Charlie said, 'Have you?'

I had been hoping she wouldn't ask, and it would be so easy to lie. She would never find out, as I was certain the evidence had been erased and my co-star in the only other home sex movie I'd made was highly unlikely to tell. I didn't want to lie, though, and didn't think I had any need to.

'Once,' I said.

Charlie was quiet for a long time, so long that I thought she'd fallen asleep.

'With Harriet?' she said, just as I was about to drift off myself.

'No. She wouldn't have . . . She would never have wanted to do anything like that.'

From my position, with Charlie's head on my chest, I couldn't see her face, just the top of her head. But I could feel how tense she was. Again, I was tempted to lie. But I couldn't.

'It was with Karen,' I said.

Charlie sat up rapidly. 'I need to go to the toilet,' she said. She almost ran out of the room, naked.

When she came back, she sat on the edge of the bed, wearing my dressing gown. 'I want to see it.'

I had been close to dozing off again. I squinted at her. 'What?'

'I want to see the tape you made with her.'

'You can't, Charlie. It doesn't exist anymore. We made it as a bit of a joke, using her phone, watched it – not even the whole way through, because it was too cringeworthy – and then deleted it straight away.'

'Are you sure she hasn't kept a copy?'

I reached out for her but she shrank away. 'I'm certain, sweetheart. I deleted it myself. And there's no way I'd want you to see it anyway.'

'Why?'

'For fuck's sake, Charlie. If there was a tape of you having sex with another guy out there, it would be the last thing I'd want to see. Jesus.'

She didn't respond.

'Please, come back to bed. Don't spoil the evening.'

But she wouldn't move. 'Do you ever wish you were still with her?' she asked.

I laughed. But when I saw her expression I said, 'You're serious?'

'Yes,' she whispered.

'You mean, leave *you* and go back to *her*?'

She nodded.

'Why on earth would I want to do that? Karen and me – it was just a fling. It came with a built-in expiry date.' I reached out for her. 'We're not like that, are we?'

Like a bubble bursting, her expression changed back to a smile. 'Sorry. I was being an idiot.'

She slipped back beneath the quilt and cuddled up to me.

I told her that I loved her.

'You swear?' she said.

I laughed. 'You want me to swear?'

She laughed too. 'Yes. Yes, I do.'

'OK,' I said, holding up my hand like a Boy Scout, pleased that the conversation had swerved from serious to silly. 'On my life. On my sister's life. I love you.'

She propped herself up on her elbows and stared at me. She had stopped smiling and I felt confused. Were we messing about or was she taking this seriously? 'Forever?' she said.

'Scout's honour,' I replied. 'Until the day I die.'

In the middle of the night, I woke up needing the toilet. Charlie wasn't in the bed. I got up and went into the dark living room.

'What are you doing?'

I walked over. She was sitting, wrapped in a towel but goose-pimply with cold, staring at the little screen on the video camera. She was watching us having sex.

She looked up at me, her face flickering in the glow of the camera.

'We're perfect together,' she said in a whisper, her eyes wide like she was telling me she'd just discovered that aliens really existed or that she'd found God.

I put my arm around her and took her back to bed.

Thirteen

I woke up late the next morning, having forgotten to set the alarm. Charlie was buried beneath the quilt and as soon as I saw the time – 10:20 a.m. – I nudged her.

'Charlie, you're really late for work.'

She made a low groaning noise. 'I'm going to call in sick. I'm too tired to move.' She groped for her phone and called the hospital, putting on a very convincing sick voice. I was impressed.

I knew I ought to get up and do some work but with Charlie sleeping beside me, and after such a weird night, I told myself I'd catch up later.

Charlie and I had lunch together, and she was trying to decide whether to go home or stay, when my doorbell rang.

'Postman?' Charlie asked.

'I don't know.' But as I was going down the stairs, I remembered. It was Wednesday.

'Hello Andrew,' Kristi said, as I opened the door. 'Oh. What is wrong?'

'Huh? Oh, nothing. Come in.'

'Am I late?' She pulled her phone out of her bag and frowned at the screen.

'No, no – it's me. I'd completely forgotten you were coming.' I noticed that she had a bruise on her cheek, and the hint of a black eye. 'Are you OK?'

'Yes,' she said firmly. 'Why you ask?'

'Oh. No reason.' I didn't want to pry into her private life. I followed her up the stairs, the smell of cigarettes wafting off her. As we entered the flat, Charlie was standing by the door, her bag on her shoulder.

'Hello,' Charlie said, smiling at Kristi. This was not Charlie's genuine smile.

'Hello.' Kristi turned straight to me. 'Andrew, you want me to do my usual?'

This was ridiculously awkward. 'Yes, of course. We're just going out. Let me give you the money now.'

I opened my wallet. It was empty.

'How much is it?' Charlie asked, opening her bag.

'Sixteen pounds for two hours,' Kristi said, looking around. The flat was messier than usual and probably stank of sex and the cannabis we'd been smoking occasionally. The bin was full of condoms and the bed wasn't made.

Charlie handed Kristi £20 and told her to keep the change, as I always did. Then we left her to it.

It must have been zero degrees outside, the sky heavy with the threat of snow.

'She looks like a model,' Charlie said.

'Who, Kristi?'

She rolled her eyes. 'Who do you think I'm talking about? A model who's been beaten up.'

'Maybe she had an accident.'

'What, she walked into a door?' Charlie craned her neck to look up at my flat.

'What do you think I should do?'

Charlie sighed. 'There's probably nothing you can do. It's a shame, though.' She touched her own face, staring up at the building. 'She really is beautiful. Shame she's being exploited.'

'Please don't start that one again.'

Charlie narrowed her eyes and for a moment I thought she was going to launch into another tirade. But she merely said, again, 'It's a shame.'

The next day, I had a meeting with Karen to show her the work I'd done on her site, after which I was due to see Victor to talk about the Wowcom project.

Karen was less than enthusiastic when I showed her the mock-ups I'd been working on – that were overdue, in fact.

'I think it needs some work,' she said, casting her eye over the simple white and purple design I'd created. 'It's a bit . . .' She pulled a face.

I was taken aback. I thought it looked elegant and professional. 'But this is what you said you wanted.'

We were in the same coffee shop as before but her mood was completely different. Gone was the playfulness and ironic conversation of our last meeting. I had seen her like this before, when she was overtired or had had a run-in with her ex or a difficult client. Maybe that's what had happened. She'd been given a hard time and was paying it forward.

'I'm sorry Andrew, but I imagined it completely different to this. I thought it would have some more "wow." My friend Cassie has just set up her own site. It looks better than this and she used a template she found online.'

I wondered who she'd been talking to. Had someone told her she was being ripped off?

I headed to Victor's office in a bad mood, having agreed to re-do the work, which would mean at least another couple of days on it without any extra money. En route, I felt the need for friendly human contact, so I fired off a text to Charlie.

Fucking Karen doesn't like the work I did – I have to do it all again. SO annoying. Xx

Charlie replied immediately. *What a bitch! I'm sure the work was brilliant. You should refuse to do it. xxx*

No, I need the money. This is what it's like being a freelancer but I'm sure she's taking advantage of me. xxx

I think she's always taken advantage of you. x

I wasn't sure what to say to that, so decided to change the subject. *Do you want to go out for dinner tonight? New Thai place just opened in H Hill. xxx*

She replied. *I'm knackered. Quiet night in OK? Love you xxx PS, have you called Tilly lately, checked she's OK? You should.*

Good thinking. Quiet night in sounds good. Love you too. xxx

I called Tilly. Her mobile rang out so I tried the landline. Rachel answered.

'You haven't been fired then,' I said, without thinking.

'No thanks to you.'

Oh dear. 'I'm sorry. She kind of forced it out of me. She knows you were just trying to help though. Anyway, I'm glad you answered. How does she seem at the moment?'

Her voice dropped a few decibels. 'She's all right, yes. She seems brighter. I found her crying the other day—'

'Oh God.'

'—but she told me I shouldn't worry about it. She said it's just that she misses your mum and dad sometimes. And I think she misses you too.'

Rachel had a habit of stabbing me right where I was most vulnerable. Right in the guilt glands.

'I'll try to come down more,' I said.

I remembered a conversation I'd had with Tilly after I'd bought my flat. 'So,' she had said. 'Did you buy a flat on the fourth floor with no lift so I wouldn't be able to visit you? Or are you planning on setting up some kind of winch and pulley system so you can haul me up the front of the building?'

I had been mortified. It genuinely hadn't crossed my mind, when I had bought that flat, that Tilly would never be able to visit it. I was gripped by self-loathing and vowed to visit her frequently. Of course, she had been nice about it and told me not to worry, that she knew it was a bargain and that I wouldn't be there forever. 'Next time, though, get a ground floor flat, eh?'

'I'll come down soon,' I said to Rachel now. 'I'm sure Charlie would like to come and see Tilly too.'

'Hang on, she's coming,' Rachel hissed, and then I was exchanging pleasantries with my sister. She didn't have much time to talk but told me, quite impatiently, that she was fine, that I didn't need to worry about her, but that she couldn't wait to see me and Charlie again.

'You've got a good one there,' she said. 'Try not to fuck it up.'

In contrast to Karen's reaction to my work, Victor was full of enthusiasm about what I'd done for Wowcom.

'You're on fire,' he said. 'Now you've toned down the naughtiness a bit. I've gotta say, I never saw you as the controversial type. Must be the influence of your new bird.' He looked me up and down. 'You've lost weight too. Banging you ragged, is she? You lucky bastard.'

I didn't know what to say.

Victor sat down on the adjacent sofa in his office.

'Take my advice. Don't marry her. Don't have kids. Don't even let her move in.'

I gestured at the large, happy family portrait on his desk: his cool-looking wife, Amanda, with her bleached blonde hair, and his tweenage son and daughter, big grins showing gappy teeth.

'You're telling me you'd rather have a casual girlfriend than your lovely family?'

He looked at the picture too, beaming with pride. 'Nah, of course not. My family are everything to me. But those early days of a relationship – all that passion, the constant shagging, the lack of bickering about money and housework. Sometimes I'd like to go back to those days. Just for a week.' He winked at me. 'Maybe a month.'

'Maybe you and Amanda should go away on holiday for a week, leave the kids with a babysitter.'

'Maybe. Anyway, Andrew, there's something I want to talk to you about.'

'Right?'

He fixed me with his most sincere look. 'The work you've done on Wowcom has been first class. Just like your work always is. I'm impressed. And I was wondering if you'd be interested in coming and working for me. Here.'

'You mean . . . as part of the company?'

'Yeah. We've got a position available: senior designer. Darren, one of our seniors, is going off travelling or something ridiculous like that. As soon as he told me, I thought of you.'

I must have looked dumbstruck as he went on, 'You don't have to say yes or no now. I know you like working from home – lounging about in your pyjamas all day, not having to put up with office politics or share a bog with anyone else. But, I dunno, if I were you I'd get a bit lonely.'

'I'm not lonely,' I said, without much conviction. I looked out through the glass wall of his office at all the cool young people – a girl in a tight T-shirt stopping to chat to a guy with a beard; a pair of blokes heading outside for a cigarette break. There was lots of serious work going on, but Victor's staff also appeared to like it here. It was a small business that punched above its weight.

'Don't make a decision now,' he said. 'I'll email you the job spec and details of salary and all that boring stuff.' He cleared his throat. 'I know you've only been with this bird a month or whatever, but if you are thinking it might get serious, down the road, maybe you'd be better off with something more secure than freelancing.' Perhaps sensing he was pushing it, he added, 'But don't let me twist your arm. All I'm saying is, there's a job going, I'd love you to have it, and if you'd rather stay working at home in your jim-jams then I'll probably be able to keep chucking work your way.'

Perhaps if I wasn't feeling so pissed off about Karen rejecting my work or if Victor hadn't slipped that 'probably' into his final sentence, I might have made a different decision.

I had always worked freelance, since leaving university. Because of the money I'd had from my parents' insurance, I hadn't needed a student loan and I hadn't felt pressured to find a job immediately. I'd fallen into freelance work when a friend of a friend asked me to do some work for him and it had grown from there.

By the time Charlie came round, I had made up my mind. I was going to accept the offer Victor had emailed to me.

'The money's excellent,' I said to Charlie. 'And it's secure. I won't have to take on shitty little jobs like the one for Karen where I end up doing twice as much work as I'd originally estimated.'

Charlie sat down at the table, bottle of wine already open. Her cheeks were pink from her walk from the train station through the bitter cold. Snow was forecast for tomorrow and England was bracing itself, unprepared as usual.

'I understand about that bit,' she said. 'But otherwise I think you're mad.'

I was disappointed. I wanted her to be enthused. 'Really? Why?'

'You don't know what it's really like, working in an office. You're so lucky being able to work here, and for yourself.'

'But the people at Victor's office are cool.'

She furrowed her brow.

'Not as cool as you, obviously.'

I was trying to make her smile but her expression remained grim.

'Sorry,' she said. 'I'm in a bad mood. Shitty day at work.' She sank half a glass of wine. 'Go on, tell me all about it.'

I did, recounting the entire conversation with Victor, explaining my reasoning, telling her that I was sick of being on my own all the time.

'Maybe I should quit my job and then we could spend the days together,' she said.

I laughed. 'Yeah, right.' I was fired up with excitement. 'It will also be great for me professionally. I'll learn so much working for Victor, and just being around other designers.'

She looked at me over her wine glass. 'Sounds like you've made your mind up already.'

My gaze slipped away from hers. It was awkward, what I was going to say. It made me uncomfortable. 'Charlie, before I met you, I lived in a kind of self-imposed solitary confinement. I found going out into the world . . . difficult.'

I was speaking so quietly that she leaned closer, straining to hear. 'I've been like that since my parents died. It's hard . . . it's hard to explain, but I shut down after that. Like a flower closing up.' I illustrated this by clenching my fist. 'Even at uni I kept to myself, studied hard, didn't make many friends apart from Sasha. I say I fell into freelancing, but I also allowed it to happen because it suited me.'

Charlie stretched out her hand to take mine.

'But since meeting you – and I know it hasn't been long – I feel . . . stronger. More, um, equipped to go out into the world. Like I'm finally unfurling.' I opened my fist, fingers curling outwards. 'It's all thanks to you, Charlie.'

She nodded, slowly, squeezed my fingers. 'I was the same,' she said, 'after I lost my parents. Like, if I'm an orphan, I'm *really* going to be an orphan, you know?' I thought she was about to tell me more, open up about her past. But she said, 'It's great . . . it's really great that you feel better, or different or whatever, because of me.'

There was an extended silence.

'So you've made your mind up?' Charlie said, startling me out of my thoughts.

'I have. I'm going to accept. I'll text Victor now.'

I sent the text then held up my drink. 'A toast? To orphans, making it in the big bad world.'

She arched an eyebrow. 'How about just a toast to us?'

After dinner, we watched TV for a while then went to bed and made love. I suggested to Charlie that we watch our DVD, which she had edited at home and presented to me as a gift, but she said she was too tired. I drifted off.

An hour later, I woke up. Charlie wasn't in bed.

I went into the living room, where she was sitting at the computer. This was starting to become a habit: me getting up in the night to find my girlfriend doing something in the dark in the front room.

'Charlie?'

She didn't respond. Getting closer, I saw that she was on Victor's company website. Old Street Design. Specifically, she was on the 'Meet the Team' page, an area of the site that profiled the staff. Each person who worked there had a photo along with their name, job title and a couple of factoids: favourite cartoon character, what they wanted to be when they grew up, that kind of thing.

'So this is who you'll be working with,' she said.

She scrolled up and down the page.

'Does Victor only employ attractive young people?'

'Not only,' I said, feeling groggy. 'But yeah, I guess mostly.'

She glared at the screen. 'He should be taken to a tribunal. I bet if he interviewed two equally qualified women he'd give the job to the prettier one. Actually, he'd probably give the job to the prettier one even if she was less qualified.'

'I don't think that's true,' I said. 'Why don't you come back to bed?'

'I wish you weren't going to work there,' she said.

'You're being stupid,' I said. I was tired, fed up. This was the harshest thing I'd ever said to her. 'And it's too late now. I've already told Victor I'm going to accept the job.'

I went back to bed, leaving her clicking around the screen, zooming in on the images of one young, attractive woman after another.

———

The next morning, I woke up to find Charlie sitting on the bed holding a plate loaded with scrambled eggs and toast, a steaming mug of coffee already on the bedside table. As I pushed myself into an upright position, she handed me a folded-over piece of paper. On it she had drawn a caricature of herself, a frowning girl with a tear rolling down her cheek, an arrow pointing to her with the word IDIOT.

Inside, it said SORRY. C xxxx.

'I love you,' she said. 'And I really am sorry. I know it's a brilliant opportunity for you.'

I kissed her. 'Why were you so weird about it?'

She shrugged. 'I don't know. I guess I don't like change.'

'But it's change for me, not you.'

She took the plate and set it to one side. 'Let's leave it, can we?'

She slipped back into bed beside me. 'I've got five minutes,' she said.

Fourteen

I left the flat not long after Charlie had headed to work, the taste of her still on my lips. The parked cars had thick ice on the windscreens; the woman in the flat downstairs worked on hers, scraper in one gloved hand, a big can of de-icer in the other.

'It's going to snow,' she said, flicking a glance towards the sky.

I looked down at my inappropriate footwear: trainers, more like plimsolls, really. I ought to go back up, change into some boots. But I couldn't be bothered to go back up four flights, so decided to risk it.

My eyes had been bothering me, feeling dry and scratchy for the last few days, so I went to the optician's in Brixton to get some drops. Apparently, this was a common after-effect of the kind of operation I'd had. Floaters came and went too, each one making me worry that it was going to happen again. But apart from that, I was in high spirits.

I wanted to buy Charlie a present, so I spent an hour or so browsing around the shops and exploring Brixton Market. Although she'd bought me lots of presents, I'd hardly bought her anything apart from a couple of books – a volume of love poetry and an erotic novel that we read to each other in bed – and a cuddly dog that she called Bones.

I didn't feel confident about buying her something she'd like. In the end, I found a silver locket in a vintage shop that was probably over-priced but that I thought she'd love. I bought a silk scarf too to wrap it in.

After that, I headed on the Tube to Oxford Circus. I needed some new clothes for work. I didn't want to turn up on the first day wearing my holey jumper and paint-splattered jeans. I was going to be working with lots of trendy kids and I wanted to fit in, though I didn't want anything too self-consciously hip.

I was deep in thought about clothes and work and what it was going to be like on my first day – my mouth went dry when I contemplated it – but when I emerged from the Tube station into the open air I gasped.

Snow was flurrying down, flakes as big as moths spiralling towards the pavement where it attempted to cling on, only to be trampled underfoot by the crowds. It was beautiful, like a scene from a Christmas movie, and I knew that in most other, less-frenetic places across the capital, the snow would by sticking to the ground. Children would be crossing their fingers for a day off school. Trains and buses would be cancelled. The usual chaos that erupted across Britain whenever it snowed heavily would ensue. As a nation, we moaned about it but we loved it really.

I hurried into Top Shop, where Charlie and I had gone that first night. It seemed so long ago but was only, what, four weeks?

Four weeks! My relationship with Charlie had got very serious, very quickly. I was deeply, seriously in love with her, beyond lust or infatuation. Already, I couldn't imagine a future without her. Her comment that morning – 'I don't like change' – made me believe that she felt exactly the same way. I had no doubt that she liked me as much as I liked her, and that made me feel secure and happy.

Perhaps, by most people's standards, it had moved too fast. But I really didn't care. We felt how we felt, and it wasn't like we were talking about eloping or even moving in together. I was, however, planning to ask her if she wanted to go on holiday at Easter, somewhere warm. I was also thinking about taking her to see my mum and dad's graves, down in Eastbourne, the closest I could get to introducing her to my parents. Or was that too morbid? I wondered if she'd want to do the same with her own deceased parents. Things like that, the coincidence of us both being orphans – though I hated that word – made me think that our relationship was serendipitous. The same with us having such similar surnames. *We were meant to be.* Charlie whispered that to me all the time.

'You know the Greek myth?' she asked. 'That Zeus split humans in two and that we all wander the earth looking for our lost half? Well, we're the lucky ones, Andrew. We found our missing half, the half that makes us whole.'

In addition to embracing Greek myths, like many couples we mythologised the beginning of our relationship. *If I hadn't dropped that coin. If you hadn't had to wait so long at the Tube station.* And then Charlie had lost her phone, been unable to contact me. What if I'd met someone else during that short period? Oh, we had overcome so many obstacles to be together, laughed in Fate's cruel face!

I mulled all this over as I explored the shops of Oxford and Regent Street. By the time I had finished shopping, the rooftops were white with snow and the pavements were slippery with slush. It seemed like lots of people were leaving work early, keen to get home before public transport shut down, keeping their fingers crossed for a snowed-in day tomorrow.

I joined the crowds pushing into the Tube station. I was already beginning to regret buying so much as I was laden with bags full of shirts and jumpers and shoes. My pathetic trainers were soaked through, my socks damp and cold. The snow was still coming down hard.

To enter Oxford Circus station, there are several stairways that lead down from the intersection of Oxford and Regent Street. We were lined up six across to get into the station. I wondered if it would be more sensible to get a bus back to Tulse Hill. But I was caught up in the crowd now, bodies pressing behind me. It was like leaving a football match or stadium gig, everyone trying to get into the station at the same time. I hoped commuting wasn't going to be like this or I might regret my decision.

I finally reached the front of the crowd at the top of the steps that led down into the belly of London. From in front of me I could hear shouting; someone had slipped on the concrete steps.

A voice shouted, 'Hold up!' from below. I stopped, allowing the stairs to clear in front of me. I was stuck in the middle of the crowd, halfway between the wall on one side and the central handrail on the other, unable to use my hands because of all the bags I was holding. I hesitated – and as I did I felt the crowd surge behind me, could hear shouting, the pedestrian equivalent of cars sounding their horns in a traffic jam, the thin veneer of civilisation being torn down by impatience and anger.

What happened next has replayed itself in my dreams many times since. I started to descend the steps, putting one soggy foot in front of the other, head down, treading deliberately and carefully.

And then I was falling, arms flailing, a whoosh of air in my belly as I went down head first, unable to stop my fall because of my full hands, and in a blur of darkness and light, I tumbled, fast, trying to grab hold of the rail, my foot jarring on a step, knee twisting, the bright flash of agony shooting up through my leg, and then I was lying on the ground at the bottom.

I remember flickers of what happened next. How most of the people in the crowd poured past and over me, so that I seriously feared I would be trampled to death. How a young black man pulled me to one side and his girlfriend fetched a couple of Underground workers, who acted like I was causing them a massive inconvenience. Then someone was asking me if I could walk. I couldn't; my knee felt like it was on fire and the slightest pressure sent spears of pain through me. I was carried out of the station by a pair of paramedics and taken to the nearest hospital where I joined a queue of people in A&E who'd slipped in the snow, the nurses looking harassed as the walking wounded were brought in one after another.

In the chaos, I had lost my shopping bags, which concerned me even more at that point than the pain in my knee. I texted Charlie, playing down what had happened, telling her I'd see her at the flat later if she could make it round. Then, finally, I was wheeled in to see the nurse and made to wait some more for an X-ray.

'You've sprained a knee ligament,' the nurse said, eventually. 'Nothing too serious, but you're not going to be able to walk on it for three to four weeks. Are you on your own? Do you have someone who can come and help you get home?'

This was just like when my retina had detached. Except this time, I did have someone who could come and be with me. I called Charlie and told her what had happened.

'Oh, Andrew! I'll be right there.'

Two hours later I left the hospital, my swollen right leg swaddled in a tight bandage, on a pair of crutches. I had ten days' supply of codeine, forty pills, and instructions to rest. 'For goodness sake, don't go out on your crutches in this snow and ice,' the nurse said, looking at me as if she was sure that was exactly what I was intending to do.

Charlie called a minicab which took us home. My street was carpeted with snow and the taxi could barely get up the road, the driver complaining and cursing as he inched his way towards my flat, headlights illuminating the swirling snow-flakes. Charlie insisted that he take me to my front door. Then came the worst part: getting up the steps, all four flights. I did it backwards, on my bum, pushing myself up, trying not to bump my leg, shards of white-hot pain exploding every time I did. By the time we reached the top I was almost in tears, sweating and shaking.

Charlie, her face etched with concern, helped me onto the sofa, pushing the coffee table away so I could sit with my leg propped up on a cushion.

'My poor wounded soldier,' she said.

'I need a drink,' I said.

'Is that wise, with the codeine?'

'I don't care. Please.'

She opened a bottle of red and I gulped down a glassful quickly. I had taken two painkillers at the hospital and they were finally kicking in.

It was so good to have her beside me. What would I have done without her?

'You really must be more careful,' she said, smiling gently. 'I've only just got you. I can't bear to think of losing you.'

'I'm sure,' I said, 'that someone – some bastard in the crowd behind me – pushed me.'

She looked shocked. 'Did you see them?'

'No. But I felt hands on my back. I'm sure I did.' My blood chilled as I thought of it, like the snow was inside the room; inside my veins.

I looked down at the bandage on my leg. Outside the window, the snow was falling even more heavily. Four flights of stairs, and outside, the pavements were slick with ice. With a sinking heart, I realised I was trapped.

Fifteen

The snow didn't stop falling for days. From Land's End to John o' Groats, from London to Glasgow and everywhere between, Britain shivered beneath a white shroud. I pulled a chair over to the window and watched it eddying past my window, Christmassy scenes that, under other circumstances, I would have enjoyed. The heating was cranked up, I had plenty of food and drink in the house, lots to entertain me. But I didn't feel cosy or safe: I felt stuck, anxious, a lame polar bear at the zoo.

One of the first people I called the morning after it happened, after an uncomfortable night flat on my back, the pain in my knee keeping me awake, was Victor.

'I'm not going to be able to start Monday.' I told him what had happened, leaving out the part about believing I'd been pushed. I didn't want him to think I was paranoid.

'Ah, bollocks,' he said. 'Talk about the shitty end of the stick.'

We agreed that I would carry on doing freelance work from home and, to my great relief, he said I could start my new job as soon as I was able to make it in.

'As soon as the ice and snow are gone, and I can get around on these crutches, I'll be there.'

'Take your time, Andrew,' he said. 'Maybe I'll come round and see you, bring you some grapes.'

'That would be great.'

'They got you on painkillers?' he asked.

'Yeah. Industrial-strength codeine.' The tablets were huge, like ones you'd give to a horse. I was supposed to take one every four hours during waking hours, but had been cheating a little and was often unable to wait the full interval, taking them every two to three hours. I wasn't worried: I'd be able to get more from the hospital when I ran out.

'Love that stuff,' Victor said. 'And what about your missus? She looking after you?'

'Yeah, she's coming round straight after work. Listen, Victor, I'm really sorry about all of this.'

'Don't worry, mate. There's no great rush. Look at it this way: it's a bit more time without me being your boss, after which I won't be nice to you any more.'

He spluttered with laughter and I put the phone down, feeling a little better until a stab of pain pulsed inside my cast.

I took a codeine tablet.

⌣

'How are you feeling?' Charlie asked when she turned up in the early evening, her hair dotted with melting snow, carrying a small suitcase and a couple of carrier bags.

'Frustrated,' I said.

She gave me an exaggerated comedy wink. 'I can sort that out.'

'I didn't mean that kind of frustrated. I meant I hate being stuck here, unable to go outside.'

'I know. Did your sense of humour get knocked out when you fell down those steps?'

'Sorry.'

She kissed me. Her lips were cold. 'It's OK. Now, look, I brought you some presents and I'm going to cook you dinner.'

She gave me some books, magazines and *The Sopranos* box set because she'd been horrified to discover I'd never watched it. Then she set about making dinner.

'What's with the suitcase?' I asked, watching her chop basil and tomatoes, spaghetti waiting in the pan.

She turned to me. 'I thought I'd better come and stay with you for a bit, look after you.'

'That's really sweet,' I said. 'But I'm not sure I like being looked after. It makes me feel like you're mothering me or something.'

She put the knife down and came over to me. 'Don't be daft. I'm not going to put on a nurse's uniform and wipe your bum for you. But you're going to go crazy stuck in here on your own, aren't you? I come here nearly every night anyway, so I thought it would be easier if I left some stuff here. Then I won't have to keep going back to my place every day.'

'All right. Thank you. I'm sorry.'

She went back into the kitchenette.

'Did you talk to Victor?' she asked.

I recounted our conversation and she nodded. 'That's good. I know your leg hurts and you hate being stuck indoors. But you should try to enjoy it. Just chill out, rest, watch *The Sopranos*. I wish I could take some time off work but this project is at a critical stage, fucking pain in the arse that it is.'

She turned, pointing the tip of the knife in my direction.

'Have I told you about that dick, Michael?' She recounted an argument she'd had with one of the consultants at the hospital, jabbing the knife forward to emphasise the parts she was most annoyed about.

'Shit, Charlie, you look like you want to stab him.'

She looked down at the knife and smiled. 'Hmm. If I could get away with it I'd stick this in his heart and shove him in the incinerator.'

She turned back to the worktop.

I took a sip of wine. 'I hope I never get on your bad side.'

She sliced a cucumber. 'Don't worry, handsome. You never could.'

The days bled into one another in a codeine- and boredom-induced haze. I did some work on Karen's site, emailing the new draft to her. I tinkered with the Wowcom campaign. What else did I do? Looking back is like straining to see through misted glass, or watching a slow-moving, faded movie in which all the scenes have been chopped up and jumbled.

I watched TV. I browsed Facebook and eBay and Buzzfeed until my eyes throbbed. I tried to read, but the words wouldn't go in and I would read the same paragraphs over and over before giving in. I waited for Charlie to come round. I tried to ignore the itching beneath the cast.

A lot of the time, I slept. The codeine gave me vivid dreams that would have impressed and terrified Salvador Dali, dreams in which I floated on clouds with talking tigers, or was a member of an American street gang, mowing down motherfuckers with an Uzi. I had that Miley Cyrus song, 'Wrecking Ball,' stuck in my head and it went round and round and round so many times that I wanted to cut my own head off to escape it.

And all the while, the snow kept falling. In one of my codeine dreams, I imagined the snow burying the streets, reaching my fourth-floor window and causing me to mount a daring escape, gliding across the vanished city on a tea tray to rescue Charlie. Except I was the one who needed rescuing: I was Rapunzel, or that guy in *Rear Window*. I felt like I was going mad, and only Charlie, who came round every evening and stayed over, kept me from slipping into insanity.

'It's your own fault for buying that fourth-floor flat,' Tilly said, teasing me. 'Otherwise I'd come round and visit. If you lived on the ground floor, we could get you a wheelchair and could have races.'

'You'd whip my arse.'

'True dat. Oh, guess what? Rachel's got a boyfriend. His name's Henry and he's a Hells Angel.'

'Really?'

'Actually, they're not real Angels, are they? The Eastbourne and Pevensey Motorcycle Club.' She sniggered. 'You should see him. He's about seven foot tall, with a beard almost that long, and more tats than David Beckham. Nice chap, though.'

'That's so sweet. Do they go out riding together?'

'Yeah, she gives him backies.' She laughed dirtily.

'And what about your love life?' I asked, somewhat tentatively.

'You see the weather outside? Cold, bleak, no sign of a thaw? Well, it's like that.'

'Maybe Henry has a friend?' I could just see Tilly in the arms of a hairy biker.

'Oh, puh-lease.'

Talking to Tilly cheered me up. I was trying hard not to feel sorry for myself. I couldn't help, though, thinking it was desperately unfair that I'd suffered two medical dramas within a year. My 'eye thing,' as Tilly called it, hadn't kept me confined to the flat – though walking round with a gas bubble in my eye was not much fun – but it had been more worrying. I knew my leg would heal. I just had to be patient. Like Charlie urged, I tried to enjoy the downtime, and after a few days of going slightly crazy, I got a grip and spent more time being constructive, taking on a new mini-project for Victor.

I remembered that I hadn't received any feedback from Karen about the second version of her site, so emailed her asking if she was happy with it. She didn't reply straight away and I decided to give it a couple of days before chasing her. I felt anxious about it, and told Charlie so in an email. She asked if I wanted her to go round and 'sort her out.'

You don't have any boys to send round, she wrote, *so I'll do it.*

I replied with a LOL.

Sasha called and texted and arranged to come round. She was finally going to get to meet Charlie, who was still adamant that Sasha wouldn't like her but agreed it was crazy they hadn't met yet.

'Why are all your friends girls?' Charlie asked after I'd set up the 'date' with Sasha.

'I've got male friends.' I tried not to sound indignant. 'But most of my friends are scattered around the country or still in Eastbourne.'

'I suppose you don't meet that many new people, being free-lance.'

'Exactly. And what about you? You never talk about your friends at all, apart from people at work.'

She walked over to the fridge, poured herself more wine. 'I've got plenty of friends . . . But I haven't lived in London very long, have I? They're all back home in Leeds.'

'Do you miss them?'

She shrugged. 'Yeah, a bit.'

'We should go up there, when I'm walking again. You can show me where you grew up, introduce me to your mates.'

'Maybe.'

I remembered something. 'That night we first went out, you stayed with someone in central London. Who was that?'

'Huh?'

'I just assumed you have a friend who lives in central London.'

'Oh. Actually, I lied to you that night.'

I looked at her.

'I wanted to go home with you, but knew that you'd think I was a total slut or that it was just a one-night stand. And I didn't want the awkwardness of getting a cab to drop us off separately. So I lied.'

'Oh.'

'I waited five minutes then got a taxi home. Sorry.' She leaned into me and kissed my cheek. 'I didn't want you to know how irresistible I found you. Do you forgive me?'

'Yeah, of course. It's no big deal. Though I wouldn't have thought you were a slut, you know. I was smitten within ten minutes of meeting you.'

'Ditto.'

The codeine was starting to wear off and I felt a twinge in my knee. I needed another pill.

'Maybe you and Sasha will become friends,' I said, hobbling over to the kitchen to retrieve the painkillers. I had enough for a few more days, even though I'd been taking more than I should.

'I'll try, Andrew,' she said.

'I'm sure you're wrong about her not liking you. She'll think you're awesome.'

She pretended not to hear, staring at something on her phone.

I swallowed the codeine tablet.

Six days had passed since my fall and Charlie went off to work, leaving me in bed with my laptop. I had given her my keys so she could let herself in and out, and I spent most of the day sitting around looking forward to hearing the scratch of the key in the lock.

It hadn't snowed for over twenty-four hours but, according to Charlie, the ground outside was treacherous, in need of gritting.

'I've seen around ten people slip over in the last week,' she said. 'You're lucky, being safely cocooned in your little flat.'

'Don't forget Sasha's coming round tonight,' I said as she left.

She rolled her eyes. 'How could I?'

She texted me a dozen times during the morning, telling me lots of filthy things she wanted to do to me.

Shortly after lunch, the doorbell rang. Fortunately, I had remembered that Kristi was due and was up and dressed. I buzzed the door and listened as footsteps ascended the stairs.

A middle-aged woman appeared on the landing. She had frizzy hair and a face that looked like it should have been a warning picture on a cigarette packet. Wheezing, she approached me and said, 'I cleaner.' She handed me a card bearing the logo of the cleaning agency.

'Where's Kristi?' I said, as she peered over my shoulder into flat.

She shrugged and scowled.

I led her into the flat and showed her where the cleaning stuff was. She couldn't take her eyes off my crutches.

'So . . . is Kristi on holiday or something?'

The woman, whose name was Maria, stared blankly at me. 'Sorry. English, I . . .'

I was surprised by how disappointed I felt that Kristi appeared to have been replaced. Perhaps she *was* on holiday, but it seemed unlikely. I remembered the bruises she'd had on her face the week before. What if something had happened to her? Unable to rest, I needed to find out.

I called the agency and, after being put on hold for an interminable length of time, listening to their hold music (R. Kelly's 'Clean This House'), I eventually got through to a man who sounded like he'd just heard that his dog had died.

'Kristi's not with us anymore.'

'Oh. She's left?'

A long pause. 'I'm not allowed to give out personal information about our staff.'

'I wasn't asking for personal information. I just wanted to check if she would be coming back.'

'I'm sorry, Mr Sumner, but like I said, she isn't able to work at the moment.'

Wasn't able?

'Maria is one of our most experienced cleaners. I'm sure she'll do a great job for you. But if for any reason you're dissatisfied please get in touch.'

I hung up and listened to Maria clean my bathroom. I felt glum. I'd liked Kristi, though maybe if I was honest with myself it was only because she was attractive and mysterious. She had been terrible at her job.

Maria came into the room, carrying a bin bag full of rubbish she'd collected from around the flat, a business-like expression on her face. I could read her mind: she was thinking I was a dirty boy, a pig who lived among his own mess. I flushed with shame because, if she was thinking that, she was right. Since Charlie had come into my life I'd turned into a slob.

By the time Maria had left, leaving the flat looking and smelling better than it had in months – surfaces gleaming, carpet spotless, rubbish removed and the musty smell I hadn't even noticed banished from the air – I'd stopped worrying about my old cleaner.

Sixteen

When I was a kid we had a plump and loveable tabby cat named Claude, whom Tilly would carry around like a baby, dressing him in doll's clothes, while I let him sleep on my bed and fed him pieces of contraband ham from the fridge. When Claude was getting on a bit, Tilly started pestering for a kitten. Mum and Dad compromised and got a rescue cat, a year-old neutered tom whom we called Speedy. When we introduced Speedy to Claude, the old cat hissed, arched his back and pissed on the carpet while the newcomer trembled under a chair.

When Sasha walked into the living room, where Charlie waited, hovering awkwardly by the sofa, it reminded me of that terrible introduction. They didn't hiss or spit or soil the rug. They were civil, smiling and shaking hands in that soft way that girls do. But the atmosphere shifted in the same way, like a disturbance in the universe, stress fissures in the fabric of the air. I was tempted to hit the abort button, get Sasha out of there, but I badly wanted them to like each other, to get along.

I was sure alcohol would help.

'Do you want wine, Sasha? White or red? Here you go.' I hobbled over, crutch under one armpit, bottle in my free hand. 'Charlie got this from a wine merchant near the hospital, didn't you?'

Charlie made a 'no big deal' face and Sasha pulled an 'ooh, la-di-da' expression. The two of them exchanged chit-chat for a few minutes, about the snow, my accident – 'He's such a klutz,' said Sasha – and some other stuff that I can't remember because I was too busy wracking my brains for a topic they could bond over. They were both into music, films, books, though Charlie's tastes were at the darker end of the spectrum, more cerebral, difficult stuff that Sasha would have called pretentious.

'Andrew tells me you're an artist,' Sasha said, sitting stiffly on the edge of the sofa. She had come straight from work and was dishevelled, her hair going curly from the damp, make-up faded, a grease stain on her top. Still, this was how Sasha usually looked; it was part of her charm.

Charlie, by contrast, had just spent an hour in the bathroom and looked immaculate in a soft green dress with salon-fresh hair. I had seen Sasha flick her eyes up and down Charlie's body in a judgmental way when she came in to the flat. I didn't like that look; it wasn't the kind of thing Sasha usually did, and it made me feel protective of Charlie.

'I don't even know if I call myself an artist anymore,' Charlie said. 'It's been so long since I painted anything.'

'What a shame.'

'I simply don't get time anymore.'

Sasha looked at me. 'Yes. So I hear.'

Charlie affected ignorance of the meaning behind Sasha's words. 'It's mainly because of work. It takes up all my energy, doesn't leave much time to be creative.'

'Sucks having to work for a living, doesn't it?'

Charlie smiled. 'Yes, it really does.'

'And Andy here—' She never usually called me Andy. 'Andy is going to be joining us work drones soon.'

'Hmm.' Charlie put her hand on my arm. 'I think he's crazy.'

Sasha furrowed her brow. 'Really? It's a great opportunity.'

'Yes, it is,' I said. 'As soon as I'm off these bloody crutches . . .'

'You need to take it easy,' Charlie said, rubbing my arm. 'You don't want to rush things and aggravate the injury.'

'Oh, he'll be fine,' Sasha said. 'He's a typical bloke, that's all. Have you seen him with a cold yet?'

Charlie shook her head.

'You wait. You'd think he was dying from Ebola. You should have seen him when he had his eye thing. I know it was horrible, but I've seen more stoic toddlers.'

'Hey, that's a bit unfair,' I said.

'I think he's really brave,' Charlie said. Every time she spoke to or about me, she touched me, stroking my back, squeezing my elbow. She looked at me lovingly. 'It can't simply be kissed better, though I've tried.'

Inside her head, I knew Sasha would be making vomiting noises.

'Hey,' Sasha said. 'Remember that time at uni when we went on that country ramble with the bloody fell-walking club – you thought it would be fun to join but they were such a bunch of humourless wankers – and you didn't have any proper walking boots so wore your trainers and you spent the next week moaning about your blister?'

'Did I?' I had a vague memory of this.

'Yeah, you were a nightmare. Then there was that time we took E and the next day you were convinced you were going to die? You drank pints and pints of water because you'd seen something on the news about a girl who died of dehydration and you were sure you were having some sort of delayed reaction.'

'You make me sound like a right hypochondriac.'

'Then there was that time we—'

'Excuse me, but I need to sort out dinner,' Charlie said, knocking back her wine. Sasha had finished hers too and I refilled both their glasses. I was so woozy from the codeine that I was taking it easy, had had only a couple of sips of mine.

While Charlie prepared dinner – something she had insisted she wanted to do – I sat and chatted to Sasha.

'How's everything going?'

'Hmm?' Sasha had her eyes on Charlie, whose back was to us. I wanted to tell Sasha to stop being so hostile. What was it about Charlie that she didn't like? So far, Charlie had been polite and completely inoffensive, even if she'd been a bit OTT with the touching and comments about kissing it better. Sasha was being unreasonable. She had decided she wasn't going to like my girlfriend before she'd even met her. She had to accept this was the woman I loved.

But I couldn't say all this – any of it – with Charlie in the room.

'Any news about Lance or Mae?' I asked.

Sasha tore her eyes away from Charlie's back. 'Oh God, yes. I had an encounter with him at work.' She shivered. 'I was in the stationery cupboard, getting a new notebook, and he came in.'

'What happened?'

She took a deep breath. There was a lull in the music and Sasha lowered her voice, talking almost in a whisper. 'He looked horrified to see me, tried to completely frigging ignore me. But I wasn't having that, I was so angry, like I'd been repressing it all for ages and suddenly, there he was and it all came bubbling up.'

I waited while she swallowed more wine.

'I shut the door – you should have seen his face – and told him to tell his bitch of a wife to stop sending me messages, that if I got one more text or email from her I was going to have him up for sexual harassment. I mean, older, rich man, impressionable young woman made to believe that if she didn't respond to his advances she'd be fired . . . I'd definitely have a case.'

'Fucking hell,' I said.

'Sorry,' Charlie said. She was standing over us. 'I couldn't help but overhear. I don't think that's a good idea.'

'What?' Sasha said, her mouth staying open.

'It will be your reputation that suffers if you do that. A friend of mine in Manchester went through the same thing. The guy ended up looking like a hero, everyone thinking he was a big stud, his wife standing by him, and the girl was made to look like an idiot. This boss of yours sounds like a disgusting creep, but perhaps you should put it down to experience and move on.'

Sasha blinked at Charlie like she couldn't believe what she was hearing. I expected an outburst, but she said, 'I'm sorry, Charlie, but it's none of your business.'

'I know. I just wouldn't want you to make a mistake.'

'It does sound like it would end badly,' I said, trying to work out how quickly I could end this conversation. 'Even though he would deserve it. What did he say, anyway?'

'He said that I should stop making threats. Then he walked out.'

Charlie had gone back over to the kitchen.

'Maybe you should look for another job,' I said.

Sasha shook her head vehemently. 'No way. Why should I be the one who loses out? I'm lucky it's so hard to get rid of employees in this country. He knows he can't fire me without ending up in court.'

Over dinner – which was excellent as always; even Sasha admitted as much – things calmed down. We talked about safe topics: our favourite box sets, the redevelopments in Herne Hill, the price of property in London.

We talked about a film we'd all watched recently, in which a woman murdered her husband and covered it up, getting away with it in the end.

'The perfect murder,' Charlie said. 'What would you do, Sasha, if you wanted to murder someone? Like your boss, for example.'

Sasha grinned. 'Hmm . . . I don't know. I think you'd have to make it look like a suicide. Get them to write a note at knife-point.'

'I reckon if you wanted to murder someone, the best way to do it would be to make it look like a drug overdose,' Charlie said. 'Death by misadventure.'

'You two!' I said. 'You're terrible.'

As I washed up, Charlie and Sasha had a civil, though stilted, conversation about *Breaking Bad*. They were both one glass short of drunk and Sasha seemed a lot more relaxed than she had been. Pretty soon, she announced that she needed to go. We called a taxi, because I didn't want her to walk home on her own in the dark.

'Lovely to meet you,' Charlie said, moving in for a hug, after the taxi arrived.

Sasha held back for a moment before accepting the awkward embrace.

'I'm sure we'll see each other soon,' she said.

I saw Sasha out. At the front door of my flat, at the top of the stairs that I couldn't get down without extreme difficulty, she said, 'You really love her, don't you?'

I was taken aback. 'Yes. I think she's amazing.'

Sasha looked like I'd just told her I was moving to the other side of the world.

'She's too good to be true,' she said.

'What do you mean?' I had said these words about Charlie myself, but I didn't believe it anymore.

Sasha frowned. 'I don't know. There's something not right about her.'

'Your taxi's waiting.'

'Don't hate me for saying it,' she said.

'I don't. Come on, you're drunk. I'll call you.'

I watched her go down the stairs, trying to keep my anger locked down. When I went back inside, Charlie said, 'I told you.'

I wished I could tell her she was wrong but all I could do was say, 'I'm sorry. She's not normally like that.'

Charlie walked over to me, balancing with one crutch, and said, 'Do you think I did something wrong?'

'No, not at all. You were lovely, as always.'

She kissed me. 'You're lovely.'

The peck on the lips turned into a longer kiss, with me leaning against the wall. When Charlie broke away she was breathing heavily, her chest rising and falling.

'Let's go to bed.'

In the bedroom, where she had already lighted the candles, she pulled her dress up over her head while I sat on the bed and watched, unbuttoning my shirt. She was wearing red underwear, her milky skin flickering in the candlelight. She straddled me and ran her hands over my chest, kissing me again as she unbuckled my belt. Carefully, she pulled my jeans off and, kneeling on the floor, took me in her mouth, her tongue and lips so warm, gripping the base of my cock in one hand, stroking my balls with the other.

I closed my eyes, lost in bliss. She crawled onto the bed and unclipped her bra, pulling me up so I could lick her nipples, flicking my tongue across them rapidly in the way she liked.

'I need to fuck you,' she said, unrolling a condom onto me, positioning herself over me and guiding me into her. She rocked and rotated her hips, increasing the pace, stroking her own breasts then running her nails across my chest, panting hard, coming quickly.

'What's wrong?' she asked, seeing my expression.

'I can't come,' I whispered. 'It's the codeine. It numbs me.' My penis slipped out of her.

She looked thoughtful, then reached over into the drawer and took out the little bottled of jasmine-scented massage oil, squirting some onto her breasts, rubbing it in, then turning her attention to me. She pulled off the condom and chucked it aside. Her hands were warm too, and gripped me firmly, pumping my slippery cock, fast and slow. But still I couldn't come.

She sat up, looked like she was contemplating her next move.

Over the next hour, she tried everything. She whispered filthy words into my ear. She moved into every position I could imagine and many I couldn't. She varied the speed and rhythm. I tried to tell her to leave it, that I didn't need to come, that I was fine. But she wouldn't give in. Finally, after going down on me for a long time, while I lay there half in ecstasy, half in maddened frustration, all mixed up with guilt and admiration, Charlie made me come.

She lay panting on the bed beside me, her body drenched with sweat like she'd just run a marathon.

'I love you, Charlie.'

She got up from the bed and stood looking down at me, drinking from a glass of water, her whole body glistening. Her expression was serious as she leant towards me.

'I love you the most,' she said. 'Don't ever forget that.'

.

Seventeen

When I woke up the next morning Charlie had already gone to work, leaving a note in her neat handwriting next to the bed.

You were completely zonked out and I didn't want to disturb you. You look so sweet and innocent when you're asleep . . .
Last night was intensely good.
I'll call you at lunchtime.
Love you forever.
C xxxxxxxxxx

I lay in bed for a while, thinking about the day ahead. I had some work to do for Victor, some additional pages for the Wowcom micro-site we were now working on. As Wowcom were potentially Victor's biggest client, he was paying particularly close attention to my work, which added some pressure. But apart from that the day stretched out emptily. I was already looking forward to the evening and Charlie coming round.

My thoughts turned to Sasha, and the way she had acted around Charlie. It was a side of her I'd not seen before. She and Harriet got on really well and were still in touch. But the way she had behaved last night, and the stuff she had said about Charlie on the doorstep, made me not want to talk to her, not until I was less angry. I decided I'd give it a few days and then call her. I wasn't sure what I would do if she didn't warm to Charlie. Could I still be friends with her if she hated my girlfriend?

I dozed off and when I woke my knee was throbbing. My packet of codeine was in the bedside drawer and, to my horror, when I opened it I found I only had three left. Stupidly, I shook the packet. Three left? I was sure there were around ten, enough to get me through a couple more days. This meant I would run out before the end of the day. My skin prickled with anxiety.

I grabbed my crutches, limped into the bathroom and washed at the basin, having first gulped down one of the remaining tablets with water straight from the tap. In the living room I checked the weather outside – no snow but there was still ice on everything – then dug out the notes I'd been given at the hospital, including the phone number for the ward where I'd been treated.

I got straight through to a nurse and explained who I was.

'Let me just find your notes.' She had a soft Irish accent.

The line went quiet for a little while until she finally returned.

'So, you were prescribed forty 100 mg codeine tablets, to be taken four times a day for ten days. That was eight days ago.'

'I know. But I've almost run out.'

A silence at the other end. 'You do know you're not supposed to exceed the stated dose?'

'I know.' I was aware of how pathetic I sounded. I laughed nervously. 'But the pain has been awful. I think I took too many in the first few days.'

'Hmm. I'm sorry, but we can't prescribe you any more.'

Cold goose bumps rippled across my flesh. 'What?'

Her Irish accent didn't sound so soft anymore. I had been a bad patient and she wanted me to know it. 'I'm sorry, Mr Sumner, but we can't let you have any more. Codeine is addictive.'

Tell me about it, I thought. 'But . . . what am I supposed to do?'

'If you're still in pain I recommend Paracetamol or ibuprofen. I think ibuprofen would be better.'

'But that's not strong enough.'

'I'm sorry, Mr Sumner. When are you due in to see us?'

'In just over two weeks.'

'And how's the leg?'

'It hurts.'

She laughed and I hung up. How dare she laugh at me? If I could have stomped I would have. Instead, I limped over to my desk and sat down, prepared to write a stern email to the hospital. But by the time I'd found an email address the wind had dropped from my sails. I was OK. It didn't hurt at the moment; the nurse was just doing her job. I had some Nurofen in the cupboard. I'd take that tonight after the codeine had all gone.

———

I spent the next few hours working, then sent the results to Victor. Just after lunch I noticed that the room was brighter than normal and went over to the window. The sky was blue, cloudless; the sun had returned like a hero from war. My spirits immediately lifted. If it stayed like this for a day or two, the ice would thaw and I should be able to go out again.

I switched on the TV, hoping to catch the weather forecast. I flicked to BBC News and staggered over to the kitchen to make myself lunch.

As I opened the fridge, a snatch of the news report caught my attention.

. . . young woman attacked in south-east London . . .
I walked over to the TV.

Police are appealing to anyone who might have witnessed a horrific crime in West Norwood last Friday. A young woman was seriously injured when acid was thrown into her face by an unknown assailant.

The victim, an Albanian immigrant who worked as a cleaner, is being treated at King's Hospital. The young woman is reported to have lost the sight in one eye and to have suffered horrific burns to her face . . .

I stared at the screen.

West Norwood. That was a ten-minute walk from my flat. Albanian cleaner.

I put my hand to my mouth. It had to be her. It had to be Kristi.

Eighteen

'What's her name?' I said aloud to the TV.

But the news moved on to something else – a story about Lucy Newton, the so-called Dark Angel, who had been slashed across the face by another prisoner – and I was left flicking around the news channels trying to find more about the cleaner.

Giving up, I turned to my computer, went onto Google News and typed 'acid attack West Norwood'. The page filled with results.

The second result was from my local paper, *The Norwood Examiner*, with the headline ACID ATTACK VICTIM NAMED.

Heart in mouth, I clicked the link.

Police have revealed the name of the victim in a horrific attack in West Norwood last Friday, February 9th.

Kristi Tolka, 23, is originally from Albania but now lives in Streatham Hill and works as a cleaner.

She was on her way home from work last Friday evening when she was attacked by a man who threw sulphuric acid in her face. The attack has left her blinded in one eye and with severe chemical burns to her face, neck and hands.

The attack took place on Gipsy Road at approximately 6:15 p.m. and police are appealing for witnesses.

Detective Inspector Tom Jenkins, who is leading the investigation, told the Examiner:

'The victim has described her assailant as slim-built and of medium height. He was wearing a balaclava and a black leather jacket. She says he appeared from behind a wall, as if he was waiting for her. She believes he ran off in the direction of Norwood Road. Unfortunately, because of the poor weather, there were very few people around.'

Tolka is being cared for at King's College Hospital and is described as being in a stable condition.

Poor, poor Kristi. I could barely imagine it: the pain, the shock, and then much worse – her face ruined, her eyesight half gone. I had watched a documentary about a model who had been attacked in the same way; in that case, as I recalled, it was an ex-boyfriend or a spurned admirer . . . I couldn't quite remember. Was the person who had done this to Kristi the same person who had left bruises on her face? Her boyfriend, assuming she had one? Surely he must be the most likely candidate. But if the police were looking for witnesses now, almost a week after the event, it seemed that the most obvious solution wasn't necessarily the correct one. Or was Kristi protecting this guy? When I thought about Albanians in London, I couldn't help but think about gangsters and people trafficking, all those clichés. Was Kristi mixed up in that somehow?

All these questions rattled through my brain. Overall, though, I mostly felt terrible sympathy for her. I wondered if I should send something – a card, flowers? As if that would do any good. Besides, I was just some bloke whose flat she cleaned once a week. She probably didn't even know my full name.

I would ask Charlie when she came round if she thought I should send something. She would know. Women are better at that kind of thing.

I took another codeine tablet. I now had only one left but the little twitch of panic this thought invoked was, I realised, pathetic compared to what Kristi was going through.

I awoke the next day knowing that I had no codeine left. I hadn't told Charlie that I'd run out because I didn't want her to worry about me. We'd had a relaxing evening, eating a curry, watching a Johnny Depp film, going to bed early. She'd told me that it would be a bit weird to send anything to Kristi but that maybe I should ask the cleaning agency if they had a collection for her, which seemed like an excellent idea.

The sun was out again and although it was cold and icy outside I felt optimistic that I would be able to go outside soon. This hope helped get me through the morning, but by lunchtime the pain had crept back into my leg so I swallowed a couple of Nurofen. It took the edge off. But as I tried to work in the afternoon, I couldn't concentrate. I felt sick and the computer screen hurt my eyes, no matter how I fiddled with the brightness controls. The inside of my head felt tight, like there were metal bands squeezing my brain, and the noise of the traffic in the distance penetrated my skull. I could feel the blood throbbing in my veins.

Codeine is addictive, I heard the nurse from yesterday say, and I realised: I was dependent. The moment this thought entered my head, even though the ibuprofen was keeping the pain mostly at bay, I *needed* codeine. Could think about nothing else. When I was seventeen, during my most nihilistic period following my parents' deaths, I had taken up smoking. I smoked for only a few years but

I would never forget the struggle to give up, how I had barely been able to think of anything else as the nicotine left my system.

I paced about the flat on my crutches, then went for a lie down. What now seemed like a harsh winter sun penetrated the windows, causing little dots to dance about in front of my eyes. *Oh my God*, I thought. *My retina is detaching again.* I stared at the white sheet – I had forgotten to put the bedding in the wash yesterday and it stank of sweat and semen – and tried to work out if there was a dark shadow in my eye.

Get a grip, I told myself. *It's the withdrawal, making you paranoid.* I lay down and closed my eyes, remembering something with a start.

The bottle of pills Charlie had left in the bathroom cabinet – or, to be precise, the bottle that Kristi had put there along with the toiletries. That had been codeine!

I jumped up from the bed, momentarily forgetting all about my sprained knee. I yelled with pain and fell onto my side. Ah, fuck. That hurt. I lay there for a moment laughing at myself. *For God's sake, man, sort yourself out.*

I hauled myself up and, back on my crutches, made my way into the bathroom. There it was, right at the back of the cabinet: the little brown bottle with *codeine* printed on the label.

I tipped a couple onto my palm. They looked different to the ones I'd got from the hospital. Yellow and white capsules as opposed to the little white tablets I'd been taking. I downed one, thought about it, then added the second.

I went back to the computer. I was sick of being cooped up. *If I don't get out of here soon*, I thought, *I'm going to lose my mind.* I was in that state where I was so bored that I couldn't make myself do anything to relieve the boredom. I wanted some chocolate, a cigarette, a drink, a wank – anything to take my mind off the crushing tedium of my daytime existence.

Instead, I browsed the web, clicking listlessly from page to page, bored but unable to stop.

I was scrolling through a list of '21 kangaroos having a bad day' when I started to feel sleepy. My eyes were heavy. My whole body felt leaden. I checked the time. Four o'clock. Could I squeeze in a nap before Charlie got back?

No, I should try to stay awake. Napping during the day almost always made me feel groggier than if I fought through it.

Temporarily giving up on the holiday idea, I went onto Facebook. I decided to look at Sasha's page, to see if she had posted anything interesting since the other night. I wanted to contact her but still felt angry and unsure of what to say to her.

Sasha hadn't written any posts, but an old university friend of ours, Tabby, had posted a link to a story about students on our course. I read it, and then, curious, decided to see what Tabby had been up to recently. But I couldn't see anything on her timeline. She had unfriended me.

Another one! I went through to my list of friends. I was pretty sure I'd had about 250 friends last time I'd looked. Now it was down to 210. OK, so the numbers fluctuated all the time, but to lose forty friends in a month? That was worse than careless. What had I done? I tried to remember if I'd posted anything that might be deemed offensive or controversial. No, I hadn't. In fact, I'd barely been on Facebook since meeting Charlie. That must be it, I decided, feeling that heavy weariness sweep over me again. My friends were bored with my lack of updates and were culling me.

I checked the time again. Four-thirty. Had half an hour really passed? How had that happened? I rubbed my eyes. So tired. So very tired. It felt like my blood had been replaced with syrup. My brain was finding it hard to formulate thoughts. My limbs were heavy, as were my eyelids. I couldn't feel any pain though; my legs were numb, rubbery. Charlie's codeine was doing its job.

I pushed myself up from my chair and almost fell over. OK, I really did need to lie down. The bed was too far though. The sofa was just a few steps away. I made it and lay down.

My phone chirped. With great effort, like all my muscles had wasted away, like the air in the room was crushing me to death, I found my phone in my pocket and squinted at it. The words in the little grey speech bubble on the screen floated about but, with a Herculean force of will, I was able to make out that the text was from Karen – Karen? Who was Karen? Oh, yes, my older woman, my Mrs Robinson – and that it said *Please call me urgently x*

One last struggle to stay awake, to stay afloat, concentrate . . . and then I gave in.

Ninteen

'Andrew. Andrew? Can you hear me?' The voice was soft, kind. A hand on my cheek, then stroking my hair. I was rising, floating up through the dark water, breaking the surface in a froth of bubbles.

'Mum?'

A gentle laugh. 'No, handsome. It's me, Charlie.'

I opened one eye, then the other. There was a sharp pain behind my eyebrows and my mouth felt like I'd been crunching on spoonfuls of sand. I was warm, too, and I looked down to see that I had a blanket over me, the thick woollen one that I kept rolled up in the top of my wardrobe. I was on my sofa.

And there was an angel smiling at me, an angel with glorious flaming hair and big intelligent eyes.

'Andrew?' the angel called Charlie said, tilting her head. 'Stay with me. Don't go—'

I slipped beneath the water again.

I woke up with Charlie kneeling on the carpet in front of me, holding a glass of water and gazing at me with concern. As soon as I opened my eyes she said, 'Oh, thank God. Please try to stay awake this time.'

'There are cobwebs in my head,' I said. 'Spiders crawling around my brain.'

She looked at me with alarm.

'No, I don't mean literally.' Was this what delirium felt like? 'I mean . . .' I couldn't find the words to complete the sentence.

She held out the water, told me to drink some.

'How are you feeling?' she asked.

'I can't . . . I don't . . .'

She smiled, showing her teeth. She had a little chip on the right front tooth. Had I noticed that before? 'OK, don't worry. I know what it's like.' I must have looked confused because she said, 'I mean, I've been there. When I first took Temazepam. Oh, that's what was in that little jar.'

It took my brain a few seconds to work out what she was talking about. 'Not codeine?'

'No. I put them in that jar for safekeeping. They're sleeping pills. I've been carrying them round in my bag for a long time . . . a couple of years at least. I got them when I was having trouble, well, sleeping when I lived in Birmingham.'

'You lived in Birmingham?'

'Yes. For a short while. I had a contract there. But that's not important. The point is that the pills came in a huge box, in foil . . . and I popped them all out and put them in an empty jar I had. I guess they must have fallen out along with that other stuff – the shampoo and whatnot. How many did you take?'

I thought about it. 'Two.'

She shook her head. 'No wonder you were out for so long. One is enough to knock you out for a whole night.'

'How long was I out?' I looked towards the window. It was light.

'Well, I don't know when you took them exactly, but it's two p.m. on Friday now.'

I had taken them on Thursday afternoon. 'Oh . . . shit. I've been asleep for nearly twenty-four hours.'

I sat up, my body creaking like a geriatric's. My bladder felt like it was on fire.

'And I've been here,' she said. 'All the time. Looking after you.'

Charlie ran me a bath and sat on the edge while I let the hot water bring my limbs back to life.

'I called in sick,' she said, trailing her hand through the water. 'I didn't want you waking up with no one here, wondering what the hell had happened.'

'Thank you. God, I think my brain evaporated while I was asleep.' I splashed my face and rubbed it. 'Why did you have those pills?'

She looked away. 'I told you. A couple of years ago, I was having trouble getting to sleep.'

I waited for her to continue. When she didn't, I said, 'What was wrong? Why couldn't you sleep?'

She shrugged. 'It was just a phase. No big deal.'

But this hoarding of her past was beginning to bother me. For once, I pushed her.

'Come on Charlie, there's more to it, isn't there?'

She fidgeted. Looked all around the room like she was seeking an escape route.

'Can you look at me?'

She drew a breath and looked at me, tight-lipped.

'I broke up with someone,' she said.

'Oh.'

'It was a difficult break-up. Very . . . unpleasant.' Her hand in the water was motionless.

'What was his name?' I asked.

Another long hesitation. 'Leo.'

'Was he a lion?'

She smiled at last. 'No, he was a rat. A love rat.'

'He cheated on you?'

She stood up, went over to the basin. The mirror on the cabinet was steamed up and, as she spoke, with her back to me, she traced lines in the steam: jagged lines, slashes in the condensation.

'He was a bastard. A total fucking bastard. He was one of those guys, always eyeing up attractive women, like I'd be sitting with him in a restaurant and his eyes would be roaming about the room, perving over anyone with a bit of cleavage showing or legs on display. Very early on in our relationship he slept with someone else when he was on a business trip. But his excuse was that we'd only been seeing each other a few weeks, he didn't know we were exclusive, it was a meaningless shag. So I gave him another chance.'

The condensation was all gone now, so I could see Charlie's face in the mirror, frowning.

'That was the worst mistake . . .'

'You ever made?'

Her eyes had gone blank, and I knew she'd gone deep inside her head, had left my bathroom and withdrawn into her memory. The tap dripped. Plink. Plink. Plink. I counted. After eleven drips, Charlie came back into the room.

'Are you all right?' I said.

'Yeah. I'm sorry.' She shook her head and smiled, like the whole topic was forgotten, like we'd been talking about our favourite chocolate or childhood TV shows. 'Want me to join you?'

Before I could answer, she had stripped off, chucking her clothes on the floor, and jumped into the bath, and while I wanted to ask her about her ex, Leo, and the worst mistake Charlie had ever made, yet again my body took over, told my mind to shut up, stop worrying. Enjoy the ride.

———⌣———

I leaned on my crutch by the front window, dried and dressed. Maybe it was because of the long sleep, but my leg felt less painful today, nothing a couple of normal painkillers couldn't cure. And although I had mild cravings for codeine, I was able to distract myself, not think about it too hard.

'The snow and ice have all gone,' I pointed out to Charlie, who had been in the bedroom drying her hair.

'I know. The thaw finally arrived.'

'I want to go out,' I said.

'Are you sure that's a good idea?'

'I'm going completely stir crazy here. If it's not slippery, it will be fine. You'll just have to catch me if I fall over! Come on, I'm not going to be dissuaded.'

Ten minutes later we stood on the street, after a wobbly journey down the stairs, wrapped in our coats against a bitter wind. But the cold breeze felt wonderful, like inhaling mints, filling my lungs, making my heart beat faster, my blood pump harder.

'Let's go to the park,' I said.

It was far more challenging to walk on crutches outside than in the confined space of my flat, but Charlie stayed close to me, teasing me about being a 'poor wounded soldier.' I soon settled in to a rhythm and when I relaxed I felt more alive than I had in two weeks, like I'd been let out of prison.

'Well, I'm glad you haven't been institutionalised,' Charlie said when I told her this.

'You have been an excellent cell-mate though.'

'Hmm. More like a warden.'

We passed through the park gates.

'That gives me an idea,' Charlie said, a wicked twinkle in her eye. 'We could play prison guard and inmate. I'll get some handcuffs and a big stick, and you can wear a jumpsuit.'

'Kinky.'

'If you behave yourself, you'll get special privileges. But if you're naughty, if you disobey me . . .'

'You scare me sometimes,' I laughed.

The park was beautiful. Tree bark glistened with frost. Spidery branches were framed by the steely-blue sky. Chunks of ice floated in the lake where Charlie and I had made love, though I shivered to remember the feeling of being watched and the second-hand memory of the boy who had drowned here, on a day just like this. I stopped to give Charlie a kiss, leaning on my crutches, and we walked on, up to the big house where we bought hot chocolate with cream and marshmallows and watched some pre-school kids running about on the grass.

'Do you like kids?' Charlie asked.

'Kids? Yeah, definitely. I mean, I'm not ready to have any yet, but one day. How about you?'

'I'm pregnant,' she said.

I spat out my hot chocolate.

'Just kidding.' She laughed uproariously.

'Charlie! Don't do that to me.'

'Judging by that reaction, you're definitely not ready. No, I do like kids. I sometimes have dreams where I have a little boy who has hair the same colour as mine and he's wearing a stripy T-shirt and he holds my hand and tells me he'll love me forever.'

'That's sweet.'

'They never do though. Boys, especially. They always leave their mums.' She watched a pair of little girls running in circles, shrieking. 'I don't know how I'd feel about having a daughter though.'

'I'm sure you'd be an excellent mum. You're so caring and nurturing.'

She laughed. 'Really?'

'Yeah. You look after me.'

She ruffled my hair. 'You're my little boy. You won't leave me, will you?'

'Never. But the little boy thing is a bit creepy.'

'Yeah. Sorry about that.'

On our way out of the park, we passed a woman with long blonde hair, wearing an expensive-looking black coat. She could have been a model, with sharp cheekbones and huge eyes.

'See something you liked?' Charlie said, after the woman had passed and was out of earshot. A switch had been flicked and Charlie's mood had changed in an instant.

'Huh?'

'That girl. I saw you staring at her.'

Charlie stopped walking and I was forced to stop too.

'Staring? What are you talking about?'

'I saw you. Your tongue fell out of your mouth. You were practically drooling.'

'No I wasn't.'

She moved in front of me. 'So tell me you weren't staring at her.'

'Charlie, this is ridiculous. I looked at her, sure. But . . .'

'Looked at her?'

'Yes, but just an, I don't know, appraising look.'

'*Appraising?*'

Her voice had grown louder and I looked around, worried someone might hear. It was embarrassing. But there was no one nearby.

'That's the wrong word,' I said. 'Charlie, this is ridiculous. You're accusing me of what? Fancying her? Planning to track her down and . . . hobble off with her?'

'No. But you were wishing you could be with someone like her. Instead of me.'

I was flabbergasted. 'Charlie, I think you're the most beautiful woman I've ever seen. I have no interest in other women. None. I promise you. This is crazy.'

Her face twisted into what I can only describe as a snarl. She jabbed a finger at my chest and hissed, 'Don't call me crazy. I am not fucking crazy.'

And she started to cry.

'Charlie.' I leaned on one crutch, reached out and pulled her against me, which wasn't easy, especially when she resisted. Her muscles were wound tight, her back as hard as rock. But then she gave in, relaxed slightly, letting me embrace her awkwardly. I whispered reassurances to her, told her I loved her and didn't want anyone else. She apologised and promised she would stop being so stupid.

But I was worried. She'd shown a few signs of being prone to jealousy before, but not this level of irrational insecurity. I was certain I hadn't looked at the passing woman with my tongue hanging out, as Charlie had put it. But had I stared at her, shown signs of desire without even realising it? I tried to imagine how I would feel if it was the other way round, if some gorgeous bloke walked past and Charlie had looked him up and down, shown obvious signs that she found him attractive. I wouldn't like it, that was for sure. I wouldn't, though, accuse her of wishing she was with him. I wouldn't have got upset about it.

Then it struck me. The conversation in the bathroom.

'I'm not like him, you know. Leo.'

She looked up me.

'I'm not going to cheat on you. I'm not going to start staring at other women. I'm not like that. And it's hard to say this without sounding corny as hell, but I've only got eyes for you.'

She held me tightly, the chilly wind whipping around us, her head pressed against my chest, until my leg began to ache.

'Come on,' I said. 'Let's go home.'

Twenty

It was a glorious sunny winter morning, mild and bright, and I opened the windows to let some of the mustiness out. A couple of days had passed since I'd awoken from my long sleep. Maria was due that afternoon but I decided to have a pre-spring clean, to sort out some of the admin of my life.

I emailed Victor to ask if it was OK for me to start work next Monday and he replied immediately: 'The sooner the better!' Knowing I would soon have some regular income, I went online to buy replacements for the clothes I'd lost when I fell. The postman brought the necklace I'd ordered as a gift for Charlie, which prompted me to buy some more gifts for her: a couple of lavish art books and, remembering our conversation in the park, some handcuffs with pink fluffy bits that I thought would make her laugh.

I even managed to get through all my unread emails. I contemplated sending a message to Sasha, whom I'd had no contact with since the unsuccessful night with Charlie, but decided against it. I would leave it a few more days. I didn't want to risk anything spoiling my good mood.

As I ate my lunch – mushroom soup that Charlie had prepared and left in the fridge for me – I felt more relaxed than I had for ages. My hibernation period was over; not just the last two weeks, stuck inside in a codeine haze, but the last fourteen years, ever since my parents' deaths. This felt momentous. I was about to embark on a new chapter of my life. No, not a chapter – a book. Andrew Sumner: Volume 2. Or was it 3?

Whatever, it felt like things were changing. And as I went around the flat tidying up and sorting out the messy piles of DVDs and books and clothes, I thought about asking Charlie to move in. I was confident she'd want to. She was here all the time and still paying rent on her own place – which I still hadn't seen. It made sense. Or was it still too soon? It might be a good idea for me to see her place before asking her to move in. What if it was an apocalyptic mess? What if she had a collection of creepy porcelain dolls that she'd want to bring with her?

I opened the wardrobe, still mulling over these questions in an unhurried way. I began pulling out old clothes, ones that I knew I would never wear again, and bagging them up. My leg was feeling a lot better and I was able to put a little weight on it, was limping about with no crutch, though it was still something of a struggle to lug bags around. By the time I'd half-emptied the wardrobe I was sweating, and I sat down on the edge of the bed to catch my breath.

I stared into the darkness of the wardrobe. There was a niggle at the back of my mind: something was missing, or different. I got up and peered inside, realising what it was.

When I'd last sorted out the flat, shortly after splitting from Harriet, I'd put all of my memorabilia of our relationship – photos, cards, notes and postcards – into a large reinforced paper bag. This bag already contained mementoes of my previous relationships, such as they were, along with a load of other bits and pieces that I didn't want to throw away – fliers from university nights, a couple of mysterious Valentine's cards whose sender had never revealed herself, my degree certificate and some silly letters that Tilly had written to me while I was at college.

Beneath all this, in a bag within the bag, were other personal treasures. These were items that were too painful for me to have on display, even though the rational, lucid part of me knew it would be better, healthier if they were out there. These items included photographs of my mum, with her long red hair, and dad, mainly during his eighties fashion-disaster period, when he'd sported a moustache and glasses with oversized frames. There were family pictures too: the four of us, Tilly and me as little kids, on holiday on a beach somewhere, or with our dog, Benji, a cocker spaniel who had died when I was twelve.

Along with the photos, there were other souvenirs of my parents' lives. Their wedding certificate (Tilly had the rings and the photo album). Cards that my mum had written to me when I was too young to read, telling me how much she loved me, how proud she was of her only son. Most precious of all, there was my baby book, in which she had recorded not just the basic information like my birth weight and time but her feelings upon meeting me, her firstborn. Stuck into this book was a picture of her and my dad holding me when I was a couple of hours old. My face was pink and puffy but they were gazing at me like I was the most beautiful thing on earth.

Although Tilly had her own mementoes, every trace of my parents that I owned was in this bag.

It was missing.

I moved aside clothes, lifted shoes, pulled boxes and folded jackets off the top shelf. Then, frantic, I pulled everything out, chucking everything on the floor, coat hangers flying, until the wardrobe was empty. I checked on top of it, behind it. Under the bed in case I'd moved it absent-mindedly. I looked inside every cupboard in the house.

It was gone.

I sat on the floor of my bedroom, my good mood obliterated, replaced by a dark, cold sickness.

The doorbell rang and, slowly, I got up to answer it. When Maria came in, and saw the clothes scattered about the room, she looked at them, then at me. Huffing and puffing, she systematically set about sorting everything out, while I sat in the other room, trying not to throw up.

———

As soon as Charlie came round, I said, 'I've got something I need to ask you.'

Her eyes widened. She could tell from my face, I hope, that I wasn't about to ask her to marry me or move in. Since discovering that my bag had gone missing, I hadn't even thought about my idea to ask her to live with me.

'In my wardrobe, I had a bag of stuff.'

I watched her face grow pale.

'Oh God,' she said. 'I'm so sorry, Andrew. I was hoping . . .' She broke off. 'I was hoping it would turn up before you noticed it was gone.'

I stared at her, conflicting feelings shooting about beneath my skin. Anger. Horror. Confusion. Even sympathy. She looked so contrite and scared.

'What happened?' I asked quietly.

'I found it the other night. You know, when you were in your sleeping pill coma. I was getting that blanket out to cover you? Well, I saw the bag and I couldn't help but look inside – I'm sorry, I know it's your private stuff but I couldn't stop myself. I found the pictures of your mum and dad and the cards and all that stuff. And I started to think what a shame it was that it was all just stuffed in a bag in your wardrobe.'

I got up and poured us both a glass of wine while she talked.

'I was planning to take some of the pictures of your parents and get them framed, maybe get a few of them made into an album. But before I could sort it all out, you woke up. And then the next morning, when I was leaving, I didn't get a chance to pick out the pictures I wanted so I took the whole bag, smuggled it out without you seeing.'

I had a horrible feeling I knew what she was going to say.

'And on the way to work, the bus was really busy, and then the Tube was even worse, and I . . . I forgot it. I'm *so* sorry. I'm sick about it. I stupidly left it somewhere – I don't even know if I left it on the bus or the train. I've been wracking my brains, but I was half-asleep and engrossed in the book I was reading and—'

'Have you reported it?'

'Yes. Of course. I've been ringing London Transport's lost property office every few hours, asking if it's been handed in. They're getting sick of hearing from me.'

I stared into my wine. I didn't know what to say.

Charlie grabbed my forearm. 'Please, Andrew. Please don't be mad with me. I feel like shit, I really do.'

'I'm not mad,' I said.

'If you want to stop seeing me, I'll understand.'

'Don't be silly. I'm not going to break up with you over something like this.'

She inched closer. 'You look like you're going to cry.'

That was exactly how I felt. All my stuff. My only connection to my parents. Gone. At least Tilly still had some things. I could probably get copies made, even though we didn't have the negatives of any of the pictures. Negatives – it sounded so old-fashioned. These days, if you lose a photo you just get another one printed. These ancient artefacts, pictures from the 1980s and 90s, were irreplaceable. Gone forever.

'The guy at the lost property office said it's likely the cleaner would have thought it was rubbish. I mean, it's not the kind of stuff someone would steal, is it? And I've looked into it, thinking maybe I could go to the rubbish dump, but depending on where it was chucked out, it could have gone to one of half a dozen dumps, and they destroy stuff really quickly. Like the same day.'

'Oh Charlie,' I said.

'Do you hate me?'

'Of course not. I just think . . . Maybe I should be on my own tonight.'

She looked at me like I'd suggested that she jump into a fire. 'You want me to go home?'

A large part of me wanted her to stay, hated not being with her. But I heard myself say, 'Yes. I think I need to have a night to myself.'

She nodded sadly. 'OK.'

But after she'd been to the loo and got her coat on and was standing by the front door looking as miserable as a dog who'd just been told off, her hair hanging in her eyes, I said, 'I've changed my mind. Stay.'

'Really?'

'Yes. Come on. Take your coat off. I'll pour more wine.'

She hooked her hands over my shoulders and pressed her body against me. 'I love you. And I'm so sorry. Do you want to go to bed?'

I peeled myself off her. 'No. Not yet. I'm not in the right mood. Just . . . please stop saying sorry.'

'OK.'

'So . . .' I took a deep breath. 'Let me tell you what else happened today.'

That night was the first night that we didn't have sex. Although we cuddled, we kept our underwear on. I feigned exhaustion and Charlie was soon asleep, her arms still wrapped around me.

I lay and looked at her in the semi-darkness. Her chest rose and fell, her hand twitched in her sleep. She made little murmuring noises. I loved her. There was no doubt about that. But, for the first time, I wasn't sure if I believed her.

Twenty-one

Monday arrived. I woke up early with butterflies in my stomach and had a last-minute panic while cleaning my teeth. Was I doing the right thing? I had a word with myself in the bathroom mirror, an out-loud pep talk that made Charlie ask, 'Who were you talking to?' when I went back into the bedroom.

'Myself.'

'First sign of madness.' She looked me up and down. I was wearing my new work clothes. It wasn't the kind of job that required a suit (if I'd turned up wearing one I think I would have been sent home) but I had new jeans, a new white shirt, new Converse train-ers. 'You look hot.'

'Thanks. So do you.'

She examined herself in the full-length mirror, at her own work clothes: the pencil skirt, the blouse with the Peter Pan collar. 'No. I definitely don't look hot when I'm Charlotte.'

'But it was Charlotte that first attracted me,' I reminded her.

'Yes. In an eye clinic.' She glanced at her watch. 'Better go. You don't want to be late on your first day.'

I stood at the door, crutch in hand. I didn't need it to walk around the flat any more but still found it necessary when walk-ing any distance. Charlie and I had agreed not to travel to work together because, Charlie told me, she was always grumpy on her journey into work and she didn't want me to suffer, especially when it was so important for me to arrive at the office feeling relaxed.

'I'm nervous,' I said.

Charlie came over and kissed me on the cheek. 'You'll be great. Don't worry. Call me at lunchtime, OK?'

'Maybe we could meet for lunch?'

She ruffled my hair. 'I expect your boss or new colleagues will take you out for lunch. You normally get treated extra-special on your first day.'

On the bus, I couldn't help but think about the lost bag. Charlie told me she was calling the lost property office every day but it hadn't turned up. I had given up hope. Maybe it was on a landfill site somewhere. Most probably, as Charlie had said, it had already been destroyed. I had called Tilly and she'd offered to make copies of some of her photos of Mum and Dad. They wouldn't be perfect but I didn't have any other option. This time, I wasn't going to hide the pictures away, unable to look at them. I was going to get them framed, put them on display.

I wasn't sure why I hadn't believed Charlie's story. Something about the way she had told it, or the incredible absent-mindedness needed for her to have left it on the bus. But then, people did that kind of thing every day. I had once left my expensive laptop on a train. And why would she lie? What else would she have done with the bag? I could imagine her getting upset about the mementoes of my exes. But she hadn't been afraid of showing her hurt when she felt insecure, like with the girl in the park, and I couldn't imagine her sneaking the bag out of my flat and secretly destroying it. It was completely out of character. If she could do that then . . . well, it would show I didn't know her at all.

So I cast my doubts aside, told myself I was being stupid, that it was nothing but an accident. I forgave her. Thinking, cynically, that it was one in the bank for me, if I ever did something like break one of her favourite teacups or shrink her clothes in the washing machine. All couples must go through this at some point: in our case, it was unfortunate that she was trying to do something lovely and ended up doing something that hurt me.

I changed buses and, before I knew it, I was heading past Old Street roundabout and towards Victor's office. I was using a single crutch now, and only outdoors, but it was still slow going.

The office was on the second floor of a converted warehouse, like so many of the offices around here. A few steps led up to a solid metal door, the names of the companies in the building – all of them something to do with the media or internet – written in bright colours beside a row of buzzers. I was ten minutes early and I stood and looked up at the building, giving myself another little pep talk – silent this time.

A police car was parked outside the office in front of the steps. As people arrived and went inside, they all looked at the car. A couple of smokers stood and had a conversation beside it. I recognised one of them, was sure she worked for Victor. I'd seen her in the office and also on the Meet the Team page Charlie had been looking at. An attractive young woman with short white-blonde hair. She saw me looking and said, 'Are you Andrew?'

I went over. 'Hi. Yes, I start today.'

She and the guy she was with – trimmed beard, thick glasses – stared at my crutch and she said, 'Awesome. I'm Amber. This is Pete. We heard about your accident. Very dramatic.'

'It was more sit-com-like,' I said.

'So, what, did you just, like, fall?' Pete asked.

As with Victor, I didn't want to tell them my suspicions about being pushed. It would make me sound paranoid. 'Yeah, it was snowing and really slippery.'

'Tough break,' Amber said. 'But you're all better now and here you are! Oh my God, we are so busy. You're starting just in time. Victor has been telling everyone how amazing you are. Like, the Wowcom stuff you did? That was amazing.'

I probably blushed.

'Weird shit happening in the office this morning, though,' Amber continued. 'I got here early—'

'Employee of the year,' said Pete.

'Fuck you. I got here early and Victor was already here, like he always is—'

'That why you get here early? To see Victor, eh? Naughty girl.'

'Will you let me finish, you twat?' She rolled her eyes and Pete guffawed. He was obviously in love with her. 'Where was I? Oh yeah. Victor has got a couple of cops in his office, sitting on the sofas with him, a man and a woman. I couldn't see their faces but Victor looked *sick*. Like they were giving him really bad news.' Her expression changed. 'Fuck, I hope everything's OK with, like, his wife and kids.'

'Oh, it's probably something to do with his parking tickets,' Pete said. 'He was telling me once he's got something like ten unpaid congestion charges. He refuses to pay it on—'

He was interrupted by the metal door opening and one of the police officers emerging: the WPC. To my surprise, she was followed out by Victor, his head down, not looking at anyone, bald spot on display, the male PC coming out behind him. We watched as they put him in the back of the police car and slowly drove off.

'Oh my days,' said Amber.

'What the fuck?' said Pete.

We went upstairs to the office. My first day at work wasn't starting as I'd imagined it. I trailed after Amber and Pete into the open-plan room, where almost everyone was standing looking dazed and worried, gathered around the receptionist's desk. The receptionist herself, whose name was Claire, looked like she'd just been told World War 3 had started and nuclear bombs were cruising towards London.

'We just saw Victor getting in a police car,' Amber said.

The babble of voices was so confusing, voices overlapping, everyone saying nothing very much at the same time, that it was impossible to work out if anyone had any useful information. I saw a few people look at me, this stranger in their midst, as if I were somehow to blame. Then a voice called out from halfway down the office: 'Guys! Look at this!'

We swarmed down the office, with me at the back of the group on my crutch, Amber darting towards the front of the crowd.

There were lots of 'Oh my Gods' and 'Fucks' and 'Holy shits'. Lots of people, having seen what the bloke who'd called out was looking at, hurried off to peer at their own machines, giving me enough space to shuffle forward so I could see what was on the computer.

It was a web page, with Victor's photograph at the top. The title of the page jumped out at me: Victor Codsall – Dangerous Paedophile. I couldn't read the rest of the text from where I stood, but Amber began to read out extracts.

'Victor Codsall is a paedophile who preys on pre-pubescent girls . . . When we baited him and sent him a message purporting to be a twelve-year-old called Lucy, he responded and arranged to meet for sex . . . Codsall was fully aware he was meeting a twelve-year-old. He also boasted of downloading vile images of underage girls . . .' Amber broke off. There were tears in her eyes. 'I can't believe it.'

'It's got to be bullshit,' said a young man standing next to me.

'There's no way . . . He's got kids,' said someone else.

Apart from that, the office was hushed, with just the sound of keyboards tapping and mice clicking breaking the stunned silence as more and more people went to their machines to look at the web page. I got closer to the desk and made a mental note of the URL.

As I turned away, two more police officers came into the room and went into Victor's office. A few minutes later they came out, carrying his desktop computer and a laptop. Everyone watched, mute.

'What should we do?' someone asked.

A brunette in a polka dot dress stood up. 'I feel sick. I can't believe we work for a paedo.'

'He's not a paedo!' Amber snapped.

'What the hell's going on?'

I looked up. A smartly dressed woman with a blonde bob had come into the office. This was Emma, the chief operations officer, Victor's second-in-command. She put her bag down on her desk and her hands on her hips. 'Well, is somebody going to tell me?'

I sat down and waited while Victor's employees crowded round Emma, filling her in, her eyes widening and jaw dropping as she made sense of the babble. But she gave the impression that this was the kind of situation she was born to deal with. Pretty soon, she had everyone back at their desks, and she was in Victor's office, talking animatedly on the phone.

I knocked on the office door and she gave me a 'Who on earth are you?' look.

'I'm sorry, but I'm meant to start work today,' I said.

'Oh. Andrew, is it?' She beckoned for me to come in and sit down. 'Hang on a minute.'

She searched through the papers on Victor's desk, huffing and tutting.

My eye caught the photo of Victor's children and his wife on his desk. There was no way, surely, that he was guilty of what the web page alleged. But how well did I know him?

I thought about him getting into the police car, refusing to look at anybody. The accusations on the website made me want to throw up. Twelve-year-old girls?

'For goodness sake,' Emma said. 'Vic emailed me and said he was going to sort out your induction himself. He hasn't left proper instructions.' She sighed. 'Listen, Andrew, I think it might be best if you go home, rather than hang around here with nothing to do. Until this . . . mess is sorted out, or at least till I've had a chance to talk to Vic.'

'But . . .'

'Yes, I think that's best.'

Having made her mind up, she ushered me out of the office and told me she'd call me.

I stood outside, in a state of shock. My job seemed to have ended before it had even began. Maybe Victor would be back tomorrow, the police would be apologising, the whole thing would be laughed off. But if the allegations were true, my misfortune was trivial. It wasn't my life that had just been destroyed.

Twenty-two

I texted Charlie to tell her what had happened, but she didn't reply so I guessed she was in a meeting. I didn't want to hang around for three hours waiting for her lunch break so I headed home, the buses half-empty now, my head reverberating from the shock of what had just happened. Beneath the concern for Victor was a little self-interested voice: what was I going to do for money now? How long would it take for the mess to be sorted out? And if Victor didn't come back quickly, would Emma or whoever was in charge now decide they didn't need me after all?

By the time I got home I was in a muted state of panic. I checked my bank account online. I had enough to keep me going for another month, but that was it. Apart from Victor, and Karen, I hadn't done any work for anyone for over six months. My contacts book was so creaky it wouldn't have mattered if Charlie had left it on a bus instead of my bag of mementoes. I was going to have to send some emails, go fishing for work.

I made myself a coffee and tried to rein in my growing panic. This whole thing might blow over by tomorrow. I could afford to wait a day or two to see what happened before I started reaching out for work.

As I was about to switch off my computer, I remembered something: Karen still hadn't told me if she liked the new site, meaning I couldn't invoice her yet.

And that triggered another memory, something I'd completely forgotten. Just before I'd passed out from taking the sleeping pills, I'd received a text from Karen. What had it said? I tried to recall . . . Something about calling her urgently?

I checked my phone. There was no such text. The last text from her was from the day of our last meeting, when we'd been arranging where to meet. That was it.

I stared at the screen of my phone. I must have dreamt the text, hallucinated it as I'd slipped into my twenty-four-hour slumber. I sent Karen another reminder email and temporarily forgot about it.

⌣⌣⌣

At lunchtime, I called Charlie and gave her a rundown of the situation. She was shocked.

'I'm worried about money,' I said. 'If this doesn't turn out to be a big mistake – which I'm praying it will, for everyone's sake – and whoever takes over from Victor decides they don't need me, I'm going to be in deep shit.'

There was a pause at the other end and I knew what she was going to say before I heard the words. 'Maybe I could move in. Then I could pay half the bills. I mean, I'm there all the time anyway.'

These were exactly the same thoughts I'd had a few days ago.

Before I could respond, she said, 'Well, let's not make any decisions now. Maybe we can talk about it when I get home.' She paused. 'Oh, can you do me a big favour and take my suit to the drycleaner? It's on the chair at the end of the bed.'

'Sure.' I was tempted to point out that it wasn't that easy for me to run errands while I still wasn't properly on two feet, but didn't want to be a wimp.

'Thanks, gorgeous.'

It was only later that I realised what she'd said before. Home. *When I get home.*

I took Charlie's clothes – one of her 'Charlotte' outfits, a slim-fit grey trouser suit – to the drycleaner in Herne Hill, about ten minutes away. It didn't look dirty to me but my standards were clearly lower than Charlie's. I paid for the super-express service and, while waiting, went over the road to the park.

I stood by the lake where Charlie and I had made love. The ice had melted now and the ducks looked relieved. Standing by the low metal fence I closed my eyes and remembered that evening: the delicious surprise, the slap of the cold water, Charlie's pale skin in the moonlight, the spark in her eyes. It still overwhelmed me, the way she affected me physically, that giddy intoxicated feeling that came over me when I looked at her, the naked need to touch her, to have her close to me. The taste of her kiss, the little murmuring sounds she made in bed, the earthy scent of her flesh. A great rush of love surged through me, compelling me to take out my phone and send her a text.

I want you to come live with me. Share my nest. I love you and want to be with you forever xxxxxx PS I wish you were here right now so I could kiss you . . . everywhere xxxxx

She replied almost straight away. *Where exactly do you want to kiss me? Xxxx*

I think you know . . . xxxx

I went back to pick up Charlie's suit, then walked home, still buzzing from the text exchange, passers-by glancing questioningly at my dizzy grin. Whatever else happened in my life, as long as I had Charlie, everything would be OK.

Walking back to the flat, I felt my phone vibrate in my pocket. Thinking it was probably Charlie again, I put the suit down on a wall and wrestled my phone into the open.

The message was from Sasha.

Hey you. Hope you're OK. Can you call me? I need to talk to you. X

I contemplated the message. I hadn't spoken to her for two weeks, though I had been meaning to get in touch. Sasha's friendship was still important to me, even if I was going to have to find some way of having her in my life if she and Charlie couldn't get on.

I sat on the wall, Charlie's suit beside me, and called her straight back.

'Andrew. Thank you so much. I didn't know if you'd call.'

She sounded oddly formal, but when I spoke, I did too. 'That's all right. I've been meaning to call you for ages. Are you OK?'

It took a minute or two for the conversation to shift, the ice breaking off the edges, until it felt natural again, though still not like our normal easy exchanges. Not yet anyway.

I told her about Victor and we speculated about what it might mean for the Wowcom contract. Sasha told me that Wowcom had terminated contracts with suppliers in the past because they were worried their 'brand might become contaminated'. This possibility hadn't occurred to me.

'Do you think he's guilty?' she asked.

'No. I mean, I don't know. He never struck me as . . . the type.'

I could almost hear her rolling her eyes. 'You mean he didn't wear a grubby mac and have a box of puppies in his car.'

'You know what I mean.'

'Yeah, sorry.'

An awkward silence fell between us. My eye was sore. I had noticed that this happened increasingly when I was stressed. Something to do with eye pressure, perhaps. The little bubble of excitement I'd been floating in, thinking about Charlie moving in with me, had well and truly popped.

'What did you want to talk to me about?' I asked.

I heard her take a deep breath. 'It's kind of difficult to explain without sounding ridiculous or mad. Can you meet me after work?'

Here it was: the difficult moment that would repeat all the while I was friends with Sasha. 'I'm not sure. Charlie's coming round.'

Sasha was silent.

'Are you still there?' I asked.

'Yes. I wouldn't ask if it wasn't important. But it's all right. I'll find someone else to talk to. Don't worry.'

'Hang on.' I really wanted to see Charlie tonight, but it wouldn't do any harm to meet Sasha for an hour, would it? 'I'm sorry, Sash, of course I'll meet you. Where and when?'

'My place at six-thirty?'

I texted Charlie and told her I'd be out for a little while with Sasha. She didn't reply.

———

Sasha texted me at six to ask if we could meet in The Commercial as she didn't want to go straight home. *Will all make sense later!* the text read.

She was already at the pub when I got there, with a glass of red wine that was so big it was more like a bowl. I asked for what she was having and as I neared the table, Sasha got up and hugged me.

'I really hate to admit it, but I missed you,' she said.

'Yeah, I kind of missed you too. A smidge.'

'A smidge? A *smidge*? Bloody cheek.'

'So tell me what's been going on,' I said.

Before answering, Sasha looked around like a spy in a black and white movie. She wasn't doing it ironically though; she genuinely appeared concerned that someone might be listening in. The pub was busy with the after-work crowd. There was an important match on later which the pub was showing on a big screen, so the pub was filling up with a second wave of drinkers: young men, mostly, in football shirts. It was noisy and Sasha should have had to raise her voice to be heard. But as she spoke, the background hubbub dropped away so all I could hear was her voice.

'Someone's been following me around,' she said.

'What do you mean?'

'Just that. I first noticed it a couple of weeks ago, when I was coming home from work.'

'When it was snowing?'

She nodded. 'Yes. I was, like, struggling home, head down like this, because the wind was trying to blow my face off, and there was hardly anyone around . . . That was when I started to think someone was behind me, like I could feel eyes on me.'

'Go on.'

'But when I looked round there was no one there. The street was empty. There was a van over the road and I was convinced they were hiding behind it.'

'What did you do?'

'I headed home as fast as I could. I tapped in 999 and had my thumb hovering over the call button, just in case. And that wasn't the last time. It's happened at least twice more, once when I was coming home from the pub, quite late. And once at the weekend, in the middle of the day. I was walking through the park and I was sure someone had followed me in and all the way through. But every time I looked round there was no one there.'

'Do you think you imagined it?'

'I'm not completely gaga yet, Andrew. But, actually, yeah, I did wonder that. Of course. But that time in the park, I retraced my footsteps and someone burst out of the bushes and legged it across the grass. Nearly gave me a heart attack.'

'Christ. What did they look like?'

'Dressed all in black. Slim. Wearing a hat. I mean, if there was a uniform for a burglar or stalker, he or she was wearing it.'

'He or she?'

'Yeah. Well, they looked very slim . . . like it could be a woman. But they were moving pretty fast and were obscured by all the bushes and trees.'

I stared at her. 'You know, I was followed by someone. Or I thought I was. That night after I watched *Blair Witch* at yours. And so was Charlie – someone followed her through the park. But when we went to look for them there was no one there.'

'That's weird,' she said. 'But, actually, if it wasn't for the other stuff—' She held up a hand to let her continue. 'If it wasn't for the other stuff, that would make me feel better. Make me think that it wasn't me they were targeting specifically. I mean, if there was a mugger or some weirdo in the area, who was following anyone who happened by at the right time, I wouldn't feel so paranoid.'

'But?' I asked.

She stood up. 'I'm going to need another drink. Same again?'

'Sasha, what is it?'

She glanced around her and leaned forward. 'I haven't told you about the other stuff yet. The *really* creepy stuff.'

Twenty-three

Sasha came back from the bar and pushed a fresh glass of wine towards me. The football had started and people were shouting encouragement and abuse at the screen but I could barely hear them. I hadn't noticed before how pale and ill Sasha looked. Dark circles under her eyes, a waxy complexion, bloodshot pupils, lank hair. She had looked like she was suffering before, when she first split with Lance, but her appearance had worsened considerably since I'd last seen her, when she came round for dinner.

'Tell me what's happened,' I said.

'OK. Well, firstly, someone's been in my flat while I was out.'

The hairs on the back of my neck stood up. 'What do you mean?'

'It happened twice. The first time, I think it took me a little while to notice, but then I realised: some of the stuff in my flat had moved. For example, I've got these three zebras that stand on my mantelpiece.'

'Yeah, I've seen them.'

'Well, someone turned them the other way round, to face the wall. And that's not all. You know I have my books arranged in strict alphabetical order by author?'

'Your library, you mean?'

'Exactly. A lot of the books had been rearranged, put out of place. DVDs had been swapped around too, so the wrong ones were in the wrong cases. I never do that. It's one of my things.'

'I know.' I had once found myself at the end of a barrage of insults for returning one of Sasha's box sets with several of the DVDs in the wrong place.

'At first I thought I was going mad, that I must have done it when I was cleaning.'

'You don't have a cleaner?'

'No, we're not all as middle-class as you.'

'Hey, I only—'

'I'm kidding. I haven't got to the weirdest bit yet. I've got a load of fridge magnets – you know, those little plastic letters. The second time this happened, I got home and found that someone had left a message on the fridge door for me. KEEP AWAY. Spelt out mostly using the red letters.'

'Oh my God.'

She nodded. 'I know, right. And get this – my butcher's knife was lying on the worktop above the fridge. I'm certain I'd left it in the block when I went out. When I found it, I completely freaked out. I had to go and stay with my mum for a few days. When I got back I chucked my toothbrush away – I mean, you hear all those stories, don't you? – and scrubbed and bleached everything.'

'Did you call the police?'

'Huh. What's the point? There's no evidence, is there? They'll think it's me, that I'm bonkers or making it all up. Anyway, that part of it has stopped. I installed a camera, pointing at the door. It's rigged up to trigger if someone comes in. I've been running it for the last week and no one has entered the flat apart from me. But there's been other stuff happening.'

'Like what?'

'Someone standing outside my flat at night, for one. Hang-ups on the phone. My doorbell ringing and there being no one there when I answer.'

'Oh, Sasha.'

I reached out and took her hand. It was shaking.

'I'm really scared,' she said.

'You need to go to the police,' I said.

'No. Because . . . because I know who it is. What it's all connected to. It's Lance and Mae, maybe her brothers. It has to be.'

I stared at her. 'Are you sure?'

'Who else would it be? Lance is still angry with me for threatening to do him for sexual harassment. And, well, I did something stupid. I went round to his house when I knew his wife was out at her gym class. We always used to meet on Tuesday evenings, when Mae was doing spinning. He said what we were doing was *his* exercise.'

I pulled a 'yuk' face.

'Hey, I did love him, you know. Or I thought I did. We all make stupid mistakes, don't we? Anyway, I went to their house, but she wasn't out. She opened the door and started screeching at me. She went berserk.'

I wasn't sure I could blame her, but I didn't say that to Sasha. 'Why did you go round there?'

'Because I wanted to smooth things over. This was just after I came to yours for dinner and I was feeling wound up. It was two days later that I first thought someone was following me. I told you about the threats Mae made back when she found out about the affair, didn't I?'

'Yeah, you did. But how would Mae or her brothers get into your flat?'

Sasha looked away. 'Lance had a key. I gave it to him so he could let himself in. We had this thing where – oh, this is really embarrassing – sometimes he would let himself in during the night and sneak into my room, get into bed with me and have sex with me, then slip out without saying anything. Don't look at me like that. It was exciting.'

'It sounds like he was using you, Sasha.'

She shook her head. 'We were using each other.'

'Please tell me you've changed the locks now.'

A great roar swept across from the other side of the pub. Someone had scored. Sasha said, 'No.'

'For God's sake . . . why not?'

'I was hoping to catch whoever it is. So I'd have some evidence. But I'm going to change the locks tomorrow.'

'What a nightmare,' I said. I paused, then added, 'I think Charlie's right. You should look for a new job, make a clean break.'

She scowled. 'Why should I be the one who suffers? That prick will probably be fucking another impressionable young woman in a year's time.'

'Sasha, you just told me you were using him too.'

She seemed to deflate, putting her head in her hands. 'I know. You're right. I just don't want to leave that job. I love it too much.'

I gave up. It wasn't my place to tell her what to do. But I could make sure she was safe. 'You really have to get the locks changed tomorrow. Don't walk around on your own. I guess the police won't do anything unless they have evidence of a crime taking place, but I think you should talk to them, get it logged, just in case. OK?'

'OK.'

She downed the dregs of her wine. 'Will you walk me home?'

'Yes, of course. I was going to insist on it.'

We ended up getting a taxi as I couldn't face the long walk with my crutch. I was physically exhausted. When we got to the flat, I said, 'Let me come in, just in case there's anyone there.'

She nodded, her face etched with worry.

Inside the flat, she looked around, checking the book case, the fridge, the bedroom. 'It all looks normal. I don't think anyone's been here.' She took a bottle of wine off the rack. 'Do you want another drink?'

'I don't know – I should get back.'

Sasha made an 'under the thumb' gesture.

'It's not like that,' I said.

'You're not going to get rolling-pinned if you're late?'

'You're hilarious.'

Sasha crossed to the window and looked out. She was visibly trembling.

'Sasha, are you going to be all right? I'm really worried about you.' I joined her by the window. The street was deserted, trees bending in the wind, litter swirling in the dark corners.

Her voice was quiet. 'I'm worried. What if one of Mae's brothers tries to get in during the night? Rapes me in my bed? I can see it happening, the night before I actually get the locks changed.'

'I'll stay,' I said.

'No, don't be silly.'

I wasn't sure how Charlie would react to me staying over at Sasha's. But Sasha was my best friend. There was no way I could leave her in this state. 'I'll stay here on the sofa. I'll be your guard dog. Then tomorrow, we'll call a locksmith, get this situation sorted, and talk to the police. All right?'

Her eyes were wet. 'You're a good friend, Andrew.'

'Yeah, yeah. I know. I haven't been much of a friend recently though, have I?'

She sat down on a beanbag in front of the TV. 'I'll make more of an effort with Charlie, I promise. I know how important she is to you. And if I'm still going to be your friend, I'm going to have to get on with your missus, aren't I?'

'It would help. Thanks Sasha.' I took out my phone. 'Right, I'd better call Charlie, let her know what I'm doing.'

I looked over at the dry cleaning bag, which I'd left by the door. I didn't think Charlie needed the suit tomorrow. Regardless, this was more important.

'What's that?' Sasha asked.

'Oh, just a suit of Charlie's. I had it cleaned today.'

She laughed. 'You're turning into a good little house-husband, aren't you?'

'Sasha.'

'Yes?'

'Fuck off.'

—⁀—

Sasha dug a blanket and spare pillow out of her airing cupboard and I lay on the sofa, uncomfortable but pretty drunk. Sasha and I had polished off a bottle of wine after we'd got back, then she'd ordered a delivery pizza and we'd spent the evening watching television, taking the piss out of reality TV contestants like we were students again, though our hearts weren't in it. Every now and then, Sasha would get up and look out the front window, but there was never anything to see.

To my relief, Charlie had been cool about me staying over at Sasha's, making a joke about how it was my loss, and I was pleased to have made things up with my best friend. The unspoken falling out had been stupid and I wouldn't let it happen again.

I must have fallen into a drunken sleep after a long time fidgeting on the sofa. The next thing I knew, someone was hissing my name.

'*Andrew.*'

I opened my eyes, groggy and confused. 'What? What is it?'

'I think someone just tried to get in.'

I sat up. Sasha was in a pair of fleece pyjamas, holding a bread knife.

'What the hell are you doing with that?' I asked.

She just looked at me with wild eyes.

'Sasha, put it back. What happened?'

'I put the chain on the door before I went to bed. I just heard it rattle. Someone was trying to get in.'

I pulled on my jeans and hobbled over to the front door. I wouldn't be much use with my bad leg if I needed to chase someone. Or run away. The door seemed securely closed, the chain in place. I slid it back and opened the door, looking out into the hallway, which always smelled of some kind of meat stew.

'Hello?' I said, my voice echoing in the darkness. I stepped into the hall.

'Don't go out there,' Sasha said, peering through the doorway behind me.

'It's fine. There's no one here.'

Sasha went back inside and I heard her pad over to the window. Then she shouted, 'There!'

I rushed in, as fast as I could – which was frustratingly slowly – and found her pointing at the street.

'Down there,' she said, her voice squeaking. 'I saw someone. They went behind that van.'

'Call the police,' I said.

'But—'

'Please, Sasha. Just do it.'

She went off to find her mobile in the bedroom. When she came back, her face was so pale it was almost transparent.

'There was a new message on my phone,' she said. 'Like the ones I got before. But worse.'

She gulped.

'What does it say?' I asked, still looking at the street. I couldn't see anybody out there. The wind was still blowing hard.

'Take a look,' Sasha said, handing me the phone.

There were two words on the screen, written in block capitals. YOU'RE DEAD.

Twenty-four

Neither Sasha nor I could get back to sleep after that. I sat on the sofa drinking weak coffee while she paced the room, staring out the window and checking the chain was on the door every two minutes. By the time the sun came up I was exhausted, had that post-red-eye flight feeling, scratchy eyes and fuzzy brain.

The text had been sent from a blocked number. A quick Google search showed us how easy this is to do: there are numerous apps that allow you to either create a fake number to send from or block the caller ID altogether.

As soon as it got light, Sasha called a locksmith, telling them it was an emergency, and they promised to arrive within the hour.

'You need to call the police next,' I said.

She chewed her lip. 'I really don't want to. What am I going to do, tell them I suspect the boss I had an affair with, or his wife? It's going to cause so much shit. I'll be humiliated. It will be the talk of the office and most people will think I deserve it. Oh God . . .'

I took her by the shoulders. 'Sasha, you have to do it.'

'OK, OK.' She took a shuddering breath. She held the phone to her ear and dialled the police station, and I listened to her tell someone what had happened. 'They're going to send someone round a bit later.'

I tried to bite down on a yawn but she saw.

'You look knackered. You should go home.'

'No, I'll stay and wait for the police to come.'

This time, I was unable to suppress the yawn. I was dizzy and my body was screaming at me to let it sleep.

'No, honestly. You get back, get some kip. I'll be fine. The locksmith will be here soon and then I'll wait in for the police. You don't need to be here for that.'

'All right. If you're sure.'

'I'm sure.' She gave me a hug. She was still trembling. 'Thank you so much for staying the night. I don't know what I would have done without you.'

'That's what friends are for, Sash.'

I practically floated home. I couldn't remember the last time I'd been this tired. It was about ten thirty when I let myself in the front door and entered my flat, dropping Charlie's dry cleaning in the hallway and heading straight into the bedroom.

'Jesus, you made me jump!'

Charlie was lying in my bed. As soon as I came in she sat up, in a move that reminded me of Nosferatu sitting upright in his coffin, a smooth elevation. And she looked like the living dead: her eyes were ringed with mascara smudges and streaks, her face white, her red hair sticking out at crazy angles, matted and stiff. She stared at me vacantly. She was wearing a pink camisole which looked like it had been scrunched up; there was a black stain on the front, like dried blood.

'Charlie, are you all right? What are you doing here? I thought you'd be at work.'

She said something in such a low voice I couldn't hear it.

'Pardon?'

'I said, did you enjoy fucking her?'

I hadn't really been paying much attention, had been too tired, too busy trying to take my shoes off. Now, though, my head snapped towards her.

'What?'

Her face twisted with anger, lip curled into a sneer. 'I'm not. Going to. Fucking repeat myself. *Andrew*.'

Ice water had replaced the blood in my veins. I sat on the edge of the bed, reaching out to her and saying, 'Charlie, why are you—'

She shrank away like a vampire from garlic. 'Get away from me. You stink of her.'

I had never had to deal with a situation like this before. What was I supposed to do? Part of me, the very tired part, wanted to ignore her and curl up with the quilt over my head. But this was not a mild attack of jealousy. She was shaking, and all I wanted to do was hold her, reassure her, make her feel better. Get this sorted out. The other option – getting defensive, starting an argument and telling her not to be so fucking stupid – barely entered my mind.

'Charlie, sweetheart, what are you talking about? I slept on her sofa. Actually, I barely even slept. Sasha—'

'I bet you didn't. You were too busy fucking her. How does she like it, huh? Is she really dirty? No, no, that's not right. She's far too repressed, probably only wants it in the missionary position. Is that what you like, Andrew? You don't actually want a woman like me, someone who is free, a proper, hot-blooded woman. You want that stuck-up, rude, cheating little bitch, someone who will fuck her boss and then boo-hoo-hoo about it like she's the fucking *victim*.' The last word came out as a strangled yelp.

I had no words.

'What?' Charlie said. 'Are you just going to stand there with your mouth gaping open like a fucking goldfish? Not going to defend your girlfriend?'

'You're my girlfriend,' I said.

She spat out a laugh and pushed herself up onto her knees. That was when I noticed the knife on the pillow: my sharpest kitchen knife, black handle, the one Charlie so often used to chop vegetables. Some dark substance clung to the blade.

'I'm your girlfriend. Yes, yes I am. So why – *why?* – do you spend the night with another woman? Answer me *that*.'

My voice, when it came out, sounded weak. 'But I told you I was going to stay over. You said it was fine.'

She didn't respond, just stared at me with a thunderous expression.

'Sasha has been having loads of weird stuff going on and she wanted me to stay over, make sure she was safe. You knew that.'

She tipped her head to one side. 'The knight in shining armour. Saving the poor little damsel in distress. Come on, tell me, how many times did you fuck her? What are her blow jobs like? Better than mine? What's her cunt like, eh? Nice and fucking tight?'

'Oh my God. Charlie. This is ridiculous. Come on, please.'

Her face was red with rage. She jabbed a finger at me but her voice was quieter. 'You can tell her . . . tell your bitch, that if she wants you she's got to get past me first. I'm not the kind of woman who'll sit back and let another woman steal from her.'

Tears dripped from her cheeks and the flesh was mottled pink around her collarbone, the same flush she got when she was aroused. The smell of stale sweat and alcohol came off her, which led me to spot the two bottles of red wine, one on the bed, folded in the quilt, another tipped over on the floor, a stain like blood on the carpet.

She picked up the knife from the pillow. I was sitting sideways on the bed, my torso twisted towards her. I backed away, held my palms up towards her. 'Charlie, put that down, please.'

She didn't put it down. She pulled up the front of the camisole with her free hand, revealing two long slashes across her belly, one either side of her navel. They were shallow, more like scratches than cuts. She held the long blade of the knife against her stomach, across her belly button, and stared at me staring at her.

'Oh my God.' I moved towards her.

'Don't,' she hissed.

'Charlie. Please. I love you. I promise, nothing happened. Nothing will ever happen between me and Sasha. Please, put the knife down. Don't hurt yourself.'

She continued to stare at me.

'I see Sasha like a sister. A friend. That's all.'

I edged closer. Her arm was rigid, knuckles white where they gripped the knife handle. I reached out, terrified she would cut herself, a little part of me scared that she would lash out at me. She was silent, tears running down across her face, snot glistening in her nostrils, breathing audibly, deep, wet breaths.

My fingertips touched her arm. With all my might, I forced my hand not to shake.

'Please, sweetheart,' I whispered. My fingers closed around her forearm, and I felt her relax slightly. She let me gently pull her arm away, extricate the knife from her hand. I threw it across the room, where it skidded and spun beneath the chest of drawers.

I tugged the front of her camisole down and, shuffling towards her on my knees, pulled her into an embrace. Her body was rigid at first, but as I whispered to her and told her everything was going to be all right, she slowly relaxed. Finally, she hugged me back and started to sob.

We stayed like that for a long time before either of us spoke.

'I'm sorry, so sorry, so sorry, oh Andrew, I'm so—'

'Sshhh. It's OK, it's OK.'

It was so quiet in the room that I could hear children playing in the grounds of the school three streets away, could make out the song on a radio playing somewhere else in the building.

Finally, Charlie pulled away from me and said, 'Let me go to the bathroom.'

After she'd left the room I wandered into the living room. The TV was on and muted, the sink full of food, pasta splattered up the wall. A smashed glass lay on the floor.

The picture of me and Sasha on holiday had been taken down, removed from its frame, torn into strips and left on the carpet. I picked it up, shook my head. I could picture Charlie here during the night, drinking, going crazy, like a wild animal in a cage. I was amazed that she hadn't bombarded me with calls or texts, hadn't done so at all. Perhaps she hadn't wanted me to know how she felt, had wrestled to control it, but finally lost the battle.

Charlie was taking ages in the bathroom and concern sent me into the bedroom to check she didn't have the knife with her. I remembered it was under the chest of drawers and was bending to retrieve it when she came into the room behind me. I stood up and turned to meet her.

She had washed her face and pinned her hair up. Although she was still very pale, she looked a lot better, the mascara tears scrubbed away, her wild hair tamed. She wore a loose T-shirt and pyjamas bottoms. Her expression was sheepish.

'Come here,' I said, hugging her. My body felt alien, adrenaline draining, replaced by a profound tiredness. I guess I was in shock.

'I'm so sorry,' she said.

We sat down together on the bed, holding hands.

'I don't want to make any excuses,' she said. 'I was fine when you told me you were staying over, at first. Then I started drinking, got quite drunk, and I looked up and saw the photo of you and

Sasha and started to feel paranoid. I guess . . . I worked myself into a frenzy over the next few hours.'

'How's your stomach?' I whispered.

She pulled up her T-shirt and looked down. The scratches were shallow. 'Quite sore. But I'm too much of a wimp to really hurt myself.'

'Have you . . . have you done that before?' There were no scars on her body so I knew she had never self-harmed in that way.

She shook her head. 'No.'

'I promise you, Charlie, there is nothing between Sasha and me. I have no interest in any other women. I love you.'

'I know. I'm an idiot.'

'I'm so tired. Can we talk more later?'

'OK. I'm exhausted too. You won't believe what happened—'

She held up a hand. 'Later. Please.'

'All right.'

I undressed and slipped into bed beside her. We held each other. My brain was whirring, popping. The emotional storm echoed in the room, keeping us awake. Soon, we were kissing silently, and Charlie shrugged off her T-shirt and I ducked beneath the quilt and pulled off her PJ bottoms, and then we were making love, word-less, intense sex where we couldn't get close enough to each other, though we tried, kissing hungrily, pressing our bodies together as hard as we could bear, arms and legs wrapped tight, like we were trying to melt into one another. A corporeal bliss touched every inch of my skin, buffed away the emotional pain. It was the best sex we'd ever had.

Twenty-five

I awoke in the early afternoon, lay there for a while listening to the rain lashing against the window. Charlie was deeply asleep and I left her there, hair splayed across the pillow, while I spent the next hour clearing up the mess she'd made during the night. I binned the wine bottles, threw away, with a flare of sad anger, the ripped-up picture of Sasha and me. When I'd finished I peeked into the bedroom: Charlie was still asleep, the picture of tranquil innocence. She'd slept through my futile attempts to scrub away the wine stain on the bedroom carpet.

I made myself a coffee and sat at my desk. I checked my phone. Sasha's locks were changed and the police had been round. She had to go to the station to make a statement. She ended her text with *Thank you so much for last night. I don't know I'd have coped without you. Love S xx*

My thumb hovered over the text. Should I delete it? If Charlie saw it, it might cause another outbreak of jealous rage. I put the phone down. I couldn't start hiding things, modifying my behaviour. The moment I did that, our relationship would be tainted. Doomed.

But what was I going to do? I had seen glimpses of Charlie's jealousy before, like with the girl in the park, but this? This was something new. Something deeply disturbing.

A friend of mine called Belinda, whom Sasha and I had known at uni, had a jealous boyfriend. She told us about him after they finally split up, because she said she was too ashamed to tell anyone while it was going on. She said that if she ever spoke to another man, if she was late home from work, if she got a message or a text from any other young male, he would go mad.

'He'd go quiet at first, which was when I knew what was brewing. Then he'd start asking snide questions, making sarcastic comments. Eventually, he'd get angry, start shouting, throwing things. He never hit me but he'd scream at me and threaten me and whoever it was he was convinced I was screwing. After that was over he'd be contrite, crying, telling me he was sorry, that he would get help. But he never did get help. It happened over and over again and every time I forgave him.'

'Why?' I asked.

She shrugged. 'I loved him. Because the rest of the time he was lovely. But it was always there, like a little . . . gremlin that lived in our flat, hiding, waiting to come out.'

I had shaken my head. 'If that ever happened to me, I'd be out of there like a shot. There's no way I'd put up with it.'

I looked towards the bedroom. It's easy to feel certain of how you would act when you don't have a real situation, real emotions, to deal with. I was shocked and upset by what Charlie had done, what she'd accused me of. I had a sickening vision of a future in which I could never relax, would repeatedly find myself in dramatic, disturbing scenes, a life where I could never accept the innocent offer of a lunchtime drink from a girl at work, never click 'like' on the picture of a woman I was friends with, eventually give in to the pressure to break contact with my female friends.

But when I pictured another future, one without Charlie in it, where I was alone again, the pain was even sharper. I was in love with her. Besotted. When we were together, the rest of my life felt sepia, dull, a black-and-white movie. The thought of losing her made me panic.

I hated to think of her suffering too. I wanted to make everything all right, make her happy. Perhaps, a little voice murmured, I *had* been in the wrong. I shouldn't have spent the night at my friend's flat, leaving Charlie here on her own, especially when we had been planning to talk about her moving in, when we were both expecting a fun evening together.

No, I told myself firmly. You are not in the wrong. You were being a friend to Sasha, that's all. Charlie should understand that. And even if she was upset, she shouldn't have reacted like that.

I knew that I was going to have to do something about this. Nip it in the bud.

I woke the computer from sleep and Googled 'jealousy'. Unsurprisingly, the internet was awash with information. I quickly found an article about something called 'morbid jealousy', which is also known as the Othello syndrome, a suitably dramatic label. Morbid jealousy, I read, is where a person is convinced their partner is being unfaithful despite having no proof. They are delusional and become obsessed with the notion, torturing themselves and their other half.

The more I read, the more worried I became. The articles and Wiki pages were stuffed full of terms like 'psychological illness', 'mental disorder', 'insecure attachment' and 'extreme obsession'. There were endless news reports of people – mostly men, which gave me some reassurance – who had become violent and attacked their partner because of perceived infidelity. Othello, if I remembered correctly, murdered his wife, but most sufferers of morbid jealousy kill nothing more than their relationship.

I read on. Apparently, for women, jealousy is more likely to be triggered by emotional infidelity than by sexual betrayal. I thought about Charlie's rant about what she believed I'd done with Sasha.

It had been intently focused on sex. But maybe, really, the attack was caused by me offering Sasha emotional support, my closeness to her similar, in Charlie's mind, to a romantic attachment.

Charlie had, I was sure, a psychological issue, probably with its roots in something that happened in her childhood. She was so sketchy when it came to talking about her past that it seemed logical that there was something hidden in her past that she didn't want to face; a history that was causing her to be jealous now.

Pleased with myself for finding a rational explanation, I sat back.

We would find Charlie a counsellor, a therapist. Someone who could help her get to the root cause of her jealousy. Then, I assured myself, everything would be all right.

⌣

I made coffee for Charlie and took it in to her, gently shaking her awake.

Her eyes were wild for a second before she focused on me.

'What time is it?' she asked as if she had somewhere she urgently needed to be.

'It's three o'clock.' I handed her the coffee. Sitting up, she took a sip, grimaced and put it on the bedside table. 'Listen, Charlie, I've been thinking, about this morning.'

'Oh God.'

'I think that we should find you help. You know, like a counsellor or a therapist.'

She looked at me sharply. 'I'm not crazy.'

I was aware that I was talking to her like I would a child who'd done something very naughty. I changed my tone. 'I know you're not. But jealousy . . . It must be rooted in some . . .' I struggled to find the right words. '. . . self-esteem issue or insecurity.'

She groaned and pulled the quilt over her head.

Flummoxed, I said, 'Charlie?'

'Yes,' she said eventually from beneath the quilt.

'Will you please talk to me?'

She slowly pulled the quilt down to reveal her face. 'Do we have to talk about this now? I feel like shit and I don't want . . . I don't want to make a big deal out of it. Can't we just forget it happened?' She reached out and took my hand. 'I promise it won't happen again.'

'That's what Belinda's bloke used to say.' I wished I could remember his bloody name.

Charlie blinked. 'Who?'

I explained about Belinda and her jealous boyfriend.

'And you think that's what I'm like? A jealous nutter?'

I sighed. 'I don't think you're a nutter. But this morning, well, you scared me.'

She put her hands over her face. After a long pause she said, 'Is it a condition of us staying together?'

'What?'

'If I don't see a therapist, will you dump me?' Her voice trembled on the last two words.

I was about to say no, to back down, but I stopped myself. I needed to be strong. 'I think so. Yes. I don't want anything to spoil what we have, Charlie.'

She stared at me with liquid eyes. 'I don't either. But this morning – it wasn't me.'

'You've never done that before? With anyone else?'

'No. That's why it got so out of control, I think, because I didn't know how to cope with the feelings, with the . . .'

'The what?'

She sank back into the bed. 'I don't want to talk about it any more.'

'But we have to,' I said.

'No. No we don't. It won't happen again. That's all you have to know.'

This was so frustrating. But I was coming to see this was typical of her, clamming up, refusing to talk about things she didn't want to face. 'I want you to see someone, Charlie. Please. For me. Because morbid jealousy . . .'

'Hang on,' she interrupted. 'Have you been Googling this? Trying to diagnose me?'

I didn't reply.

'Ha. You have. And you're probably feeling pleased with yourself because Charlie has a problem and Andrew is going to fix it. Like I'm a leaky tap and the therapist is a plumber. You're such a typical man.' She pulled back the quilt and got out of bed, turning to face me, covering her breasts with a forearm. The scratches on her belly were red and livid.

'Sometimes people act out of character. They get irrational. Do stupid things. That's what this was. An aberration. But if you want me to see a therapist, fine. I'll go. OK?'

She walked out of the room.

Twenty-six

I walked out of the hospital, thankful that for the second time in just a few months I had been discharged from medical care. My leg was all better, though still a little stiff and sore, and I made a solemn vow to myself: no more accidents. I was going to be more careful from now on.

I was supposed to be meeting Charlie for lunch near Moorfields, but she'd texted me to say there was some kind of crisis going on at work. I didn't want to go straight home so decided I would have lunch out by myself, but would first drop by Victor's office to see what was going on there.

A week had passed since he had been arrested and I hadn't heard anything. I guessed I was very low priority. With every day that went by I became more convinced that my career as a senior designer had ended before it had begun. I'd sent a number of emails and enquiries to rival agencies and a few other contacts, but everyone came back with the same response: sorry, but they didn't need any work at the moment, maybe after Easter . . .

Charlie assured me things would be OK, that I didn't need to find a job, and last night we had talked again about her moving in, a topic that I'd avoided since her jealous meltdown.

'So, do you still want to come and live with me?' I asked.

'Hmm, it depends . . . Do you promise not to take me for granted?'

'I could never do that, Charlie.'

'Not even in bed?'

'I definitely won't do that.'

She had smiled slyly. 'Oh, I don't know. Within a month, I'll be in bed alone with an erotica novel and you'll be staying up playing video games. Then you'll get annoyed with me for rearranging the bookshelves and taking over the wardrobe. You'll expect me to cook your dinner every night while you lounge around in a pair of stained underpants drinking beer.'

I laughed. 'Hang on, I thought it was you who wanted to move in.'

'I thought it was something we *both* wanted.'

'Sorry. Yes. It is. I mean, I do want it.'

'It's settled then.' She looked around the living room. 'I can't wait to completely redecorate this place.'

'Hey!'

I smiled now at the memory. Charlie was going away on a training course in a few days' time and we had agreed she would move in when she got back from that. I felt excited and a little nervous. I had considered bringing up her jealousy again, to say that if I had to promise not to take her for granted, she needed to promise not to have any more jealous outbursts. But she had made an appointment with a therapist and I had decided to leave it at that, to carry on as normal and deal with if it happened again.

The therapist was a woman called Dr Branson, whose practice was based in Islington, not too far from Moorfields.

'It's costing a fucking fortune,' Charlie said when she told me about making the first appointment.

'I'll contribute.'

'No. You haven't got any money. And it's my problem, isn't it? I still think it's unnecessary, but I love you so I'll do it.'

I was buzzed into Victor's building and took the lift up. The offices were quiet, most of the staff sitting with headphones on, gazing at their screens. Among them was Amber. I approached her desk.

'Oh, hi,' she said. 'No crutch? '

'No, I'm all better. Do you know if Emma is around?' I asked.

She sighed heavily. 'I think she's at a meeting, trying to persuade the client that just because the head honcho has been accused of being a paedophile, it doesn't mean they should cancel their contract.'

'Not Wowcom?'

'I don't think so. Though they've been in, going on about their brand image.' She rolled her eyes. 'They're all bastards. What happened to innocent till proven guilty, eh?'

'Do you know what's going on with Victor?'

'You haven't heard anything from him? He's been released on police bail but he's hiding out at home. He said he can't face seeing anyone at the moment. Plus his wife doesn't want him to leave the house.'

'You've spoken to him?'

'Yeah. He swears blind that he's innocent, that this web page is a total fabrication. He said no one ever contacted him making out they were a twelve-year-old girl, that he definitely wouldn't have responded if they had, and he has no idea how the porn got onto his computer.'

'Hang on – porn?'

She leaned forward. 'They found loads of kiddie porn on his work machine, apparently. Really sickening stuff. That's what they're doing him for, because the people who set up the website are remaining anonymous and they haven't provided any proof. Victor is arguing that loads of people could have got onto his computer. The cleaners, anyone who works here. He reckons it might even have been done remotely, though I don't know if that's possible.'

She looked at me hopefully.

'I have no idea.'

'Hmm. Well, anyway, I hope it all gets sorted out quickly because it feels like we're living under a black cloud. The trial is months away though.'

I left the office feeling even more worried about money than before. I stood outside and tapped out an email to Emma on my phone, but it seemed to me that if they were so worried about losing business they would be reluctant to take anyone new on. The chances of starting my new job receded with every day that Victor was off work. If Emma didn't reply with good news, I was heading towards deep financial trouble. Even with Charlie moving in, I still needed a regular income. I didn't want to become dependent on her, to become a kept man. The thought was anathema to me.

Sure enough, Emma replied almost straight away.

Sorry Andrew. We have a freeze on new hires at the moment, while this mess is sorted out. But we'll be in touch as soon as we know more . . .

If I'd still been carrying my crutch I would have chucked it at something.

My blood sugar was low and I needed to eat something. I walked down Old Street towards Hoxton, deep in thought. With the freelance situation looking gloomy, I was going to have to find a job. As I was mulling over what to do, I felt my phone vibrate in my pocket. It was Sasha.

The police have been to see Lance. He denies everything. X

I replied: He would. Do they have any way of tracing that text? X

No. Can't trace blocked numbers. Also, he had an alibi so says he couldn't have come to my flat that night. But his alibi is Mae! Police say nothing more they can do at mo esp as nothing has happened since. X

I went into a cafe – a kind of ironic greasy spoon – and got my laptop out, connecting to the wifi. As the waitress brought me my all-day breakfast, I started working on my CV, using a template I found online. I had decided: I didn't want to be a freelancer any more. I was tired of being on my own all day every day. I wanted to meet new people. As this thought entered my head, it was chased by another: Charlie wouldn't like it. It almost made me change my mind back immediately, to stay working freelance. I didn't want to upset her . . . But then I asked myself what the hell I was thinking? I couldn't modify my behaviour, go against my own needs like that. I wanted a job and I was going to find one.

As I worked on the CV, I felt eyes on me. I looked up and a guy across the cafe looked away quickly. He was younger than me, with a little beard, and was wearing a black beanie hat. There was an iPad on the table in front of him which he now appeared absorbed in.

I returned to my CV and my online portfolio, trying to pick out my best pieces of work so I could link to them from the CV. After about ten minutes, I became aware that the guy in the beanie hat was looking over at me again. As I turned my face towards him he ducked his head so fast it must have hurt his neck.

I hesitated. Who was he? I tried to catch his eye but he swiftly packed up his stuff, almost knocking his chair over in his haste to get out, paying his bill at the counter on the way out.

I stood up, craning to see which way he had gone, but he crossed the road and vanished. I was tempted to go after him, but he'd be long gone by the time I'd paid and got outside. Besides, maybe he was simply interested in my computer.

By the time I'd finished messing around with my CV and was ready to leave, I'd put the incident from my mind.

Heading home, I realised I wasn't too far from Karen's place. She still hadn't told me if she was happy with my work, which meant I still couldn't invoice her. She wasn't answering her phone either. I couldn't afford to let it go, especially not now. I stood on the street for a moment before deciding I would go to see her. It would be embarrassing, but what the hell. I needed the money.

I jumped onto a bus and, fifteen minutes later, found myself standing outside Karen's place. She lived in a beautiful Georgian conversion on a ludicrously expensive street. The first time I'd visited I'd told myself that, one day, I would live in a place like this. She could certainly afford to pay me my £500.

I rang the buzzer. There was no reply. I sighed. She was most likely out, seeing a client, shopping, lunching or whatever it was she did with her days. Five hundred pounds was nothing to her. Why was she taking so long to pay up? Most likely she couldn't imagine why anyone would make such a fuss about what to her was a trivial amount. Well, I was going to set her straight. I'd wait here all day if I had to . . .

I pulled the brakes on my train of thought. What was wrong with me? This issue with the money was making me resentful and angry. But I had warm memories of my time with Karen, liked her and respected her. I didn't need to be an arsehole about what was almost certainly an oversight. I'd call her when I got home, let her know that it would be extremely helpful if she could pay the invoice without any more delay.

As I turned to leave, an elderly man wearing a cravat came out of the front door. He had a small black and white terrier on a lead, and the dog nearly sent me flying as it jumped up at me.

'Sorry about that,' said the man, squinting at me like he recognised me. Maybe he did. I'd been a frequent visitor here once. 'Were you looking for someone?' he asked. The dog was sniffing my leg furiously and I wished he'd pull it away.

'Yes. Karen in flat 3?'

His face creased with pain. 'Oh dear. Are you a friend?'

I felt my blood drain. 'Yes. I've been trying to get hold of her but she never answers her phone.'

He looked up and down the road, as if searching for help.

'Perhaps you'd better come inside.' To the dog, he said, 'Come on, Dickens.'

He dragged the terrier back inside the building, with me following. My stomach fluttered, the kind of feeling you get when a doctor pauses before giving you the prognosis.

'I'm Harold, by the way,' he said, opening the door of the ground floor flat, which was stuffed full of antiques and *objets d'art*, statues and African masks, so many books crammed into the bookcases I was surprised the floorboards could hold them. He gestured for me to sit in an armchair that almost swallowed me.

'I don't know if I should be the one to tell you this,' he said. 'Were you very close?'

'We used to be,' I replied.

He exhaled noisily. 'Would you like a drink? Scotch? Malt whisky?'

Normally, I would have said no – I wasn't a big drinker of spirits and it was only two o'clock – but I understood that he was telling me I might need one. He got up and poured Scotch into two large tumblers. I took a sip. It burned and I coughed.

Harold stared at me with his milky eyes while the dog sat at his feet.

'So . . . Karen?' I said.

He ignored me. 'What's your name?'

'Andrew.'

I didn't like the way he was suddenly looking at me.

'There's something following you, Andrew,' he said in a hushed voice, leaning forward. I leant back. On the wall behind him was a canvas with a disturbing image: a woman with no eyes in her face, reaching out while flames danced around her. I looked at the nearest bookshelf: fat tomes with titles like *English Magick: The Dark Art* and *The Life and Eternal Death of Aleister Crowley* stood out.

'Following me?' I said.

His earlier smile had vanished. 'Something has attached itself to you. A . . . a dark spirit. It's hiding – or trying to hide.' He peered closer, and I looked behind me to see what he was staring at, half-expecting to see a demon, crouched and giggling behind its wing, on the back of the chair.

'You won't be able to see it, Andrew. But it's there.' He gasped.

This was extremely unnerving.

'Tell me,' he said. 'Have you suffered a lot of . . . bad luck recently?'

I hesitated. 'I've had some.'

'I thought as much. It's a mischief maker, this spirit. It likes to create chaos.' He narrowed his eyes and his voice dropped to a whisper. 'It's dangerous, Andrew. But I could help you rid yourself of it. Perhaps.'

My flesh was coarse with goose bumps. 'No offence, but you're giving me the creeps.'

He smiled. 'You're a sceptic. Most people are, unfortunately. But when it's too late, then you'll believe.'

I stood up, setting the Scotch aside. I couldn't wait to tell Charlie about this later. She would laugh at my description of the old man and his portentous warnings. 'Can you tell me about Karen? Where is she?'

He frowned and said, 'Oh dear' again.

'What?'

'I'm sorry to have to be the one to tell you, Andrew. But she's dead. She died some days ago.'

Twenty-seven

Trains clattered in and out of Victoria station, lovers kissed good-bye, mothers tilted buggies into carriages, commuters headed home, pigeons fluttered and crapped, cleaners cleaned, guards guarded, bodies streamed and jostled and shoved. And among it all, I stood as still as death, fixed in place while the entire world – or so it felt – jostled past me, and I half-listened to the eardrum-pounding announcements: *I am sorry ... Due to an accident ... The 17:45 to Orpington is currently delayed ... A person being killed on the tracks.*

I had called Charlie, who told me she was going to have to work late, wouldn't be back till after eight at the earliest. I tried Sasha. She wasn't answering. But I needed to talk to someone. If I didn't see a friendly face I might be driven crazy by the voices in my head. Tilly. I would go to see Tilly. It would get me out of London too, if only for an evening. The news of Karen's death had sent me spinning. In my head: a clamour of voices, swirling question marks, sparking connections. I couldn't process it all, couldn't think straight. I couldn't even make sense of the displays and the announcements at the station, getting in everyone's way as they tutted and pushed me. If you want to know what it would be like if civilisation broke down, go to a train station in London at rush hour, where it's every man for himself, every woman too. The state

I was in now, I would be one of the first to perish in a dog-eat-dog world. One of the first to die.

A dark spirit has attached itself to you.

Harold Franklin, Spiritualist – that was the job title on the business card he pressed into my palm when he saw me out – didn't know how Karen had died.

'It was all very mysterious,' he said, trying to conceal how he relished the intrigue of it. 'An ambulance turned up in the middle of the night. Next thing, they're carrying her out . . . Two days later, her sister is here, cleaning out the fridge and no doubt helping herself to anything she fancied. All she told me was that Karen was dead. Such a pity. She was a beauty, wasn't she?'

'Can't the spirits tell you what happened?' I asked.

His face darkened. 'There's no need to take that attitude, young man.' And with that, he ushered me out.

Somehow, I made it onto an Eastbourne-bound train, crammed in by the luggage racks. All the way to the coast, I kept picturing Karen the last time I'd seen her. She hadn't looked well. Certainly not the vital, sexy woman I'd once known, the woman with a zest for life and a don't-give-a-shit attitude. She had once told me that the most important lesson she'd learned in life was a simple one. 'It's short. Much too short. And I intend to make the most of every minute of it.'

She hadn't realised how brief her own life would be. Karen was, what? Forty-one, I think. She should have been halfway through her time on this planet; not even that. What the hell had taken her away? How had it happened?

The train sped south, and questions ricocheted around my skull, almost making connections. Almost.

———

'What are you doing here?'

'That's a nice greeting, sis.'

Tilly looked up at me from her wheelchair. 'Sorry, it's just . . . I haven't seen you for ages. Has something happened? Is Charlie OK?'

'She's fine. She's at work. Can I come in?'

'Yeah, of course.'

I followed her into the living room. The smell of perfume hung in the air, threatening to make me sneeze. I looked at Tilly properly. She was dressed up, wearing a pair of black trousers and a tight top, her hair curled and voluminous.

'Oh shit, are you going out? Have you got a date?'

Tilly laughed. 'I am going out, yes. You should have called. But it's not a date. I'm going out with Rachel and her bloke.'

'The Hells Angel?'

She grinned. 'Yes! The very same. His name's Henry. But they're not real Hells Angels. It's just a motorcycle club.'

'Oh, yes, you told me that, I think.'

'He's actually very nice.' She appraised what I was wearing. 'You're a bit scruffy but I'm guessing Henry won't be wearing a suit. You'll be fine.'

'What are you talking about?'

'You can come with us. I was worried about being a gooseberry. I'm so glad you've come to rescue me.'

A horn sounded outside and Tilly said, 'That'll be them. Come on.'

'But there's something I wanted to talk to you about.'

'You can tell me over dinner. Unless it's something private.'

'Well . . .'

She looked at me seriously. 'It's not . . . your old problem, is it?'

I shook my head quickly. 'No. I'm fine.'

This wasn't something I wanted to talk about. Not now, not ever. My sister knew this and I was irritated with her for even alluding to it.

'OK. So maybe . . .' I saw the face she always pulled when she was about to say something rude.

'No,' I said, cutting her off. 'I'm not suffering from any sexual problems, I haven't got an STI, Charlie's not pregnant.'

'Oh. I was going to ask if you were going to tell me you've proposed to Charlie. She told me that you're moving in together.'

I stared at her. 'You're in touch with Charlie?'

'Oh yes. She friended me on Facebook. We chat all the time. She's hilarious. And she's mad about you. Actually, she must be mad, if she loves you as much as she seems to. She talks about you like you're some dragon-slaying hero, a cross between Brad Pitt, Mr Darcy and Nelson Mandela.'

'But . . . Charlie's not on Facebook,' I said.

'Yes she is.' From outside, Rachel and Henry beeped their car horn again. 'Come on, we've got to go.'

Sitting in the back of Rachel's converted MPV, I made small talk with Henry, who was a giant of a man, barely able to fit inside the huge vehicle. I was slightly disappointed that he wasn't wearing a bandanna or a leather jacket. Instead, he wore a checked shirt that looked like it was going to pop open at any minute. He was like the Incredible Hulk with white skin and a ginger beard. When he laughed, which he did frequently, the car shook.

'Do you normally ride a Harley?' I asked. 'Rachel took me on the back of hers. It was terrifying.' Although, really, I had found it exciting, exhilarating even.

'I'll have to take you for a ride sometime – if you think Rachel rides fast . . .' His laughter boomed and reverberated around the people carrier and he squeezed Rachel's knee.

'Not when I'm driving,' she said, keeping her eyes on the road.

He smiled at her but Rachel's expression remained unamused. Henry gave me a look that said 'Women, huh?' before turning back to the front. I wondered if they would argue about it later, if he would be annoyed that she publically rejected him, if he would see it like that.

I looked back at Tilly.

'Why would Charlie tell me she wasn't on Facebook?'

She didn't seem to think it was a big deal. 'I don't know. Maybe she doesn't want you stalking her on there. Watching what she's up to.'

'She probably wants to avoid that whole "in a relationship" dilemma,' Henry said.

I mulled this over. 'I can understand that she might have felt like that at first. And if she said she didn't want us to be friends on Facebook because it's a bit naff or awkward or whatever, that would be cool. But I'm surprised she lied to me about it.'

'Ah, it's only a white lie,' Tilly said.

I got my phone out, went to my Facebook app and found Tilly's account. Scrolling through her friend list I found Charlie, using her unshortened name, Charlotte. I tried to look at her wall but I was completely blocked from seeing her posts. I felt genuinely hurt that she'd lied to me about it.

'She never lets me go to her flat, either,' I said, almost to myself. 'I feel really worried now. What's she hiding?'

Henry snorted. 'Maybe she's leading a secret life. She's probably married, with kids. You're her dirty secret.'

'Oh yes, you hear about things like that, don't you?' Rachel said, pulling in to the car park of the country pub where we were having dinner.

The three of them laughed like it was the funniest thing they'd ever heard. But this, piled on top of Karen's death – and everything else – made me feel cold and nauseated.

Before we got out of the MPV I sent Charlie a friend request. I wanted to see what she'd do.

———⏜———

I wasn't hungry, and picked at my food while the other three laughed and joked. Henry really was a nice bloke, a bit gruff and rude, but funny. Rachel talked to him like he was a naughty child, a role he played with relish. Tilly seemed in excellent spirits too, much better than she had at the turn of the year. I hadn't seen her so happy for a long time. It turned out she'd found out today that she was being promoted at work and getting a decent pay rise.

'What's up, bruv?' she asked, eyeing the way I was picking at my food. 'You're not really worried that Charlie has a secret husband, are you? There's no sign of one on Facebook. Not that *you'd* know.'

They all started laughing and I said, 'Karen died.'

The laughter stopped.

'Karen?' Tilly said. 'What, that older woman you had a thing with?'

'That's right.'

'Oh my God, what happened?'

'I don't know. I saw her a few weeks ago. I did some work for her. I went round there today because she owed me for the work, and her neighbour told me she was dead. He didn't know what caused it.' I rubbed my arms. 'He also told me some really spooky shit about a dark spirit following me around, causing all my bad luck.'

Henry gave me a serious look. 'A dark spirit? Really?'

'Don't tell me you believe in all that stuff,' I said.

'Yeah, I do. Spirits are real. My mum's a clairvoyant. She talks to them all the time.'

I couldn't help it. I started laughing, and I couldn't stop. The three of them – and everyone around our table – stared at me as I doubled over, tears streaming, my stomach convulsing at the image of Henry's mum, who I pictured as a middle-aged female biker, chatting with ghosts in her kitchen.

Seamlessly, the laughter turned into tears, and instead of laughing, I was weeping, my face in my hands, body shaking, and I felt a broad arm around my shoulders and could feel all the eyes that had been staring at me turning away.

'Come on, mate,' Henry said. 'Let's go and get some air, eh?'

'No, it's fine. I'm just going—'

I dashed off to the gents and locked myself in a cubicle, sitting on the closed toilet lid, letting the last of the tears come. When I'd finished, I blew my nose, left the cubicle and washed my face.

I rejoined the others at the table.

'Are you OK?' Tilly asked, a concerned expression on her face.

'Yeah. I'm good. I just – I don't know. It's not just Karen. So much stuff has happened recently. I think it all just hit me at once.'

'What else has happened?' Tilly asked. 'Apart from your accident.'

'Accident?' Henry asked.

I told them everything. Falling – or being pushed – down the steps at the Tube station. My new job being scuppered when Victor was arrested for being a paedophile. The weird stuff with Sasha and Lance and the 'You're Dead' text. How I was sure I'd been followed, as had Charlie, and the guy staring at me in the cafe that afternoon. Charlie losing the bag of mementoes.

'Even my cleaner,' I said, remembering. 'She was attacked in the street – someone threw acid in her face.'

'What, the really pretty one you told me about?' Tilly said.

'Yes. Now this, with Karen.'

Henry had been watching me solemnly through the whole tale. Now he nodded. 'It sounds like that neighbour was right. Something has attached itself to you.'

'Henry,' I said. 'With all due respect, that's bullshit. I really don't believe in all that stuff.'

'Then how else do you explain it?' he asked, pointing at me with his fork.

'It's just bad luck.'

Tilly seemed far less bright than she had before my laughing-crying fit. 'That's a lot of bad luck, Andrew, for one person.'

'Maybe. But I've always had bad luck. Right back to Mum and Dad . . . And my detached retina last year.'

'Perhaps it's a curse,' Henry said seriously. 'You haven't crossed any gypsies, have you?'

I spluttered. 'Please. You'll set me off again.'

The waiter brought the dessert menu to the table. I didn't want anything. All I wanted was to get drunk, and I downed my third large glass of red wine.

'So,' Henry said, after he'd ordered key lime pie with cream *and* ice cream. 'All this stuff that's happened – is it since you've met your bird? This Charlie chick.'

'You think she might have something to do with it?' Rachel said to Henry. As our designated driver, she was stone-cold sober.

He shrugged his massive shoulders. 'I don't know the girl. But it seems like a lot of this stuff has happened since Andrew met her.' He addressed me. 'If you don't believe in spirits and curses, there are only two possible reasons: one is sheer chance, or bad luck as you say. The other is that someone is behind it.'

'That's even more ridiculous than blaming a gypsy curse or an evil spirit,' I said.

But even as I said the words, I felt something crawl beneath my skin, an itch in my head, like the questions that had darted around my head since I'd heard about Karen's death were trying to connect, to knit together.

Henry took a big mouthful of lager, then shrugged. 'Yeah, well, maybe. It does seem pretty crazy, doesn't it? I mean, the amount of planning, the level of obsession required to do all the stuff you list . . . Fuck, you'd have to be some kind of maniac. Clever too.'

'And why would she do it?' Rachel said.

Henry's dessert came and he shovelled it in, thinking while he chewed. 'I don't know. Because she wants him all for herself? Look at the people who've been affected: a woman he used to shag, his best friend who happens to be female, a cleaner who was apparently a real fittie before she got acid chucked in her face. Then two things have happened to stop Andrew starting his new job, where he'd be working with other women. A bag full of pictures of all his exes goes conveniently lost. Fuck, the more I think about it, the more likely it seems!'

A cold, clammy sweat had broken out across my body. I stared at Henry. He didn't even know about the other stuff: Harriet being burgled and presents I'd given her stolen; my female friends vanishing from Facebook; my book containing nude photos going missing.

'Is she the jealous type, this Charlie?' Henry asked.

Before I could make my mouth work – and I was going to lie, say no, because I didn't want to tell them – Tilly banged the table and said, 'For fuck's sake, this is insane!'

We all looked at her.

'Charlie's lovely. She's sweet and funny and cool and she's completely besotted with you, Andrew. To say she could be responsible for all the stuff that's happened to you – all this random, unconnected stuff – it's bullshit, like the ramblings of an insane conspiracy theorist. What are you going to say next, that she somehow caused your retina to detach last year?'

I shook my head weakly in the face of Tilly's fury.

'It's bad luck, that's all. The world throwing shit at you. That's what happens in life. We had a huge pile of shit thrown at us when we were kids, killing our parents and landing me in this fucking wheelchair. And now life's chucking crap at lots of people you know. I mean, fuck, it's actually pretty egocentric to think it's all down to you. The only thing that's happened to you directly is that you slipped down some icy steps and, from what you've told me, Charlie was there afterwards to look after you.' She was red in the face. 'My God, if Charlie could hear all of this. You should be ashamed of yourself.'

I think I must have been red in the face too, but from embarrassment, not anger.

'Well,' said Henry, puncturing the silence that followed, moments after swallowing the last piece of pie. 'That told us.'

Twenty-eight

'Where have you been?'

Charlie was waiting for me when I got home, curled up on the sofa, the TV on with the volume muted. She sounded like she was trying hard to keep her voice even.

I was drunk, hardly able to walk in a straight line, especially with my sore leg. All I wanted to do was go to bed and not think or talk about anything. So my voice came out harsher than I intended. 'I was with my sister. Didn't you get my text?'

'No. I've been trying to call you all evening. I was worried sick.'

I examined my phone. The text I'd sent Charlie had an exclamation mark beside it, meaning it hadn't sent.

'Twenty-three missed calls?' I said. 'That's a bit fucking excessive, isn't it? I'm going to bed.'

She stared at me with wide eyes, as silent as the TV.

<hr>

A while later, I felt her crawl into bed beside me, then put her arm around me, nestling against my naked back. She stroked my chest, moved her hand down to my belly, but when I didn't respond she gave up and soon the pattern of her breathing changed.

Even though I was drunk and exhausted, I couldn't sleep, was unable to get the conversation with Tilly, Rachel and Henry out of my head. I had decided, perhaps because it was what I wanted to believe, that Tilly was right. To blame Charlie for all the weird stuff that had happened lately was like embracing a crazy conspiracy theory. Everything had a logical explanation. Charlie hadn't been anywhere near me when I'd slipped down the steps. Sasha's problems were almost certainly down to her affair with Lance. Kristi had either been targeted by a random nutter or attacked by a spurned boyfriend. None of it could be connected.

I felt terrible. I had been horrible to Charlie when I'd got home. She didn't deserve it. I wriggled around, put my arms round her and kissed her. She stirred and I whispered that I loved her. Her lips twitched into a smile and pretty soon I fell asleep.

The next morning, I woke early and made Charlie breakfast, taking it to her in bed. Scrambled eggs on toast, coffee, a note telling her how much I loved her.

'What's all this for?' she said, rubbing the sleep from her eyes.

'I was a dickhead last night. This is my attempt at saying sorry.'

'It's OK. But you should have let me know where you were.'

'I know. I didn't realise my text didn't send.'

'All right. But I was worried. And I wanted to see you. You know I'm going away on my course today?'

I frowned. The course was in Newcastle and I wouldn't see her for four days. But when she got back, she'd be moving in.

'I'll sort the flat out while you're away,' I said. 'Make room for your stuff.'

She gave me her sweetest smile. 'I can't wait. But you don't have to. I don't have much stuff. A lot of it is here already.'

As she ate her breakfast, I told her about my visit to Victor's office and about Karen, which made her gasp. I told her about the old man, too, but left out the part about the dark spirit. I would tell her another time, when I was able to turn it into a joke. I had thought I'd be able to do that already, but as I opened my mouth to talk about it I went cold and the joke died in my throat.

'Oh, how did the session go with the therapist?' I asked. The first one had been the evening before.

'It was fine.' She paused. 'I don't really want to talk about it. It's private. But I think it's going to help. Actually, I think it's helping already. Like, last night . . . I didn't accuse you of being with another woman, did I?'

'No.'

She was quiet for a moment. 'You weren't, were you?'

'Of course—'

'I'm joking, Andrew. And by the way, I got your Facebook friend request.'

'I was going to ask you about that.'

'I'm really sorry. It's just that I knew that you would want us to be friends on there if you knew I had an account, but I think it's silly. I mean, why do we have to communicate online when we can do it in the flesh? I know couples who talk to each other more on Facebook than they do verbally. It's stupid. I don't want us to be like that. I want our relationship to be special. Does that make sense?'

'I think so. Charlie . . .'

'Yes?'

'You haven't ever . . . been on my Facebook account on my computer . . .'

She interrupted. 'No, of course not. What are you talking about?'

'Nothing. Just being an idiot.'

The women who unfriended me on Facebook must have done it themselves. Maybe they were tired of reading about my new girlfriend and my leg injury. I had been pretty boring on there recently, I had to admit.

'I'm going to miss you,' I said a bit later, as she stood in the doorway with her little suitcase.

We hugged and kissed. I had tears in my eyes.

'It's only a few days, silly,' she said.

'I know.'

'And when I get back—'

'We'll be living together.'

She kissed me and ran her hand over my chest. 'How am I going to get through four days without your body?'

'I don't want you to go, Charlie.'

She laughed. 'Oh God, look at us. Lovesick before we've even parted.' She gave me the naughty look I liked so much. 'But our reunion will be fun.'

I went downstairs with her and waved her off. I watched her walk along the road, her black coat flapping about her, red hair whipped by the breeze. She turned and blew me a kiss. She was lovely. How could I ever have doubted her?

My mobile rang as I was going up the stairs.

'All right, mate?'

'Victor!' I was lost for words temporarily. 'How are you?'

He made a familiar groaning noise. 'A lot fucking better than I have been. I'm in Brixton at the moment. That's near you, isn't it? Fancy meeting for a coffee? Oh, and by the way, I'm not a fucking paedophile.'

———

We met at a coffee shop in the market and as I approached the table Victor stood and gave me a bear hug. His eyes were moist and he smelled of cigarette smoke.

'You OK?' I asked. I had never known him to be tactile before and was sure he didn't smoke.

'Yeah, yeah, I'm good. Do I smell of fags?'

I nodded.

'I need to quit again. You know, I hadn't even thought about smoking for ten years. Then as soon as all this shit kicked off, the only way I could get through it was by chain smoking.' He drummed his fingers on the big wooden table. He was all nervous energy, twitches and tics. 'I got a call from the police this morning. They're dropping all charges.'

'Oh, that's brilliant.'

'Isn't it? Though they shouldn't have charged me in the first place. I mean, me, a paedo! I'm the kind of bloke who thinks people like that should be strung up by their bollocks in public. The thought of it . . . Jesus.'

'So – what happened?'

He blew on his coffee. 'The police don't know who's behind it, but someone set that site up to stitch me up. This whole thing about me going to meet a young girl . . . I'll tell you what happened.'

I waited while he pulled the words together in his head.

'So, a few days before this all kicked off, I had this weird friend request on Facebook. Someone called Sarah Smith. Middle-aged, quite attractive, same age as me. I thought it must be some old classmate I don't remember and accepted it. Didn't think nothing of it.

'Then I started getting messages from her, saying I looked really fit in my pictures.' He laughed humourlessly. 'So I made the mistake of responding, didn't I? Flirting. I mean, I thought it was just a bit of harmless fun. I wasn't going to *do* anything.' He sighed. '*Then* she suggested meeting up and I said yes.' He pulled a face. 'That's the bit my missus is upset about. But I really wasn't intending to do anything. I was just, I don't know, curious.'

He fiddled with a cigarette packet as he spoke, turning it over and round in his hands, picking at the edges, the gruesome image of a man with a throat tumour rotating in front of my eyes.

'Except she didn't turn up, which to be honest was a massive relief. I went home and the next day the police turn up and show me that website. They've got all these screenshots from Facebook—'

'I've seen it,' I said.

'I thought you might have. But the screenshots were Photoshopped and Sarah Smith's profile was changed to that of a twelve-year-old girl. Same profile but new photo, new age, new everything. And there were photos of me at the meeting point, lurking about looking shifty. Someone must have been taking pictures of me with a long-lens camera.'

'Oh my God.'

'Yeah. Anyway, the police tracked down the IP address of this Sarah Smith, who was obviously a made-up person, to an internet cafe here in Brixton. No CCTV or anything, though, not that the police are really that interested.'

'Is that why you're here?'

He nodded. 'I wanted to check the place out. See if I saw anyone I recognised. But no joy, just a load of students.'

'What about the images on your computer?'

He rubbed his face. 'Christ. The police showed me the pictures. I'm never going to get over it, mate. Little kids . . . Actually, I can't even talk about it. Heartbreaking stuff. The kind of stuff that makes you want to seriously hurt the people responsible.'

'I don't even want to imagine it.'

'Vile stuff. Anyway, the police accept that they have no evidence that it was me who downloaded the pictures. Loads of people have access to my computer – the cleaners, the IT department. Plus we had a break-in a few days before this all happened. I didn't report it because nothing got nicked and I didn't want the hassle. So the police thought I was lying at first.' He sighed. 'Anyway, my lawyer was able to persuade them they didn't have a leg to stand on and they've finally dropped the case.'

'Thank God for that.'

'Too right. Come on, let's go outside. I need one of these.'

We stood outside in the cold and he lit up. 'I'll quit soon. Maybe I should try one of those e-cigarettes. Anyway, there are two things I need to talk to you about. The first one is the job. I'm really sorry, mate, but business is pretty bad at the moment. Emma and the others did their best while I was away but there are a lot of twats out there who decided they didn't want to do business with us anymore. Now I've been cleared I'm hoping they'll come crawling back. But in the meantime, I can't afford to take anyone on. I feel crap about it, but . . .'

'It's fine.' I tried not to show my disappointment. 'I'm just happy the mess is being sorted. What was the second thing?'

He blew out smoke and squinted at me. 'Have you . . . heard about Karen?'

I stared at the ground. 'Yes. Awful. Do you know how it happened?'

'It was a heroin overdose.'

'What?'

'Yeah. I heard from her sister, Violet, who's a friend of the missus. They had the coroner's report yesterday. Heroin. I can't believe Karen was into that shit.'

I couldn't either. 'She wasn't into drugs when I was with her. The odd spliff. We took E together once because she'd heard it was meant to be an amazing experience. But heroin?'

'I know. I spoke to her a few weeks ago, just before all this paedo crap happened. God, that seems like a long time ago now. We mainly talked about me but I've been wracking my brain trying to think if she seemed different in any way. Like I'd be able to tell. Most drug users function pretty normally, especially early on.' He tutted. 'We talked about you a bit. She told me she was really happy with the work you did for her, in the end anyway. She thought it was a bit weird though.'

I hadn't been listening properly, because I'd been remembering the phantom text I'd received from her the night I'd taken the sleeping pills, asking me to call her. The text that I was sure I'd hallucinated. I snapped out of my reverie. 'What was weird?'

'You. Sending your girlfriend round there to get your money.'

It took a moment for this to sink in. 'What?'

'Karen said that you sent your bird round to see her, to have a go at her about making you do all that work again. She was really surprised, thought you'd turned into a right wanker. Karen said your bird said something about how no one could get away with trying to take advantage of you anymore. Hey, are you all right, mate? You look like you're about to have a funny turn.'

I sat down. All I could think about was what Charlie had said the night Sasha had come round for dinner. *If you wanted to murder someone, the best way to do it would be to make it look like a drug overdose.*

'I think I'm going to be sick,' I said.

Twenty-nine

Victor took me back to my flat in a taxi and escorted me up the stairs, huffing and puffing behind me and exclaiming loudly about how someone 'should put a fucking lift it here.'

Sat down at the table with a cup of tea – three sugars – in front of me, Victor said, 'Fucking hell, Andrew, talk about an attack of the vapours. I thought I was going to have to carry you to the cab.'

'It's the hangover,' I said. 'Low blood sugar.' I sipped the hot tea, the sweetness bringing me back to life. But my heart was skittering, banging.

'Whatever you say.' Victor had found a can of Coke in the back of the fridge, which he cracked open, a little wisp of condensation rising and catching my eye. 'So are you going to tell me what's going on?'

I couldn't meet his eye. 'Finding out about Karen – that's all it is. It's such a shock.'

He scrutinised me. 'So you knew your girlfriend had been to see her?'

'I . . . Yeah. I didn't want her to, but . . .' I trailed off, unable to force the lie out.

'Pretty shitty thing to do, if you ask me,' Victor said. 'Maybe I got you all wrong, Andrew. Maybe you're not the decent bloke I thought you were.'

I couldn't speak.

'Anyway, I need to get home. The missus is cooking a special celebratory dinner tonight.'

'All right. Thank you for, well . . .'

'Yeah. Whatever.' He smiled sardonically. 'Better make sure I don't piss you off, hadn't I? Don't want your girlfriend paying me any unexpected visits.'

I watched from the window as he headed off down the road, then sank onto the sofa, head in hands.

I hated lying to him, but I had no other choice, not until I had all this straight in my head. If I had told Victor that I hadn't known about Charlie going to see Karen he would have started asking questions – questions which would lead on to me telling him all the things I had suspected her of, before Tilly had sprung to her defence, including setting him up. And if I told him that, he would go to the police.

I couldn't have that, not now. Not before I had figured it all out. I couldn't risk it. I loved her. If she was innocent and got the slightest hint that I suspected her of doing these terrible things, I'd lose her. No relationship could survive such an accusation.

I made myself a coffee, splashed my face with freezing water from the tap. My head felt clearer.

Here was what I knew: Charlie had said, albeit in a jokey way, that if she were going to murder someone, she would fake a drug overdose. Karen, who had never been into drugs, as far as I knew, had died from a heroin OD. Charlie had secretly visited her shortly before Karen died. Also, she had said to me, by text, that she thought Karen had taken advantage of me – the words she had used when she went to see Karen.

If I was on a jury, would I convict her on that basis? It was – what was it called? – circumstantial evidence. Charlie's defence would be that she was only kidding about the heroin overdose, that she would never actually kill anyone.

What about her motivation?

That was simple: jealousy. Charlie hated me working for Karen, loathed me having anything to do with her. Maybe she thought I was still interested in her, that we would have an affair. But I hadn't shown any signs that I was still into Karen, had been moaning to Charlie about how annoyed I was with her. I could picture Charlie going to see Karen on my behalf, thinking she was doing me a favour, getting my money. But why do it without telling me? And where was the cheque? She hadn't given it to me.

I tried to think it through, how it might have happened. Charlie goes to see her, on the pretext of getting my money, and then – what? Did she always intend to kill her or was it only something that happened after she'd met Karen? Did Karen say something that enraged her, that made her flip out, her jealous fury driving her to do something terrible? She hadn't done anything on their first meeting, so she would have had to go back.

How do you give someone a smack overdose anyway? I imagined the possible scenarios: Charlie slipping a loaded syringe out of her bag, plunging it into Karen's arm; hiding in her flat when she was asleep and slipping the needle into her skin; holding a gun to her head and instructing her to inject herself. None of these scenes, especially the one involving the gun, seemed realistic. They were like snatches from *noir* films, with Charlie in the role of the deadly *femme fatale*. Maybe Karen really was into drugs. Thinking about it, it did fit with her experimental, hedonistic persona. She had told me on many occasions that she was willing to try anything once, that she believed in having as many interesting experiences as possible before she died. Karen had seemed ill and pale the last time I'd seen her; her tardiness in paying my invoice was uncharacteristic. If she had been addicted to heroin, and Charlie had somehow found out, all she would have to do would be to turn up with a narcotic peace offering, some extra-pure gear that Karen couldn't cope with.

The light-headed sensation was returning, like there were huge, rubbery bubbles floating in my skull. Could I picture Charlie doing those things? I'd already been through this once, had shared my fears with the group the night before, and convinced myself it was ridiculous. Charlie was lovely. Warm, generous, kind, nurturing, sensitive. Almost everything she had done for me had been sweet and selfless, the actions of a woman in love. She had a strong moral core too: she loathed exploitation, as I had seen when she'd discovered I had a cleaner; she cried if she saw someone being bullied on TV; she refused to watch films or programmes in which children were hurt because it affected her too much. She had told me she worked for the NHS, when she could have made more money accepting contracts to work for private companies, because she believed in the cause.

'They helped my mum when she had cancer,' she told me. 'For a while, I wanted to be a nurse or a doctor, but I wasn't cut out for medicine in the end. Hence project management.'

The Charlie I knew and loved was a good person.

And yet. There was her jealousy. The explosion of fury and self-destruction the night I'd stayed over at Sasha's. She had shown a violent side that night, even if it had been directed at herself. She could be confrontational. The very first time I'd been out with her, she'd started an argument in the pub. She definitely had a dark side, a wild aspect to her personality that made her do things that most other people wouldn't do: like have sex in a freezing lake in the middle of winter. These were just the things I knew about. Because as Henry had said, all the weird stuff in my life had started after I met Charlie.

I vacillated. Could she have done it? As I grappled with the question, a voice inside my head shouted at me to stop. The word 'love' wasn't strong enough for how I felt about her. I could hardly imagine life without her. So how could I entertain the notion that she was a killer? This notion was like a virus invading my bloodstream, and my love made antibodies that fought and rejected every negative thought.

I got up and made another coffee, leaned on the worktop – one of the many places in the flat that bore a ghostly imprint of our lovemaking – and waited for the kettle to boil.

What did I really know about Charlie? I hardly knew a thing about her past. She was cagey about her entire existence before she'd met me; was equally secretive about the parts of her life that didn't involve me now. I'd never been to her place, though she told me it was because it made sense for her to come here, where we had privacy, no housemates listening outside the door.

I had never met any of her friends. But she hadn't lived in London long, said she didn't know anyone here.

I imagined myself in court again, a witness – for the prosecution! – explaining my relationship with Charlie. Would I look like a fool? The guy who doesn't know anything about the woman he's been sleeping with for the last two months, who he's about to move in with. I tried to justify it to myself. It had been an insane rush, passionate, exciting, with no pause for reflection. Charlie had a talent for diverting me if I asked her anything. I had been concerned about it at first, about how little she gave away, but then I decided to let it go. All I really cared about was what she was like in the present, who she was when she was with me. There would, I had thought, be plenty of time for us to share stories about the past.

This was agony. I knew people would say that if I refused to go to the police, I should talk to her about it. But what was I supposed to say? 'Charlie, did you kill Karen and arrange to have me pushed down the stairs? Oh, no reason – just curious.'

It wasn't funny though. It really wasn't. Because this was not just about me and Charlie and the things I thought she might have done. It was also about what she might do in the future if I didn't act.

If Charlie had killed Karen, then surely any woman I had a relationship with would be in danger. Like Sasha, I realised. Could Charlie be responsible for the stuff that had happened to her too? Sasha was convinced it was Lance and Mae, but she might change her mind if I told her about Charlie's jealousy. There was Harriet, too. She'd already been burgled – and the thief appeared to have targeted the lingerie I bought her, a detail that made my head hurt. What if that was only the beginning? Again, I found it painful to contemplate. But if Charlie was really behind this, then everyone I knew, including me – especially me – was in danger.

What could I do? I tried to think of it in a legal way again. I either needed hard evidence or, failing that, I needed to know more about Charlie and her past, find people who knew her. Did she have a criminal record? Had anything like this ever happened before? Maybe I would uncover an alibi for the night Karen died.

I grabbed a piece of paper from the printer and listed the various crimes Charlie might be behind, starting with the attacks on other women:

Karen's death.

That was the big one, the worst. Could Charlie really be capable of murder? Had her jealousy really spun so far out of control? With a swirling sensation in my gut, I carried on.

Threats against Sasha.
Harriet – burglary.
Kristi – acid in face.

My hand trembled as I wrote these down, each name. My best friend, my ex, my attractive cleaner, whose now-ruined face had been so pretty. To do these terrible things, my girlfriend would have to be insane. Could I really be sleeping with someone who was capable of these terrible things? I moved on to the other weird occurrences that had impacted on my life since I'd fallen for Charlie.

Victor framed for paedophilia.

Why would she do this? To stop me working for Victor. But why – to stop me working with a bunch of cool, attractive women? There was a certain warped logic to it. But was Charlie capable of such a complex set-up?

The thing was, I didn't know what she was capable of. Large parts of Charlie's life, her past, were still shrouded in secrecy. I shook my head, was tempted to screw up the paper, rip it to shreds. Was I the crazy one, entertaining these possibilities? I forced myself to carry on, to write down the last suspected crime.

Me pushed down steps.

Why would she do this? If she loved me, why would she want to hurt me? The answer came quickly:

To keep you trapped in your flat. To stop you starting your job. To make you her prisoner, like a pet in a cage.

Was that her idea of love?

I got up, paced the room, feeling light-headed and nause-ated, then returned to the list, trying to view these possible crimes coolly, rationally.

All of them had a logical explanation that didn't involve Char-lie. She definitely hadn't been there the day I'd fallen down the steps. Did that mean she had enlisted someone else's help? The more I studied the list, the more my head hurt. Perhaps I should go to the police, let them gather the evidence . . . No, I couldn't. I didn't want to risk her leaving me before I knew for certain. But if I distrusted her enough to suspect her of any of this, could I really love her as much as I claimed? Yes, yes I could.

Another little voice in my head whispered: *And if she is guilty – would you forgive her? Would you want to be with her anyway? Maybe it excites you, turns you on?*

I shook my head violently.

It came down to this: I loved her. I wanted her to be innocent but I didn't know if she was. I needed more proof before I went to the police or confronted her. And if, as I prayed, she *was* innocent, I could clear my head of all this and we could go on as before. But she could never know I had suspected her. I had to be discreet.

I walked across the room, thinking about secrets stacked upon secrets, and as I reached the window, something crashed into the glass.

'Jesus!' I cried out. What the hell was that?

I looked down. A small bird – a sparrow or starling – lay dead on the tiny balcony. I rubbed my arms and heard Karen's neighbour's voice in my head. *A dark spirit has attached itself to you.* I shivered. It was getting dark outside, the streetlights flicking on. I stared at the dead bird, with its broken neck and mashed beak, and realised I needed to retrieve it so it didn't rot and start to stink.

I pushed the sash window up and went to look for a carrier bag. As I was hunting beneath the sink, where dozens of plastic bags lived inside other plastic bags, the doorbell rang.

I pressed the intercom. 'Hello?'

The voice at the other end sounded faint, nervous.

'Hello, Andrew? Can I come up? It's Rachel.'

Rachel? What on earth was she doing here?

Thirty

Rachel came up the stairs and stood blinking at me, her shoulders hunched inside her leather jacket, crash helmet in hand. Her short dark hair was squashed and she had grey crescents beneath her eyes. She was wearing her full biker gear: leather trousers, boots, gloves. She smelled faintly of petrol and fresh sweat.

'I've left the bike outside. Is that OK?'

'Yeah, sure. Er . . . come in.'

She followed me into the flat. She looked like a fox that had evaded the hunt, eyes darting about nervously. Taking off her biker gear made her appear even more vulnerable, like she was removing her armour, a turtle rolling over to reveal its belly. Having her here made me feel nervous too. A young woman in my flat. But Charlie was hundreds of miles away. She would never know.

'Are you on your own?' she asked.

'Yes. Charlie's on a course in Newcastle.'

'Oh.' She relaxed a little.

'What is it, Rachel? Why are you here? Is Tilly all right?'

She gripped her crash helmet. She was trembling. As she answered me she put her hand in front of her mouth. 'Yeah, she's fine. Sorry, I didn't mean to worry you.'

I was perplexed but decided to let her tell me in her own time. I offered her a tea and she accepted gratefully.

We sat down and I waited.

'I like your flat,' she said, glancing around.

'Thanks.'

It was dark outside now and I hadn't removed the dead bird. I'd have to do it in the morning. I went over and shut the window, wondered if I should offer Rachel a blanket. She was still shivering.

'I'm really sorry to barge in on you,' she said. 'But I couldn't think of anyone . . . You're the only person I know in London and I had to get out of Eastbourne.'

'What's happened?'

'It's Henry. I needed to get away from him.'

She burst into tears. Awkwardly, I went into the bathroom and came back with a loo roll which I passed to her. After she'd stopped crying and blown her nose a couple of times, she apologised again.

'It's OK, Rachel. What's happened? What's Henry done?'

She was, I realised, terrified. Her voice dropped to a whisper. 'He attacked me. I thought he was going to kill me.'

'Oh my God. What . . . why?'

'He . . .' She trailed off, squirmed in her seat. 'I don't . . . really . . . I can't. I'm sorry.' Her hand crept up to obscure her whole face. 'I'm sorry.'

'Hey, it's OK. I don't need to know.' I paused. 'He seemed like a nice guy.'

'Despite what he looks like?'

I smiled.

'That's what I thought. He was at first. Sweet and funny but with that edge of danger. It's attractive, you know?'

I nodded. 'I know.'

'But I'm scared. I don't know what to do.'

'You should go to the police,' I said, fully aware of the irony.

'I don't want to. What will they do? He'll deny it and then it will be even worse for me.'

'Did he actually . . . hit you?'

She stood up and took off her leather jacket and for a moment I thought she was going to show me her bruises. Instead, she sat back down and said, 'It was more like pushing and shouting and . . . he spat at me. In my face.'

'Fuck.'

'It's next time I'm worried about. He said they'd get me.'

'They?'

'Him and the other bikers. His mates. I think it was just an idle threat, but . . . He said I'd tricked him. Made him think I was into him.'

'I see.'

'But he was always pestering me to go out with him and, in the end, I thought why not? I haven't been with anyone for ages and I thought going out with Henry would be fun, just like going out with a friend. It was when it came to sex that . . .' Her words trailed off.

'You don't have to tell me any more,' I said, embarrassed for her.

'Thanks. To be honest, I don't think he even noticed that I didn't really fancy him . . . I mean, I like sex, don't get me wrong, I love it, but not with . . .' She trailed off again.

I squirmed. This really was embarrassing.

She gathered herself. 'It was when I tried to end it, after I realised what a stupid mistake the whole thing was, that he went mad.'

A horrible, selfish thought struck me. 'Hang on – does he know you've come here?'

She shook her head quickly. 'No!'

'You're sure he didn't follow you?' My pulse accelerated at the sound of a motorbike on the street and I rushed to the window. But it was some guy on a little Honda.

'He's at work. He definitely didn't follow me. Don't worry.'

'OK. So what are you going to do?'

'I don't know. I just thought if I could get away for a few days, then I'll talk to him. My sister lives in Cardiff. I'm going to head up there tomorrow.' She met my eye for the first time. 'I don't want to be with him anymore. But maybe if I give him a few days to calm down, he'll leave me alone.'

'My God, Rachel. If he continues to threaten you, you have to call the police.' I sipped my tea but it had gone cold and I spat it back into the mug. 'Does Tilly know what's going on?'

'Yes. But don't worry, she'll be safe. He's not going to attack her. He really likes her.'

'You're sure?'

'Yes. Don't worry. I wouldn't have left her alone if I wasn't one hundred per cent confident.'

I looked at my watch. It was five o'clock. 'I think we should open some wine. I could do with a drink.'

'I'll give you some money for it.'

'Don't be silly.'

I opened a bottle of red and poured two glasses. It slipped down, making me feel better almost immediately.

'So is it OK for me to stay the night?' she asked.

'Yeah, of course. You have my bed and I'll have the sofa.'

'Oh no, I couldn't.'

'Rachel. I insist.'

By nine o'clock, after we'd eaten a delivery pizza and watched a rubbish film on TV, Rachel told me she was exhausted and asked would I mind if she went to bed. She'd spent the evening checking her phone compulsively. I wasn't sure if she was receiving messages from Henry; the phone didn't beep but it could have been on silent. She didn't appear to reply to any.

A short while after she'd shut the bedroom door, my phone rang.

'Hi sexy.'

'Hi Charlie.' My heart surged and I forced myself to stay calm, sound normal. 'How's it going? How's the training?'

'Oh God. Boring with a capital B. But there's this cool woman on the course from Birmingham and I'm going to the bar with her in a bit. I'm just in my hotel room. The bed's all lovely and springy. Wish you were here.'

'I wish *you* were *here*.'

'Yeah, me too. But hotel rooms can be very sexy.' She paused and, with a smile in her voice, said, 'I'm getting changed. I'm just sitting here in my underwear at the moment.'

'Really?'

'Uh-huh. What about you?'

'Oh, you know, just lounging about in my posing pouch.'

'You're funny. Hang on.'

It had almost become a regular part of our relationship, Charlie sending me pictures of herself in a state of undress. A few seconds later, the photo arrived, her body from the neck to the tops of her thighs, clad in red underwear, stretched out on the hotel bed.

'Like what you see?' she asked.

I swallowed. Was I talking to a killer? Of course, the photo was glorious. She was glorious. Perhaps another man would have found the extra layer of danger, the possibility that Charlie was a murderer, exciting. I had kissed and touched every inch of her. I had spent almost every waking minute since we'd met thinking about her. But looking at the photo now, I felt lost. Did I really know her? Who was she? I felt sick with anxiety.

'I'm touching myself,' she said. 'Stroking my clitoris.' She let out a long, breathy sigh. 'Ah, that feels amazing. I'm so wet, Andrew. Why don't you touch yourself?'

'I am,' I whispered. But I was lying.

'Are you hard?'

'Rock hard.'

She giggled. 'I love your hard cock. Why don't you tell me what you'd like to do with it.'

I was aware of Rachel in the next room. Would she be able to hear? I got up and shut the living room door.

'What was that?' Charlie asked, her tone changing.

'Oh, nothing. I shut the door.'

'Why? There's no one there to hear you, is there?'

'No. It's just . . . cold. I'm trying to keep the warmth in the room.'

She was quiet for a few seconds. 'You've broken the spell now,' she said. 'The mood's gone.'

'I'm sorry.' I was relieved.

Charlie sighed. 'It's OK. I've got to meet Brenda anyway. Maybe I'll Skype you later. Then I'll be able to see you.'

My eyes filled with tears. 'Sounds good.'

'All right. I love you.'

'I love you too.'

I awoke with a stiff neck and fluff in my mouth. I groaned and sat up. My sofa was not designed to be slept on. Charlie hadn't called me back, just sent me a text at 1 a.m. saying she was drunk and going to sleep.

Rachel stayed for breakfast then told me she was going to head to Cardiff.

'On your bike?' I asked.

She grinned. She seemed brighter this morning. 'How else?'

'Well, be careful.'

'Are you relieved there isn't a gang of bikers parked outside?'

'Nah, I was hoping they'd turn up so I could take them on. I've got a big rolling pin.'

She giggled. 'They'd be terrified.'

I saw her out. She hesitated on the threshold and, on the spur of the moment, I gave her a hug. She looked like she needed one. Her muscles were so tense that it was like hugging a statue.

'Thank you so much,' she said, shielding her mouth. 'You saved my life.'

'Slight exaggeration perhaps, but you're welcome.'

After she'd gone, I retrieved the dead bird from the balcony and stuffed it into the bin, tied up in a carrier bag. I found the list on which I'd written Charlie's possible crimes from my pocket and stared at it. I needed to get started.

But where was I going to start? The logical place had to be her house. I could meet her housemates, take a look through her stuff, even though this made me feel deeply uncomfortable. I needed an excuse for going round there, but I'd think of one.

The bigger problem was that I didn't know her address. All I knew was that she lived in Camberwell.

I went on to Google. There were hundreds of Charlotte Summers, dozens in London alone, but none with an address in Camberwell.

Then it struck me: Charlie had loads of stuff in the flat. There was an old bag of hers in the wardrobe, a coat, various items of clothing, including her work suits. I went through to the bedroom and retrieved the bag, searching through it. A hairbrush, lipstick, an empty packet of contraceptive pills, numerous hair grips, packets of tissues, a box of condoms, a loose key . . . All this detritus tumbled out. Among it, an envelope, folded in half. I opened it and inside was a payslip with her address printed in the top left.

'Bingo,' I said.

Thirty-one

Charlie's building was not at all what I expected. I thought, like me, she would live in a converted Victorian house, although I wasn't sure where that impression had come from. Instead, the address I'd found on the envelope was of a large 1960s building, a former local authority block housing thirty or forty small flats. It sat just off a busy main road near the Arts College and, in the dying light, looked foreboding and depressing, the England flags that were draped from several windows making the place appear even more unwelcoming.

I went up three flights of steps and found Charlie's door. There was no one around. Apart from the smell of lunch being prepared and the muffled bark of a dog inside one of the flats, the whole block could have been deserted, ready for demolition. I looked around nervously before I knocked.

I waited by the door. From inside I could hear the faint sound of a TV. I still couldn't picture Charlie living here. I had an image of her coming to the door, a couple of kids round her ankles, a shocked expression on her face. But that was impossible, of course. She had spent far too many nights at mine to be leading a double life.

I knocked again and heard a toilet flush. A male voice called out, 'Hang on.'

The door opened.

I don't know who was more shocked: me or him.

It was the guy who had been watching me in the cafe in Hoxton the day before. He was tall, maybe six-foot-four, the absence of his hat revealing a mop of curly blond hair.

I must have been more shocked than him because he recovered first, saying, 'What are you doing here?'

'I'm . . . looking for Charlie.'

'Go away.' He tried to close the door but I stepped forward, blocking it with my foot.

'If you don't let me in I'll call the police, tell them you've been following me.'

'What?'

'I saw you yesterday.'

He sneered. 'That was a coincidence.'

'But you were looking at me like you knew me. I've never seen you before, so . . .'

'Oh for fuck's sake. You'd better come in.'

I followed him into the living room. He picked up the remote and turned off the TV. A half-full ashtray and can of beer sat on the coffee table. Apart from the TV and an iPod dock, a few magazines and books stuffed untidily onto a bookcase, the room was bare. No pictures on the wall, nothing to make it look like a proper home.

'Charlie's stuff is all in her room. Boxed up. Ready for when she moves in with you.' He shook his head. 'I'm Fraser. I'm having a beer. Want one?'

It was only noon. I shook my head.

'Suit yourself. I'm having one.'

He came back and handed me a dirty glass containing tepid tap water, then gestured for me to sit down.

'So, are you Charlie's flatmate?'

He laughed. 'Yeah, you could say that.'

I decided to come back to that one. 'Why have you been following me?'

He seemed wired, his left leg twitching up and down like it wanted to detach itself and make a run for it. He stared at me, his eyes wide and unblinking, and I wondered if he was on drugs. Was *he* a smackhead? He was wearing a thick jumper so I couldn't see his arms, couldn't tell if they were covered with track marks. He was chewing gum, even while drinking his beer, and his jaw jerked in time with his leg.

'I told you, I wasn't.'

'Then why were you staring at me?'

'Because I recognised you, didn't I?'

'You mean . . . Charlie showed you a photo of me?'

He barked out a laugh. 'Yeah. Something like that.'

'What are you smirking at?'

'I've seen you in the flesh before, too.' I didn't like the way he said it. It was hot in the room but I felt cold inside. 'The first time I saw you was back in December. That night you and Charlie hooked up.'

So that was where I had originally recognised him from. That night, coming out of the nightclub. He had seen us and crossed the road. I'd hardly thought anything of it at the time.

He picked up his beer can but fumbled it, knocking it over. Beer gushed onto the carpet between his feet.

'Oh, bollocks!' he shouted, springing up and running to the kitchen, coming back with a cloth. 'Charlie will be well pissed—' He stopped himself. 'Ha. Force of habit. I don't need to worry about all that shit anymore, do I? She's your problem now.'

'What do you mean by that?'

He impersonated me, using a whiny voice. '*What do you mean, what do you mean?* You ask a lot of questions. I mean, you've got her now, haven't you? You're the one who has to deal with her issues.'

I stared at him. 'Were you and Charlie . . . together?'

Fraser snorted. 'Yeah, we were. For nine months. We moved in here together after we'd been with each other for about a month.' He looked around the empty room. 'Good times.'

'I had no idea she still lived with her ex.' At least I knew now why she hadn't wanted me to visit her place.

He picked up the almost-empty can, raised it and sucked out the dregs. 'Likes her secrets, does Charlotte.'

I almost said *What do you mean?* but stopped myself.

'When did the two of you split up?' I asked.

He frowned. 'Do you really expect me to just sit here and answer all your stupid fucking questions?'

He stood up and I shrank back, suddenly fearful of him. He was bigger than me, though he didn't look particularly strong. His face twisted into a snarl of hatred, then suddenly relaxed, and he flopped back onto the sofa. He put his face in his hands.

'I thought we were going to be together forever,' he whimpered. I realised, with horror, that he was crying. I shrank back in my seat, wishing it would swallow me up. Eventually, he wiped his face on his sleeve and groped on the table for a cigarette.

'We split up just after Christmas. That was—' He gulped, his Adam's apple bobbing. 'That was the worst week.' I could see him picturing it, like he was reliving a nightmare. Just after Christmas. That meant they were still together when Charlie and I had gone out that night.

He gathered himself. 'I don't want to talk about that week. It's too . . .' He trailed off.

That first night, Charlie had told me she was going to stay with a friend. 'Did she stay here? That first night I saw you?'

'Yeah.' He smiled with one corner of his mouth. 'She was really turned on that night. Horny as hell. I suppose I should thank you for that.'

My insides went cold.

'And now *you* get to fuck her. Amazing, isn't she? Unbeliev-able. That girl . . . I'd give anything, everything, to spend another night with her.' He stared at me as he sucked his cigarette.

'You haven't . . . slept with her since I was with her?'

He laughed coldly. 'No. I've hardly seen her. She's never here. And now she's moving in with you and I'll probably never see her again. But that's good, it's for the best. I mean, I'll be able to move on. Get my life back on track.'

I waited for him to say more but he changed the subject. 'Why are you here?'

I trotted out the lie I'd prepared. 'I want to surprise Charlie by arranging to move her stuff. I wanted to see how much there is.'

He swept an arm towards the hallway. 'Feel free. Second door along.'

I left the room, leaving him curled into a ball on the sofa. I wanted to go, to get the hell out of here, but I had come here look-ing for information. This could be my only chance. I had already found out why Charlie had taken so long to contact me after that first night. She had been with this loser. I had taken an instant dislike to him, but I wasn't sure if I believed him about yesterday. Had he already been in the cafe when I went in? I couldn't remem-ber. On balance, he was probably telling the truth about it being a coincidence.

Charlie's bedroom was almost as empty as the living room. Half a dozen boxes were piled up in the corner, along with a few carrier bags stuffed full of clothes. The bed was stripped to the mattress, the walls bare. The room smelled stale, musty.

Then I spotted half a dozen canvases leaning against the wall, one against the other. I crouched and studied them. A couple were abstract: jagged lines and swirls, blood reds and blacks. They looked angry. Another was a charcoal sketch of a man, but he had no face. Was it supposed to be me? The canvas at the back startled me. It was a collage of photographs arranged in the shape of a female body. The photos had been cut out of a book: my Rankin book, to be precise. Various models, either naked or nearly nude. Charlie had painted sharp, jagged lines in red across their flesh. It was a powerful picture. But why hadn't she asked if she could take the book if she wanted to cut pictures out of it?

'Not much, is there?' Fraser said, startling me. He was leaning in the doorway. 'You could probably take it home on the bus.'

'She never had much stuff,' he continued, swaying in the doorway, his eyes pink and unfocused. 'I used to joke that she always acted like she was preparing to go on the run.'

'How did the two of you meet?' I asked.

'I was working at King's.' Kings College Hospital was just up the road from this flat. 'I'm in IT and she was on a temp contract there, just before she started at Moorfields.'

'And do you know where she lived before that?'

He stared at me and a sly smile crept on to his face. 'She's as secretive with you as she was with me, isn't she? It used to drive me crazy. Trying to get any info out of her about her past was like trying to get a cat to go walkies. Her line was that it didn't matter, that it was all about the here and now.'

He walked into the room, came up close. His breath stank of warm lager and I shrank away as he grabbed my arm and leaned in close, his nose inches from mine. 'Do yourself a favour, mate. Don't let her move in. Get away while you can.'

I pulled my arm free. 'Why are you saying that? A minute ago you were saying you'd do anything to spend another night with her.'

'Yeah. A night. Not a *day*.' He pulled up the sleeve of his jumper and I gasped. The skin was criss-crossed with slashes, most of them scars but some fresh, scabbed over, the skin between the knife-marks looking like it was going to peel off.

'See this. This is what Charlie did to me. She fucked me up.' A noise came out of his mouth that was half laugh, half sob. 'She really fucked me up.'

I waited for him to calm down.

'What did she do?' I asked quietly, dreading the answer.

He sat down on the edge of the mattress, picked at one of the long scabs on his arm. 'It's hard . . . it's hard for me to talk about. But you know her. You must have seen it. Signs, at least.'

I didn't want to give anything away. I had no idea if I could trust him. And with the conflict raging inside me, the internal war between virus and antibodies, I didn't want to say anything negative about Charlie. I was still hoping that, any minute, the lights would come on and the truth would be illuminated – the truth being that Charlie was innocent of everything but being jealous, that this guy was a liar or a nutter or both, and that my girlfriend and I could get on with our lives. Walk into our bright future together.

'I'm talking about how possessive she is,' he said. 'How jealous. Even though I never did anything to make her jealous. Christ, why would I want to look at other women when I had her? It didn't make sense. I used to tell her, it's irrational, illogical. Stupid.'

'What was her reply?' My throat was so dry I could barely get the words out.

'That love isn't rational or logical. That it's meant to be like this: like a tropical storm, a hurricane. Exciting and destructive and unpredictable. She said that when two people love each other they have to give themselves completely. It has to be all or nothing. No one else is allowed in.'

I wondered if this conversation was awaiting me in the future.

'She hated me seeing other women. Being in IT, I mainly work with a load of greasy blokes, but I have female friends, acquaintances. Charlie went mental if I so much as went for a coffee with them.'

'How long had you been together when she started being like that?' I asked.

'I dunno. Three months? Everything kind of snowballed after that. I mean, it just went crazy. Intense. Her temp contract ended and she persuaded me to quit my job so we could be together all the time. She wouldn't let me go out. We got all our shopping delivered. I mean, we became hermits. We stayed in *all* the time. I lost contact with everyone: my mates, my family. My mum would ring me every day, worried sick, and Charlie wouldn't let me answer it, said that I shouldn't need anyone else, even my mum. And I was so scared of her leaving me that I gave in. She had a violent temper too. She smashed up loads of my stuff, all my old vinyl, because she said I'd listened to the music with other women so it was tainted.'

'Jesus.'

'I had one album, an old Pixies album, with a picture of a topless woman on the cover. When Charlie saw it she went mental. Accused me of fancying this picture more than I fancied her. She burned it, right there in the middle of the living room. I thought she was going to burn the fucking flat down. She was screaming at me. I'm amazed the neighbours didn't call the police. But afterwards, the sex . . . That's why I stayed.' He hung his head.

I could understand. Not because he was thinking with his penis – though that was probably part of it. I could understand how you could get trapped in a bubble, the intensity and excitement addictive, this twisted version of love providing rush after rush. It was the opposite of boredom. It was being alive.

I had tasted that with Charlie too. But I wasn't like Fraser, the poor sap. I was in control now. I had told Charlie she needed to seek help for her jealousy. I wouldn't let her control me. I understood the draw of the dark side of love, knew how seductive the stormy waves could be, but I was strong enough to resist.

Wasn't I?

'I asked her to get help,' Fraser said. 'To see a counsellor about her jealousy, and she told me she was going to see one, but she lied.'

I swallowed. There were barbs in my throat.

'Then,' he said, 'it all changed. Suddenly. She went out one day and came back announcing that she had a new job, a contract at Moorfields. She told me I should get one too, get out of my pit, as she said. It was so sudden, like she'd simply got bored and decided she wasn't interested any more. She stopped wanting to have sex with me. I tried to talk to her and she said that I was being pathetic, that I shouldn't expect it to last forever. But I couldn't suddenly change the way I felt about her.'

I looked at him, at this shell of a man. Chewed up and spat out. Was this my future?

'That's when she met you,' he said. 'I followed her that night, I admit. I watched you both. I saw her kiss you goodbye. I texted her straight away, telling her that I was going to talk to you, tell you what she was really like, put you off, if she didn't come home with me. We spent the rest of that week here, talking. Fucking. I called you at one point, but chickened out and hung up. I hid Charlie's phone, which made her go mad. And at the end of that week, I was worn out. I knew I couldn't cling on anymore, that I had to let her go. We agreed that she would stay here for a little while, and she moved her stuff into the spare room. This room. And that was it – she went. Leaving me like this.'

It was raining outside now. In the silence that followed his words, I heard it beating against the window.

'What about other people?' I said. 'Did anything . . . happen to any of your friends while you were with her?'

He stared at me like he didn't understand the words. 'What?'

'Your friends. Especially female friends. Ex-girlfriends. Did anything weird happen to any of them?'

'I don't understand,' he said. 'But as soon as I let Charlie in, I broke contact with everyone, like I told you. I didn't have any female friends left. And Charlie was my first proper girlfriend.'

I let this sink in. So there had been no one to threaten the relationship from the outside.

'Do you promise you haven't been following me or Charlie around?' I said.

He nodded, but I wasn't sure if I believed him. I still didn't trust him.

'I'd better go,' I said.

I walked past him into the hallway, my legs unsteady. My injured knee throbbed and there were spots dancing before my eyes. I had an almost irresistible urge to go home and put the duvet over my head, blot the world out. Stay there forever.

'There are probably others,' Fraser said, as I opened the door.

I turned back. 'Others?'

'Like me. Other men, from her past. I bet she's left a trail of fucked-up blokes and squashed hearts. And you'll be next.' He pointed a shaky finger at me. 'Think of me, when she decides to leave you.'

'I bet you're hoping she will,' I said. 'Because you'd have her back, wouldn't you? You'd want her back, anyway.'

He shook his head. But I knew he would. He'd have her back in a heartbeat.

Thirty-two

I leaned my head against the window of the bus, welcoming the vibrations into my skull. The man in the seat in front was talking earnestly to his companion about how Jesus had come to him in a dream and told him that the world would end on April 1st. 'And it won't be no April Fool's joke!'

I had found out nothing to prove that Charlie was either innocent or guilty of murdering Karen. But I had been given a terrifying glimpse into what life with Charlie might be like. Did I still want to prove her innocence? Maybe I should go to the police now, tell them my suspicions. Explode everything. Go back to being alone.

But even as I thought this, a text arrived on my phone.

Hi handsome. What are up to? Feeling REALLY rough this morning. Can't concentrate. Why the hell do they have to do training at the weekend? Call me later – maybe we can Skype? Finish what we started yesterday. Love and miss you. xxx PS Can't wait to live with you :) Exciting! xxx

I sighed. How could any of it be true? How did I know Fraser wasn't lying or exaggerating? He didn't seem like the most stable person on earth, and the more I thought about it the more convinced

I was that he was lying about following me. Even if a lot of what he'd said was true, that had been *his* relationship with Charlie, not mine. He was weak. He had caved in to all her demands, pathetically grateful that she was his girlfriend. The dynamics in their relationship were all wrong; they created bad weather. I would never allow anything like that to happen. Knowing that Charlie was prone to jealousy, possessiveness, even obsessive behaviour, didn't put me off her. I didn't want a boring girlfriend and as long as it didn't get out of control, it would be worth it. I suppose there was also part of me that relished the challenge, that wanted to be the one who rescued her, an atavistic urge that lay deep within my psyche, the need that we men feel to be the gallant prince, the hero, the only man able to tame the wild woman. I wasn't proud of this. It was just the way it was.

I wanted to rewind time, just a few days, back before I had started to wonder about Charlie. Back when everything was straightforward.

Instead, I still needed to prove her innocence to myself.

I texted her back, still pretending everything was normal.

Hi gorgeous. Not up to much. Miss you too. Def Skype later. I'll wait up. xxx

I sat back and tuned out the doom-mongering warnings of the guy in front. Being on the bus prompted thoughts of the bag Charlie claimed to have left on one just like this. I was now certain that she had been lying. I could picture her rifling through it, spying on my past, feeling sick as she discovered the old photos and letters from ex-girlfriends. Then, in a jealous rage, she had decided to destroy the bag. Dump it in a bin somewhere. She wouldn't have been able to come up with a story to explain removing just the items relating to my exes; she'd needed to get rid of the whole thing. Then she made up the tale about losing it on a bus, pretended that she had been calling London Transport every day in a desperate bid to find it.

There was, of course, a big difference between the things I knew or strongly believed she'd done – cutting up my photography book, destroying my bag of mementoes – and killing someone. I now knew that she could be jealous, secretive, a liar. But those were things I could deal with, could talk to Charlie about. I didn't expect her to be perfect. Nobody is.

The crux, I reminded myself, was whether she was jealous, secretive and duplicitous enough to be the one thing that I would never be able to forgive her for. A murderer.

I stared at the filthy streets as they rolled by. I knew where I needed to go next, who I had to talk to.

Harold's expression changed from puzzlement to delight when he opened his door, his little dog, Dickens, bounding about at his feet.

'You changed your mind?' he said.

'Can I come in?'

'Yes, please, do. I was just making tea.'

I followed him into what I guessed he would call the sitting room. A fire burned in the hearth and Harold's dog, Dickens, lay on the rug, chin on paws. The scene reminded me of going to see my grandparents, my mum's parents, when I was little. They had out-lived my parents – I remember them at the funeral, him stoic, her sobbing – but died a few years later within weeks of one another. Couples in my family die in pairs.

Harold came and sat in the armchair opposite mine, putting the tea tray on the table between us and tossing half a biscuit to Dickens, who snatched it up and swallowed it in one gulp.

'How have you been?' Harold asked, leaning forward and looking not only directly at me but at the air around me, his eyes roaming about my periphery. It was disconcerting.

'Not bad.' I didn't want to give too much away. 'I wanted to ask you a couple of questions – about Karen.'

He nodded very slowly. 'That would be fine. But only if you agree to do something for me.'

I knew what he was going to ask.

'Let me read your aura.'

What harm could it do? It wasn't like I believed in any of his hokum. As long as I didn't let what he said worm into my head, it would be fine.

'All right.'

He rubbed his hands together. 'Marvellous.'

'Do I need to do anything to prepare?' I asked.

'Yes, please take off all your clothes, dear boy, and leave them on the chair.' He smiled wickedly at my expression. 'I jest. You don't need to do anything except stand here, in front of the white wall, and relax.'

He stood before me and reached up, his hands hovering over my head, one on either side, then slowly moved them down so they were a couple of inches from my cheeks. I closed my eyes. Harold had terrible breath, like he had rotting meat trapped in his teeth, and I tried not to breathe through my nose. He made a low humming noise as he studied me. Despite the halitosis smell and my scepticism, I could feel my muscles unknotting like I was having a deep tissue massage. At the same time, I felt a prickle on my scalp; my stomach gurgled. My legs felt weak. I lost track of time, went deep inside my head, though when I emerged I couldn't recall what I'd been thinking about.

I opened my eyes. Harold stood before me, a grave expression on his face. He sat down and picked up his teacup, took a sip, screwed up his face like it was bitter.

'What did you see?' I asked, returning to the seat opposite.

His face was covered with his hand, his fingers pinching the bridge of his nose. I had expected a full run-down of what he had seen, expected to see a theatrical report, but he looked exhausted, grumpy. Wiped out. His voice was reduced to a cracked mumble. 'Your aura . . . It's like a bruise surrounding you. Purples and browns and greys . . . Ropes of black and blood red.'

He looked up at me, his eyes watery, unfocused. 'I don't want to alarm you.'

'Tell me.' I wasn't worried. I didn't believe in it. I wasn't sure why I was whispering. I knew I shouldn't allow him to suck me in. This way madness lay.

'Very well.' He recovered his voice a little. 'The mix of brown and grey and pink . . . That usually indicates terminal illness. Cancer or something equally dreadful.'

Now I was alarmed.

He waved his hand before I could speak. 'But I don't think that's it . . . It's more like . . . a cancer of the spirit. An emotional, spiritual sickness. There's black there too, which shows that you're experiencing great trauma, and grey, which indicates depression. It's hooked into your chakras, here and here—' He pointed to my chest and throat. 'And here.' This time he pointed at my groin.

'This is a very generalised interpretation, you understand. I could go into far more detail.'

I shook my head. 'Is it all negative?'

His mouth twitched. 'No. Not all. There's pink there too. The pale pink of love and the more vivid pink of sexual desire.'

I nodded.

'But there's something else . . . The spirit that has attached itself to you . . . It communicated with me. Showed me a vision. A woman, a woman who is obsessed with you, who believes what she feels to be love. The spirit is acting out her desires, causing havoc, what it sees as mischief.'

I studied him. I wasn't sure if he believed all this stuff or if it was a deliberate con. If the latter, what was he trying to get out of me? I guessed he would offer me more sessions, help to deal with the negative energy and the dark spirit, at which point he would charge me. Such help wouldn't come cheap. If it was a con, he was an excellent actor, because he appeared genuinely disturbed and shaken. So perhaps he was genuine, but anyone could have guessed my state of mind. We had met when I'd come here asking about a dead woman. This wasn't rocket science. The very fact, though, that he had lasered in on my biggest concern, my current obsession, made me feel cold and uneasy.

'There's a cord hooked to your crown,' Harold said, pointing towards the top of my head. 'It's draining your life force.'

'What do you suggest I do?' I asked, my voice still a whisper.

'I should do a cord cutting. It's not as alarming as it sounds.'

'No.' I really didn't want to get involved in any of this. I felt like I was having to turn down a persistent salesman. 'I don't really believe in this stuff.'

He looked at my harshly. 'Then all I can suggest is that you stay away from this woman.'

On the rug, the dog stretched and yawned, breaking the spell.

'I need to go,' I said.

He seemed terribly disappointed. As I headed for the door he said, 'You came here to ask me something?'

In my eagerness to get out – away from the images he had, despite my efforts, implanted in my head – I had almost forgotten why I'd come here.

'Oh, yes. Of course.'

I showed him my phone, a recent photo of Charlie on the screen, smiling at the camera.

'Is this your girlfriend?' Harold asked.

'Yes. Have you ever seen her near here?'

'I don't know. Maybe.' He squinted at the picture. Then, unexpectedly, he grabbed my arm. His fingers were sharp and dug into the bone of my arm. 'But this woman . . . there's a darkness about her aura too. It's screaming at me, even through a photograph. Black and red. Blood red. She's dangerous, Andrew.' He hissed in my face, a noseful of halitosis. '*Dangerous.*'

I snatched my arm away, rubbed at it. I felt terribly claustrophobic, scared, desperate to get away.

'Be careful,' he said, as I yanked open the door. 'Please. Be careful.'

———

There was one more place I needed to go before I went home. King's College Hospital, which dominated Denmark Hill, not far from my flat. Charlie's old workplace, where she'd met Fraser. I remembered reading in the newspaper reports about Kristi's attack that she was being cared for there. It had been weeks ago but I guessed she would still be there, given the severity of her injuries.

As I entered the hospital, I had a growing sense of a clock ticking. I needed to resolve the swirling questions in my head before Charlie got back. Otherwise, how would I be able to act normal around her? So far, all I had were questions and doubts. Everything was ambiguous.

I wasn't sure which ward she would be in but, after consulting the board in the lobby, I figured she would most likely be in the Brunel Ward, where patients undergoing facial surgery stayed. I would try there first.

I felt queasy with nerves as I negotiated the maze-like corridors. Would she agree to see me? Would they let me? I had no idea, but I had to try.

I eventually found the Brunel Ward and, acting as confidently as I could, told reception I was here to see Kristi Tolka. The woman behind the counter said, 'Bed thirteen' and I inwardly thanked God for providing me with this stroke of luck. Dark spirit, be damned.

Bed thirteen had a plastic curtain drawn around it, and I could hear voices from within. I paused. The voices were speaking a language I didn't recognise. Albanian, I assumed. I cleared my throat and said, 'Excuse me.'

The curtain was jerked back and a young woman with black hair and suspicious eyes peered up at me. Now I wished I'd brought flowers.

'Yes?' she said in a thickly accented voice.

'I . . . er . . . I came to see Kristi.' I couldn't see beyond the curtain to the bed.

'Who are you?' the woman asked.

'My name's Andrew Sumner. Kristi was my cleaner and I, er, heard about the terrible . . . thing that happened. I just wanted to check how she is.'

Then Kristi said something in her native language, addressing the other woman as Dita. Reluctantly, Dita gestured with her chin for me to step beyond the curtain.

I took a deep breath as Kristi came into view. She was sitting up in bed, a pillow propped behind her, a thin hospital quilt pulled up to her collarbone. The right side of her face was covered with a bandage, which wrapped around her skull and across her chin. Her lips were visible through a slit in the bandage. Only the upper left-hand side of her face, including her undamaged eye, was visible.

She fixed that eye upon me now and said, in a weak, restricted voice, 'Hello?'

'Hi Kristi,' I said, in what I hoped was a friendly, light tone. 'How are you?'

She looked at me, her eye blinking slowly. I cringed.

'How do you think she is?' Dita asked.

'I'm sorry.' I turned back to Kristi, who picked up a beaker and sucked up some juice through a straw. I noticed that there were no cards or flowers beside the bed and wondered how many people she knew in the UK. Would she go back to Albania after this? I found her future impossible to envisage. But I knew it would involve pain and suffering. 'Have they caught the person who did it?'

Dita replied for her. 'Fucking police are not even looking. Why do they care about some immigrant?' She spat out the last word.

Kristi said something to her in Albanian and Dita said, 'She is asking what you want.'

It had dawned on me that by coming here, I was making myself a suspect, particularly in the eyes of these two women. And what I needed to ask Kristi would seem strange to say the least.

I spoke to Dita, while continuing to look at my former cleaner. She had been so beautiful. It's easy to say that beauty is only skin deep, but I imagined myself trotting out that cliché now. It would be like a barb in her heart. 'I need to ask Kristi something. I want to show her a photo and ask if she recognises this person.'

I thought that, if Charlie had been behind the attack, she would have had to follow Kristi at some point so she knew her route home, which would tell her where to lie in wait. The report had said that the attacker was a man in a balaclava and black leather jacket. But wouldn't it be easy for a woman dressed like that to be mistaken for a man? Especially if it happened quickly, in the dark, and the victim was half-blinded? I wanted to know if Kristi had seen Charlie.

'I need to know if you ever saw this woman,' I said. Dita translated.

I brought up my girlfriend's photo on my phone and held it close to Kristi's face. She reached up with an arm that was also wrapped in bandages and took the phone.

She scrunched her one visible eyebrow. 'Your girlfriend,' she said in English.

'Yes. You saw her at my flat. But did you ever see her anywhere else? In the street.' Again, Dita translated.

The wait for her response was agonising. She stared at the picture. I could hear her breathing, a wet, rasping sound that emerged from the slit in the bandages.

She spoke to Dita in Albanian, and I waited impatiently for the translation.

'What did she say?'

Dita stared at me, her face pale and hostile. 'She says that your girlfriend is crazy. That she offered her money to stop cleaning your flat.'

My blood ran cold. 'When was this?'

The two women spoke and Dita shrugged with one shoulder. 'She doesn't know exactly. A day or two after she first met her? This girl, your girlfriend, was waiting outside the cleaning agency office when Kristi went to get wages. She asked Kristi to refuse to clean your flat, that she would give her £100 to stop.'

They spoke together for a moment.

'Your girlfriend had translated her words into Albanian on the internet – she had words printed out.'

'What did Kristi say?'

Another exchange.

'She said nothing. She just laughed at her. Laughed in her face.'

Thirty-three

I walked home from the bus stop, picturing myself surrounded by a bruise-coloured halo, invisible hooks and cords turning me into a living marionette, and when I went inside I was shivering and sniffing from the damp, clinging cold. Harold's and Kristi's words echoed in my head.

I could picture Charlie's reaction when Kristi laughed at her. The anger that would have bubbled up. Anger that could lead to her attacking the woman who had rejected her offer. Would Charlie really go that far? All I knew was that Charlie had felt threatened enough by Kristi to try to stop her cleaning my flat. My cleaner, who was attractive, yes, but whom I had never shown any sexual interest in. If Charlie had done what Kristi said – and I couldn't see any reason why Kristi would have lied about it – then some of the other things I suspected Charlie of seemed more in character, like setting up Victor to stop me working in his office and becoming 'exposed' to all those attractive women.

As if that wasn't enough, when I got home I found an email from Sasha in my inbox.

Hey A

How's it going? Just wanted to let you know all is quiet here at the moment. No more threatening texts or weird things going bump in the night (I have to joke about it because otherwise I'd spend every day hiding in bed, unable to go out!).

I'm sure I saw Charlie yesterday afternoon in Farringdon. She was going into the chemist's. I tried to catch her eye, not wanting to be unfriendly, but she blanked me. Hope all is good with you two. I'd like to meet up with her again, try to make amends for last time. I don't want there to be any crap between us, anything that makes it harder for me to see you.

Anyway, hope all good with you. Call me.

S xx

I called her immediately.

'I just got your email,' I said.

She mimicked my voice. '*Hi Sasha, how are you? I'm fine, thanks. How about you?*'

'Sorry. It's just . . . are you sure you saw Charlie yesterday afternoon?' I was light-headed, the walls of the flat closing in on me.

She hesitated. 'I'm pretty sure it was her, yeah. Like I said, she blanked me. Though I don't—'

'What time was it?'

'Um. I finished work early, got back into Herne Hill about four, so it would have been just after that.'

'It can't have been her. She's in Newcastle on a training course.'

'Oh.' There was a long pause. 'Well, I didn't see her face. Not properly. She was ducking into the doorway.'

'But you said you tried to catch her eye.'

Again, she took ages to respond. 'Yeah. I meant I was waiting for her to turn her head. Maybe it was someone who looks like her, wears similar clothes.'

'That must be it. Sorry.'

I hung up before Sasha could say any more. Had Charlie lied about going to Newcastle? She had given me the name of the hotel she was supposedly staying at so I looked up the number and called it. A young woman with a light Geordie accent answered.

'Hello. I need to speak to one of your guests. Charlotte Summers.'

'Do you have her room number, sir?'

I told her I didn't.

'Hold on.'

The line beeped for a while, then started ringing. If they were trying to put me through, at least that meant she was indeed at the hotel. I looked at my watch. It was five-thirty. Surely her training would have finished for the day. But then I was talking to the receptionist again. 'Sorry, sir, there's no answer. Can I take a message?'

'No, it's fine. Can you tell me when she checked in?'

An intake of breath. 'I'm sorry, I'm not able to do that. But I can take a message.'

'It's all right. I'll try her mobile.'

I stared at my phone. Sasha must have got it wrong. Of course she had. Normally, I would have known that straight away, but with everything that was going on . . . I sent Charlie a text, asking her to call me when she got a minute. After that, I looked in the fridge and took out a bottle of wine. I needed to get drunk.

When Charlie called me, a couple of hours later, I had almost finished the wine. I didn't ask her whether she'd been in Herne Hill yesterday afternoon, unable to think of a way of asking it without revealing all my suspicions. She told me about an amusing incident on the course, said that she missed me, told me they were going out in Newcastle but she didn't really want to go.

'What are you doing tonight?' she asked.

'Nothing. Staying in, watching TV.'

'You should go out. Why don't you go and see Sasha?'

'Really?'

A soft sigh. 'Yes, really. I know there's nothing going on between you, and she's your best friend. Apart from me, I mean.' She laughed. 'I need to make an effort to be friends with her.'

I felt like my brain was being ripped in two. 'She said something very similar earlier.'

'You saw her today?'

'No, she emailed me.'

'Oh, right. Well, that's good. You don't want the women in your life to be at war, do you?'

I couldn't tell Charlie that I didn't want to go out because I had no energy, that I was worried sick, that all I wanted to do was hide in my flat. So I said, 'No, I think I'm going to stay in. There's a film on that I want to watch.'

I woke up late the next day with another hangover, having polished off nearly two bottles of red wine. *This needs to stop*, I thought, running myself a hot bath, planning to sweat out the alcohol.

Charlie would be back the next day and, sitting in the bath, I made my mind up. I was going to ask Charlie about everything. I would tell her I knew about her offering Kristi money and visiting Karen. I would also tell her I knew she lived with her ex-boyfriend. It was the only way forward. I would be able to gauge her reaction to the news that Karen had died of a drug overdose, see what she had to say about Kristi and Fraser. I would look into her eyes as we spoke and, I felt confident, I would know.

I didn't know, however, what I would do with this knowledge.

I got out of the bath and walked, dripping and naked, into the bedroom. The heating was cranked up and the flat was tropical, the windows steamed up. I was sick of winter, was reaching the point I got to every year where I started to crave sunshine, my body starved of vitamin D. It had been a long winter and now even the brightness Charlie had brought into my life was diminished, black clouds over the sun. I wanted to get that brightness back.

The phone rang. It was Tilly.

She went straight into the conversation without niceties, in the same way I had with Sasha the day before.

'Did Rachel stay at yours on Friday night?'

'Yes . . .'

'And what did she say she was going to do afterwards?'

'Why? What's happened? You sound like you're about to have a panic attack.'

'No, I'm fine. I'll explain in a second. Just tell me, please.'

'She said she was going to ride up to Cardiff to stay with her sister. She left here Saturday morning. What's going on?'

I sat on my bed wrapped in just a towel, the last droplets of water on my body evaporating. I could hear the couple downstairs arguing. I wondered vaguely what colour my aura was at the moment. Red, probably. *Cabernet sauvignon.*

Tilly's voice tightened, like she was on the verge of tears. 'She never got there. Her sister waited for her all afternoon. Rachel's not answering her phone, either. I've tried to ring it a hundred times but it goes straight to voicemail, like it's turned off.'

'Oh Jesus.'

'I'm so worried, Andrew. We've been on to the police but there haven't been any reports of motorbike accidents.'

'Maybe – I mean, I don't like to say it, but what if she went off the road somewhere remote and the bike's . . . concealed somewhere.'

'In a ditch, you mean.'

Neither of us spoke.

'How did she seem Friday night?'

I realised straight away what Tilly was asking. 'You mean did she seem suicidal? No, she didn't at all. She was scared, shaken by what had happened with Henry. But she struck me as someone who very much wanted to survive.'

'That's what I told the police. Listen, they've got your name and address. They might come round to talk to you.'

'OK.' The couple downstairs had stopped arguing and were now having sex. 'What about Henry?'

'I don't know. The police asked me a *lot* of questions about him. I told them what he'd done.'

'You think he caught up with her, intercepted her?'

'Oh God, I hope not. But that's the most probable explanation, isn't it?' Her voice caught. 'I don't know what I'd do without her. I couldn't cope.'

All I could do was reassure her, say words I didn't believe. Tell her everything would be all right. But inside I was thinking, *She's dead. Another one.* And I heard Harold's voice again, talking about the dark spirit. Rachel had stayed with me – and now she was dead.

It was my fault.

Monday morning. Charlie was due back later. There was no news about Rachel, except that the police had arrested Henry, were questioning him. I kept the news channel on, waiting for a story about how the body of a female motorcyclist had been found. But there was nothing.

I needed to change the bed. The sheets smelled and a ridiculous part of me was worried that Charlie would be able to smell

Rachel on them. I stripped the sheets and opened the wardrobe to get out a clean set.

A few of Charlie's clothes had slipped off their hangers onto the wardrobe floor, including a coat and the suit I'd had dry cleaned. I picked them up and took down some coat hangers. As I held the coat, something struck me. If I was looking for evidence, surely here was somewhere else to look.

I felt terrible delving in her pockets, but reassured myself that the ends justified it. Besides, I had already looked through one of her bags, and I didn't really expect to find anything, anyway.

The coat contained nothing but a few balled-up tissues, an old Oyster card and a pair of gloves. Next I checked the trousers of the suit. Empty.

Finally, I tried the pockets of the suit jacket. There was just one pocket, on the inside, and I could feel, immediately, that there was something inside. A small brown envelope, sealed. I took it out and held it in my hands. Had the envelope been there when I'd had it dry cleaned? I hadn't checked, had just taken it out of the wardrobe and put it in a bag.

If I opened the envelope, Charlie would know. Unless I went out and bought an identical envelope, which wouldn't be hard. This one had no marks on it, no writing.

I had to do it. I ripped it open and something dropped to the carpet.

I stooped to pick it up. It was a little plastic bag, as big as a credit card. It was quarter-filled with pale brown powder.

Thirty-four

I waited in the interview room at the police station, sipping from a plastic cup of coffee. It was, I imagined, exactly like the coffee dispensed by the machines at the eye hospital, the coffee that had given me an excuse to talk to Charlie that first day. I set it down on the table. I couldn't stomach it.

The policeman at the front desk had listened to the beginning of my story with an inscrutable expression before holding up a hand to stop me. Twenty minutes later, during which I almost changed my mind and went home, a guy in a smart-but-inexpensive suit came out and gestured for me to follow him. This was Detective Constable David Moseley. I had seen enough cop shows to know this was the lowest detective rank, and Moseley had the air of somebody who was ambitious and impatient to progress. He took me into an interview room and I showed him the little bag of heroin, began to tell him my story. As I spoke, DC Moseley stared at me, occasionally glancing at the little packet of powder on the desk between us. Then he disappeared and left me waiting for another twenty minutes.

Now, DC Moseley came back into the room. This time he had a notepad with him. He licked his index finger and thumb and flicked the pad open.

'OK, Mr Sumner. Let's go over all this again. Start by telling me how and where you found what you believe to be heroin and how you believe it relates to Karen Jameson's death.'

He had taken the packet with him last time he'd left the room.

'Are you saying it might not be heroin?' I asked.

'We need to check that.'

'Have it analysed, you mean?'

He rocked his head back and forth and made a non-committal sound in the back of his throat. 'Please tell me again how you found it.'

So I recounted the tale, and then went back and told the whole story from the beginning. Trying to stay calm, though my heart was trying to burst out of my chest, I told him all the things I suspected Charlie of doing, from murdering Karen using the heroin I'd found in my flat, right back to Harriet's burglary, taking in the attack on Kristi, the framing of Victor and all the other odd and worrying things that had happened over the last couple of months. My voice cracked as I told him about going to see Fraser, what Kristi had told me in the hospital, about Charlie's jealous rage. As I spoke, DC Moseley wrote everything down in his notepad in a series of bullet points. He kept writing for a few minutes after I stopped talking, catching up while I tried to catch my breath.

He sat back and tapped the pen on the table.

'That's quite a litany of accusations,' he said.

'I know.' I sank my face into my hands. I hated this. Hated it. 'But the only one I can prove is Karen's murder.'

The detective lifted a dark eyebrow. 'Prove?'

'Well. I mean, that's the only one with any evidence. That's probably the one we, you, should concentrate on.' My voice trailed off when I saw the look he was giving me.

'Leave the detective work to us, please, Mr Sumner.'

'Sorry.'

He tapped his pen on his teeth, studied his notes. 'How well do you know this woman, Charlie Summers?'

'I told you. She's my girlfriend. Or she *was* my girlfriend.'

'Hmmm. Would you describe it as a close relationship?'

'Yes, very.'

He remained quiet, waiting for me to fill the silence. Although I suspected this was a technique he'd been taught, I still surrendered.

'Very . . . intense.'

'Intense, eh?' That eyebrow lifted again. 'And Karen Jameson, the deceased, is an ex-girlfriend.'

I met his eye. 'She wasn't really a girlfriend. But we had a relationship, yes.'

'Were still having a relationship?'

'No! It ended a long time ago.'

'So why would Ms Summers be jealous enough to want to kill her?'

'I told you this too. Because Charlie is obsessive. I was working for Karen and Charlie must have hated it.'

'Must have? She didn't tell you she hated it?'

'No. Not in those words.'

I wasn't sure exactly what I'd expected, but it wasn't this. I had imagined the police being keenly interested, treating me as some kind of tragic hero, understanding the pain I was putting myself through. How naive can you get? My story sounded like the invention of a lunatic or a fantasist. But the bag of heroin was real. Surely the police could see that this proved that Charlie was the killer?

'All right,' DC Moseley said. 'Let's go through it again.' As I started to protest he said, 'Just the last bit, involving Karen Jameson.'

'You need to talk to Harold,' I said. 'He lives in the ground floor flat in Karen's building. He might have seen Charlie . . .' I paused. I didn't want to start talking about Harold reading auras. I could imagine how that would go down with the detective. 'Victor Codsall too. Karen told him that Charlie had been to see her.'

DC Moseley doodled a number of swirls and stars around his notes. He said, 'OK, thank you. Leave it with us.'

He stood and I looked up at him. 'What are you going to do?'

'We'll talk to Ms Summers.' I had already given him details of Charlie's movements.

'And you'll be in touch?'

'We will indeed.'

I stood outside the police station with no idea of what to do next. Charlie was due back in London in a few hours. I knew she would come straight round to mine. But I couldn't be there, not now I'd found the heroin. I needed to head her off. I had no other choice: I would have to lie.

I sent her a text.

Hi Charlie. Have had to leave flat. Suspected gas leak. Why don't you go back to yours and I'll text you with the all-clear later?

I agonised over whether to put a kiss at the end. If I didn't, she would definitely know something was up. I decided to add a couple. What harm could it do? As soon as the police went to talk to her she would know I had been lying anyway.

She texted back a minute later. *Oh, OK. What a nightmare. See you later. xx*

I went to a coffee shop and sat at a table on the pavement, embracing the cold. I felt utterly miserable, more unhappy than at any time since my parents had died. It felt like all my emotions had been put into a spin dryer which was churning and tossing them around inside me. I didn't know it was actually physically possible for a heart to ache, but right now, mine did.

I had just lost the woman I loved, the woman who had made me so happy over the last couple of months. Regardless of what she'd done, I loved her. You can't turn your feelings off like a tap. Love doesn't die like that. Look at all those husbands and wives who stand by their spouses even after they've been found guilty of the most terrible crimes. Picture the mother who stands by her murderer son. Even if they know their spouse or offspring is guilty, even if it goes against everything they believe to be right and decent, they still love them. Love is hard to break. Adultery, violence, betrayal, cruelty. Love can survive them all. Although I didn't expect Charlie's love for me would survive what I'd done. She had, I believed, committed murder. But, in a way, my crime against her was even worse. I'd betrayed her behind her back.

I missed my girlfriend. I wanted to erase the last couple of weeks, to go back. I had a kind of waking dream in which Charlie and I were lying in bed, her head on my chest, talking to me, laughing, and the only other sound I could hear was the rain beating against the window.

'You all right, mate?'

I looked up. One of the baristas from the coffee shop was looking at me with a mix of concern and amusement. And who could blame him? I was sitting in the middle of a downpour, the rain lashing down on me, drenching my skin and hair, plopping into my coffee. I hadn't even noticed.

I went to Sasha's, sat outside on the steps till she got home. Luckily, the rain had stopped.

She took one look at me and said, 'Andrew? What the fuck's happened?'

'Can I come in? I'll tell you all about it.'

We sat on her sofa and she listened while I poured out the whole story, for the second time that day, though it came out as more of a jumble this time, jumping back and forth, Sasha constantly stopping me to ask questions, gasping, swearing, her mouth hanging open. It all came gushing out, like telling it to Sasha was a kind of exorcism. When celebrities write their autobiographies they always, without fail, say it's been a cathartic experience. That's what this was like. Sasha was particularly interested in the part where I described Charlie's jealous frenzy the night I stayed over with her. There was part of me that thought Sasha was enjoying this tale a little too much. Though I couldn't blame her. It was a great story, involving people she knew, and the baddie was someone she hated, who she'd warned me about.

'You haven't said *I told you so* yet,' I pointed out after I'd finished. I was spent.

'I'm not going to. How the hell were you supposed to know she was . . . like that?' She laid a hand on my arm. 'How are you coping?'

I hung my head and fought back tears. 'Not well, to be honest. I miss her, Sash. Despite everything. I love her.'

Sasha stroked my hair. 'I know. I feel the same about Lance, despite all the shit he's done.'

'How is everything with that?' I asked.

'Oh, he's gone quiet. I saw him at work today and he ignored me but he didn't look at me like he wants me to die. I think he realises I'm not going to leave Wowcom but that I'm not going to cause any trouble for him. I mean, it makes me sad to see him but a little less sad every day. So tell me—'

'I don't want to talk about it any more.'

'All right. I understand.' She squeezed my knee. 'Let's get drunk.'

'I don't—'

'Come on. You could definitely use a drink. You look like you haven't eaten for days as well.'

She was right. I had barely eaten anything since meeting up with Victor on Friday.

'I'll pop out,' Sasha said, 'get us a takeaway and some booze. What do you fancy? Fish and chips?'

I nodded. I wasn't hungry. But the booze, and the prospect of temporary oblivion, sounded perfect.

Sasha came back with two bags, the greasy smell of cod and chips emanating from one, the other containing two bottles of gin that clonked together. She put the food onto plates and poured us both a large G&T.

'Put the TV on,' she said. 'Unless you'd prefer music.'

'Telly's fine.'

It was strange being with Sasha sometimes, like we were an old married couple, completely at ease with each other. It came from when we'd lived together for two years at uni, our bedrooms adjoining. We did our food shopping and cooked together to save money, went out together all the time. Spent many nights sitting up putting the world to rights, dreaming of our futures. Most people thought we were a couple, which Sasha blamed for her lack of success with men, but we were firmly in the friend zone.

The news came on and Sasha told me to switch it over to something more light-hearted, but just as I was about to change channels, a familiar face appeared on screen and my finger froze.

'Sasha – that's Rachel!'

She came over to join me by the TV as the newsreader intoned over the photo of my sister's missing personal assistant.

Police are appealing to anyone who might have seen Rachel Marson, 27, who went missing on Saturday while riding her motorcycle from London to Cardiff. Miss Marson, who lives in Eastbourne, East Sussex, called her sister to tell her she was setting off at just after 10:30 a.m. Since then, no one has seen or heard from her. She was riding a black and purple Harley Davidson, wearing a black leather jacket and trousers and a purple crash helmet.

They went on to recount her licence plate number and to give out a phone number for anyone who might have seen her.

'Do you think she might have simply done a runner?' Sasha asked, passing me my plate.

'I hope so.'

'You should turn your phone off,' Sasha said.

'Eh?'

'You keep looking at it. All the time. It's quite distracting.'

'I can't help it. I keep thinking I'm either going to get a call from the police telling me they've arrested Charlie or a call from Charlie herself.'

Sasha took the phone from its spot beside my plate and switched it off. 'Now you can concentrate. Come on, drink up.'

I finished my first G&T and pushed the glass forward for her to refill it.

By ten, we were both wasted. Sasha had turned off the TV and put music on, and was lying across the sofa, gesticulating with her arms and legs as we talked. We were reminiscing about the old days. My anxiety was a constant buzzing at the back of my head, but it had got to the point where the front of my brain was able to ignore it, treat it as ambient noise.

'. . . And do you remember that Halloween party, the time that girl doing sociology turned up dressed as The Demonisation of Human Sexuality?'

'Oh God,' I said. 'Wasn't she completely naked?'

Sasha laughed. 'She was wearing a flesh-coloured bodysuit.'

'Oh no, I'm disappointed. I knew I should have worn my glasses that night.'

I stood up to go to the loo, and had to hold on to the back of a nearby chair to steady myself.

'Whoa,' I said.

Sasha squinted up at me. 'Where are you going?'

'To find my flesh-coloured body suit.'

She laughed again as I staggered to the bathroom. As I peed, I felt my pockets for my phone, then remembered Sasha still had it. I closed my eyes and swayed. I really was drunk. I wanted to lie down. Lie down and never get up.

When I re-entered the living room, a half-formed joke about the sociology student in my head, Sasha was sitting up, a serious, but still inebriated, expression on her face.

'I've got something to tell you,' she said.

'What is it?' I sat down on the sofa beside her.

'It's about Lance.' She took a big gulp of vodka. She was drinking it neat now. I hadn't seen her this drunk for a long time.

'What about him?'

She looked at me. 'Something I haven't told you. When our affair ended, he – he tried to kill me.'

Thirty-five

'Do you want to talk about it?' I said as softly as I could.

She nodded, not meeting my eye. 'Can you turn the music down?'

'Of course.' I got up and turned it down so it was barely audible. I thought Sasha might want some physical space so sat in the chair opposite, leaning forward so she could speak quietly.

'It happened the day he told me he didn't want to see me anymore. He said he wanted to meet me at the hotel we went to sometimes. That's when he told me he wanted to end our relationship – just after we'd had sex.'

'He waited till after?'

She stared into her glass, where the last couple of ice cubes were clinging to life. 'I know. Bastard, right? We were naked, in bed, and he told me he needed to talk about something. That's when he told me it was over. That his wife had found out about us and he'd promised her he'd end it.'

'What did you do?'

She poured more vodka into the glass. As she talked, her words slurred and she wobbled from side to side. Her face had that sloppy, unfocused look really pissed people get just before they pass out.

'I told him I was going to talk to her, to tell her exactly what we'd done together. All the really pervy stuff. I haven't told you all of it. I told him I'd tell Mae that he told me she was an ugly old bitch and that I was so much better than her in bed.'

'You wouldn't really have done that, though, would you?'

'Of course not. I was upset, angry. I wanted to scare him. Because I knew, from that moment, that he'd get away with it. He'd had his fun, got to fuck a young girl from work, and would now walk away unscathed.'

'And that's when he attacked you?'

She shook her head. 'Not at that moment. He told me to get dressed. I went into the bathroom, suddenly didn't want him to see my body, certainly didn't want to look at his shrivelled old cock. I stood in the hotel bathroom and cried. I was in there for ages, hoping he'd go before I came out.' She looked at me. 'I loved him, Andrew. I know it was stupid, that I should have known the rules. And I did feel terrible for his wife. I still do. But I couldn't help the way I felt about him.'

'I understand.'

'When I came out of the bathroom, he was still there. That was when it happened. He grabbed me by the throat, like this.' She mimed him squeezing her neck, fingers pressed hard against the underside of her jaw. 'He pushed me against the wall. He said if I went near his wife, he would kill me. He told me he knew people who could dispose of bodies. He said he could buy anything, any service.'

'Did you tell the police about this?' I asked. I felt more sober now, her story a slap round the face.

'No.'

'Oh, Sasha. Why not?'

'What's the point? There's no evidence. It's just my word against his.'

'I know. But you still have to tell them.'

She pouted. 'In case he does it to someone else?'

'Exactly. Please, Sash.'

Very reluctantly, she nodded.

'Let's do it now.'

'But it's nearly eleven.'

'I know. But the police are there all night. Come on. Where's your phone?'

I called the police station for her, before she could protest any more, and once I'd been put through I handed the phone to her. I listened to her explain everything to the police officer on the other end.

'They said they'll send someone round to talk to me first thing tomorrow. Now, I need to go to bed.'

'OK.' I stood up too, waited for her to leave the room, but she didn't move. 'What is it?'

'Will you sleep in my bed?'

'Sasha, I—'

'I don't mean sex, stupid. I just – don't want to be alone. Is that OK?'

She took hold of my hands in hers.

'Come on then,' I said.

⌣

I was woken by the insistent sound of the door buzzer. I lifted my head and it was like being punched in the face. The room was bright with sunlight and I didn't know where I was. Then I looked beside me and saw Sasha, the covers thrown off, arms and legs akimbo. She was naked. I was naked too.

Oh shit. We hadn't . . . had we? I tried desperately to remember. But the last thing I could recall was crawling into bed, Sasha asking me to hold her. No sex. I didn't think we had, was sure I would remember it.

The buzzer sounded again, like a giant angry wasp. Sasha moaned and rolled over, exposing her pale buttocks. I covered her with the quilt, pulled on my jeans and T-shirt, which were dumped at the end of the bed, and walked into the living room to look out of the front window to see who was ringing so insistently.

It was Charlie. I stepped back quickly from the window, just as her head turned. Her face was flushed with anger. I was sure she had spotted me.

I noticed my phone on the sofa, and switched it on. It immediately started vibrating with notifications: seven missed calls from Charlie this morning, a couple from my sister, a text from Charlie that was so long that it filled the screen. Before I could read it, the phone, which had been on one per cent battery when I turned it on, died.

The door buzzed again, and Sasha came into the room, a dressing gown wrapped round her. She looked like one of the walking dead, her hair Medusa-like, eyes like a dying panda's.

'It's Charlie,' I said.

She peeked out the window. 'Don't let her in.'

'I don't want to hide from her,' I said.

'Why not?'

'Because—' I couldn't find the words. Because I was a man, not a mouse? Because I felt I owed Charlie the common decency to talk to her? Or was it that I wanted to see her? This was the real reason. I missed her, was worried about her. Had she spent the night in a cell? Was it cold? Were they horrible to her?

My thoughts must have been evident on my face because Sasha said, 'Go on then. Go and talk to her. Just, please, don't tell her about last night. I don't want her coming in here trying to kill *me*.'

Before I could respond, ask Sasha if she remembered what had happened when we'd gone to bed, she had locked herself in the bathroom.

I put on my socks, shoes and coat, went down the stairs and, after taking a deep breath, opened the front door.

Charlie looked over my shoulder into the hallway before turning her attention to me, her face stony, eyes cold. But despite her expression she looked lovely: her hair looked just-washed, her long black coat hugging the contours of her body, her face clear and fresh. I closed the door and stepped onto the pavement.

'I knew it,' she said.

'Are you OK?' I asked softly.

She ignored the question. 'I knew you'd be here. With her.' Her lips twisted into a bitter smile. 'Don't worry, Andrew. I'm not going to cause a scene. I just think it would have been decent of you to tell me where you were or answer my *fucking calls*.'

Her voice was very quiet and even, right up until the final two words.

'I'm sorry. I thought—'

She interrupted me again, her voice returning to its previous quiet tone. I found this more unnerving than if she'd screamed and shouted. Plus something here didn't make sense. She wasn't following the script I had sketched out in my head.

'I've been at your flat all night, trying to stay calm, wondering if you'd had an accident. I even phoned the hospital. Then I figured it out. That you'd be with her.'

I blinked. 'Hang on. Haven't you been with the police?'

She frowned at me. 'What the hell are you talking about?'

I was speechless. She hadn't been arrested. She hadn't even been questioned. My mind raced.

Charlie had already moved on. 'So are you going to deny it this time? That you fucked her?'

I think I must have looked very stupid at that moment, my mouth gaping open, unable to defend myself because I didn't know if I'd had sex with Sasha, was still reeling from the news that Charlie hadn't been arrested. What were the police playing at?

I managed to get a grip of myself. 'Come on, let's go somewhere else to talk.' I reached out for her arm and she snatched it away like I was made of shit.

'What? Don't want to upset her? Is she up there, listening out of the window? Doesn't want all the neighbours to know what she is? A serial home wrecker.'

'Please, Charlie, come on. It's nothing to do with Sasha.'

Reluctantly, she followed me down the road and around the corner, where there was a small park with a couple of benches and a few bare trees. The sky was almost white, like it was going to snow again. I sat on a bench that glistened with frost and gestured for Charlie to sit beside me.

'No,' she said.

I didn't know what to do. If the police hadn't talked to her, she wouldn't know anything about all the things I suspected her of. Karen, the heroin, Kristi. All of it.

'Come on then,' she said. 'What do you want to say to me?'

I couldn't tell her. I simply couldn't get the words out. All I could say was, 'I'm sorry.'

She sneered. 'Sorry? *Sorry?* You think that means anything to me? Jesus Christ, last week you made me sign up to see a fucking therapist – who I didn't go to see, by the way, so stick that in your pipe – because of my "issues". But I was justified, wasn't I?' Her eyes blazed. 'Everything . . . I was fucking justified.'

Quietly, I said, 'Do you really think so?'

'What?'

'I know everything, Charlie. I know what you've done.'

She stared at me. 'What *I've* done? What the hell are you talking about?'

'Everything. Karen, for one. I've got evidence.'

She looked around, as if trying to see if anyone could overhear, but there was no one around, just a couple of thrushes pecking fruitlessly at the hard ground.

'I have no idea what you're going on about.'

A wave of nausea washed over me, almost dragging me under. I had the urge to put my head between my knees. An elderly man came into the park and walked past us. We watched him go.

'Have you been fucking Sasha the whole time we've been together?' Charlie asked. Her eyes had taken on a manic sheen. 'How did you have the energy? The time?'

I shook my head. 'You should have gone to see that therapist, Charlie. It might have helped your defence. Shown that you were trying to seek help for your problems.'

She gawped at me, her face full of shock and disgust.

'I went to your flat,' I said.

'What?'

'I met Fraser. He told me all about your relationship, about what you put him through. I guess that was the start of it. A kind of practice run. At least, with him, no one got hurt. No one died.'

'I can't believe you went to my flat.' She pointed at me. 'How dare you?'

'I've been to Karen's flat too, spoken to her neighbour. He saw you, can identify you.'

This was a lie, but I wanted her to believe she had no way to escape.

'What the hell are you talking about?' she said.

I stood up. 'You should hand yourself in, Charlie. They'll help you. You'll get psychiatric care.'

But she wasn't listening. She stared into the air beside my head, her mouth open, face flushed. Her eyes were darting about; I could feel waves of nervous energy coming off her.

'Fraser is a lying shit,' she said. She narrowed her eyes at me. 'I love you, Andrew. You told me you loved me. You promised me.'

'I do. I did.'

'You swore on your life. You swore on your *sister's* life. And then you betrayed me.' Without warning, she let out a terrible noise, a high-pitched wail that rose with distress and then dipped with fury.

'Charlie . . .' I began.

She pointed at me again, her eyes ablaze with hatred. 'You'll never be happy,' she said. 'You think you can just walk away from this. But I'm going to haunt you, Andrew. I'm going to fucking *haunt* you.'

Before I could respond, ask her what she meant, she was gone, running across the little park and out through the gate.

I could barely breathe. I needed to talk to the police but my phone was dead. I didn't want to go back to Sasha's, didn't want to face her right now (had we had sex?), so I made my mind up. I would go home, plug my phone in, call DC Moseley.

My flat was only ten minutes' walk from the park. I felt so sick, my head thumping with every step, that I could only walk slowly. After what felt like the longest walk of my life, I reached my building. As I felt in my pockets for my keys, I heard a car door shut and looked up.

It was DC Moseley. Great. That would save me from making the call.

'Mr Sumner,' he said, sauntering over to me. 'Will you come with me, please?'

'What for?'

'I need to ask you some questions.'

Thirty-six

This time, there was more than one detective in the room. Beside DC Moseley sat a female officer with chestnut hair, wearing a suit that, unlike Moseley's, looked cheap and worn, though she was a higher rank than him. This was Detective Inspector Hannah Jones. She sat back in her chair, head crooked to one side, regarding me like I was an interesting yet slightly repulsive painting in a museum. They had kept me waiting in the room for over an hour and a half before coming in to talk to me.

'Why didn't you talk to Charlie?' I asked. 'She came to find me. I'm worried that she's going to—'

Jones cut me off. 'We will talk to her, don't worry. But we want to talk to you first.'

'Ask me more questions, you mean?'

They exchanged a glance.

'Tell us again about finding the bag of heroin in your flat,' Moseley said.

I went over it for what felt like the hundredth time. This was how the police wore people down, tripped them up if they were lying. They asked you to repeat the same story again and again until you got so tired that you let your guard down, made mistakes. This thought was chased by another: *Do they suspect* me?

'You don't think I had anything to do with Karen's death, do you?'

Jones motioned for Moseley to do the talking.

'Our lab analysed the substance you brought in,' he said. 'It is indeed heroin. As you told us. We also had the plastic container fingerprinted. Can you guess what I'm going to say?'

'That Charlie's prints weren't on it?'

'Correct. Actually, we don't have Charlotte Summers' prints on record. But we do have yours.'

I swallowed. A dim memory surfaced, of a cop in a different station pressing my fingers into a pad of ink.

'And there was only one set of prints on the bag, Andrew,' Moseley said. 'Yours.'

'I'm not denying that I touched it. You know I did. I handed it to you! But Charlie must have worn gloves.'

Moseley stared at me. 'Here's what I think happened. You and Karen Jameson had a disagreement over the money she owed you. Or perhaps it was a lovers' quarrel. Karen was jealous of your new, younger girlfriend. You murdered her, injected her with a dose of nearly pure heroin while she slept beside you, then panicked and came up with this crazy story about your girlfriend doing it.'

'Pretty nasty,' Jones said. 'Killing one girlfriend and trying to frame the other for it.'

'This is mad,' I said. 'It was Charlie. I can't believe you haven't talked to her. She's still out there. Listen, if you don't get her in custody, I have no idea what she'll do. I'm worried she's going to do something to Sasha.'

Moseley raised an eyebrow. 'Sasha? Who's that?'

I didn't like his expression. 'A friend.'

The two detectives exchanged a glance. 'Quite the Casanova, aren't you? It's always the quiet ones.'

I could sense Jones sizing me up, a slight curl to her lip. It was dawning on me that maybe I should ask for a solicitor. It would have to be the duty solicitor as I didn't have enough money to hire my own. But would that seem like an admission of guilt. This whole thing seemed so ludicrous that I couldn't believe the detectives weren't going to break into laughter at any moment, point at me and say, 'Gotcha!'

'If I was guilty, why the hell would I come here and bring you the heroin? As far as I know you weren't even treating Karen's death as suspicious until yesterday.'

Moseley leaned back and the look he gave me chilled my blood. 'This isn't the first time you've done this, is it, Andrew?'

My words could barely squeeze past the lump in my throat. 'What are you talking about?'

'Come on. Don't act the innocent.' He actually said those words. 'We had a look at your record.'

The door opened and another plain-clothed policeman stuck his head in, gesturing to Moseley.

'Excuse me,' he said, pausing the interview, and both he and Jones left the room, leaving me alone in a horrified daze.

I knew exactly what Moseley was talking about.

It was a memory that was so painful, that so conflicted with my current image of myself, that I kept it locked away in a conscious-ness-proof box. Sometimes, the memories seeped into my dreams and I would wake up feeling ashamed and jittery. But if they tried to escape during waking hours, I would push them straight back into the box.

'That was a long time ago,' I said to the empty room, my voice weak.

But sitting there in the interview room, punch drunk, weakened and exhausted, I no longer had the strength to hold the box shut. The lid flew open and, like wasps escaping from a bottle, all the memories came flooding out.

After our parents died, when I was sixteen and Tilly fourteen, I went to live with Uncle Pete (my dad's brother), Aunt Sandra, and their kids in Hastings, a few miles along the coast from our family home. Their daughter, Michelle, was my age, and my other cousin, Dominic, was thirteen. It was just me because Tilly was in Stoke Mandeville Hospital, which had a specialist department for dealing with people like her: accident victims who had broken their spines. We visited her every weekend, driving up to Aylesbury, the whole journey like a trip on a rollercoaster. Every lurch of the car sent bubbles of panic through my blood. I held my breath every time we passed a truck. It was terrifying and I had to be dragged into the car every time like a dog being dragged into the vet's. Uncle Pete, a no-nonsense, balding bank manager with the emotional intelligence of a goldfish, was a firm believer in getting back in the saddle, in embracing your fears. After a while though – and, I'm sure, some stern words from Sandra – Pete relented and let us go by train. I could cope with his passive aggressive comments about the extortionate costs and the stale buffet sandwiches far better than I could handle being driven on motorways.

Because Hastings and Eastbourne are only thirty minutes apart, I was originally going to return to my old school to study for my A-levels. But on my first day back I realised I couldn't handle the pitying looks, the soft voices, the sympathy. At lunch time, I sat on my own, chewing food I couldn't taste, an invisible force field around my table. A couple of upper sixth form girls came over to talk to me, and if I'd been a different kind of person I could have milked it, let them look after me. They could have passed me around, the sad orphan virgin, and made me merely a sad orphan.

Instead, I went home that night and announced to Pete and Sandra that there was no way I could ever go back. A week later I was enrolled at Hastings College, where no one knew my history. I was just another gangly teenager. I didn't tell any of my new friends about my parents or my sister. When they asked if I wanted to meet up at the weekend, I made up an excuse about a part-time job. I invented a back story for myself, one in which I'd been to private school in Los Angeles, where my dad worked in the movie industry and my mum was a soap opera actress, but they'd sent me over to England to learn about the 'old country'. No one ever asked me why I had a Sussex accent; it's easy to live a lie when everyone around you is a self-absorbed teenager. And I discovered that making up stories made me feel better about my real life. I became addicted to lying. I even began to believe the fiction myself – it was easier to inhabit this invented world than live in the real one and deal with the terrible, all-encompassing grief that made my bones ache, the urge to cry as constant as the need to breathe. It was comforting to think that my parents were living the good life in Hollywood.

The only people who knew my real past were my new family, though I hated thinking of them like that. Everything about them, compared to my former life, irritated me. Uncle Pete and his boring stories; Aunt Sandra and her cooking which was nothing like my mum's (she used the wrong kind of meat in shepherd's pie, for a start); Michelle, who was much cooler than me, with an older boyfriend who took her out every night, driving up and down the seafront with the other boy racers. Then there was Dominic. Thinking about Dominic makes me prickle with shame. I haven't seen him in over ten years. I'm sure if he saw me in the street he would hide. One day, when Pete or Sandra die, we will have to attend their funeral together. The prospect of that day stays firmly locked in my box.

Dominic was a typical thirteen-year-old boy in most ways. Spotty, awkward, addicted to his PlayStation. He was also somewhere on the autistic spectrum. Brilliant at maths and chess, but fragile and cripplingly shy, barely able to cope with the social side of school. I am not exactly sure whether he was ever given a special educational needs statement, even if such things existed in those days. I was too wrapped up in my own problems, not privy to my aunt and uncle's conversations. All I knew was that Dominic made me feel awkward and uncomfortable. He would ask me questions that I didn't want to answer, questions about the accident, about what it sounded like when we hit the lorry, whether I knew the velocity of the car when it collided with the truck, whether I remembered our Nissan rolling over and how loudly Tilly had screamed. Thinking back, I guess he was trying to make mathematical sense of it, find a neat way in which he could understand it. Being asked these questions though, mere months after it happened, repeatedly, made me want to punch him. I avoided him as much as I could. I didn't want to hit anyone. I didn't like or understand these feelings of rage and the urge to commit violence. I had never been like this.

I had been assigned a bereavement counsellor after the accident, a man with nostrils like the entrance of a great forest, who wanted me to talk to him about my feelings. I tried, at first. I didn't tell him about the sadness and fear and anger that would swoop down out of nowhere, when I was waiting to cross the road, or that were provoked by a misplaced word, like Dominic's questions. I pretended I was fine, tried to convince him. I lied to him, told him things I thought he'd like to hear, based on a TV documentary I'd watched.

The only person I could be honest with during this whole period was Tilly, on the rare occasions I was left alone with her, flat on her back in the hospital, the rest of the family gone to the cafeteria, nurses coming by every so often to turn Tilly to prevent bed sores. Tilly and I would talk about Mum and Dad, but also the future: Tilly was going to get better and I would look after her. She was going to be a paralympian athlete. She would hold my hand and cry and I would whisper that I was sorry, that it should have been me.

Between my made-up life at college, the lies I told my counsellor and pretending to be fine in my new home, my visits with Tilly were what I clung to, little moments of reality that allowed me to hold on to my true self.

Christmas was coming and we had arranged to visit Tilly on Christmas Eve then stay overnight in Aylesbury so we could be with her on the day itself. I was desperately looking forward to it, had starting to hype up this event in my head as a turning point, a day on which I would begin to claw back some happiness.

Then Uncle Pete announced that, because the trains on Christmas Eve were going to be 'a nightmare', we would have to drive.

I begged him to let us take the train. Since we'd stopped travelling to the hospital by car, the auto journeys had taken on a near-mythical horror in my imagination. I couldn't picture myself in a car on a motorway without bloody, fiery disaster striking – and Dominic would be there recording the velocity and decibel levels as the car burst into flames around us. I saw his charred skeleton in my daydreams, reciting numbers and poking at a calculator with a blackened, smoking finger.

'The trains will be a nightmare,' Pete repeated, and Sandra agreed. They understood my fear, but I was worrying about nothing.

'Your uncle will drive carefully, sixty in the slow lane all the way. Won't you, Pete?' Sandra tried to reassure me, but I didn't trust my uncle. He didn't say yes at all convincingly.

I managed to enlist Dominic, who didn't want to go by car either, mainly because he hated being squashed in the back between Michelle and me. He complained and moaned about it, and asked if he could stay at home on his own, but that just made Uncle Pete laugh and start talking about Macaulay Culkin. Dominic went into a major sulk, locking himself in his room, while I stoked his resentment by reminding him constantly how awful the journey was going to be.

As December 24th approached – and my excitement about Christmas curdled into dread – I began to panic. How could I stop us going? I wanted to see Tilly, but I couldn't get into the car. I had become like one of those people who is terrified of flying, who would need to be given a general anaesthetic before getting on a plane. I needed to do something.

We had the internet at Pete and Sandra's, unlike most people in England back then. When everyone was out one afternoon I dialled up and searched for ways to disable a car engine. My plan was to sneak out the night before Christmas Eve, do something to the car that would mean we'd have to get the train.

I found the answer pretty quickly – or as quickly as anything could be found online in those days. Sugar in the petrol tank. Simple. I crept downstairs after everyone had gone to bed, grabbed a bag of granulated sugar from the cupboard, along with a plastic funnel, and went into the garage. I poured a pound of sugar into the tank then went to bed, confident that we would be travelling by train the following day.

But that's not what happened.

The next day, when I got up, I asked Sandra where Pete was.

'He's gone to the petrol station to fill up before the journey,' she replied.

I walked out to look in the garage. The car was indeed gone. My plan hadn't worked. I started to tremble. But then the phone rang inside the house. It was the police. Uncle Pete had been in an accident.

What I hadn't realised, hadn't discovered through my internet research, is that a car with sugar in the tank will start up and travel a little way before it breaks down. Pete had been halfway across the busiest crossroads in town, the roads full of last-minute Christmas shoppers, when his car had suddenly broken down. The car behind went into his rear, another car ploughed into that; it caused a four-vehicle pile-up. Uncle Pete was all right apart from minor whiplash and the fact that his precious motor was written off. The woman in the car behind was less lucky; she banged her face on the steering wheel, suffered concussion, broke her cheekbone.

When the police and insurance companies got involved, they quickly discovered the sugar in the tank. When the police turned up on our doorstep and told us what had happened, questioned everybody, I had known there was only one thing I could do.

Thirty-seven

'You told them you saw your autistic cousin do it,' Moseley said, tutting. He and Jones had been gone for ten minutes before returning, their expressions even graver than before. 'Pinned it on Dominic. Seems like that's your way of operating, isn't it? Point the finger of blame.'

'But I owned up in the end,' I protested.

'And why was that?'

I stared at the surface of the desk. 'Pete looked at the history on my computer.' I didn't know you could delete it, not back then.

'So you didn't actually own up. You were found out. How long was this after the incident?'

I had a feeling he knew the answer. 'About a week.'

'During which time your poor cousin had been through hell, I bet.'

'He denied it, said it was me. But they didn't know which one of us to believe. Until they found the evidence.'

They both shook their heads slowly, looked at me like I was a kitten killer, the lowest piece of scum who'd ever sat in front of them. It was exactly how everyone had looked at me back then, when I'd been found out.

'I was a different person back then,' I said, thumping the table. 'I was a *kid*, one who'd just lost his parents. I was fucked up, confused. Terrified of going in that car.'

'I understand that, Andrew,' Moseley said. He was a few years younger than me but he talked to me like I was the guilty sixteen-year-old liar I'd been that Christmas. 'But in our job, you know what we see more than anything? Patterns of behaviour. People who do the same things, make the same mistakes, over and over again. This is your nature. You fuck up, and you blame someone else. You make accusations. You know what else I think, why you came to us in the first place? You want to get rid of this girlfriend of yours, Charlotte, but you're too much of a coward to go about it the manly way. So instead of telling her you don't want to be with her anymore, you go extreme and decide to get her arrested.'

'No . . .'

'You saw a way of killing two birds with one stone.' He smiled at his own joke.

'I want a solicitor,' I said.

'Oh really? Very well. Duty solicitor OK, or have you got your own?'

'Duty,' I said quietly.

'All right. We'll arrange something.'

He knocked on the door of the interview room and a uniformed constable came in.

'Put Mr Sumner here in a holding cell,' Moseley said. 'We're postponing our little chat.'

'Am I allowed a phone call?' I said.

He rolled his eyes. 'We'll arrange that too.'

'Listen,' I said, before they escorted me from the room. 'Have you talked to Harold, the old man in the ground floor flat? He can verify what I'm saying. He'll tell you how shocked I was when I heard that Karen was dead. You need to go round there.'

'We have,' Moseley said, his voice flat.

'And? What did he say?'

'He didn't say anything,' said Jones from behind me. I turned around and thought the look she was giving me might turn me to stone. 'He's dead.'

I stared at her. 'Harold?'

'Trying to pretend you didn't know?'

I swung round to face Moseley. 'It must have been Charlie. She did it to stop him talking. Must have thought he'd seen her. When did you find him? How long has he been dead? Oh my God.'

That poor old man. The dark spirit that he had warned me about, that had been following me around – well, now it had visited him. Yet again, it was my fault.

'We thought you might be able to tell us that,' Moseley said.

I sank back into my seat. I was too shocked to respond. When had Charlie done it? Thinking that Harold had spotted her and could ID her, she must have gone straight round there this morning after I'd spoken to her, while I was being kept waiting here. Now I knew why the two detectives had left the room halfway through my interview. If I'd had any last lingering doubts about Charlie before, I didn't now. And, I realised with a lurch, it was my fault. I had lied to her about Harold definitely seeing her. His death was down to me.

'If he died this morning, while I was here,' I said, raising my face, wondering how pale I looked, 'then how can I know what happened to him?'

I could tell that Harold's death had complicated things for Moseley. Probably, they were waiting for the coroner to tell them the time of death. I could see in the DC's head that he was trying to work it out, figure out how I fitted in to everything. And they weren't going to let me go till either the time they were allowed to hold me for ran out or they solved the puzzle. The most maddening thing was that I knew the solution, had told them – and they wouldn't believe me.

'Please, tell me,' I said. 'What happened to him?'

The two detectives exchanged a look and, this time, Jones answered.

'We don't know the exact cause of death yet, Mr Sumner. But it looks like he had a fall, hit his head on the fireplace. Whether he fell or was pushed, we don't know yet.' He cleared his throat. 'Unfortunately the scene, the body, had been disturbed somewhat by his dog.'

Moseley studied my face, trying to work out what was going on beneath the surface of my reaction to this horrific piece of news. Then he lifted his chin in the direction of the uniformed PC, and I was escorted from the room, my legs so shaky I could hardly walk.

The cell was small and stank of nervous sweat. I sat on a bench that appeared to have been designed to hurt your buttocks as quickly as possible, and stared at the wall, trying to wrestle my thoughts into some kind of order.

I had mostly managed to get the memories of what had happened with Pete, Sandra and Dominic back into the box, but now I forced myself to remember the rest of it, so I could play it through, exorcise it once again. Move on to the current nightmare I was trapped in.

After the truth had come out, Dominic didn't speak to me anymore and Uncle Pete communicated with me only when he had to. He had wanted me to be charged – vandalism, reckless endangerment, I forget the rest – but Sandra had pleaded with him and he'd backed down. Because of the injuries to the woman in the second car, and the involvement of the insurance companies, it hadn't been simple. There had been compensation claims, an out-of-court settlement that, eventually, came out of the death benefit I received. There were no criminal charges brought in the end. But the story of what had happened – in its black and white version, stripped to the facts – obviously remained on my record.

The worst thing had been how I had destroyed my relationship with my surviving family. I felt a terrible guilt. In a way, what I'd done, the blast of fear and regret that followed, helped me. It was the short sharp shock that people say should be meted out to young offenders, and it worked for me. It brought me out of the cocoon of fantasy and lies I'd been living in, made me face up to what had happened. I was finally able to grieve properly for my parents. I opened up to my counsellor at last, and I did everything I could to act like a model nephew for the next two years.

By the time I left Hastings and headed to university almost two years later, I was different. I had grown up. This doesn't mean I didn't have my demons. I had more than my fair share. I still felt, in my heart, out of step with the world. I found it easier to seek solitude than fall into crowds. And I guess, without trying to psychoanalyse myself, it led to the loneliness that made me so vulnerable and open – desperate, even – when Charlie came along and promised to make me whole.

None of my history with the law had crossed my mind when I'd reported Charlie. Perhaps if it had, I would have thought twice about going to the police, even though the circumstances were so different.

My thoughts returned to the present. Where was Charlie now? What was she doing? I guessed she would run, go far away. If she had killed Harold while I was at the police station, did she really think she could get away with it, that the police would blame me? Although she wouldn't have known I was here, that I had the best alibi it's possible to get. Was she going to go to my flat and leave something of Harold's there, some fake souvenir? And how had she killed him? *Frightened to death.* Yet again, I thought of the dark spirit and thanked God I wasn't superstitious, then laughed humourlessly at the irony of this.

I banged on the cell door. After a while, a policeman in a uniform with a white stain like baby sick on one shoulder, came to the door.

'After room service?' he said.

'I need to talk to DC Moseley or DI Jones.'

'You'll have to wait,' he said. 'Try to enjoy the facilities.'

'But Charlie will be getting away. She's probably planting something in my flat right now, trying to frame me.'

He chuckled. 'I'll pass that on.'

'What about my phone call? I want to call my sister. And my solicitor? You can't keep me here indefinitely.'

'Patience is a virtue,' he said, shutting the door in my face.

Fifteen minutes later, it opened again. I rose from the bench, expecting to hear that I could make my call or talk to my solicitor. But it was the policeman with the baby sick stain again, and he was escorting someone else into the cell.

It was a tall middle-aged man, balding but fit-looking. I must have gawped at him because he gave me a dirty look before going to sit on the bench and putting his face in his hands. A moment later, he sprang up and stared pacing around, muttering to himself.

'What are you staring at?' he snapped.

His voice was middle-class, private educated. He was wearing an expensive watch and the kind of suit I could never afford.

I had recognised him the moment he'd entered the room. Had seen his picture on his own website.

It was Lance.

Thirty-eight

I was sharing my tiny cell with the man who had terrified and attacked my best friend. I had never met him before, despite the work I'd done for Wowcom, so he had no idea who I was. The police must have gone to talk to him after Sasha's call this morning, had brought him in for questioning.

I could have kept my mouth shut. But I was so agitated that I couldn't help myself.

'I know who you are,' I said, as Lance continued to pace the cell. He stopped dead.

'You're Lance Hendrix. From Wowcom.'

He eyed me warily. I expect he thought I had seen his profile in *Wired* or a Sunday newspaper, that I was going to hit him with a business idea, pitch for an investment. Or, more likely, he was worried that when I got out of this cell I would leak news of his arrest. I am sure he had a lawyer to match his expensive watch and suit, someone who would be doing everything they could to not only get their client off but keep his face out of the papers.

'You deserve everything you get,' I said.

I wished in that moment that I could have taken a picture of his face, of his jaw literally dropping, and send it to Sasha.

'What the bloody hell are you talking about?' he said when he'd recovered.

I stepped closer to him. 'I'm talking about what you did to Sasha.'

He stepped back. 'You know that little bitch?'

'She's my best friend. And she's told me everything – your sordid affair, what you did to her in that hotel room, the threatening texts, the way you set your wife on her. All of it.'

He sneered at me, though his face had turned white. He looked me up and down. 'What are you doing in here? Did she tell a pack of lies about you too?'

'What? No. But I know—'

He jabbed a finger at me. 'I have no reason to explain myself to you, whoever you are. But this girl is a liar. I never had an affair with her. In fact, for your information, I have never, ever been unfaithful to my wife. I certainly never attacked the silly girl.' He twisted and turned as he spoke, a ball of kinetic energy. 'I was barely aware of her existence until the police turned up at my office this morning.'

'Bullshit,' I said. 'How can you say that? She works for you.'

'Hundreds of people work for me. Do you think I know them all?'

I ignored him. 'And I know you had an affair. She told me all about it. She told me all about your . . . proclivities.'

'My *what?*'

'She told me what you like to do in bed.'

He stared at me, then burst out laughing. 'Did she indeed?' He seemed genuinely amused. 'Tell me, does your friend have mental health issues? We normally screen for that sort of thing, but a few slip through the net. Psychometric tests aren't foolproof, unfortunately.'

Now it was my turn to be affronted. 'No, she hasn't. Is that going to be your defence in court?'

He sat down on the bench, suddenly calm and collected. 'It will never get to court. Sarah or Sasha or whatever her name is – she's a liar. A fantasist. She's invented the whole thing.'

'I don't believe you,' I said.

He shrugged. 'You know what? I don't care.'

Before I could say any more, or make sense of this, the door opened and the officer with the baby sick stain beckoned me out.

'You can make your phone call now.'

He pointed to a pay phone on the wall opposite. I hadn't used a pay phone in years, was barely aware they still existed. I picked the receiver up and realised I was going to have to pay for the call myself. I fished in my pockets and found two 20p pieces. I pushed one into the slot and dialled Tilly's mobile number, one of the few phone numbers I knew by heart.

She picked up after four rings, but all I could hear was a great rushing howl. It was like she was standing at the centre of a hurricane, or there was extreme interference on the line.

'Hello?' I said. Then, raising my voice when there was no response, said it again. The howling continued, a blast of static that looped and roared. I pulled the handset away from my ear. It was like I was trying to call someone in Hell.

'Tilly, are you there?'

'Hello? Andrew?' Her voice was faint but it was unmistakeably my sister.

'Can you hear me?'

'Yes. Sorry, it's really windy here.' She laughed. 'It's like the start of the *Wizard of Oz*.' Her voice was a little clearer now, though I had to press the receiver hard against my ear. Beyond her voice and the roar of the wind, I could hear the faint background sound of seagulls, their cries cutting through the static.

'Where are you?' I asked, gripping the phone with frustration.

'Beachy Head.'

'What the hell are you doing up there?'

Beachy Head is a famous chalk cliff on the outskirts of Eastbourne and is a notorious suicide spot. It's well known as the most popular place in England to kill yourself. I remembered reading that around twenty people a year throw themselves off the cliff, its fame no doubt adding to its popularity among the suicidal. The Samaritans had a huge billboard on the clifftop, encouraging people to call the charity helpline to be talked around. Despite its bloody reputation, it was a beautiful place, offering breathtaking views of the churning English Channel below, the red and white stripes of the lighthouse, the continent just beyond the horizon.

Her reply was swept away on the wind and as I said, 'What?' the phone beeped and the display flashed *Insert another coin*. Jesus. I stuck my second and final twenty pence piece into the slot.

'Sorry, Andrew,' she said. 'Maybe I should call you back when I'm inside. I think we're going in the pub in a minute.'

She sounded happy and I wondered if she was on a date. Or maybe Rachel had turned up. But I needed to tell her about my own predicament – it was important that someone knew where I was – so I said, 'Listen I need to tell you something . . .'

She wasn't really listening. I heard her say, 'It's Andrew,' to whoever she was with.

'Tilly . . .' I said, impatient.

'What's the matter? You sound really worried. Don't tell me you think I'm going to wheel myself off the cliff?'

'No, Tilly . . .'

'That thing at the start of the year, it wasn't that serious. I'm absolutely fine now, OK? How many times do I have to tell you. I. Am. Fine.'

I heard her say something to whoever she was with. Then she addressed me: 'I think I should call you back. Do you want to talk to her first?'

Little shivering tendrils of dread reached out for me. 'Tilly,' I said. 'Who are you with?'

'Charlie.'

It was as if the gales blowing across the clifftop came down the wires and through the phone, knocking me backwards, a blast of ice that penetrated my entire body. The police officer who'd escorted me to the phone furrowed his brow as I staggered, grabbing hold of the payphone on the wall and almost collapsed.

I could hear Charlie's voice from just a few hours ago. *You swore on your life. You swore on your* sister's *life.*

I frantically tried to work it out. Could Charlie have got round to Harold's in north London then down to Eastbourne in the time I'd been here? Yes, just about, with the hours I'd been kept waiting in the interview room and then in the holding cell.

'Yeah, she came to see me,' Tilly said in her chirpiest voice. 'She wanted to take me out as a treat. Hold on, she wants to talk to you.'

Before I could shout out a warning to Tilly, Charlie came on the line.

'Hello Andrew.'

Her voice was calm and measured. As she spoke, the wind seemed to drop, the roaring noise dropping to a low, undulating hiss.

'Charlie. Whatever you're planning to do, please, don't do it. Tilly has never done anything to you.'

She laughed. It was the coldest sound I'd ever heard.

'We're having a lovely time,' she said. 'It's hard to believe that so many people die every year in such a beautiful place.'

'Charlie!'

There was a pause of a few seconds and I figured that Charlie was taking a few steps away from Tilly so she wouldn't be overheard.

'Tilly doesn't know what you did to me,' she said.

'I know,' I blurted. 'She's innocent. Charlie, I'll do anything, say anything. Just please, please don't—'

The police officer was watching me even more closely now.

'I can't hear you,' Charlie said. 'Too much interference on the line. You know, this is probably the last time we'll ever talk.' She sighed, sadness entering her voice. 'I loved you, Andrew.'

'Charlie, I loved you too.' My voice was shaking. 'Maybe we can—'

'Shut up,' she hissed. 'You betrayed me. Do you really think I could forgive you?'

'Charlie—'

The phone beeped. *Insert another coin.* I didn't have any more coins.

'I'm going to go now, Andrew. I'll hand you back to Tilly.'

'Please—'

The phone beeped urgently.

'Say goodbye to your sister,' Charlie said, and the line went dead.

Thirty-nine

I stared at the dead receiver in my hand. I was on the verge of hyperventilating. I scrambled in my pockets for another coin but had nothing. I wanted to scream.

'Everything all right?' said the police officer, coming over.

'No. Please, I need you to call Eastbourne police, get someone to Beachy Head.' I was almost sobbing. 'She – Charlie – is going to kill my sister. She's going to push her over the cliff, make it look like an accident. Oh God, it's probably too late already.'

He put his hand on my arm.

'Calm down,' he said. I guess he was used to dealing with crazy people, drunks, nutters. He was looking at me like I was one of them.

'I can't fucking calm down,' I said. 'You have to let me go. And call Eastbourne police. You have to!'

'Let's get you back to your cell . . .'

'No!'

I shoved him in the chest, and in a flash I was surrounded by uniformed police. They came out of nowhere, and one of them had my face against the wall, yanking my arms back, sending spasms of pain into my shoulders. He cuffed me, and I was dragged back to the cell and shoved inside. The door slammed shut behind me.

'She's going to kill her!' I shouted at the door. I kicked it and screamed curses at the unrelenting metal, shouting till my throat was shredded and hoarse. Tilly, oh Tilly. I could picture the stunned look on her face as Charlie shoved her chair, the sea and the rocks rushing up to meet her. I closed my eyes, sank to my knees, sobbing. It was too late. She would already be dead.

I had invited the dark spirit into my life. Its name was Charlie. It had stolen from Harriet, disfigured Kristi, ruined Victor, murdered Karen and Harold. It had wreaked havoc in my life, tried to cut me off from everyone. What had happened to Sasha and Rachel – was that Charlie too? Were Lance and Henry merely convenient patsies? Everyone I cared about, all the people I liked and loved. The dark spirit had poisoned their lives too, destroying everything. And now, the final straw, the coup de grace. It – she – had taken my sister.

Eventually, I stopped crying and looked up to see Lance gazing at me with a mixture of contempt and amusement.

'You're as mental as your friend,' he said.

A little while after that, Lance was taken from the cell, for questioning I assumed. I sat on the hard bench, numb and drained. I had given up trying to get the police to open the door or talk to me. All I could do now was wait.

If Tilly was dead, the only person I had left in the world now was Sasha. I was terrified that Charlie would target her next. She hated Sasha anyway. A terrible thought struck me: what if she had already done something to Sasha before heading to Eastbourne? That would be logical. She knew Sasha was at home. What would she do? Make it look like another death by misadventure? An apparent suicide?

The door opened and DC Moseley entered the room.

I jumped to my feet.

'I need to talk to you,' I said. 'Urgently. I tried to tell the—'

Moseley put up a hand to silence me then gestured to the uniformed officer who had cuffed me. Moseley took the key and unlocked the cuffs.

'You're free to go,' he said.

I stared at him. 'What? Why?'

He rubbed his neck. He looked tired but alert, like he was running on adrenaline. 'Some new evidence has come to light.'

'What?'

'I'm not able to tell you right now.'

'Oh, for God's sake . . .'

The officer holding the cuffs gave me a meaningful look and I shut up.

'Go home,' Moseley said. 'We'll be in touch.'

'What about my sister?' I said. 'Did you speak to the police in Eastbourne? Has anyone?'

He sighed wearily. 'Just go home, Mr Sumner. Have a shower.' He wrinkled his nose. 'You reek.'

'You have to call them. I'm reporting a crime. You can't ignore that.'

'All right. Jesus.' He had reached the end of his tether with me. 'I'll call them now. OK?'

'Thank you.'

A few seconds passed. 'What are you still hanging around for?'

'I'm waiting for you to call Eastbourne.'

'For fuck's sake,' he muttered. 'Go home. I'll ring you shortly. OK?'

I walked home in the rain. It was that fine, drizzling rain that soaks you from head to foot within seconds. My wallet must have been at

Sasha's, probably on her bedroom floor, so I couldn't get any money out to pay for a cab or get a bus. I needed to get home as quickly as I could so I could plug my phone in and try to call Tilly and Sasha. Plus I would phone Eastbourne station myself, make sure someone was checking out Beachy Head. I alternated running and walking, jogging as far as I could each time until my lungs burned and my legs were on the verge of collapse.

It took me just over an hour to get back, by which point I was drenched, water trickling down my face and stinging my eyes. I let myself in and went up the stairs, opening the door and going into the warmth. I dropped my coat on the floor, kicked off my shoes and stripped off my wet top and socks, headed into the bathroom to grab a towel.

I looked at myself in the bathroom mirror. My hair stuck up from my scalp, my skin looked like the surface of the moon, my eyes were sore and pink. But I didn't have time to stand around studying the wreck I'd become. I needed to call Tilly, the police and Sasha, in that order.

My phone charger was plugged in next to the bed, so I went into the bedroom, sat down in my damp jeans and plugged the phone in, holding it and urging it to switch on, jiggling my knees up and down and muttering 'Come on, come *on*.'

After what felt like an eternity in purgatory, the Apple logo appeared on the screen and a few dots appeared to let me know I had a signal. I immediately called Tilly. It went straight to voicemail. While I was leaving her a message, telling her that I prayed she was OK and to please call me the second she could, the phone vibrated a few times. When I looked at the screen, I saw I had two voicemails. The first was from Tilly. It had come in just after I'd spoken to her in the police station.

I listened to it. The wind was howling behind her but her voice was clear.

'Hey, bruv. I tried to talk to you but you were gone. Are you all right? You sounded really stressed out. Call me back. Charlie's just going to take me up to the cliff edge so I can take some photos of the lighthouse.'

My heart jumped and skipped and I chewed my knuckles, the phone still held to my ear. While I was frozen in that pose the second voicemail message began to play. It was a gruff male voice, thick London accent.

'This is a message for a Mr Andrew Sumner. This is the Lost Property office at London Bridge. Your bag has turned up. Yeah, someone at the bus depot left it in a cupboard in their office and it's just made its way to us. The young lady who reported it left us this number to call if it turned up.' He laughed. 'I recognised it as soon as it came in because she used to ring us every day. We're open—'

I had stopped listening.

My bag of mementoes. Charlie really had left it on a bus. She *really had* reported it to London Transport and chased it daily. I stared at the phone screen, the guy from the lost property office still chattering away, as if the truth might leap out from it. I had been certain Charlie was lying about the bag.

If she hadn't been lying about that, did that mean . . . ?

Something went *bang* in the living room.

Somebody was in the flat.

It couldn't be Charlie. There was no way she could have got back from Beachy Head in time. But she was the only other person with a key. Then I realised what it must be: another bird, flying into the front window. My stomach settled and I stood up and walked into the living room to check.

Sasha was sitting on the sofa. Her bag lay by her feet, half its contents spilled out like guts on the carpet. She had a cushion on her lap. She didn't get up, or move, but rolled her eyes towards me.

She must have been in the flat when I got home, but I hadn't looked in the living room.

'Sasha. What are you doing here?'

She opened her mouth to speak but nothing came out. I went over and stood in front of her, my mind racing all over the place, hearing voices. Lance saying that Sasha was a fantasist, that she had invented everything. The man from the lost property office telling me that Charlie hadn't been lying.

'I'm sorry,' Sasha said. Her voice was very quiet, a forced whisper.

'What for?' I didn't want to get too close. All of a sudden, I was afraid of her.

She opened her mouth to speak but again, nothing came out. What was wrong with her?

I crouched on the carpet before her, keeping my distance. 'Sasha, I saw Lance at the police station.'

She stared at me.

'He said that you made the whole thing up, that you were a fantasist.'

She shook her head and said a single word. 'Liar.' Her face creased with pain and it hit me: why had I believed him, a stranger, over the woman I had known and trusted longer than any other? Sasha hadn't been lying. Lance was the fantasist.

'I believe you,' I said, and her lips twitched; the faintest flicker of a smile.

Then she coughed and drops of spittle flew from her mouth, flashing red in the light that streamed in from the window.

I scooted closer, put my hands on her upper arms. She was freezing, her body like marble.

'Sasha, what's wrong? What's going on?'

She looked into my eyes and coughed again, blood droplets splattering my face.

My voice went up an octave as I spoke, panic mounting. 'Sasha, what's happened? What's wrong with you?'

She made a guttural sound, trying to speak, but could only manage a single syllable. 'She . . .'

'What? She what? Do you mean Charlie?'

Sasha stared into my eyes and pulled the cushion away from her lap with great effort, as if it was heavier than a rock.

I couldn't believe what I was seeing.

'Oh Jesus. Oh fuck. Sasha . . .'

There was a hole in her stomach. A gaping wound, dark blood trickling from it, down between her legs onto the upholstery. A wild, ridiculous thought entered my head, that not even Maria would be able to get those stains out, and at that moment Sasha toppled sideways, rasping, a line of blood running from her mouth, and I caught hold of her. She flopped. A dead weight.

'Don't touch her.'

The voice came from behind me. After gently laying Sasha on her side and closing her eyes, I turned and stared at the woman who had just murdered my best friend.

Forty

'Stand up. Get away from her. But keep your hands up, like this. I want to be able to see them.' She smiled as she said this. The butcher's knife in her hand glinted.

I did as she asked, catching sight of myself in the mirror above the fireplace. Sasha's blood ran in streaks across my naked torso.

Rachel looked at me affectionately, the way you might look like at a child who'd spilled his dinner over himself. 'We're going to have to get you cleaned up. Come on, strip the rest of it off. Let's get you in the shower.'

'Rachel . . .'

She was wearing her biker gear – the leather boots and trousers – and there was a holdall by her feet. There was a dark patch on the front of her black T-shirt. The muscles in her arms appeared to ripple, reminding me that I had once envied her athletic build, developed from all those months of lifting my sister.

But though she looked the same, she held herself differently. She seemed more open, confident. Her hand didn't move to her mouth as she spoke. She seemed fully relaxed. Here she was, for the first time since I'd met her, showing her true self. Her real, terrifying self.

'Quiet,' she said. 'Take your clothes off. Stop fucking around.'

Trying hard not to look at Sasha's body, I unbuttoned my jeans and pushed them down, kicking them off. I felt curiously calm.

Where was my phone? Still charging in the bedroom. I glanced around for a weapon but there was nothing within reach. Certainly nothing that could take on the huge knife Rachel held. Plus the leather outfit acted like a suit of armour. Anything I threw would bounce off her.

'Underpants too,' she said.

'Come on, Rachel.'

'Off.'

I obeyed, and stood before her, naked and completely vulnerable. I guessed that was her intention. She looked me up and down, slowly, like I was a statue in a Roman museum.

'Beautiful,' she said. 'But dirty. You've got that bitch's blood on you.' She looked at Sasha, tutted and shook her head. 'You shared a bed with her last night, didn't you? What was she like?'

I had my hands cupped over my shrunken genitals. The flat was warm but I was shaking. 'Please Rachel . . .' I still couldn't remember if I'd had sex with Sasha. I didn't think so, was sure I would know if I had.

'Save it. It doesn't matter anyway. It's only the future that matters now.' She took a step towards me. She was smiling. 'Come on, let's get you into the shower.'

She escorted me into the bathroom at knifepoint. Again, I looked around for a weapon. There were some razors in the cabinet. A small cup that held the toothbrushes. That was it. Holding the knife pointed towards me, she turned on the shower, which hung on the wall above the bathtub, with the other hand. When the water was hot and steam began to rise into the air, she ordered me to step into the bath. I stood beneath the scalding water and she handed me a bar of soap, told me to scrub. Sasha's blood ran down my body in thin, pink rivulets.

'Wash it all,' Rachel said. 'I want you clean. That's it, wash off all the whore's blood. I want all traces of her scrubbed from your skin.'

'Why are you doing this?' I asked, as I did what she commanded.

She looked at me like I was stupid. She shrugged.

'Because I love you, Andrew.'

I looked around the bathroom. Rachel barred the door and there was no other way out, just a tiny window that had been painted shut years before. There weren't any heavy objects in the room that I could smash it with. Even if I did smash the window, all I would be able to do was shout for help. By the time anyone heard me, Rachel would have stabbed me to death. There was already one body in the flat. If she was caught, she would do life for murder. It wouldn't matter if there were two of us or one.

'You killed them, didn't you?' I said. 'Karen and Harold? And it was you who threw the acid at Kristi?'

'The cleaner? No, that was nothing to do with me. A happy coincidence.'

'But the others?'

Her face twisted into a glassy-eyed smile again. 'Oh yes. You can thank me later.'

My only hope was that Rachel believed she loved me. The people she'd hurt so far had been the people around me. There was one little bright spot in this fucked-up, terrifying situation. Tilly must be OK. When Charlie said 'Say goodbye to your sister,' that was exactly what she meant. It wasn't supposed to be a permanent goodbye.

I had been so wrong about Charlie. But I didn't have time to think about that, because Rachel reached up and turned the shower off, pointing the knife at my face.

'Into the bedroom,' she said.

I got out of the shower, shivering and dripping, and Rachel jabbed the tip of the knife into my back, beside my spine. I gasped with pain and she said, 'Oh for goodness sake.'

'Rachel . . .'

'Shut up, Andrew.' She took a deep breath. 'Please don't make me lose my temper.'

We entered the bedroom and she instructed me to lie on my back on the bed. There were handcuffs attached to the bed frame. She snapped one over each wrist. Then she cuffed my ankles together. If I had been scared before, now I was terrified. I turned my head and saw that my phone was gone. She walked out of the room and came back carrying the holdall.

'How did you get in?' I asked. I needed to keep her talking, try to connect with her, talk her round. Find out what she wanted.

'You keep a spare key in your bedside drawer,' she said matter-of-factly. 'I thought you meant for me to take it.'

I took a deep breath. 'And the little bag of heroin. You put it in Charlie's suit pocket.'

She smiled at me. 'Clever, aren't I? You'll soon realise, Andrew, that all those other women – Sasha, Karen, Charlie – they're nothing compared to me. I thought maybe Harriet was a threat too, but I could tell from your emails that you stopped caring about her a long time ago. I don't think you ever loved her.'

As she talked, she put the holdall on the bed and removed some items from it. From my prostrate position I couldn't see what they were, could only see a flash of silver, something catching the light.

'You've read my emails?' I said.

'Hmm. All I needed was your iCloud password. Once I had that all I had to do was set it up on my iPad and I had access to everything, including all the texts you send and receive on your iPhone. Easy.'

'But how did you get it? My password?'

She smirked. 'I installed a piece of keystroke-recording software on Tilly's computer. I wanted to keep an eye on her emails, see what she was saying about me. And when you stayed at Christmas you logged in to your iCloud emails and your Facebook. The software stored your passwords. That was the best Christmas present I ever had.'

I was stunned and horrified. With one password she could access everything because I used my Apple computer and phone, using my iCloud account, to send all my messages. And my Facebook password gave her even more access to my life.

'And you deleted loads of my Facebook friends.'

'Only the sluts.' She smiled at me. 'You didn't notice me for a long time, did you? I know you merely thought of me as the poor sap who looked after your sister, who did the job you didn't want to do.'

I opened my mouth but she put a finger to my lips. 'Don't worry, I don't blame you. Some people are meant to be carers – like me – and others are supposed to be cared for. Like you. The first time I met you I knew that it was actually you I was supposed to look after.'

She put a hand behind my head and tilted it upwards, put something on my tongue. Before I could spit it out, she poured water into my mouth from a plastic bottle and the pill slipped down my throat.

'What was that?' I said, gasping, water running onto my neck. The rest of my body was still damp, cold.

'Just something to relax you.'

'Rachel, come on. Why don't you uncuff me? We can talk about everything.'

She shook her head. 'Later. When I've finished.'

'Finished what?'

She leaned over me and I saw that she was wearing something familiar. It was a helmet – the same helmet Mr Makkawi had worn when he'd performed my eye operation. It looked a little like an old-fashioned miner's helmet, a brilliant light attached to the front.

'Rachel, why are you wearing that?' I could barely speak. On top of everything else, the sight of the helmet had brought back memories of the pain of the eye examinations I'd undergone. The awful torture as they shone brilliant lights into my eyes, the veins filling my vision like bloody corals, the horror of being trapped, my eyes forced open, the laser they used for the follow-up surgery causing the nerves in my eyes to scream, like when a dentist pokes a nerve in a tooth.

She didn't reply. Instead she took a couple of small objects from her holdall.

'You know, Rachel isn't really my name,' she said. 'But I like it. Makes me feel pretty.' She spoke in a strange sing-song voice.

A deep shudder went through my core as I realised what she was holding.

Eye clamps.

'No, please, Rachel, please don't . . .'

She ignored me. 'Did you know I worked at Moorfields for a while? Fascinating place. I took this helmet when I left. That's where I first saw you, when I realised that we should be together. You were coming out of your operation. You were unconscious. You looked so beautiful, like an angel lying there. I looked up your details. One of the other nurses told me that you'd told her about your sister, that she was in a wheelchair. You told her that she was looking for a personal assistant. It seemed like fate. What better way for me to get close to you, to watch you.' She wagged her finger at me. 'Though I was disappointed you didn't visit more often.'

She snapped the clamps onto my eyes, forcing them open. I stared at her face, tried to turn my head, but she grabbed my chin and forced me to look at her. Tears pooled in my eyes and ran down my cheeks. She dabbed them away with a tissue. The hard metal of the clamps dug into my eye sockets, the pressure intense, like someone pushing the end of a spoon into my eye. I tried to kick with my legs, but Rachel straddled me, leather on my bare skin, pinning me down.

'When I got Fraser to push you down those steps, I was hoping you would break your back. I was very disappointed. I thought, if I could get you to have an accident, I could be *your* personal assistant. I could look after you. We'd be together all the time.' She licked her lips. 'But that didn't work. Fraser . . . what a fuck-up he is.'

'Rachel . . .'

She ignored me. 'This will be better than a broken back, though. I don't really want you paralysed, Andrew, because then you wouldn't be able to make love to me.' She leant forward and kissed me on the lips. She ran her knuckles over my shrunken penis. 'So beautiful. I could look at you all day. Soon, I *will* be able to look at you all day.'

She pulled a gag out of her holdall and strapped it around my mouth.

'Don't want you screaming and bringing the neighbours running, do we?'

She held up a scalpel.

'When you're blind, you'll need someone to care for you. It's going to be wonderful, living together. And it's perfect because you won't be able to look at any other women ever again.'

She raised the scalpel and held it above my left eye. 'I'm the last thing you'll ever see, Andrew. My face will be imprinted in your memory forever.'

She brought the blade towards my eye and I started screaming into my gag.

Forty-one

There is a fine membrane that covers the surface of the eye, called the conjunctiva. This membrane protects the sclera, or the white part of the eye. I knew this from staring at a poster in a waiting room at Moorfields. Iris, retina, pupil, cornea, optic nerve. These words tumbled through my brain at lightning speed, on rapid repeat—

iris, retina, pupil, cornea, optic nerve

—as I screamed and begged for Rachel to stop, screaming abuse, begging for mercy—

iris, retina, pupil, cornea, optic nerve

—every noise I made muffled by the gag in my mouth, the neighbours so close but oblivious to what was happening to me—

iris, retina, pupil, cornea, optic nerve

—and the hard pain of the clamps that dug into my eye sockets intensified as I tried desperately to buck and writhe and get a hand free from the cuffs. But I couldn't move, not with Rachel straddling my body, not with the handcuffs that secured my wrists like a carpenter's vice. And the drug she had given me had made me weak, my muscles heavy and pathetic. While my brain leapt and sparked and screeched, my body lay there like a newborn baby's, stranded, helpless. At Rachel's mercy.

With the calm precision of a surgeon, Rachel sliced through the conjunctiva of my left eye and into the sclera, then across, slashing through the cornea and pupil. She hummed something under her breath as she drew the blade across my eye.

I blacked out.

When I came to, she was still on top of me, dabbing at my cheek with a cloth.

The pain in my eye hit me like a tsunami and I almost went under again, craving oblivion. But she slapped my cheek, kept me awake.

'Look at me,' she said softly.

My left eye, the eye that the surgeons had worked so hard on to repair last year, was blind. My remaining good eye swivelled towards her, the clamp digging into the bone. It kept filling with tears which dripped down my face. I made a choking noise and she pulled the gag away from my mouth.

The first words I tried to speak came out as a rasp. She tipped some water down my throat, smiling kindly. I managed to speak. 'I'm begging you, Rachel. I'll live with you. I'll do anything you want. Just please don't make me blind. Please.'

She carefully removed the clamp from the wounded eye and I squeezed it shut. The pain was like nothing I had ever known. Indescribable.

She leant forward and kissed the bloody eyelid.

'Take a good look, Andrew,' she said in that velvet-and-nails voice. 'I want you to remember what I look like. I want you to be able to see me in your head when we make love.'

'Please Rachel, please don't blind me.'

She moved the blade towards my remaining good eye as I struggled and tried to throw her off. But I couldn't get any leverage and my limbs were limp and useless.

I spat in her face.

She sat back, a look of stunned horror on her face. For a fleeting moment, I felt good. 'I'd rather fuck a dog than fuck you,' I said. But she smiled at me like I was a toddler who'd said something silly.

'You shouldn't have done that,' she said, yanking my jaw and slipping the gag back onto my mouth, pulling it tight. 'You've got to be a good boy. When I'm looking after you, if you do naughty things, you will be punished. Like this.'

She leaned away and slashed the scalpel across my chest. Compared to the pain in my eye, it was a scratch. I wanted to scream at her. Tell her to do her worst. I wanted to die, but more than that: I wanted her dead. I conjured up every bit of strength I had left and bucked and thrashed and struggled, but whatever she had given me meant I hardly moved, and she laughed.

She brought the blade back towards my eye.

The front door opened with a rattle and click.

Rachel sat up, looking at her watch, as if she had been expecting someone, but not so soon. I realised I had been holding my breath, and exhaled through my nose, relief flooding through me. Rachel dismounted me and picked up the butcher's knife from the bedside table where she'd left it, moving slowly, careful not to make a noise. I shouted into the gag.

A voice called out. 'Hello?'

It was Charlie.

I tried harder to shout, to warn her. But all I could do was turn my head and watch with my remaining good eye – *Oh God, I was blind in one eye* – as she came into the room. As she took in the scene – Rachel with the knife, me naked and bloody on the bed – her mouth fell open and she tried to back out of the room. But Rachel grabbed her by the arm with her free hand, pulling Charlie and throwing her across the room. She crashed into the chest of drawers and fell to her knees.

'What have you done to him?' she screamed, eyeing the knife and staying where she was.

Rachel panted, ignoring the question. 'How did you get here so quickly?'

I guessed from this question that Rachel had been expecting Charlie. No doubt Rachel was planning to kill her too, but she wanted me blind and helpless first, so I would have to listen to my girlfriend – if she was still my girlfriend – die. Charlie was the one Rachel hated the most. Because she was the woman I really loved.

Charlie climbed to her feet. Through the tears pooling in my right eye, everything was blurred, colours and shapes swimming in the bright light.

'How did you get here?' Rachel demanded, jabbing the knife towards her.

A male voice said, 'I gave her a ride.'

I turned my head. Rachel turned too. It was Henry. Huge, muscular, strong, tall Henry. Come to save us. Oh thank God, thank God. He stepped towards Rachel with his hand outstretched, a towering presence, his motorbike boots thumping on the floor. He opened his mouth and said, 'Give me—'

Rachel plunged the knife into his chest.

I watched in stunned horror – everything in slow motion – as our apparent saviour slumped to the floor, hitting the ground with a thump.

I had barely taken this in when Charlie jumped onto Rachel's back. My tormentor spun, sending Charlie flying backwards, colliding with the wardrobe. Rachel leapt on her with a yell, shifted the knife to her left hand and punched her in the face with her right. She grabbed Charlie's cheeks and smashed the back of her head into the corner of the chest of drawers, a sickening cracking sound filling the room.

I tried to cry out. Charlie!

She didn't move. Rachel stood over her, looking down, panting. Then she came back over and climbed onto me.

'Let's get this over with,' she said, replacing the knife with the scalpel.

This was it. I was going to be blind. This was my punishment for escaping injury in the crash that killed my parents and paralysed my sister. A dark spirit *had* been stalking me, ever since that day. It had tried to blind me last year. Now it was going to happen. Justice was being done on behalf of the universe, of all the laws of fate, and there was nothing I could do about it. Nothing.

Behind Rachel, I saw Charlie push herself onto her hands and knees.

I made a loud noise in my throat, thrashed my head, tried to make Rachel believe I was choking, swallowing my tongue.

Not wanting me dead, Rachel pulled the gag down.

'Under the chest of drawers,' I yelled to Charlie. 'The knife!'

The knife that Charlie had thrown during her jealous rage about Sasha. It had spun under the chest of drawers. If fate really wanted me to go blind, it would have told Maria, my new, competent cleaner, to find it, remove it, put it back in the kitchen. If there was no such thing as dark spirits, the knife would still be there.

Rachel tried to get off me, to grab her butcher's knife, and I used every shred of willpower I possessed to buck and knock her off balance as she got off. She stumbled and tripped over Henry's body, landing face-first with a grunt, but still holding onto the knife.

It didn't matter. Charlie had found my knife under the chest of drawers and scrambled to her feet with it. There was no dark spirit. No fate. No pre-destined blindness. Just luck.

Charlie stood over my attacker, over the woman who had tried to destroy our lives. Holding the knife in both hands, Charlie brought it down, with all her strength, between Rachel's shoulder blades.

Forty-two

Hi Charlie,

    I've wanted to email you for a while but have been putting it off. I suppose that's silly, but maybe I'm right to be hesitant. I wouldn't blame you if you never wanted to hear from me again, if you have blocked my email address or if you drag this straight into your junk folder.

    The other reason for the delay is that I've been dealing with the fallout of everything that happened. Adjusting.

    But this email isn't about me.

    Tilly told me you've gone away for a little while, though she's reluctant to tell me where, so maybe you're not checking your emails. But I have been composing this message to you in my head for weeks and now I feel the need to share it with you. To explain to you some of the things that have happened since . . . well, since that terrible day. And, more importantly, to say I'm sorry.

    I should never have believed you were capable of doing those things. You, the sweetest, most compassionate, life-loving person I've ever met.

    How could I believe that you could be behind Karen's death? Or the attack on Kristi? Or any of the rest of it? All you ever gave me was your love. You looked after me when I needed it. You made me happier than I ever thought possible, happiness that was off the scale. You came into my life like a great rush of joy. And what did I do?

I fucked it up.

Maybe if I tell you some of what happened, and what I've found out since, it will help you understand why I was so mistaken, so misled. That's my hope anyway. I want you to understand that you were a victim of someone else's scheme, of bad luck and bad decisions. I never meant to betray you, to let you down. If I tell you the story of everything that happened, maybe you will see that.

So let's start with the person behind most of it.

Rachel.

DC Moseley came to see me in hospital. He said that three years ago a guy called Philip Ellis was tortured and murdered, along with his girlfriend, Sophie, in Birmingham. The police thought it was a murder-suicide at first, that Sophie had done it. But then they discovered that two of Philip Ellis's ex-girlfriends had died in weird circumstances. They found Rachel's fingerprints at all of the crime scenes. She was a friend of Sophie's but there was no reason for her to have visited the exes.

By the time the police figured this out, she'd vanished. They realise now that she moved south, reinvented herself, worked as a cleaner at Moorfields, then got the job as Tilly's PA after seeing me, becoming obsessed with me and getting information about me and Tilly from one of the nurses.

When they started to treat Karen's flat as a crime scene, after I went to see them, they found Rachel's fingerprints again. The results came up on their database while they were holding me at the station. It's why they let me go. The police were out looking for her while everything was going on at my flat.

Rachel told me, while she had me handcuffed to the bed, that she had full access to my emails, messages and Facebook, because she had some software installed on Tilly's machine to record keystrokes. She knew which underwear I'd bought for Harriet from an old email receipt in my inbox. She broke in and stole it. Maybe she planned to wear it herself. She knew everything about me.

Of course, I know now that it was *her* who went to see Karen. Remember how I texted you about slagging Karen off because of my work for her? The police think that maybe she killed Karen as a kind of offering to me because I was pissed off with her. Like a cat bringing a dead mouse to its owner. She told Karen that she was my girlfriend. Karen didn't know what you look like, so Victor told me you had visited her.

The police reckon she went to see Karen twice. The first time was to have a go at her about the website work. I guess she must have decided Karen wouldn't call me. In fact, Karen texted me but Rachel deleted it. That was the night I took the sleeping pills.

Moseley says Rachel got the heroin from one of Henry's drug dealer mates and, the second time she went round, she gave Karen the same muscle relaxant she gave me, then injected her. The coroner didn't bother looking for anything like that at first because it seemed obvious she'd died of a smack overdose. Moseley said that even though they reckon Rachel originally killed Karen as an offering to me, she soon saw the opportunity to, well, kill two birds with one stone. Get rid of Karen and frame you. So she put the heroin in your suit pocket when she stayed at my flat. I suppose she didn't know I would find it. Maybe she planned to call the police herself once she'd planted the false evidence.

It's hard to say how precisely Rachel planned everything. Some of the things that led me to suspect you were, I thought originally, coincidence. Like you saying that if you were going to murder someone you'd do it via a fake drug OD. But now I know that you said the same thing to Tilly, when you emailed her about that awful dinner party with Sasha. Of course, Rachel had access to all Tilly's messages too.

And of course there was all the other weird stuff going on too. That feeling of being followed, for one. Well, now we know that Fraser was following you about because he was still hung up on you. Rachel encountered him on one of her trips up to London (she could travel quickly between here and Eastbourne on her bike). We had *two* stalkers, one each, and they joined forces in an attempt to break us up. He hasn't admitted it but Rachel told me Fraser pushed me down the stairs of the Tube station. It was because she was hoping I'd end up in a wheelchair. I expect he thought you wouldn't want to be with me anymore if that happened.

Other things that made me, stupidly, begin to feel suspicious about you . . . Well, of course, there was your jealousy. I was so shocked after that night I spent at Sasha's and saw a different side to you. Now I know that that was all it was: jealousy. But being completely honest, seeing your anger that night made me wonder what you were capable of.

There was the small stuff too: I didn't know if I believed you about losing my bag on the bus, thought you had deliberately got rid of my old photos; my female Facebook friends vanishing (that was Rachel); my photography book going missing . . .

Charlie, you should have just asked to borrow it – though if I'd known you wanted to cut it up for your artwork I'd have bought you a new copy!

What else? God, there's so much. Victor being framed as a paedophile. Again, that was Rachel, though I'm not entirely sure why she did it. Was she worried about me working with and meeting other women? Or did she want me to have no money? Maybe she thought that if I was completely skint I'd have to leave my flat, go and stay with Tilly. Who knows what twisted logic went through her head?

Anyway, Rachel set up the page about Victor and paid one of the temps in his office to plant the kiddie porn on his computer.

Finally, there was the attack on Kristi. I know that you tried to bribe Kristi to stop her being my cleaner. I don't know exactly why you did that. Did you feel threatened by her or was it because you thought she was being exploited? Maybe a bit of both. But the police don't think it was Rachel who attacked her. Moseley thinks it's something to do with Albanian gangs.

So there you go. All the reasons why I betrayed you. It's quite a list, isn't it? The kind of stuff that would keep conspiracy theorists going for years! But I know I shouldn't joke about it . . . It all contributed to my confusion and paranoia. It's not an excuse. But it is the reason.

For the record, I never, ever suspected that Rachel was obsessed with me. She worked at Moorfields before you started there. Of course, I don't remember seeing her there. Tilly says she never suspected anything either. She said Rachel talked about me quite a lot, but she didn't think anything of it.

Somehow, I unwittingly attracted a psychopath, one who became fixated on me for reasons I will never fully know or understand. I read that approximately one per cent of people are psychopaths. In London, that's 80,000 psychos. I think only a small number of them are dangerous. I was unlucky. We were unlucky. As were Karen, Sasha, Harold, Victor.

There was a profile about her in the paper. Like us, she was an orphan. But she was put into the care system, going from foster home to foster home. She kept running away, couldn't settle anywhere. There was an interview with one of the foster mothers, who said that Rachel – or Tracey, which was her real name – became obsessed with one of her 'foster brothers', tried to poison him when he rejected her advances. This woman said she used to bring home stray cats, keep them in secret in her room. Once, she found that Rachel/Tracey had broken this cat's leg so it couldn't run away.

It turned out that her dad did similar things to her mum. Beat her so badly that she couldn't leave the house because he was afraid she would leave him. One day the mum tried to escape but he caught her and killed her, then committed suicide. Rachel/Tracey saw the whole thing.

I can't help but hate the woman Tracey became, but I want to cry for the child she used to be.

I think Rachel had been patient, happy to watch me for a while, but when I got together with you it seriously accelerated her crazed actions, panicked her, made her decide that she had to eliminate all the opposition.

Certainly the easy thing, though it pains me to write this, would have been for her to kill you. So why didn't she?

In a way I wish she were alive so I could ask her. But my theory is that she wanted to weaken me, to make me as vulnerable as possible. When she eventually came to imprison me, she wanted my spirit to be crushed so I'd be compliant. It was bad enough that she made sure I was unemployed and that my friends were suffering, that I was paranoid and scared. If I also thought my girlfriend was a killer – and better yet, already jailed for it, even convicted of it – it would have been the last straw, worse even than if you were murdered. She wanted you utterly discredited and tainted in my memory and in my heart. So she set you up. Tried to make me fall out of love with you. She made up the story about Henry attacking her in order to get in and plant the heroin. Then, I guess, she staged the disappearing act so she could wait and watch until you were out of the way.

My night with Sasha and my arrest complicated things. Rachel, who was watching me, following me around, must have assumed I had slept with Sasha. Now, in her warped mind, she had another love rival – and it drove her over the edge. She must have been worried about the police too, wondering if her name had come up. She must have forced Sasha to my flat at knifepoint, wanting me to see her die when I got back from the station, then lain in wait for me. I know from Tilly that she also called you, while you were at Beachy Head, telling you I was injured and needed your help. I know this isn't easy to read, but she planned to kill you after she'd blinded me, the original plan gone out of the window. She must have known that the police were on to her too. I guess she meant to spirit me away, to keep me prisoner somewhere so she could 'look after' me. She no longer cared about whether I would be grieving for you. As long as she had me and didn't get caught.

She didn't know that Tilly would be so worried about me that she would call the one person she knew who could get you back to London quickly. Tilly told me that Henry came to see her while Rachel was 'missing', persuaded her that he was innocent, that Rachel was lying. But you know that already. Poor Henry. It would have been better for him if Tilly had believed he was a thug. But not better for me.

Another reason to feel guilty.

What else? I don't know if this interests you but the police dropped the charges against Lance after Sasha's death. But his wife has left him and is going to take him to the cleaners. Her brothers are after him too. I've heard he's going to sell Wowcom and move far away.

He told me that Sasha was a fantasist, but that was a lie. I feel deeply ashamed that I believed him, even if only for a few hours. Do you remember that someone had been in Sasha's flat, moved things around, written KEEP AWAY with fridge magnets? I wondered if it might have been Rachel, if Sasha was another target of hers, but Rachel couldn't have got in. It must have been Lance's wife, Mae, using his spare key, trying to scare her. It worked.

I still can't quite believe Sasha's gone, that I can't pick up the phone and call her when I feel down, can't go out and get drunk with her, let off some steam. I've got no one to talk about music and TV with. The other day I saw a trailer for the new season of *The Walking Dead* and went to text Sasha, to tell her. Then I remembered . . .

Things like that can knock me out for a whole day.

Seeing her mum at the funeral was even worse. You know, Sasha died a few days before her birthday. Her mum had already bought her presents and wrapped them. They put one of the parcels into her grave with her. Sasha's dad sobbed the whole way through the ceremony and when her brother got up to speak, the entire congregation was in pieces. I couldn't take it. I left halfway through, went back later and sat by the grave.

You would have liked her if you'd got to know her properly. And I'm certain she would have liked you.

Charlie, I'd love to see you, if you're around, when you get back from wherever it is you've gone. Anytime, any place. Just let me know.

Maybe you don't want to hear this, but I still love you. I think I always will.

And I'm sorry.

I hope you can forgive me.

Yours,

Andrew x

Epilogue

I walked into the coffee shop and looked around. There she was. She was as beautiful as ever, her red hair catching the spring sunshine that flooded the room. The bruise on her forehead had faded. Whether the scars inside would ever fade, I didn't know. My own psychological scars were still livid. Raw. I was on heavy painkillers – not codeine – for my ruined eye. The surgeons had broken the news within hours of the ambulance speeding me to the hospital. There was nothing they could do. Not this time.

Everyone told me I would adjust to living with one eye. The human body is clever like that. It overcomes obstacles, it adapts. And I could cope with the physical damage. It was everything else Rachel had done that kept me awake, tormented by nightmares. I had PTSD: post-traumatic stress disorder. I was seeing a psychotherapist, and just like the counsellor who had eventually helped me after my parents' death, it was doing me good. It was early days, but the vivid flashbacks – the scalpel, Rachel's leering face – were growing slightly less frequent. Harder to deal with was the lingering sense of guilt. Everybody told me that it wasn't my fault I had attracted a murderer, a psychopath. But I was the hub that connected the victims: Karen, Sasha, Kristi, Harold, Henry. I could only thank God that Rachel had never targeted Tilly, who was also in shock after everything that had happened. I guess Rachel didn't see my sister as a threat. Maybe, somewhere in that twisted mind, she was genuinely fond of her. Who knows? Any chances of finding out for certain had died in a pool of blood on my bedroom carpet.

We, especially Tilly and I, had been all over the papers and TV for a week or so. Rachel's face was on the front page of every newspaper, and the case was inevitably linked by the media to the Dark Angel case. Another carer gone bad, though Rachel's death count was far lower than that of the Dark Angel, Lucy Newton. Then Lucy Newton herself knocked Rachel off the front page when her appeal against her sentence reached the court. They say she could get off on a technicality. Something to do with botched DNA evidence.

But I digress.

'Hi Charlie,' I said.

'Hey.' She didn't smile.

I sat down opposite her. I wanted to kiss her cheek, give her a hug. No, actually I wanted her to give me a hug. But I knew that wasn't going to happen. Not after everything I'd done.

'Thank you for agreeing to meet me, to talk to me.'

She had replied to my email several days after I sent it, three days when I drove myself half-insane checking my inbox.

She stared at me now, her face serious, appraising. Then, suddenly, she seemed to relax, and she smiled that soft smile I'd always loved so much. Her red hair caught the sunlight and she had a faint tan that gave her skin a honeyed glow. How had I ever thought she could be a killer? Looking at her now, I was reminded of two things: one, that I still loved her as much as ever; two, that I had blown my best chance of happiness. I would never again feel like I had in those early weeks of our relationship. Here was my other half, torn from me once by Zeus, torn from me a second time by my own hand.

'Stop looking at me like that,' Charlie said. 'You look like a pirate eyeing up a mermaid.'

I laughed, then felt the urge to cry. The waitress came over and I ordered a latte and a slice of chocolate cake. I had lost a lot of weight during the last month and had been instructed to eat and drink more fat and protein, to try to regain my strength.

'I knew you'd look good with an eye patch,' Charlie said. 'It suits you.'

'Thanks. I've got a contact lens in the other eye. It looks too weird having glasses and an eye patch.'

She smiled again, but it slipped away quickly.

'So,' I said. 'How have you been?'

She shrugged. 'Not bad. I mean . . . I guess I'm doing OK. Considering . . . everything.'

Considering she had killed someone, had watched her boyfriend, who had accused her of being a murderer, being tortured.

'I'm sorry,' I said.

She shook her head. 'I know it's been much worse for you.'

'Yeah, but I'm not going to get competitive about it.'

Finally, I'd made her laugh.

My coffee came and I added three sugars.

'Where have you been the last couple of months?' I asked.

'Florida.'

'Really?' I had imagined her holed up in her flat, like me, watching TV and drinking.

'Yeah. Miami, to be precise. Plus I travelled around a bit. I just needed . . . to escape. To feel the sun. To be a stranger.' She looked down.

'Did you read everything in my email?'

'Yes. Through my fingers. It's just so . . .' She shook her head, lost for words.

'I know. But do you . . . understand?' I swallowed hard. 'Why I did what I did?'

Charlie looked at me. She didn't answer my question. 'Andrew, I want you to understand something. About me being jealous . . . I don't know what Fraser told you about me. But whatever it was, he was a liar. He always lied when we were together. About everything. I loved him at first and he destroyed our relationship by lying, lying, lying. He slept with at least three other women while we were together and denied it. It was like he had a disease that stopped him from telling the truth. But the thing was, I thought it must be me, doing something to men to make them cheat on me. I already told you about Leo.'

I nodded. That was the boyfriend who had previously been unfaithful to her, the break-up causing her to turn to sleeping pills.

'I thought about this a lot while I was away. The stuff with Fraser and Leo . . . that's what made me so jealous and paranoid when I was with you. It was learned behaviour from my relationships with them. I thought you must be the same as them. That every man I met would let me down, betray me.'

'I would never have betrayed you, Charlie.'

The look she gave me stabbed me in the heart.

'Maybe not in that way.' She sighed. 'When I told Fraser I was leaving him, he couldn't cope. He thought he was the one with all the power, that he would choose when to leave me. I spent that week between our first date and when I contacted you trying to deal with him. He was going psycho, threatening to kill himself. It was a real mess.'

'Did you sleep with him that week?'

She was taken aback. 'Would it matter?'

'I guess not.'

'For the record, I didn't. I couldn't stand him anymore.'

'But that night, the night we first went out, you went home with him?'

'I didn't have a choice. He texted me, saying he'd seen me with you, that he was going to talk to you. I knew he'd tell you all sorts of lies about me and, well, I liked you. I didn't want you to go off me. I spent that night trying to dissuade him from jumping off Waterloo Bridge. Maybe I should have let him.' She paused. 'I'm sorry I lied to you about that.'

'You don't need to apologise.'

'When you met Fraser you must have wondered what the hell I'd ever seen in him. I wonder that now too. But he was charming when we were first together, before I realised what he was really like. He comes across as an utter mess now – he sold all our furniture to buy drugs – but he's clever. When I was with him he basically enacted psychological warfare against me. He targeted every one of my insecurities, completely emotionally abused me, manipulated me, turned me into a mess. That's the state I was in when I met you. Desperate for a normal relationship, to start again with someone . . . normal. Someone nice. But I was fucked up. I wasn't ready for another relationship. But I thought that you could heal me.'

I didn't know what to say to this.

'It's like the thing with Kristi,' she said. 'Offering her money. It was such a stupid thing for me to do. But when I saw how pretty she was, I kept imagining the two of you together. I was so in love with you, Andrew. I would have done anything . . .' She laughed harshly. 'Well, obviously not anything.'

But I knew what she was thinking. How far do you have to travel to go from what Charlie did to what Rachel did?

I knew the answer to that. A long way. A very long way indeed.

'Anyway,' Charlie said. 'I've had a lot of time to think, to look at myself, and I know that I have a problem. I know that the way I reacted when you stayed over at Sasha's, a lot of the other stuff I did, accusing you of fancying other women . . . I know it's not normal or healthy. You were right when you said I should see a therapist. So I've done it – I'm doing it. It was the first thing I did when I got back. And it's good.' She stared at the table. 'I don't want to be that person, the person who Fraser and Leo fucked up. I'm not going to be that person anymore.'

'That's . . . really good to hear.'

'How's Tilly?' Charlie asked, changing the subject. It felt like it had taken a lot for her to say what she'd just said. 'I've been meaning to call her since I got back.'

'She's all right. She's got another personal assistant. A guy called Matt. He's really hot, apparently.'

'Why doesn't that surprise me? She must be in shock, though, after what happened.'

'I'm still waiting for it to fully hit her. But when it does, I'll be there for her.'

'That's cool. But how are *you*?'

I fiddled with the bowl of sugar, twisting it round. How could I answer that?

'I'm getting better,' I said. 'I'm going to start working for Victor. At long last. And I've put the flat on the market too. Hoping to find someone who never watches the news.'

I wanted to tell her that I would get better much quicker, would be able to cope better, if she was by my side. But the words stuck in my throat.

'And you? What are you going to do?' I said, swallowing.

She pulled a face. 'I don't know. I think I need a change of scene. Maybe I'll go backpacking or something. Go to Australia.'

'I'll miss you if you go,' I said quietly.

She stared into her coffee. 'How can I forgive you, Andrew? You thought I was a murderer. You told the police that I killed someone.'

'I know, but that was—'

'I know. I understand the reasons. I really do. But I would never have done that to you, whatever. I would have talked to you first. I would never have betrayed you like that.'

'I'm so sorry.'

She stirred the coffee with a wooden stick. 'You broke my heart, Andrew.' She smiled humourlessly. 'That hurt a lot more than when that nutter threw me into the chest of drawers.'

'I'm an idiot,' I said.

'You are. A real fucking twat.'

She smiled.

It took all my strength to say her name. 'Charlie . . .'

She shook her head. 'No.'

'How do you know what I was going to say?'

'You were going to ask if we could give it another go.'

I didn't respond. She was right.

'But I can't, Andrew. Not after what you did. You don't trust me.'

'But I will, I would. This time.'

She shook her head, looked at me with those soft, beautiful eyes.

'I'm going to go now, Andrew. It was lovely to see you again. I think I needed to. But please don't try to follow me.'

I fought back tears. 'Charlie. I love you. Please don't go.'

'I'll see you,' she said, her voice so quiet and soft I could hardly hear her.

And she walked out of the coffee shop, leaving me sitting there, all the people at the tables around me trying not to look at the sad guy with the eye patch whose girlfriend had just walked out. It sounded like he'd done something terrible. He deserved it. Besides, she was gorgeous. She could have anyone.

The coffee tasted bitter, despite the sugar. The sunshine had dimmed. The people around me looked ugly and mean. The music on the coffee shop stereo, one of my favourite songs, sounded tuneless, discordant.

Maybe I hadn't realised quite how much hope I had held for this meeting. I loved Charlie. Now that I'd lost her, I loved her more than ever.

And Rachel – although she couldn't have me herself – had won.

I don't know how long I sat there, staring at the table, counting the stray sugar grains, but the waitress came over and asked me if I wanted another coffee. I nodded. I didn't want to go home, back to my cold, haunted flat, the place that nobody wanted to buy. I would stay here as long as I could, among people. There was a couple in the corner, sitting close together, and from the way they looked at each other, the proximity of their foreheads, the touches and the smiles, I could tell they were in love. I tried not to feel envious. But all I wanted to do was cry.

I was about to go, afraid that the tears would come in public, when I heard the door of the coffee shop tinkle. I glanced up as it was pushed open, cold air entering the shop, the temporary blast of traffic noise drowning out the music inside.

The woman in the doorway had long red hair, lightly tanned skin and large, intelligent eyes. She was the most beautiful woman I'd ever seen. I caught my breath.

She walked quickly over to my table without looking at me. Still standing, she pointed at my coffee mug.

'I wouldn't drink that if I were you,' she said. 'It tastes like cow's piss.'

Once again, just like before, I groped for something clever to say. Once again, just like before, I failed.

She smiled at me.

I stuck my hand out and, still smiling, she took it. Her palm was warm and dry.

'Nice to meet you,' she said, sitting down opposite me, her chair scraping on the tiled floor. 'I'm Charlotte.'

Letter From the Author

Dear Reader,

Thank you for reading *Because She Loves Me*. Of course, I hope you enjoyed it. I'd love to hear your thoughts and can be contacted in a variety of ways:

Email me at markandlouise@me.com;
Find me on Facebook.com/vossandedwards;
Follow me on Twitter with the username @mredwards.

I love hearing from readers and always respond.

I'm going to talk a little about the inspiration behind this book. Please be aware – this contains some spoilers so please only read this if you've already finished the novel. If you haven't, don't even peek at the following paragraphs!

Because She Loves Me was inspired by a number of events that happened to me.

Firstly, like Andrew, I suffered a detached retina a couple of years ago, and spent two weeks sleeping upright with a gas bubble in my eye, imbibing a cocktail of drugs and wondering if I would ever recover my sight. It was scary. Fortunately, thanks to the surgeons at my local hospital (New Cross in Wolverhampton), I recovered. But the experience, including the horrible follow-up laser surgery, has made me slightly obsessed with my eyes.

So when I thought about what was most physically terrifying to me, and what I could inflict upon my character, the answer was obvious.

Secondly, there has been my experience of jealousy. When I was at university I had a girlfriend who made my life hell because a green-eyed monster lived inside her. She accused me of fancying every woman I met; she got angry if an attractive woman appeared on TV; she demanded that I break off contact with my female friends. Going into a lecture, I squirmed and sweated if a good-looking girl sat next to me, in case my girlfriend found out. Being a nineteen-year-old idiot, I let her get away with it for quite a long time before the relationship burned itself out.

Years later, I lived with a woman who wasn't jealous but who told me, after I broke my leg and was trapped in our upstairs flat for weeks (yes, just like Andrew), that this situation made her happy. 'I like knowing exactly where you are all the time,' she said. 'And what you're doing.'

And I have experienced jealousy myself. I know what it feels like when that darkness takes over and devours good sense, filling you up with paranoid rage and fear. It's the most irrational and nasty emotion and I'm happy to say it hasn't afflicted me for a long time.

All of this combined to make me want to write a book about sexual jealousy and how destructive it can be. And, of course, that original idea grew into something much darker . . .

This book is a kind-of companion piece to *The Magpies,* in which I focused on neighbours from hell, exploring the idea that the real monsters are not vampires or demons but the people who live next door. In *Because She Loves Me*, I wanted the terror to be even closer to home. But this time, with a twist. The main challenge of this book was making everything ambiguous, so there are at least two possible explanations for everything that happens. I hope you didn't guess it but if you did, let's hope I can get you next time!

Finally, anyone who has read *The Magpies* will have noticed that Lucy from that book gets a few mentions in this one. Lucy is hated by many, but to a large degree she has lived in the shadows of my books, never fully revealing herself. I am sure she will surface in future work — and maybe we'll get to see a lot more of her. I think she still has a lot of havoc to wreak . . .

Thanks again for reading.

Best wishes
Mark Edwards

Acknowledgements

Thanks to my very cool and beautiful wife, Sara, for reading this book first and helping me make it a lot better, including coming up with the lost property idea.

To Michele Knight and Anne Coates for helping out with my questions about aura reading.

To everyone at Amazon Publishing in the UK, including Emilie, Sana, and Victoria – I couldn't wish to work with a more enthusiastic and professional group of book lovers.

Thanks to David Downing, my editor, who is not only an excellent editor but a great guy and a good laugh.

To my agent, Sam Copeland, for dealing with all the boring stuff for me and being awesome at karaoke.

Finally, huge and heartfelt thanks to everyone on Facebook.com/vossandedwards – you're the most fun and all-around-awesome group of readers in the world.

About the Author

Mark writes psychological thrillers. He loves stories in which scary things happen to ordinary people and is inspired by writers such as Stephen King, Ira Levin, Ruth Rendell, Ian McEwan, Val McDermid and Donna Tartt.

Mark is now a full-time writer. Before that, he once picked broad beans, answered complaint calls for a rail company, taught English in Japan and worked as a marketing director.

Mark co-published a series of crime novels with Louise Voss. *The Magpies* was his first solo venture and topped the UK Kindle charts for three months when it was first released. Since its success, the novel has been re-edited and published by Thomas & Mercer on 26th November 2013. *Because She Loves Me* is his second spine-tingling thriller.

He lives in England with his wife, their three children and a ginger cat.

He can be contacted at: markandlouise@me.com
Twitter: @mredwards
Facebook: www.facebook.com/vossandedwards

Download a Free Story by Mark Edwards

In 'Guardian Angel', a young woman's obsession with missed connection newspaper ads leads to a terrifying encounter with a stalker . . .

To get your copy now, visit vossandedwards.com/free-short-story